TREASON

TREASON

➤ A NOVEL ➤

NEWT GINGRICH

AND PETE EARLEY

CENTER
STREET

NEW YORK BOSTON NASHVILLE

Copyright © 2016 by Newt Gingrich and Pete Earley

Cover design by Jody Waldrup
Cover photography by Getty Images
Cover copyright © 2016 by Hachette Book Group, Inc.

Center Street
Hachette Book Group
1290 Avenue of the Americas
New York, NY 10104
centerstreet.com
twitter.com/centerstreet

First Edition: October 2016

Center Street is a division of Hachette Book Group, Inc.
The Center Street name and logo are trademarks of Hachette Book Group, Inc.

The publisher is not responsible for websites (or their content) that are not owned by the publisher.

Library of Congress Cataloging-in-Publication Data

Names: Gingrich, Newt, author. | Earley, Pete, author.
Title: Treason : a novel / Newt Gingrich and Pete Earley.
Description: First Edition. | New York : Center Street, 2016. | Sequel to: Duplicity.
Identifiers: LCCN 2016022610 | ISBN 9781455530441 (hardback) | ISBN 9781455541652 (large print) | ISBN 9781478912996 (audio download)
Subjects: LCSH: Political fiction. | BISAC: FICTION / Political. | GSAFD: Suspense fiction.
Classification: LCC PS3557.I4945 T74 2016 | DDC 813/.54—dc23 LC record available at https://lccn.loc.gov/2016022610

ISBN 978-1-4555-3044-1 (hardcover), 978-1-4555-4028-0 (ebook), 978-1-4555-4165-2 (large print)

Printed in the United States of America

LSC-C

10 9 8

We dedicate this book to the victims of radical Islamic violence and tyranny.

"I am concerned for the security of our great Nation; not so much because of any threat from without, but because of the insidious forces working from within."

—Douglas MacArthur

CONTENTS

CAST OF CHARACTERS

Cassy Adeogo, Congressman's young daughter

Akbar and Aludra, radical jihadists

Nuruddin Ayaanie "Rudy" Adeogo, Minneapolis congressman

Jennifer Conner, teenage ward of Major Brooke Grant

Mary Margaret Delaney, political strategist

Gabe DeMoss, Pentagon liaison to National Security Council

Major Brooke Grant, U.S. Marine

Hani, Kenyan goat keeper

Mallory Harper, White House chief of staff

Ebio Kattan, Al Arabic TV correspondent

Walks Many Miles, Special Activities Division, CIA

Omar Nader, Islamic Nations spokesman

Umoja Owiti, billionaire African businessman

Wyatt Parker, FBI agent

Thomas Edgar Stanton, chair, House Permanent Select Committee on Intelligence

PART ONE

THE FIGHT COMES HOME

Those who believe fight in the cause of Allah...

—The Quran 4:76

CHAPTER ONE

Washington National Cathedral
Northwest Washington, D.C.

It was a perfect morning for jihad in America.

Fawzia Samatar held her breath as she soaked her blue jani-torial smock with turpentine. She worried the pungent fumes might cause her to faint inside the small closet. When she couldn't stand it any longer, she gulped in another breath. She wished they'd hurry.

Cans of paint and various flammable solvents used at the neo-Gothic Washington National Cathedral were supposed to be locked in a maintenance room. But a careless painter had failed to put his supplies away one night and Fawzia had snatched the tin and hidden it in plain sight on the metal storage shelves in the janitorial closet where she now was waiting.

She'd been hiding there two hours. When a Secret Service agent had checked its doorknob and found it locked, he'd foolishly assumed it was empty.

No one at the cathedral suspected Fawzia was a jihadist. *Why would they?* From her first day at work four months ago, she had presented herself as a naïve twenty-four-year-old Somali American newly transported from Minneapolis. She'd urged everyone, especially the cathedral's private security guards, to call her by her nickname, Cricket. Even the Episcopal priests had noticed her. She had a striking figure, stunning chocolate eyes, and full lips that caused men to think thoughts completely unsuitable to a church.

While speaking to a man, she would laugh flirtatiously and reach out to gently touch his arm. No one had a clue that she was married. She didn't wear a ring and she'd never mentioned her husband, who was named Cumar, to anyone at work. He'd not liked her playacting, but both of them had understood it served a higher purpose. Today's purpose.

She had reported to work before five a.m. to help clean for today's funeral and had been met at an employee entrance by a U.S. Secret Service agent who'd demanded to see her photo ID. One of the church's security guards assisting him had quickly vouched for her. "That's Cricket. She's okay. She works on the janitorial staff."

Fawzia had faked bewilderment. "Did I do something wrong?"

"The president is attending Decker Lake's funeral this morning," the security guard had volunteered.

"The president of the United States? Will I see him?"

"The president is a woman."

"Oh," Cricket had said, crinkling her nose and feigning embarrassment.

She'd walked through the metal detector without sounding an alarm. The only items in her handbag that might have aroused suspicion were an unopened pack of cigarettes and a cheap plastic lighter. Fawzia didn't smoke.

Inside the janitorial closet, she stared at the cell phone that she'd been given. A text would be her signal to burst from the storeroom into the cross-shaped sanctuary. She wasn't certain how much longer she could keep breathing the turpentine fumes before she would become physically ill.

Hurry! she thought.

Major Brooke Grant was late.

It wasn't her fault. At least that's what she kept telling herself. She knew her uncle was going to be irritated at her tardiness.

A District of Columbia Department of Transportation road crew had chosen this morning to fill potholes on Wisconsin Avenue and

Brooke had spent a frustrating sixty minutes bottle-necked in start-only-to-stop-again traffic. When she'd finally reached the National Cathedral, there was no parking. Brooke cursed and cruised through the surrounding neighborhoods until she found an open spot about a half mile walk from the U.S. government's official "National House of Prayer."

Brooke blamed herself for not accepting her uncle's offer of a ride earlier that morning. Like other high-ranking government officials, he had been chauffeured to the church's front entrance.

Brooke lowered her head and quickened her pace when she spotted a gaggle of photographers standing outside the entrance. Having her photograph taken was the last thing that she wanted. But one of them recognized her as she darted up the cathedral's front steps in her U.S. Marine Corps dress blues and she was welcomed by a chorus of electronic shutter snaps.

The cathedral's head usher had been told to close the sanctuary's doors five minutes before the funeral program was scheduled to begin. But when he noticed the blue card Brooke was holding, he waved her forward even though she was late. Blue cards had been sent only to the most elite guests. She entered the rear of the nave at the same moment President Sally Allworth was being escorted into the front of the sanctuary via the crossing, where the nave (the stem of the cross) and the north and south transepts (the bars of the cross) joined.

Because everyone had risen from his or her chair when the president appeared, Brooke was able to hurry up a side aisle and slip into her seat without drawing attention. Her uncle, General Frank Grant, who was assigned the chair next to hers, was not amused. The chairman of the Joint Chiefs of Staff did not acknowledge his niece. Instead, the sixty-three-year-old general's steel-gray eyes remained fixed forward. Lieutenant Colonel Gabe DeMoss, the general's liaison to the National Security Council at the White House, was sitting on the opposite side of Grant. He nodded respectfully.

Brooke surveyed the other dignitaries seated around them and wasn't surprised when she realized that she and her uncle were the only black faces in the first four rows of VIPs. Searching for other persons of color was an unconscious habit that she'd developed as a teenager whenever her uncle dragged her and her aunt Geraldine Grant to official functions. She was used to being a minority at these affairs.

From her seat at the end of row four, Brooke could see the back of President Allworth's head. The commander in chief was seated directly in front of Decker Lake's casket, which was copper colored and draped with an American flag.

Washington power broker Decker Lake had been responsible for President Allworth's meteoric political career. She'd been unprepared for public service when her U.S. senator husband had dropped dead from a heart attack. Under Decker Lake's tutelage, she'd claimed her husband's Senate seat from Pennsylvania and become an ever better senator than he had been—and he had been damn good. Instantly liked by the media and public, which were always eager for a fresh political face, Sally Allworth had won a long-shot campaign for her party's presidential nomination and had startled the pundits by winning in a razor-thin race. But her first term had been rocky and an international incident just a month before Election Day had sent her campaign for a second term into a tailspin. An offshoot of the Al-Qaeda terrorist network in Somalia called Al-Shabaab had overrun a newly opened U.S. embassy in Mogadishu and taken hostages. It appeared until the weekend before the election that her challenger, a Florida governor named Timothy Coldridge, would defeat her. An improbable rescue led by then Captain Brooke Grant in the Somali capital had rescued the hostages and given the president the last-minute boost that she had needed to be reelected.

Decker Lake, who'd always been fond of sports metaphors, had compared Brooke's actions to a successful Hail Mary pass in the final seconds of a Super Bowl.

All of that had happened some four months ago. Colon cancer

had claimed Lake six weeks after Allworth had been sworn in as president in late January. Now the president had come to National Cathedral to bid good-bye publicly to her beloved "Gray Cardinal."

There had been whispers at Georgetown cocktail parties that Lake had not only had access to Allworth's ear but also her bed. He'd done little to squelch those rumors because he realized the scandalous chatter buttressed his reputation as the city's most influential power broker. The president's decision to personally deliver Lake's eulogy had rekindled the gossip, but those whispers had quickly been surpassed by speculation: *Who would take Decker Lake's place as a Washington power broker?*

The turpentine soaking Fawzia's clothing felt cold and slick on her skin. She poked through her cluttered handbag with her fingers until she found the plastic lighter that Cumar had purchased for her. She was growing more and more impatient waiting for the signal. She couldn't help but fear the pain that she was about to inflict upon herself.

"*Allahu Akbar,*" she whispered. "*Allahu Akbar.*"

Allah would reward her. She tightened her grip on the lighter. She was ready. All she needed now was a text that would come from someone sitting in the sanctuary.

Brooke Grant guessed there were two thousand mourners in attendance. She knew that many of them had not been admirers of Decker Lake. Some would argue that Lake had more enemies than friends in Washington. It was part of being influential. They had not come to grieve but to make certain he was truly dead.

The jackal-like process of grabbing pieces of Lake's lucrative lobbying empire had begun within seconds after news of his death had been tweeted. Along the K Street corridor, rival lobbyists had scheduled lunches and dinners to pimp themselves to Lake's exhaustive and exclusive list of Wall Street firms and national associations. Lake had been too vain to groom a successor at his boutique lobbying firm, leaving it rudderless and unable to keep the sharks at bay.

The ripples caused by Lake's demise extended beyond the lobbyists now trampling over each other to replace him. President Allworth had lost her political champion, and power vacuums in Washington never lasted.

This was how Washington bid farewell to one of its own: with pomp, sobriety, and a thinly veiled impatience, with all eyes cast on what was to come, who would matter, who would benefit, and who would lose.

The ceremony began with a seven-man honor guard marching up the nave hoisting the stars and stripes, the colors of the military's five branches, and the state flag of Pennsylvania. Lake had served a stint as that state's governor.

Next came a processional of white-robed standard bearers carrying two large white candles on either side of a tall gold cross. A scripture reading and a few brief remarks by the Episcopal vicar served as a warm-up before the president's much anticipated eulogy.

President Allworth rose slowly from her seat in an elegant black Marchesa knee-length dress and sensible low-heeled black shoes that made a clicking sound as she walked across the marble floor to Decker Lake's casket. She knelt, placed the palm of her right hand on the burnished copper, paused to say a prayer, and then stood.

The screen on Fawzia's cell phone glowed in the dimly lighted janitorial closet. NOW. The signal!

"Allahu Akbar!" she whispered as she unlocked the door, pushed it outward, and clicked the cigarette lighter.

President Allworth first heard a woman screaming. Turning her head away from Lake's casket, she saw a burning figure running toward her. She stared at her assailant, seemingly frozen.

Brooke Grant lunged from her aisle seat, instinctively lowering her left shoulder. Fawzia had to pass by her. The twenty-nine-year-old Brooke hit the attacker one step before Fawzia reached the president.

The two women toppled onto the cathedral's stone floor at the foot of Decker Lake's coffin.

Fawzia's turpentine-soaked smock adhered itself to Brooke's blazer and white gloves. She felt the heat burning its way through her clothing. Brooke rolled from the still burning terrorist. Fawzia didn't move. She was immobile in shock.

A fog of white powder from a handheld fire extinguisher blanketed Brooke.

"Are you okay?" she heard a man's voice yell as she blinked furiously to clear the powder from her eyelids.

"Yes, yes," she answered, coughing. "Just a bit singed."

The thickness of her gloves and jacket had protected her from being seriously burned but her fingers tingled as if she had grabbed the handles of a scalding pot of water. She glanced up from the floor into the concerned faces of her uncle and Lieutenant Colonel Gabe DeMoss, who was perched above her with a fire extinguisher.

"Is the president safe?" she asked, shedding her gloves and blazer.

Secret Service agents had swarmed around President Sally Allworth within seconds after Brooke had tackled Fawzia. They had hustled her through a series of hallways to an exit. The president was now sequestered inside the presidential limousine protected by eight inches of armor plating.

"How's the Marine?" President Allworth asked.

The head of her security detail, who was listening to reports through a flesh-colored earpiece, replied, "It was Major Brooke Grant who tackled the assailant. No serious burns for the major, but your attacker isn't going to survive. We need to return to the White House."

"What if they continue with Decker's service?"

"They won't. We're going to keep everyone inside the cathedral until we exit the grounds, Madam President. We need to move you away from here."

The Secret Service had sealed off the North Road that entered the National Cathedral grounds for a quick exit. With lights flashing and sirens blaring, two D.C. motorcycle police officers led the procession. They were followed by a D.C. squad car, a black Chevrolet SUV carrying Secret Service agents, the presidential limousine, and a secondary limousine that could be pressed into service if the first became inoperable. Behind the two armored limousines were five more jet-black SUVs and two large vans.

The presidential car exited the church grounds onto Woodley Road, where it turned left in the direction of Wisconsin Avenue N.W. It was moving at a fast clip, but when it reached the intersection, it slowed to make the left turn south. As the limousine was rounding the corner, a man standing on the sidewalk darted into the street and flung his body against the president's car.

Cumar Samatar—Fawzia's husband—detonated the suicide belt hidden under the bulky hooded sweatshirt that he was wearing. Tiny steel balls packed into it blew in all directions, peppering the limousine. The explosion knocked the 20,000-pound presidential limo sideways, but it did not cause it to overturn. The vehicle's bodywork of hardened steel, aluminum, titanium, and ceramic fibers was specifically designed to stop projectiles. None penetrated the car's back chamber, where President Allworth was now lying prone on the leather rear seat. Protected behind five inches of layered glass, the president's driver continued speeding down the street away from the blast zone.

The backup presidential limo also was mobile, but the two SUVs following it were hit hard. Steel balls ripped into both like buckshot, killing the first SUV's driver and his front seat passenger. That SUV careened out of control, jumped the curb on the east side of Wisconsin Avenue, and smashed into a storefront. The driver of the second SUV swerved when the blast hit, turning his vehicle into a lane reserved for tour buses. It collided with a parked tour bus and burst into flames.

Two police officers directing traffic in the intersection were killed instantly by the blast. Half of one officer's torso was blown onto a nearby sidewalk. The other man's face was shredded beyond recognition. More than a dozen onlookers were dead, others screamed in pain from their wounds.

Two hours after the joint attack, a video made by Fawzia and Cumar Samatar appeared on the Internet. The couple gleefully identified themselves as American-born jihadists who had sworn loyalty to the Islamic State. They challenged other American Muslims to martyr themselves and promised that their deaths were only the beginning of more slaughter.

Fawzia looked nothing like the meek, childlike, flirtatious cleaning woman whom her coworkers had addressed as Cricket. Wearing a black hijab, she yelled into the camera with hate-filled eyes: "We will kill you and your children! Death to America!"

CHAPTER TWO

A beach on the Mediterranean Sea
Near Misrata, Libya

The wind is shifting," the jihadist warned as he slipped into the front seat of the parked Land Rover.

The backseat passenger behind him appeared unconcerned as he looked up from the portable computer balanced on his thighs, which was connected via a satellite phone to the Internet. He glanced out a side window into the desert.

"Yes," he replied. "I am almost finished."

Only one percent of Libya's land was arable and only a fraction of it supported permanent crops, which meant strong winds could create dust storms so thick they hid the ground. Before dawn, there had been no wind, and when the four-vehicle convoy had arrived at this beach, the air had been stale and thick with the smells of rotting jellyfish washed ashore.

The man in the Land Rover's rear seat was dressed completely in black: black combat boots, black trousers, a black long-sleeved shirt, and black gloves. His face and throat were hidden behind a snug-fitting black hood. Only his eyes were exposed, and those eyes, which peered through a narrow slit, were as black as his apparel.

To his followers and his enemies, he was known only as "The Falcon."

Unlike other radical Islamists, who would show their faces when they were among friends and their fellow fighters, the Falcon never removed his mask. None of his men would have recognized him if they had passed each other on a street.

Many believed the Falcon was an Egyptian who had first drawn blood during the Luxor Massacre in November 1997 at the Egyptian archaeological site of Deir el-Bahri. Six gunmen had murdered fifty-eight foreign nationals and four Egyptians during forty-five minutes of bloodshed. Women were hacked to death with machetes, a five-year-old child was slaughtered, and a note praising Islam was tucked inside a disemboweled body.

Others believed the Falcon was much younger. He appeared fit, with catlike movements. No matter, the Falcon had become legendary in the Arab world. He claimed Allah had shown him a vision of a united Islam and had instructed him to create a caliphate rooted in Sharia law, a unified Islamic territory where all believers—whether they be members of the Taliban, Al-Qaeda, Boko Haram, Al-Shabaab, ISIS, or hundreds of other Islamist splinter groups—would live together and create an invincible fighting force capable of crushing their non-Muslim enemies.

The Crusades, first launched by Christians in 1095, had never ended, in the Falcon's thinking. Modern-day weapons and propaganda had simply replaced the long swords, maces, spears, and arrows used by medieval warriors. The proliferation of corrupt Western culture, calls for democratic governments, demands that women be educated—all were abhorrent to him and therefore to Allah.

"All Muslims must join in our fight against America and its satanic alliance with the sons of Zion and worshippers of the Cross," he declared in weekly messages his followers posted on Internet jihadist sites. "Any Muslim who is physically able to join us but refuses is no different from an infidel and will suffer the same fate. Death!"

The Falcon typed three words—Await my orders—on his keyboard in the Land Rover's backseat and hit send. The message was encrypted and traveled through multiple relays to protect it from being intercepted and deciphered by Western intelligence.

Shutting his laptop screen, he said, "Two of our fellow fighters have achieved martyrdom. Unfortunately, they failed to kill the American president. But Allah's wishes will not be denied. The president will be dead soon and the Great Satan will be brought to its knees."

He put his laptop aside and opened a satchel at his feet. Taking a twelve-inch-long knife from the bag, he asked, "Is everything prepared?"

"Yes," the jihadist replied.

Six Coptic Christians were waiting for the Falcon on the shoreline in orange jumpsuits.

"Do you know why we behead our enemies and post videos on the Internet?" The Falcon asked as the two of them exited the SUV.

"They are infidels, our enemies."

"Tell me," the Falcon said, "do you know the group Jama'at al-Tawhid wal-Jihad?"

The jihadist shook his head, indicating no.

"The Tanzim Qaidat al-Jihad fi Bilad al-Rafidayn? Or the Mujahideen Shura Council?"

"No," the jihadist replied. "I arrived from England only three months ago through Syria and am unfamiliar with those names."

The Falcon said nothing. He did not explain that the groups he'd named were earlier versions of the Islamic State (ISIS).

Why had his young protégé not recognized those earlier incarnations? Because they had never achieved the worldwide notoriety that ISIS had the moment its members beheaded a Western journalist. A religious war needed a steady stream of believers willing to die, and while most Westerners had been appalled by the beheadings, others wanted to join the Islamic group that formed the tip of the Islamic spear.

"Why haven't you asked me?" the Falcon said as he and the jihadist approached the captured Coptic Christians. "When I removed my knife, you saw *their* book inside my satchel."

"Yes," the jihadist replied. "It's blasphemy. Pornography."

"You have not read their Book of Lies, have you?"

"I would rather gouge out my eyes."

"In the West we are considered ignorant savages," the Falcon explained. "They believe we are uneducated, even though many of us have graduated from their best schools in England and the United States. They believe we don't understand how democracy works, otherwise we would choose it for ourselves. They believe we are unfamiliar with their freedoms, otherwise we would embrace them too. But they are the ignorant ones. They are arrogant. We know all about their Western democracy and we *choose* to reject it. We know all about their freedoms and we reject them. This is not ignorance, it is enlightenment. We believe in Sharia law as delivered by the Prophet, blessed be his name. We do not need their false teachings. We live by his teachings."

The Falcon stopped walking so that he could look into the eyes of the jihadist with him.

"Their Book of Lies contains a story. A king named Sisera is fleeing from his enemies when he comes upon a tent where a woman named Jael lives. She offers him shelter. When he says he is thirsty and asks for water, she gives him milk. When he asks to rest on the floor, she makes him a bed with her finest blankets. She tells him if his enemies come to her tent, she will send them away. King Sisera falls asleep. And when he is snoring, the woman named Jael drives a stake through his head, nailing him to the ground."

The Falcon glanced at the six Christian prisoners kneeling in the sand a few feet from them.

"We will not defeat our enemies fighting here in our lands. We must take the fight into their homes and onto their streets. There are many living among them who can be recruited to do Allah's bidding. The beheadings we perform this morning will show them our resolve. And they will be the servants of Allah who will drive a stake into the heads of those who trust them when they go to sleep. We will use Americans to defeat Americans."

The wind grew stronger. Sand began pelting their faces. The Falcon stepped behind the first prisoner, glanced at the camera filming him, and lifted his knife.

CHAPTER THREE

A coffee shop
Falls Church, Virginia

Isn't that terrible?" asked the fifty-something woman serving him coffee and a bagel.

The customer seated in a corner booth at the Bean & Bagel eatery seemed confused by her question.

"The front page," she said, nodding at the morning newspaper that he was reading. "Yesterday's attack on the president—the woman who burned herself and her husband who blew himself up."

"Oh," he replied. "I was reading the sports page." He put down the sports section and glanced at the front page that he'd laid aside on the tabletop. A photograph showed people on Wisconsin Avenue bloody and despondent moments after yesterday's explosion.

"The radio said they were from Minneapolis," the waitress said. "They were Muslims, but born here. Can you believe that!"

"Somali Americans," he replied.

"You can't trust them even if they was born here. If they don't like our country, they should go back to wherever they're from."

He reached for the white plastic knife she'd brought and used it to spread butter on only one half of his toasted bagel. He put both halves together so it would melt between them.

"I knew you were going to do that." She beamed. "You come in here every Friday and always order the café misto with a cinnamon raisin bagel. You only butter one side of the bagel. You're Mr. CM/CR."

"Mr. CM—who?"

"We don't like to ask customers their names because we don't want to pry, but we recognize regulars by their orders. That makes you the Friday café misto with a cinnamon raisin guy or CM/CR. Get it?"

"An acronym."

"Yep, it's just like we never say the Bean and Bagel, it's always the B and B."

"My name is Don," he said, smiling for the first time. "What's your name, or do you go by an acronym?"

"Rhapsody, and sometimes I wish I did go by an acronym. Everyone says it's a stripper name, but it's not. My parents were musicians."

"Rhapsody," he repeated. She was too heavy set and a bit aged to be a stripper, he thought. "Well, Rhapsody, maybe next time I come in, I'll order something different. I'm not terribly fond of being Mr. CM/CR."

"Oh, don't you worry none. I'll tell everyone you're Don. We like to think of the B and B as a family. So tell me, Don, do you live around here?"

"No. I'm a regional manager for a software company and this area is part of my territory. I just happened to stop in one Friday and really enjoyed your bagels. I'm hooked now." He raised his hands as if he were surrendering and chuckled.

"That explains why I only see you on Fridays," she replied, "'cause you're just passing through town. And yes, our bagels are good." She slapped her thighs, adding, "Too good! We make them every morning fresh, or, I should say, Carlos does. I couldn't get up at four a.m. and come in here to boil bagels. Anyway, Don, it's nice to put a name with Mr. CM/CR."

He watched her return to the B & B counter. He really had enjoyed eating their bagels. He would miss them. Don wasn't his real name and he wasn't a regional software manager who just happened to pass through every Friday. He'd chosen the B & B because it was near the commuter route that he traveled into D.C. Had anyone been following him, his stopping here would not have seemed suspicious. It was convenient, but also far enough from his home and office that it was doubtful he'd bump into anyone who recognized him. He'd assumed that he wouldn't be noticed nor remembered. Rhapsody had proven him wrong. He'd become a "regular." Mr. CM/CR and now Don.

He took a bite from his bagel and was reminded of how dangerous habits could be—the simple act of him buttering only one side of a bagel, placing the exact order each visit, arriving every Friday morning had made him familiar. He'd gotten sloppy.

He glanced at the large blackboard behind the cash register where the B & B's daily specials were posted in chalk. While he enjoyed the bagels, it had been that blackboard that had drawn him here for the past several months. He'd checked it every Friday, and today—the day that Rhapsody had identified him—he'd finally seen a purple happy face in its lower right corner.

He let his eyes sweep across the coffee shop. Two customers were placing orders. Both were men wearing navy blazers and khaki pants—the unofficial uniform of federal workers. A college-age woman was answering e-mail on an electronic tablet nearby while sipping an espresso. An older couple was eating breakfast pastries near the entrance. A young man wearing denim jeans and a red Washington Nationals T-shirt was speaking too loudly on his cell phone while pacing near the counter waiting for his to-go order.

Any one of them could be watching him. No federal investigative agency ever sent one person to shadow a suspect. They dispatched dozens. Each would be dressed to blend into a crowd, much like the customers around him. But his gut told him these people were nothing more than what they appeared to be: ordinary Americans.

In addition to Rhapsody, there were three baristas filling orders behind the shoulder-high counter and array of stainless steel contraptions. Steam hissed from one device. He took note of the cashier. She was probably in her late twenties and was wearing a drab green hijab. He guessed she was Palestinian, possibly Syrian, but those were merely hunches. She was not wearing a wedding ring, but many married Muslims didn't wear them. He had never said anything to her other than telling her his drink and bagel order, but he felt certain that she was the contact who had drawn the happy face signal on the blackboard. He had once noticed chalk residue on her fingers when she had taken his order.

She would not know which of the morning customers at the B & B would be watching for the purple smiley face. She probably didn't even know what it meant. She would simply be told what to draw and when to post it.

The man returned to reading the sports page. Even if Rhapsody had not identified him as a regular, this visit would have been his last. Once a signal was posted, a new location had to be found.

He ate his bagel leisurely and when he finished, he folded his newspaper under his arm and disposed of his empty coffee cup and paper plate in a trash dispenser as he exited.

Rhapsody noticed him leaving. "Bye, Don," she hollered in a cheerful voice. "See you next Friday!"

He nodded while glancing around to see if any of the customers there appeared to be watching him. None was. Still, he couldn't be certain. If they were following him, they would have been skilled enough to not tip him off by staring at him.

As he stepped out to the parking lot, he checked his surroundings. No joggers in sight. No one walking a dog or loitering.

His Ford Fusion was parked at the back of the lot near a tall cinder block wall and the B & B's forest green trash dumpster. As he strolled toward the sedan, he spotted a crumpled white bag from a McDonald's fast food restaurant lying on the asphalt at the base of the commercial dumpster. Someone had dropped it there, possibly throwing it like a pretend basketball toward the container's open mouth and missing. He stooped down and picked up the litter, which he dropped, along with his morning newspaper, into the trash bin. Had anyone been watching, they would have assumed he was simply being a good citizen.

If the FBI was going to arrest him, now would be the time. But no cars came shooting forward to pin in his sedan and block his escape. No badge-flashing agents came darting from the B & B. Nothing. He climbed behind the wheel of his car and drove away.

About ten minutes later, he pulled into a shopping mall's crowded lot and parked. He removed his laptop from his briefcase and inserted a thumb drive. The drive had been taped to the bottom of the crumpled McDonald's bag that had been discarded at the base of the B & B dumpster. He had discreetly palmed it when depositing the bag and his newspaper into the trash container.

He typed a series of passwords, unlocking the device.

A photograph of an attractive black woman appeared on his computer screen. U.S. Marine major Brooke Grant. A series of subsequent photos showed her with a white teenage girl, identified as Jennifer Conner.

The thumb drive contained maps and more detailed information about them. He studied the drive's contents before deleting the files. Stepping from his car, he walked to the back of the Ford, where he bent down to inspect one of its rear tires. He ran his hand over its tread, as if he were checking it for nails, and while doing so, slipped the thumb drive between the tire and pavement. Returning to the driver's seat, he put the transmission into reverse and backed over the thumb drive, crushing it.

A loud blast from a car horn caused him to jam on the brakes. He'd not noticed a white Lexus SUV speeding toward him. The woman driver jabbed a finger at his parking spot, indicating that she wanted to take it. He waved apologetically and drove toward the lot's exit.

"Did you notice the plates on that car?" the woman passenger in the Lexus asked her friend. "That's a government-owned car. He's a federal worker. What's he doing shopping in a mall when he's supposed to be working?"

"We should've written down that license plate and called his boss," the driver replied.

Neither of them noticed the smashed thumb drive on the pavement as they walked from the Lexus toward the mall.

CHAPTER FOUR

Tacoma Park
Northwest Washington, D.C.

Happy birthday, husband!" Dheeh Adeogo beamed.

U.S. Representative Nuruddin Ayaanie "Rudy" Adeogo had forgotten it was his forty-first birthday. On the morning after President Allworth was attacked, the freshman congressman's mind was focused on other matters. He'd been "invited" to hold a news briefing inside Studio A at the Capitol Visitor Center, a 580,000-square-foot underground complex built below the East Front grounds of the U.S. Capitol.

Members of Congress could not hold a press conference in Studio A unless an accredited member of the Radio-Television Correspondents Gallery formally invited them, although there were exceptions. There were always exceptions, Adeogo had discovered since moving to Washington three months ago. The vice president and the Senate and House leadership could show up at Studio A anytime to address the media, but a run-of-the-mill member of Congress couldn't set foot inside the dark-blue-carpeted studio with its rich wood backdrop, podium bearing the official U.S. seal, and seats for dozens of reporters, without being formally invited. This by-invitation-only rule was in place to stop politicians from conducting self-serving news conferences that no one would attend.

That was not the case today with Rudy Adeogo.

Every reporter in Washington wanted to interview him. The failed assassins who'd attempted to kill the president were from

Adeogo's Fifth Congressional District in Minneapolis. Fawzia and Cumar Samatar were Somali Americans and Adeogo was the first Somali American elected to Congress. He was also its only practicing Muslim.

"I had this specially made by a jeweler for your birthday," Dheeh said, handing her husband a black jewelry box. She had waited until he was about to leave the Tacoma Park house that they were renting to present him with his birthday present. A taxi was outside waiting to drive him to the Capitol Hill television studio.

Adeogo quickly opened the box and discovered inside it a lapel pin shaped like a wood-handled broom. The broom had been his campaign symbol. When the Minnesota Democratic-Farmer-Labor Party had endorsed Adeogo at a press conference, Dheeh had handed him an old-fashioned stick broom and declared: "Use this to sweep out corruption in Washington." Photographers and political reporters had loved the gimmick because it was a thinly veiled attack on the Republican incumbent, who'd been caught paying a staff salary to his elderly mother-in-law even though she lived in a locked dementia ward in Florida.

"It's perfect!" he said approvingly. He leaned forward and kissed her forehead. Dheeh lowered her eyes. Theirs was an arranged marriage and even though they had been man and wife for fifteen years she was still uncomfortable with physical signs of affection.

She attached the gold pin to the lapel of her husband's off-the-rack Men's Wearhouse gray suit. "I know you will do well this morning. You practiced your statement all night."

"It is not my statement I'm worried about. You know what I'm talking about."

She did. It was a secret from his past. Decker Lake had uncovered it while Adeogo was campaigning for office and had used it to manipulate him. With Lake now dead, Adeogo should have been able to relax. But Adeogo realized that if Decker Lake had found the skeleton in his closet, someone else could too. Someone new could use it to control him.

"You are not responsible for your younger brother's actions," she said.

"You believe that, but others will not," he replied, turning to leave.

Studio A was crowded. As he stepped behind the podium, the reporters' faces disappeared into darkness. He could not see beyond the first row of chairs because of the spotlights now shining in his eyes. He could hear only their detached voices shouting questions.

"Did you know the terrorists or their families in Minneapolis?" a reporter yelled.

"No, there are more than a hundred thousand Somali Americans in Minneapolis and while we are a tight-knit community, I didn't know either of them or their families."

"The embassy in Mogadishu was attacked last year by a jihadist named Abdul Hafeez who also was from Minneapolis. Why are Somali Americans joining these radical groups?"

"ISIS is targeting men and women who are eighteen and nineteen. They were born in the United States but don't feel like they are Americans. Of Minnesota's five largest immigrant groups, Somali Americans have the highest unemployment rate—almost thirty percent. Joining ISIS gives these young people a cause and a purpose. This is why we must teach them that these groups are perverting Islam."

"But it's not actually a perversion of Islam, is it?" a voice called out.

Adeogo didn't recognize the voice and couldn't make out the reporter's face because he was seated at the back of the studio.

"You Muslims can't claim Islam is a peace-loving religion when the Quran openly calls for violence against nonbelievers," the reporter continued. "Your prophet, Muhammad, ordered Arab tribesmen, who had killed some of his slaves, to be punished by having their hands and feet cut off, their eyes gouged out, and their bodies thrown upon the ground until they died."

The room turned eerily silent. Normally, reporters would call out questions simultaneously. Now they were waiting for Adeogo to answer.

"I am not here to argue religion. But I will remind you that there are passages in the Old Testament of the Christian bible that are violent too," Adeogo said. "When Barack Obama was president, he spoke candidly about Christians slaughtering Muslims during the Crusades."

"Do you reject the Prophet Muhammad's calls for violence against non-Muslims?"

"There are 1.57 billion Muslims in the world and only a few radicals endorse what is essentially a seventh-century interpretation of the Quran."

"Western intelligence services claim radicals make up fifteen to twenty-five percent of all Muslims. Using your own figures, that's 180 million to 300 million radical jihadists who want to murder nonbelievers."

"I'm not here to debate exaggerated statistics. I'm here to talk about a thirty-percent unemployment rate among young Somali Americans in my community and those young persons' feelings of being disenfranchised."

"Representative Adeogo, the two Somali Americans who attacked the president yesterday were both employed," the reporter replied, undeterred. "More than two thousand men from Saudi Arabia have joined ISIS and they were from wealthy families in a Muslim society. I wouldn't call them disenfranchised, would you? Giving Muslim youths jobs isn't going to stop terrorism. Are you a religious liberal?"

For a moment, Adeogo considered simply ignoring his inquisitor. But none of the others in the room shouted out any questions.

"There is no Arabic word for liberal," Adeogo replied, "but if you are asking me if I am an Islamic liberal when it comes to accepting other people's religion then yes, I am. I am not an Islamic suprema- cist who believes that Islam is supreme over all peoples. I accept the legitimacy of other religions, as I believe most Muslims do. Despite your accusations about Islam, our faith is a religion of peace, beauty, and tolerance. Six days after the 9/11 attacks, President George W. Bush acknowledged that 'Islam is peace.'"

"If Islam is peace, why did two of your fellow Muslims try to murder the president yesterday?" the reporter said, interrupting him.

"I can only assume this misguided couple was radicalized by a false teacher. And that is another part of the problem that we are facing, especially those of us who are Muslims. We've allowed our faith to be hijacked by self-appointed guardians of religion who spout intolerance in mosques and through social media. These are Islamic supremacists. They vilify anyone who doesn't adhere to an austere interpretation of Islam. This is why American Muslims must speak out against this extremism, especially when radical interpretations of Islam are being taught in our mosques. We should not only be condemning radicalization, but Muslims worldwide should be leading the military fight to destroy ISIS."

"Would you today, at this news conference, demand that Saudi Arabia and other Arab states join you in condemning all Muslims who participate in a religious jihad against the United States and Israel?"

"I believe Saudi Arabia and other Arab states have already declared war against ISIS and extremists, but if you are asking me if they should be doing more, the answer is yes. The Arab world should be leading the campaign to eliminate ISIS."

"I'm not just talking about ISIS. I'm asking you if the Arab world, especially Saudi Arabia, should join the U.S. and its ally— Israel—in fighting other radical terrorists such as Hezbollah and the Muslim Brotherhood."

"Who are you?" Adeogo asked.

"I'm the Washington correspondent for a new Jewish newswire service."

Before Adeogo could react, the reporter added, "You acknowledged during your campaign that Israel was a legitimate nation, something Somalia and many Arab nations refuse to do. How are these refusals consistent with Islam being a peace-loving and accepting religion?"

"I am here today to condemn violence by radical Islamists," Adeogo said. "Not to discuss the Arab world's relationship with Israel."

"You can't discuss one without the other."

"Thank you, everyone," Adeogo said, abruptly stepping away from the podium.

When the spotlights dimmed, he searched for the argumentative Jewish reporter but all of the chairs in the back of the studio were empty.

Adeogo's public information officer was waiting for him outside the studio. "That got intense," Fatima Olol said. "But you handled it really well. I spoke to several reporters afterwards and they're going to write about your call for more jobs in Minneapolis—not the Jewish reporter's badgering questions about Israel."

She checked the time on her phone and added, "The White House is expecting you in about an hour. We need to hurry."

She led him through packs of tourists meandering inside the massive visitors' center but when they entered Emancipation Hall, Adeogo stopped her. He nodded upward at an inscription carved on a wall of the spacious lobby, which featured a thirty-foot tall ceiling and skylights, through which the U.S. Capitol dome could be seen.

"The architects originally put the inscription '*E Pluribus Unum*' in this public building," he explained. "They said it was our nation's motto."

" 'One from many,' " she replied. "I took high school Latin."

"But that wasn't the actual motto. Our country's motto is 'In God We Trust.' "

"Yes, I remember the fight. Political conservatives accused liberals of intentionally omitting 'In God We Trust' because it was a religious statement."

"The two sides actually took their argument to court. The liberals didn't want 'In God We Trust' or even the words to the Pledge of Allegiance displayed here, but they lost and so here it is for everyone to see: In God We Trust." Adeogo paused and then asked, "Does it offend you? You're a Muslim, as I am."

"When I was in high school, I stopped saying the Pledge of Allegiance. I believed swearing that oath was not compatible with my faith. But recognition of a Christian god is part of our country's religious heritage so I understand why Christians want it here. But times are changing. People are not joining Christian churches. The nation is becoming more diverse. Maybe someday, there will be mention of other great religions in our public buildings in addition to Christianity. Or maybe someday there will be no mention of them at all."

"It doesn't offend me," Adeogo said. "I meant what I said earlier. I am a liberal Muslim, a modern day one. I am not an Islamic supremacist. To me God is Allah. What someone else calls Him is not as important as believing in God. But I know many others believe there can be only one God and He is Allah."

"It's better to never talk religion in public," Olol replied. "But because you are a Muslim, you will always be asked to defend our faith."

"And because I am a Muslim, I will always be suspect."

"After 9/11, aren't we all?"

Adeogo glanced at his young protégée. She was in her early thirties, a petite University of Minnesota graduate who'd first caught his eye when she'd volunteered to work at his downtown Minneapolis campaign headquarters. He'd brought her to Washington because she was smart, willing to work a hundred hours a week for a paltry salary, and because he knew her parents. Although he was careful not to show it, Adeogo found her sexy too.

"We need to go," she said.

As they started to exit from the hall, Adeogo heard a voice call his name. A statuesque woman with red hair approached them, extending her hand toward Olol.

Adeogo's smile instantly vanished.

"I'm sure Rudy hasn't told you about me," she said. "I'm Mary Margaret Delaney."

"I'm the congressman's press secretary," Olol said, shaking Delaney's hand.

"You mean you're the U.S. representative's media contact," Delaney said, correcting her. "One of the first lessons I taught your boss was not to use the word 'congressman' since it's sexist and 'press secretary' is outdated because most of us now get our news off the Internet."

"Ms. Delaney," Adeogo said, "likes to tell others how they should think and what they should say. One of them was Governor Coldridge."

"You helped run his presidential campaign, didn't you?" Olol said.

"Yes and your boss promised to support us, but—"

"Let's go," Adeogo interrupted. "Ms. Delaney and I are not friends."

"Not friends?" Delaney replied mockingly, touching her right hand to her heart as if she'd been mortally wounded. Looking directly at Olol, she said, "I keep my promises. I don't run scared and stick a knife in someone's back at the first sign of trouble." Shifting her glance to Adeogo, she continued, "You might want to send your 'press secretary' away so we can talk privately for a moment."

"Perhaps I should stay," Olol volunteered.

"Rudy," Delaney replied sternly, "it's about our mutual acquaintance Decker Lake."

Adeogo tried not to react at the mention of Lake's name, but Delaney was studying his eyes, and she saw what she suspected was fear.

"Why don't you give us a moment, Fatima?" he said.

Delaney waited while Olol stepped several feet away from them. "Have you bedded her yet?" she asked.

Adeogo snapped, "What do you want?"

"You bedded me. The last time we spoke was at National Airport. You were scampering home to your little Somali American wife after spending several sweaty nights between the sheets with me."

"I have nothing to say to you." He started to walk away.

"Decker Lake."

He stopped.

"You were on our side," she continued, "until he got to you. He found something in your past—something you wanted kept secret—something more important than—"

"What you were using to blackmail me," he said, struggling to control his anger. "You seduced me and then you threatened to tell my wife about us if I didn't help your campaign."

"Only someone who has a secret to hide can be blackmailed, and apparently you had more than one. Decker Lake found a bigger chit than your cheating. He's dead, but that doesn't mean your secret died with him."

She'd continued to watch his eyes and now she was certain that it was fear that she was seeing. "You're an easy read, Rudy. There is something you are still hiding. I've come to tell you that whatever secret Decker Lake learned, I'm going to find it, and I'm going to use it to destroy you." Delaney spun around, waved pleasantly at Olol, who was watching them, and marched away.

CHAPTER FIVE

The White House
1600 Pennsylvania Avenue
Washington, D.C.

M adam President, thank you for meeting with me," Omar Nader said appreciatively between sips of coffee. The handsome, fifty-something Saudi Arabian was seated on one of two mustard corduroy sofas in the Oval Office. President Sally Allworth and White House Chief of Staff Mallory Harper were on another couch directly across from their guest.

"My administration is always happy to hear your organization's thoughts," President Allworth replied. She was referring to the Organization of Islamic Nations or OIN, and Nader was their official spokesman and chief Washington lobbyist.

"I've come to express our members' outrage at the actions of these two criminals who attacked you yesterday and to offer whatever assistance we may to help the United States combat homegrown terrorism. As you are aware, many OIN members also have been targeted by these radical extremists. We want you to know how thankful we are that you were not harmed."

"Yes, I was not injured," Allworth replied in a stern voice, "but those two attackers killed and wounded innocent Americans, and that is not something my administration is going to forget, forgive, or tolerate."

"Regrettably," Harper said, cutting in, "our conversation today must be brief. We only have about fifteen minutes before the president's news conference about yesterday's attacks."

"I understand," Nader said, gently placing the White House china cup on its saucer. "Yesterday's attack is why I requested speaking to you before the news conference. This couple may have professed to being Muslims, but I can assure you that their perverted beliefs are completely alien to the OIN, its members, and our beloved religion. Unfortunately, Muslims in America unfairly come under attack whenever these incidents happen and we must—"

"The couple who tried to murder me were Muslims," Allworth said flatly, interrupting him. "That's why Muslims come under attack."

"Yes, Madam President, it's true they identified themselves as Muslims, but they were not true followers of Islam, which is a religion that abhors violence and murder. And that is why it is so important for the OIN and Muslims everywhere to divorce our religion from their criminal acts. That is why it is so important for you to divorce Islam from their actions too."

"Divorcing Islam is a bit problematic, isn't it?" Harper asked, as she eyed their immaculately tailored guest. She was familiar with his credentials. Nader had attended the best private schools in England and later studied international affairs at Harvard University before joining the Saudi diplomatic corps. He'd left an ambassador posting to represent the OIN. Continuing, Harper said, "After all, the couple posted a video on the Internet proclaiming their loyalty to ISIS, which is the Islamic State."

"These radicals cloak themselves in our religion because they want to make their actions and cause appear to be a holy war," Nader replied. "They are trying to use Islam to legitimize their cause, which they claim is to revitalize the Islamic caliphate in the Middle East. But they are liars who are using Islam to hide their true intentions."

"Which are?" Harper asked.

"The leaders of ISIS are mafia criminals who engage in slave trade, sell guns, and distribute drugs. They are not religious leaders. This is why we must strip Islam from their rhetoric. This is more than mere semantics," Nader said. "If Madam President mentions

Islam this morning during her announcement, she will be granting these terrorists the legitimacy they seek. President Obama and Hillary Clinton understood this."

"Yes," Harper said, "I remember how they were criticized by Republicans for refusing to use the term 'radical Islamic terrorism.'"

"What would you have me call them?" Allworth asked.

"What they are: criminals. Or use the derogatory term: Daesh. If Madam President feels it necessary to mention Islam, we would ask that you do it in the proper context by explaining that these terrorists come from a misguided and tiny radical fraction. They do not represent a majority of our people. Surely, you understand how hurtful it is to those of us who are religious to have our beloved Islam besmirched by these murderers. It would be our preference that the words 'Islam,' 'Muslim,' and 'terrorism' are never mentioned together."

Harper had felt obligated to arrange this pre–press conference meeting because Nader and the OIN had been major supporters of the president's reelection campaign through a score of American Muslim organizations and political action committees.

"We believe the most effective way to counter homegrown terrorism," Nader continued, "is by eliminating the grievances that these criminals exploit, such as poverty and a lack of opportunity for young Muslims. I have been authorized to say that the OIN is willing to financially support community programs in Minneapolis and elsewhere aimed at eliminating the injustices and inequities that these criminals capitalize on to recruit members."

"What exactly are you and the OIN offering to do?" Harper asked.

"We would be happy to finance the building of more Islamic community centers in Muslim neighborhoods in Minneapolis and other American cities where young people can be taught that these radicals are thieves and murderers. But our presence alarms many Americans because they have been misled about our people. This is why I am here urging you to not proliferate this harmful rhetoric by referring to these killers as being followers of Islam."

"You mentioned financing projects in Minneapolis," President Allworth said. "Can I assume you are good friends with Representative Adeogo and he is aware of the OIN's willingness to help?"

For a moment, a crack appeared in Nader's polished diplomatic veneer, and Harper noticed.

"So you are not friends with Adeogo?" she interjected, turning her statement into a question.

"As fellow Muslims, we are, of course, colleagues."

"But I asked if you were friends?"

"Unfortunately, Representative Adeogo and I have, as you Americans like to say, a history. But that certainly will not prevent us from working together."

Harper wanted to continue probing, but Nader switched subjects, and when an aide appeared to escort him to the Rose Garden news conference, he ended his spiel with these words. "Please, please, Madam President, do not give these criminals the honor that they are desperately seeking. Do not give them a cloak to hide their treachery. Do not refer to them as Muslims or followers of Islam."

Minutes later, the president walked down the White House Colonnade to an outside podium in the Rose Garden. It was a cool March morning but Allworth's media advisors had urged her to stage the conference outside because it would send the public a subtle image: The president was not hiding inside the White House.

President Allworth quickly expressed her condolences to the victims of the National Cathedral attack, especially the Secret Service and District of Columbia police officers who were maimed and killed. She thanked Major Brooke Grant, who was seated in the fourth row. Without mentioning either Fawzia or Cumar Samatar by name—so not to humanize them—she described how radical extremists operating under the banner of ISIS had committed horrific atrocities in Syria and Iraq, how the Taliban had sparked political upheaval in Pakistan, how Al-Shabaab and Boko Haram had butchered men, raped women, and kidnapped young schoolgirls in Africa and sold them into the sex trade.

"Early today, a video of six Coptic Christians being beheaded on a beach in Libya was posted on the Internet. The masked figure who committed this act of barbaric cruelty goes by the fanciful name 'The Falcon.' But make no mistake; he is nothing other than a serial murderer and coward who hides his face behind a black hood. This psychopath will ultimately be held accountable for his actions because we will not rest until he is brought to justice."

Looking directly into the television cameras that were broadcasting her comments live, Allworth announced that she was appointing a blue-ribbon White House panel to investigate homegrown terrorism. She had each panel member stand as she read down the list of appointees. Major Brooke Grant, Representative Rudy Adeogo, and the OIN's Omar Nader each rose from their front-row chairs.

"All of us have a moral responsibility," President Allworth said, "to refute the notion that ISIS and these other gangs of murderers are inspired by a religious cause, because that falsehood gives legitimacy to their warped ideology. They are thugs. Criminals. Nothing more."

Nader applauded, causing those sitting near him to join in.

"If we wish to prevent future attacks by misguided Americans on our own soil," the president continued, "we must acknowledge our fault in alienating young people in cities such as Minneapolis where they are trapped in poverty and isolated with no path to achieve the American dream. This dream must be reachable for all of our citizens, not a select few."

Gazing down at her newly named members of the blue ribbon panel, she said, "I'll expect your report in ninety days. Now get to work!"

As soon as Allworth exited the Rose Garden, Nader was on his feet working the crowd. "Major Grant," he said, hurrying up to her. "Those of us in the Arab world are keenly aware of your courage, not only yesterday at the National Cathedral but also at the Mosque of Islamic Solidarity in Mogadishu where you rescued the U.S. ambassador and prevented a suicide bombing that would have killed hundreds."

"Thank you," Brooke replied modestly. "But it was a team effort."

"Yes, yes, but it was you who fatally shot the terrorist Abdul Hafeez."

"Actually it was a fellow Marine, Sergeant Walks Many Miles, who fired that shot."

"What a curious name," Nader said.

"Sergeant Miles is a member of the Crow Indian tribe in Montana."

"Perhaps I will have the opportunity of thanking him personally someday."

"May I ask you a personal question?" Brooke replied.

"Please do, but not too personal, I hope." He smiled.

"You are on the task force, but you aren't an American citizen. You're from Saudi Arabia, correct?"

"Yes. I believe I am the only non-American on the panel. I presume the president thought it prudent to include one Muslim from the Arab world to offer an international perspective."

Nader was glancing over Brooke's shoulder as they talked and he noticed Representative Adeogo was about to leave. He quickly excused himself and walked briskly toward the congressman.

"A word please," he said, stopping him. "The president has seen fit to appoint both of us on this task force. I trust we can put any past personal differences aside and present a unified Muslim perspective."

"By unified, you mean the OIN's perspective," Adeogo answered.

"As the only Muslim currently in Congress, you not only represent Muslims in Minneapolis, but Muslims worldwide. The OIN is the voice of Muslims, so I would certainly expect you to adhere to our global point of view."

"I would never presume to speak for all Muslims—as you and the OIN claim you do. And I was elected by all of the people in my district, not just Muslims, so my personal religious beliefs are secondary to my elected responsibilities."

"Stop being naïve," Nader replied in a hushed voice. "Like it or not, you are the Muslim face in Congress and you need to accept that role and act accordingly. You should not have spoken about Islamic supremacy at your news conference this morning. You should not have criticized Saudi Arabia and other Arab nations. You should not have referred to Israel as a sovereign nation during your campaign."

Adeogo started to answer him, but Nader wasn't finished. "Your statements encouraged *Islamophobia*. You should not be mentioning our beloved religion in the same breath as terrorism. The president understands this. When I met with her before her news conference, she—"

"You met with the president before her announcement?" Adeogo said, interrupting Nader.

"Yes, in the Oval Office, and I'm certain you took note that President Allworth did not use the terminology 'Islamic extremists' or 'Islamic radicals.' She called them 'thugs,' which is who and what they are."

Nader glanced around to ensure no one could overhear them. "This is not the first time we've had this conversation. I sent you a list of forbidden words to help guide you. But apparently you have not bothered to read it."

"Oh, I read your list of OIN forbidden words, such as 'Islamic militants,' 'extremist Muslims,' and 'Islamists'—basically anything that mentions our religion," Adeogo replied, "and I have ignored your list because it is *naïve*. The American public sees a connection between Islam and the actions of these Islamic radicals. Rather than ignoring that, we need to explain that their views are based on an outdated seventh-century interpretation of our religion. We need to—"

"Yes, yes," Nader said in an impatient tone. "I heard your comments this morning about how we need to do more to police our own people and mosques, and I am reminding you now that you are expressing opinions that are *not* in keeping with the Arab world's viewpoint."

"The Arab world or OIN's?"

"They are the same. We can't have you—as a highly visible Muslim—talking about how Muslims aren't doing enough to stop international terrorism. We can't have you saying radicals believe in a seventh-century interpretation of Islam. You are not an Imam. And we can't have you telling the public that our mosques are breeding grounds for terrorists and that we need to begin partnering with Israel. For your own good, I would strongly encourage you to take my advice. I will send you another copy of our list of banned words and acceptable phrases."

"Don't bother. This is America. You don't tell anyone, especially a member of Congress, what they can and can't say."

Their eyes locked, and neither attempted to hide the contempt that they felt toward the other. Adeogo turned to leave, but Nader reached out and touched his elbow, causing him to hesitate. "Tread softly, my Muslim brother," he said quietly. "Don't underestimate the power and influence of the OIN. You need me as a friend. You are a Muslim first."

"I *am* a Muslim. But I *am* an American first, and my parents didn't come here from Somalia to have anyone tell them and their children what they can and can't say in public, or how they should think, or who they can and can't support."

"The nonbelievers and Jews are not your friends," Nader whispered, "and you are deluded if you believe otherwise. You need to wake up and understand that your only true friends are your Muslim brothers and we will not be so forgiving of your blasphemies."

CHAPTER SIX

A Victorian farmhouse
Near Berryville, Virginia

Jennifer Conner heard a sound. *At least she thought she heard one.* A noise had awakened her. *At least she thought she was awake.* Sometimes her brain played tricks on her. The doctors called it a TBI. They said she had PTSD. Letters. Acronyms. Jennifer called it noodles. That was the name of a blue unicorn her best friend, Kathy, had given her four years ago when Jennifer, her older brother, Benjamin, her mother, Sarah, and father, Gunter, had traveled from the United States to Egypt. Jennifer had been ten years old then and she'd taken Noodles the Unicorn with her to Cairo.

It wasn't long after that when everything changed. When the TBI and PTSD happened. Jennifer remembered buckling a seat belt around Noodles in the family's Land Rover outside their Cairo apartment. She remembered Benjamin, who was sitting up front in the car with their mother, looking back and teasing her.

"You're too old to play with stuffed animals," he'd scolded her. He was four years older and thought he knew everything.

"Stop irritating your sister," their mother had said.

The three of them were going to see their mother's parents. Sarah and her parents were Egyptians and none of their Cairo relatives called them by their American names. Their grandparents called Benjamin "*Baabar*," which meant *lion*. They called Jennifer "*Ablah*," which meant *perfectly formed*. Everyone was gathering at the grandparents' house because it was Wafaa El-Nil, an Egyptian holiday that commemorated the yearly flooding of the Nile.

Jennifer's American father, Gunter, wasn't with them that morning because he'd been called away on business. Benjamin had told Jennifer that their father was a CIA spy but they couldn't tell anyone—especially in Egypt. That seemed odd because her father was nothing like the spies, she'd seen on television, who were handsome, knew karate, and drove fast cars. Benjamin had made her promise that she couldn't tell anyone and she hadn't, except for Noodles the Unicorn. She knew Noodles wouldn't tell anyone.

When Jennifer was finished putting a seat belt around Noodles in the Land Rover's backseat, she attached her own belt. Her mother turned the Land Rover's ignition and suddenly everything became black.

When Jennifer woke up, she was inside a huge mansion. She was alone except for Noodles the Unicorn. The mansion had lots of rooms and in each room was a window and when she went into the rooms and looked through each window, she saw different sights. Behind one window was a world where people had wings and flew. Another window looked out on purple hills covered with bright red flowers. There were frightening monsters with long fangs and scales living outside the window in another room. Jennifer was afraid when she saw them because she knew those beasts would eat her. Noodles was afraid too. Their favorite room in the mansion contained a window where people spoke to her, although sometimes what they said made her sad. A man in a white coat said her father had pulled her out of the Land Rover but he'd not been able to rescue Noodles the stuffed animal. Just the same, Noodles was with her inside the mansion and that made her happy because she had someone to talk to. A man in a black coat with a white collar told her that her brother, Benjamin, and her mother, Sarah, had been killed by a car bomb. That same man had explained that her father had brought her back to the United States from Egypt. One afternoon, her father, Gunter, had appeared on the other side of the window and said he was returning to Africa without her. *Why would he do that?* She wasn't sure, but he'd left her behind.

Sometimes Jennifer got lost in the rooms in the mansion where she lived. One day, a woman named Miriam was waiting outside the window to speak to Jennifer. She was crying. She told Jennifer that her father, Gunter, had been murdered in Germany. *He was supposed to be in Africa*, Jennifer thought. Miriam said the Falcon had killed him. *A bird? No, that wasn't right. A man. A horrible man with a bird's name.*

Eventually, Jennifer didn't leave the room with the window where people spoke to her. She liked being there. Slowly, the other rooms in the mansion began to disappear. One morning when she woke up, the mansion was gone and so was Noodles. It was as if Jennifer had stepped through the window and when she did, the mansion and Noodles had vanished. But Jennifer knew both were still somewhere inside her mind. That's why she referred to her TBI and PTSD as Noodles. It made perfect sense to her.

A psychiatrist named Wren—*no, that was the name of a bird she'd seen one morning. Bess? Maybe*—anyway, she gave her pills. They helped the mansion stay gone. Wren gave her a lot of pills. Endless pills. Yellow, red, blue, orange, and white ones. Endless physical therapy. Miriam told her that Brooke Grant was now her legal guardian. She was a Marine colonel. *No, she was a major now.* Brooke had killed bad men. They worked for that bad man with a bird's name. The Falcon. Yes, he was the bad man who had killed her father. Major Brooke had known her father in Africa. Her father had once saved Brooke's life. That's why she'd promised him to take care of Jennifer. They lived in a farmhouse. Brooke was Jennifer's best friend now. Not Noodles.

Jennifer rolled in her bed and glanced toward the window in her second-story bedroom. It was a real window, not an imaginary one. Something moved outside it. *Was it a shadow?* There was enough moonlight to see an image. A man. A man watching her. *How could a man be outside her window? Men didn't have wings, did they? The Falcon. Did he have wings? Maybe she was dreaming.*

The psychiatrist had taught Jennifer a trick to help her tell the difference between what was real and what were dreams. Turn on a light. That's what the psychiatrist had said to do. If a light came on, she was awake. If it didn't, she was dreaming. Jennifer didn't know why it worked, but it always had.

She pulled the chain. The bulb came on, causing her to blink. Jennifer looked at the window. A man was watching her and he was very real.

She screamed.

Brooke Grant grabbed her military-issue Beretta M-9A1 pistol from her nightstand when she heard Jennifer screaming. She scrambled across the hardwood floor in her bare feet into Jennifer's bedroom.

"What's wrong?"

"The window!" Jennifer said. "A man's face. He was real."

Brooke switched off Jennifer's bedside light and made her way to the window. It had an alarm, a reinforced frame, and thick bullet-resistant glass. Just the same, Brooke positioned herself along the wall and then turned to peek out the window. Brooke didn't see anyone.

The motion detection lights that edged the Victorian farmhouse had not come on. She lowered her pistol and moved to Jennifer's bed. "C'mon, peanut, just like we practiced," she said. Brooke was not about to take any chances. An intruder might have found a way to circumvent the motion detector lights.

Crossing the room, Brooke opened what appeared to be a closet door. But behind it was a reinforced steel door that led to a safe room. Jennifer scampered inside ahead of Brooke and settled onto a bunk bed near a wall of monitors. After sealing the door, Brooke picked up a phone that was a direct line to a private security company located about ten miles from the farmhouse.

"Possible intruder," she explained. "Monitors are clear. I'll turn on exterior lights and wait for your arrival."

A few seconds later, Brooke sat next to Jennifer on the bunk bed.

"I did what the doctor said," Jennifer explained. "I turned on the light."

"That was what you were supposed to do," Brooke replied. "Would you like to go back to sleep?"

Jennifer shook her head, indicating no.

"How about a snack? There's milk and candy bars in the fridge."

"Will you eat one with me? I like the $100 Grand bars the best."

"I know, because they make you feel rich," Brooke said, smiling. "I'll just be happy having a good old Payday!"

Jennifer laughed.

Brooke removed two cartons of milk and two candy bars from a refrigerator. Returning to the bed, she handed Jennifer a milk and a $100 Grand candy bar but put her drink and candy next to the bed. She ran her fingers through Jennifer's long auburn hair, soothing her. She could feel the bumps on the girl's skull, reminders of the repeated surgeries needed to remove shrapnel from the car bomb that had destroyed the front half of the Land Rover and instantly killed Jennifer's mother and brother.

Jennifer chewed the candy bar quickly, pausing only to take slurps of milk through a straw. "You liked my daddy, didn't you?" the teenager asked.

"Yes, I've told you this before," Brooke replied. "Your daddy and I were in Mogadishu, where I was a military attaché. Our embassy was overrun by an evil man named Abdul Hafeez. Everyone but your daddy and I were taken hostage. He saved my life when a different bad man was about to hurt me with a knife. Your daddy shot him. He was a hero."

"I like hearing the story. But then a bad man hurt my daddy."

"Yes, he did."

"Was it Half-sneeze?" Jennifer asked, mispronouncing Abdul Hafeez's name.

"No. It was a much worse man who always wears a mask. We don't know his real name so people call him 'The Falcon.'"

"He sent someone to kill my daddy in Germany. In a hospital."

"Yes. You remember. Good."

"Why do they call him 'The Falcon'?"

"Because he's like a bird flying above all of us where we can't see him until he does something bad."

Brooke hadn't hidden the truth from the teen. During Jennifer's therapy and recovery, Brooke had answered her questions without sugarcoating no matter what she'd asked. Jennifer's psychiatrist and therapist had agreed it was the right course. But Brooke wasn't certain if talking about the Falcon at this moment was a good idea.

"We don't have to worry about the Falcon," she said, "because I'm a Marine. And Marines stick together. You pick a fight with a Marine and every Marine out there will fight with you. That means every Marine is watching over us. Marines are like our brothers and sisters."

"Sergeant Miles is a Marine," Jennifer said, referring to the Crow Indian who'd helped Brooke thwart a suicide bombing in Somalia. "Is Sergeant Miles your brother?" Jennifer asked. She began giggling.

Jennifer was childlike in many ways. She often missed social cues because of her traumatic brain injury. But at other times, she was no different from any other teenage girl. The doctors said it had to do with which parts of her frontal lobe had been damaged and how those parts were gradually rewiring themselves.

"You know Sergeant Miles is a Marine," Brooke said, "and you know he's a good friend of mine and yours."

"I know, but he's not your brother. I think you love him."

"What's this about?" Brooke asked. "Are you jerking my chain?"

She could tell from the puzzled look on Jennifer's face that the teen didn't understand the metaphor.

"Are you teasing me?" Brooke explained.

"I was just wondering if you and Sergeant Miles were going to get married one day. You're young and you're pretty."

"Well, thank you, but I'm not that young. I'm almost thirty now and being pretty doesn't have anything to do with getting married. It has to do with being in love."

"I know you love him and I know he loves you."

"Who's putting these thoughts into your head? I'm a major in the Marine Corps and he's a sergeant. We'd both get into big trouble if we started dating. I think it's time for you to get back to sleep and quit asking me questions about Sergeant Miles."

"It would be nice if you married him," Jennifer said, handing Brooke the empty milk carton and candy bar wrapper that she was holding as she curled up on the bunk bed. "We could be a family then."

"For right now," said Brooke, as she covered Jennifer with a wool blanket, "the two of us are all we need."

Brooke tossed the trash in a container and returned her unopened milk carton and uneaten Payday to the mini refrigerator. After dimming the safe room's interior lights, she took a seat in front of a dozen monitors and checked the digital recorders that were linked to motion detectors outside the farmhouse. If an intruder had been watching Jennifer through the upstairs window, he might have tripped one of the hidden detectors, which would have activated a recorder. Brooke checked the machines. Nothing.

Jennifer must have imagined seeing a man, she thought. How many nights had Brooke been awakened by a sound and mistaken a shadow for an intruder?

A camera showed two SUVs from the private security company turning off the main blacktop onto the mile-long driveway that led up a hill to the farmhouse.

Brooke and Jennifer had moved into the green-trimmed, white clapboard Victorian three months ago. Built in 1893, it was a few miles north of Berryville, Virginia, a rural town best remembered because Confederate colonel John S. Mosby, the "Gray Ghost," had raided a Union supply train there during the Civil War and escaped with much-needed supplies. The farmhouse was surrounded by ten wooded acres and was off the beaten path, which is why Brooke had bought it. Her role in helping save a U.S. ambassador in Somalia and stopping a suicide attack in Mogadishu had given her an unwanted high profile. It had also made her a priority target of the Falcon's. Some forty million television viewers had watched a documentary on the Al Arabic network about her heroism in Somalia. She'd been fêted at the White House after she'd returned. Moving with Jennifer to the outskirts of sleepy Berryville had been a way to retreat from the spotlight.

The monitors showed the private security guards arriving outside. Six men and two women exited from the two vehicles, splitting into two teams. One began searching the grounds. The other typed a code into the house's front door's digital lock and began sweeping each room.

A movement on a different monitor caught Brooke's eye. A familiar truck was turning into the driveway. Sergeant Walks Many Miles was also responding to the alarm. Miles had rented an apartment in Berryville to be near them. She would wait for him before opening the safe room door.

He parked his weather-beaten Ford pickup next to the security guards' vehicles and hurried up to the front porch. He was wearing the Marine Corps standard combat utility uniform (MarPat), better known as camo, with its dark green woodland design. From the day they'd first met in Mogadishu, Brooke had found him handsome. He was slightly under six feet with a muscular build that came from hard labor and daily runs as well as lifting weights in a local gym. Sergeant Miles enjoyed getting his hands dirty—repairing his truck or an old Indian brand motorcycle whenever he had downtime, which was rare. Some weekends, he did construction work for a friend. She liked his rugged looks, which included a broken nose—a testament to his violent childhood on the Crow reservation. His abusive, alcoholic father had regularly beaten him

until Miles had become strong enough to knock out the old man
and leave him bleeding on the kitchen floor. Being punched as a
defenseless child had taken away any fear that he might have felt
in high school when a gang of local white boys taunted him with
racist slurs. He'd refused to turn away and had won more fistfights
than he'd lost. The Marines had been his ticket away from the
reservation, although his roots were still planted deep there. Now
in his early thirties, he'd mellowed, but he remained a man whom
other men instinctively knew would not shrink from a fight, a man
who was unlikely to stop until he was either the last man standing
or unconscious.

Brooke and Miles had developed a close bond in Somalia that
could only be understood by their fellow combat soldiers. She
trusted him with her life and he did the same.

"I didn't know you were on duty this late at night," she said,
flashing him a smile when she opened the safe room door.

"What makes you think I'm on duty?"

"You're wearing camos."

"I sleep in my camos," he replied, teasing her. "But clearly you
don't."

Brooke suddenly realized that she had darted out of bed without
grabbing her robe. She was wearing a dark red, clingy silk pajama
top and tap pants that left little about her figure to the imagination.

Sergeant Miles took it all in and he liked what he saw.

CHAPTER SEVEN

The girl was right. Someone was standing outside her bedroom window," the head of the private security team announced when Brooke and Miles joined him in the kitchen. They had come downstairs after Brooke had tucked Jennifer back in bed and grabbed a robe.

"How's that possible?" Brooke asked. "The motion detectors didn't sound an alarm and turn on the outside spotlights and the digital recorders didn't show any intruders when I watched them in the safe room."

"There's only one reasonable explanation," the security guard replied. "Whoever was here peeking in that window knew how to bypass our alarms and detectors."

"Which means," Miles volunteered, "your security was breached. The intruder had to have been given inside technical information."

"Again," Brooke said, her voice now clearly irritated, "how is that possible?"

"I've already alerted our central office and if our people leaked that information, we'll hunt them down and prosecute them," the security guard replied. "But there is another possibility."

"Which is?" Brooke asked.

"That you have a leak in your organization and one of your people did this."

"That's unlikely," Brooke said. "I did share your plans with several security experts at the FBI and Pentagon, but they have top secret security clearances and have undergone extensive background investigations. It's unlikely they leaked anything."

"Well, someone compromised the system," the guard said. "Our people will be out first thing in the morning to make modifications to prevent another security penetration. Meanwhile, my team and I will spend the night here to make certain you are safe."

"You and your crew can go home," Miles said. "I'll be staying until morning."

"No disrespect intended," the guard answered defensively, "but one man can't do the job of eight."

"There'll be two of us in the house, and I'd rather have one man I can trust," Brooke said, "than a team that may have been compromised. You can station some of your team at the driveway entrance, but the only person I want inside my house tonight with me is Sergeant Miles."

"I'm sorry you feel that way," the security guard said. "I'll tell our company head that he needs to meet with you personally tomorrow to alleviate any fears you might have about our services."

Miles escorted him outside and returned with a large black bag that he'd retrieved from his truck. He found Brooke waiting in the kitchen dressed in a red sweatshirt with "USMC" stenciled across its front and a pair of denim jeans. She had her Beretta holstered on her belt.

"How's Jennifer?" he asked, as he removed a M4A1 Close Quarter Battle Receiver—a modified assault rifle with a shortened barrel—from his bag.

"She's sleeping. Doctors told me yesterday her recovery has been truly miraculous. I just hope this doesn't set her back. She's a hero."

"So are you, and not only because of what you did in Somalia last year and yesterday at the National Cathedral. I don't know many single women in the Marines who'd be willing to take care of a fourteen-year-old girl with a traumatic brain injury and post-traumatic stress, especially one who isn't even her blood."

"I promised her father, remember?"

"Yes, I do. I was there." Lowering his voice, he added, "But I also remember Gunter Conner *wasn't* a hero. What he did in Mogadishu cost American lives."

"People make mistakes."

"People died because of his arrogance. You know that."

"I hated him when I first realized it," Brooke replied softly. "But he saved my life and I made him a promise. I can't walk away from Jennifer because of a screw-up by her father."

"Thirteen Americans died in Somalia because of him. That's more than a screw-up."

For an awkward moment, neither spoke as Miles continued removing items from his bag.

Brooke said, "I'll make coffee."

"I can do it."

"No! I tasted your coffee on the flight back to the States, remember?"

"Yeah, you said it was a bit strong."

"It was undrinkable."

He laughed as she sorted through a stash of individual serving cups for her Keurig machine.

"There's something I need to tell you," he said. "I want you to hear it from me, not someone else."

From the inflection in his voice, Brooke sensed this was serious. She immediately suspected it was about their futures. After returning from Somalia, Brooke had gotten her uncle to pull strings so she could shift from being a military attaché to working in the Marine Corps Intelligence Department at the Pentagon—a stateside job that allowed her more time with Jennifer. But Miles still worked for the Marine Corps Embassy Security Group and was overdue for an overseas posting.

"I'm returning to Somalia," he said, "and I'm not certain how long I will be gone."

"Somalia? When are you leaving and why are you going there?"

"You've been interviewed so many times by reporters that you're beginning to sound like one," he quipped.

"Somalia doesn't make sense for an embassy posting. After the attack and election, we shut down everything but a couple of front offices. Our embassy there is primarily for show. We all know that now. A few Somali locals hired to process visas while our U.S. ambassador and staff live and work in Kenya. There's no need for Marines in Somalia, and besides, I don't think a certain general there would welcome you back."

"General Haji and I are not friends, although I suspect he would prefer me coming back to having you return."

She handed him a cup and sat down at the kitchen table with her own.

"I'm not going back as part of embassy security," he said. "I've quit the Marines."

"What! That's not possible."

"I'm out."

"But you bleed Marine. And if you're not a Marine, then why are you going back to Somalia?"

"My new employer is sending me there."

For a moment she stared blankly at him. Miles had always planned to be a lifer, and he wasn't the type who would do well working for a private defense contractor. Suddenly, she understood. "You've joined SAD, haven't you?" She was referring to the CIA's secretive Special Activities Division, a covert paramilitary unit. "But why? Why leave the Marines for the agency?"

"Two reasons. Both related." He took a sip of coffee and said, "This isn't very strong."

"Who cares about the damn coffee? We're talking about your life."

"Funny," he said. "I've actually rehearsed telling you this over and over again, and each time I did it, it sounded good in my head, but now, I'm not so sure how to say it."

"Just say it."

"The first reason I quit is because I was offered a chance to be part of a six-man team with only one mission: to hunt down and either capture or terminate the Falcon. As long as he is alive, you and Jennifer will never be safe, even here in your Virginia hideaway. Tonight proved me right."

Reaching across the table, she touched his hand and said, "Thank you, but we're not your responsibility, and I don't want you sidetracking your career because you're worried about us. I can handle this."

"I know you think you can, but you'll need help. All of us do, and that brings me to the second reason, which is a bit more difficult to get out, but something I want and need to say."

He stared down at his coffee for a moment to steady his nerves and then looked directly into her dark eyes. "I want you and Jennifer to be my responsibility. I hope you know how I feel about you, about us, and as long as I was in the Corps, we'd always be a major and a sergeant and we couldn't be together. I can't accept that. Staying in the Corps is not as important to me as being with you."

"Sergeant," she said, slowly pulling back her hand.

"Brooke, I just told you that I resigned from the Corps because I've got feelings for you. Strong feelings. If you're going to reject me, at least call me Miles."

"Miles," she said, "I'm not rejecting you. But I have a teenager now who depends on me. I have to think about Jennifer too."

"And I'm sitting here knowing that, aren't I?" he replied. He studied her face, searching for a clue. To him, she was the most beautiful woman on earth.

"Your timing is lousy," she said, diverting her eyes.

"There will never be a perfect time for us," he answered, retaking her hand. "I love you, Brooke, and I deserve to know how you feel. Do you still have feelings for that man who sent you flowers in Somalia? The one you were involved with when I first met you—the French diplomat. Or do I have a chance?"

"No, I don't care about him now. But I did. I thought we'd be married. Then I discovered he already was. He had two children and I didn't even know it. He broke my heart."

"I'm not married. I don't have children. And I promise I won't break your heart. I'm in this forever, as cliché as that might sound. It's real."

"I don't want to rush things," she said, rising from the table. "Let's take it one step at a time."

"Big steps or small ones?" he asked, standing and approaching her.

"How about medium-sized ones?" she replied, smiling.

He wrapped his arms around her waist, pulled her close, and kissed her. It was their first embrace and it was electric. All thoughts of the intruder who had found his way outside Jennifer's second-story window were momentarily forgotten.

"Tell me," he said, "if I've just made the biggest mistake in my life quitting the Corps. Tell me if I've made a fool of myself just now kissing you."

"You haven't made any mistakes, Walks Many Miles. I'm in love with you too," she whispered. "I realized it when we were in Somalia. You're exactly what I want in a partner. But I'm afraid."

"I already told you that I'm not like that Frenchman."

"That's not what scares me. I lost my parents during 9/11. Jennifer has lost her brother, mother, and father because of terrorists, and you know the Falcon has threatened to murder everyone I care about in revenge for what happened in Somalia. I just don't want to make you a target."

"That's my choice," he said, "and if it comes to it, you know I'll do whatever is necessary to protect you and Jennifer."

He pulled her close again.

Some two hundred yards outside the house, hidden in trees at the edge of the clearing, a thin man was looking through Swarovski field glasses into the lighted kitchen window. He'd timed how long it had taken the security guards to respond after Jennifer had seen him outside her bedroom window and screamed. He'd carefully noted how many guards had been deployed, what weapons they were carrying, and how they'd been dispersed at the house. He'd watched a Ford truck arrive after the private security guards and a man dressed in military garb enter the house. Now, through the binoculars, he saw the light in the kitchen go dark and then a light in Brooke's bedroom illuminate.

He'd seen enough. Lowering the field glasses, he wove his way through the woods in the half-moon light. After walking about two miles, he reached a county road where his wife, Aludra, was waiting in a parked car. He startled her when he appeared from the woods.

"Akbar, did you see the child?" the woman asked.

"Yes, Aludra."

"And the woman Marine?"

"Everything was exactly as we were told, but the girl saw me and screamed before I could enter her room. I had no choice but to leave."

"How did she see you? You were told how to avoid the sensors."

Without warning, he slapped her.

"Do not question me again. Do not think you can act like some Western whore because we are now in America."

"I'm sorry," she said, wiping blood from her lip. "I was concerned about you. I thought the information you were given might have been wrong. That you were walking into a trap."

"Our source is loyal to the Falcon. He will not betray our cause."

"Yes, but he is an American. Someone important in their government. Someone they trust."

"Which makes him more valuable to us."

"But if he betrays his own people, is he trustworthy?"

Akbar raised his hand as if he were about to strike her, and she averted her eyes and looked downward in submission.

"The information about the sensors at the house that he provided was accurate. The girl simply woke up and saw me before I could enter her room and end her life and the life of the American whore who is protecting her. Let's go. I need to report what happened here."

CHAPTER EIGHT

House Permanent Select Committee on Intelligence suite
Capitol Visitor Center
Washington, D.C.

I t appears you were less than candid with me the last time we
met," Representative Thomas Edgar Stanton, chairman of the
House Permanent Select Committee on Intelligence, complained as he peered over the half-glasses on the tip of his nose.

CIA Director Payton Grainger wore the face of a riverboat gam-
bler. There was no noticeable shift in his gray eyes, no unconscious
lifting of an eyebrow, no nervous twitch. If Chairman Stanton
hoped to rattle the Harvard-educated lawyer seated across from
him in his office, he'd failed.

The fact that he could not read or intimidate Grainger frustrated
Chairman Stanton. At age sixty-eight, the snow-white-haired legislator was a legend on Capitol Hill. There were forty-six committee
chairmen in the 435-member House of Representatives, but whenever anyone uttered the phrase "The Chairman," everyone knew
they were speaking about the South Carolinian. On most days, he
came across as a grandfatherly figure. Not today. There was nothing genteel about his demeanor. He was angry because he knew
Grainger had lied to him about Somalia, and Stanton didn't take
kindly to being played a fool.

His adversary, Director Grainger, was a decade younger than
the Chairman but was equally experienced in Washington political

aerobatics. Ironically, both men had arrived in the nation's capital within a few weeks of each other. Chairman Stanton had been in his early thirties when he'd been elected to serve the first of what now was eighteen two-year terms in the House. Grainger had arrived fresh after graduating magna cum laude at Penn State and having the Navy assign him to the Pentagon. As he'd risen through the ranks, the military had paid for his Ivy League law degree and Grainger had become more of a skilled Washington insider than a soldier.

Few knew how to swim better in Washington's Capitol Hill shark tank.

Joining the two men in their meeting was White House chief of staff Mallory Harper, but she was choosing to remain silent for the moment while Stanton accused Grainger of deceiving him.

"Mr. Chairman," Grainger began, speaking without inflection, "you have accused me of being less than candid, an accusation that is both inaccurate and personally offensive."

"Excuse me, sir," Stanton interrupted, "but during our last conversation, did you not tell me that your agency had no advance knowledge that our embassy in Mogadishu was about to be attacked by Al-Shabaab?"

Grainger didn't answer that question directly. Instead, he said, "You are basing your accusation on a single NSA telephone intercept—a telephone call that was overheard in Somalia."

"Yes, that's exactly what I am basing it on. My staff has obtained a copy of that NSA intercepted call, and two Al-Shabaab terrorists can be clearly heard on it discussing how they are about to attack our embassy. And that intercepted call was, in fact, delivered to your agency four hours prior to the attack. Director Grainger, it's obvious that your agency had prior knowledge, which is not what you told me when we last spoke about Somalia. You misled me."

"With all due respect, Mr. Chairman, there are several logical explanations that do not include deception on my part."

"Then let's hear them."

"First, we receive thousands and thousands of NSA intercepts every day and—"

Stanton cut him short. He wasn't about to let Grainger dance his way through this. "I'm sure the agency receives thousands of intercepted messages, but I only care about this one—the message that warned you an attack was going to take place in four hours, an attack that ultimately cost thirteen American lives, an attack that could have been prevented. One would assume that intercept would have been a priority."

"Mr. Chairman, if you will permit me to continue, I'll answer your question," Grainger said, although he had no intention of actually doing that. "If NSA records show that the NSA delivered that intercepted call to us four hours prior to the attack, then I have no reason to doubt it. However, that doesn't mean my people were aware of the contents of that single message."

"Are you suggesting that no one bothered to read it?" Stanton replied in an incredulous voice.

Early in his career, Grainger had learned one way to avoid answering a question was by asking a question in return. "If I may make a comparison," he said. "How long does it take for a letter from one of your constituents to reach your office after it is delivered to the Capitol's internal post office?"

Before Stanton could react, Grainger added, "And, Mr. Chairman, if I may ask, do you know if the NSA translated that intercept before it was sent to my agency or if it simply forwarded it with others without indicating that it was a high priority message?"

Like the skilled lawyer he was, Grainger already knew the answer to his own question. The NSA had not transcribed the telephone intercept before passing it along to the CIA. He also knew that the Somali translator at the CIA responsible for reading NSA intercepts had gone home sick on the Saturday afternoon when the intercept had been delivered. If necessary, he could mention that complication as a possible explanation for why the CIA had failed to alert the U.S. embassy about the pending attack.

But Grainger also realized that if Stanton looked beyond those red herrings, he would find an ugly truth. Grainger had not been *transparent*—a euphemism that he preferred to lying—when he'd last been questioned by the Chairman. The CIA had been warned of the impending embassy attack four hours before it had happened. One of Grainger's subordinates had alerted Gunter Conner, the CIA station chief, and had ordered him to rush the ambassador and his staff to the Mogadishu airport for an emergency flight out of the Somali capital before they could be taken hostage. But Conner had ignored that direct command, then the embassy had been overrun, hostages had been taken, Americans had been killed, and Payton Grainger, who had built his government career on honesty, had engaged in a cover-up. He *had* lied to the Chairman to protect the agency, to protect himself, and to protect President Allworth, who had been in the midst of a too-close-to-call reelection campaign. Had the public learned that the CIA had allowed Al-Shabaab to attack its embassy, which is what Conner had knowingly done, President Allworth would have lost the election.

Until today's meeting, Grainger had thought he'd covered up the scandal, especially after Gunter Conner had been murdered in Germany. But somehow the Chairman had unearthed a copy of the damning NSA intercept, and he was on the verge of pulling a string that would bring Grainger's career to a disgraceful end, embarrass the agency, and undoubtedly humiliate President Allworth.

"I'm not interested in excuses," the Chairman snapped. "Just answer my question. Did you or your agency know in advance that our embassy was about to be attacked?"

Grainger was formulating his reply when White House Chief of Staff Harper finally decided to join their conversation. She had not asked Grainger if the CIA had known in advance that the embassy was about to be attacked. She didn't want to know. Her job was to protect the president from a scandal and, in this instance *not* asking or knowing gave her plausible deniability and seemed the prudent course. There might come a time when the White House might need to toss Grainger to the wolves, but Harper wasn't prepared to do that, at least not yet.

"Chairman Stanton," she said, "we've heard you're planning on holding investigative hearings into the Somali affair."

"Affair?" Stanton repeated, shifting his piercing stare from Grainger to the forty-something Harper. "What happened at our embassy was a bit more than an affair, wouldn't you agree? The words 'colossal disaster' and 'Benghazi' come to mind."

Up until this moment, Stanton had respected and admired Grainger. But the Chairman had never respected nor admired Harper. He thought she was pushy and arrogant, and while those traits were not uncommon in Washington, she was a political newcomer and hadn't yet earned the right to be either. The president had recruited Harper from one of the nation's most profitable Internet software companies. Coming from the corporate world, she wasn't used to having her decisions questioned or criticized. Since taking charge at the White House, she had earned a well-deserved reputation for being brash, blunt, and dismissive. Stanton had another reason for not liking her. He'd learned that opening an embassy in Mogadishu had been her bonehead idea. He also suspected that she had urged the president to open that embassy for purely political reasons, making the president's reelection a higher priority than national security.

Stanton glanced down at a stack of papers on his desk and began searching through them. "Has there been a written change in our Constitution?" he asked facetiously. "The last time I read it, Congress had oversight responsibilities."

"No, Mr. Chairman," Harper replied, without trying to conceal the disgust in her tone. "The president is not telling you what you can and can't investigate." Shooting a glimpse at Grainger, she continued, "Clearly mistakes were made in Mogadishu. And the president has asked Director Grainger to conduct an internal investigation. But holding a congressional hearing at this time would not be prudent and, in fact, could greatly aid our enemies."

"And exactly how would investigating the embassy takeover 'affair' be aiding our enemies?"

"Exposing our vulnerabilities in Somalia could make our embassies throughout Africa and the Middle East easier targets for ISIS, Al-Qaeda, or other radicals."

"Ms. Harper," Stanton said, as if he were lecturing a student, "I have been chairman of this committee a long, long time and I have never once—"

"That's correct," Harper said, daring to interrupt him. "All of us are well aware of your longevity. House rules impose an eight-year limit on how long a member of Congress can serve on this committee, but your colleagues have given you a permanent exemption for the past two decades. I'm certain you are aware of how important the president and our party's support of your leadership has been."

Her comment caught him off guard. Nearly all threats in Washington were hidden between the lines and Stanton suspected Harper was making one now. She was warning him that the president would lobby his colleagues to have him removed as chairman if he pushed for a hearing into Somalia.

"Mr. Chairman," Grainger said, rejoining their conversation, "I don't believe anyone is trying to stop you from holding a hearing into what happened in Mogadishu."

Stanton knew that was exactly what Grainger and Harper both were doing, but he let the CIA director continue speaking.

"All we are suggesting is that you wait," Grainger said in an accommodating voice. "The embassy was attacked four months ago. We need adequate time to investigate it thoroughly."

More time, Stanton thought, *for you to cover up mistakes*. Stanton decided to play their game.

"And when do you anticipate this internal probe of yours to be finalized?" he asked.

"Obviously, we are moving as fast as we can," Grainger replied, "and making great progress, but speed is not as important as thoroughness, wouldn't you agree? You mentioned Benghazi. Remember all of the accusations and confusion sparked by that embassy attack? You must give us time to collect and verify our information. Rushing a hearing also could adversely impact our search for those responsible."

"How would my conducting a hearing adversely impact your hunt for terrorists, such as the Falcon?"

"Questions asked during a hearing could inadvertently reveal our investigative techniques and sources," Grainger responded.

This is what always happens with the CIA, Stanton thought. *Claim that transparency would jeopardize national security.*

Stanton leaned back in his office chair. Why had the president sent her White House chief of staff and CIA director to dissuade him? Was it possible there was more to this scandal than what he'd already learned, something beyond the NSA intercept that had given the agency a four-hour warning? Was the White House also hiding information from him, his committee, and the American people? Stanton had heard rumors that President Allworth had secretly agreed to pay Al-Shabaab terrorists a ransom if the hostages being held in Mogadishu were freed before the November president elections. That would be a scandal on par with the legendary Watergate cover-up. That would explain why Mallory Harper was teaming up with Director Grainger to stop him from delving into what really happened in Somalia.

Early in his career, Stanton had discovered that witnesses who testified before his committee often became nervous if he simply sat quietly for a few moments and didn't immediately ask follow-up questions.

For several uncomfortable moments, he said nothing. He shifted his piercing gaze from Harper to Grainger and then back again.

Harper avoided his stare by glancing at her Fitbit. "Mr. Chairman," she said impatiently, "our president has been attacked by terrorists. I suspect voters in your district would view a hearing whose intent was to expose possible mistakes our government made in Somalia very negatively at a moment when we should be unified in our determination to defeat our adversaries."

"Ms. Harper, may I ask how many campaigns have you run?" Stanton replied in a smug voice.

"Only two," she answered, "but both were presidential campaigns, not House races, and I learned during them that the American people don't like to see our nation denigrated and dragged through the mud when it comes to how we deal with terrorists. I also learned how invaluable the support of a president and our political party can be to those who support her and our party."

Her threats are becoming more direct, Stanton thought. He would be facing another reelection campaign in less than two years.

Rising abruptly from her seat, Harper said, "I'm afraid I have other commitments, but thank you for speaking to us this morning."

Grainger rose from his chair too. Stanton did not.

Washington etiquette dictated that the official who had agreed to meet with guests in his office decided when a meeting was over. Harper was being rude.

"What shall I tell the president?" Harper asked.

"Tell the president that in the future if she wants to discuss what committee hearings I may or may not conduct, she should call me directly. Meanwhile, I will give your arguments the consideration that they deserve."

Harper turned and left Stanton's office with Grainger at her heels.

When they reached the marble staircase outside the House committee's suite of offices in the basement of the U.S. Capitol Visitor Center, Harper whispered, "Payton, I don't care if Stanton is in our party, the president needs to get that pompous bastard stripped of his chairmanship and removed from the intelligence committee. Then we need to find a way to get him thrown out of office."

She paused for a moment, and then added, "And if your agency did know that our embassy was about to be attacked in Somalia and did nothing, then you better come up with a damn good rationale or be willing to resign. The president isn't going to take a hit because someone under your watch—"

A parade of elementary schoolchildren encircled them as their teacher herded them through the center, causing Harper to stop mid-sentence.

Grainger hadn't needed to hear her final words.

CHAPTER NINE

The Al Arabic network's newest Washington, D.C., correspondent peered through the heavily tinted windows of an unmarked white van outside the Fallen Oaks Rehabilitation Center's front entrance.

"She isn't going to speak to me if she knows we're filming her," Ebio Kattan warned her camera crew. "Let's shoot first from the van."

"We can't get a clear shot through these windows," her camera operator complained.

Kattan pinned a brooch on the lapel of her bright red, one-button, Alexander McQueen patchwork blazer. "We'll get additional footage and sound through this," she said, referring to the miniature camera lens and microphone concealed in the costume jewelry. "The shaky images will add drama to my story."

A crew member fiddled with switches on a console until images from the brooch came into focus on his monitor. He shot her a thumbs-up.

"Good, because here she comes," Kattan said.

Major Brooke Grant was the first to exit the revolving glass doors, followed by Jennifer Conner and her Ghana-born nanny, Miriam Okpara.

Kattan slid open the van's passenger door. "Still good?" she asked as she stepped around the vehicle onto the sidewalk.

"Yes," she heard through her earbud.

"Major Grant!" she called out.

Brooke, who had been speaking to Jennifer, glanced over her shoulder at the figure approaching them from behind.

"I thought it was you," Kattan chirped, pretending she had simply been passing by. She extended her hand toward Jennifer as she neared them. "You must be Gunter Conner's daughter."

Brooke stepped between them, blocking Kattan from Jennifer. As she did, her eyes swept the parking lot where the white van with D.C. plates and tinted windows was parked. The glass button in Kattan's brooch confirmed Brooke's immediate suspicions.

"You're filming us," she snapped. "Miriam, take Jennifer to the car. Now!"

Grasping Jennifer's hand, Okpara hurried toward Brooke's Jaguar XF sedan, one of the few luxuries that she afforded herself.

"How dare you ambush me," she said.

Having overheard Brooke's comments through the brooch microphone, the film crew emerged from their hiding place and started toward them.

"In America, you can film anyone out in public," Kattan replied.

"No one with any ethics ambushes an underage child," Brooke replied, turning her back as she walked toward her Jaguar sedan.

"Speak to me and I'll block out her face," Kattan said, giving chase. "I would have telephoned you, but you would never have agreed to an interview."

"You're right. I've got nothing to say to you."

Kattan's camera crew dashed ahead of them toward the car, but Miriam had already tucked Jennifer into its backseat and covered the teenager's face with a shawl. Frustrated, the cameraman turned the camera on a visibly angry Brooke, who was now only steps away from the driver's door.

"Get away from my car," she ordered.

"You owe me," Kattan said. "I helped rescue that girl's father in Mogadishu. I got him an ambulance."

"You also broadcast a documentary that revealed where he was hospitalized in Germany and the Falcon murdered him."

"You can't blame me for your government's lax security. I simply report the news."

"You told the world I was on a personal crusade to kill the Falcon."

"Aren't you?" Kattan asked, happy her crew was filming Brooke hollering at her over the car top. "Don't you want vengeance?"

Brooke slipped into the Jaguar, pushed the car's start button, and spun its console dial into reverse. Before its rearview camera had time to relay an image to the dash screen, Brooke hit the accelerator and the Jaguar shot backward, nearly hitting the camera operator. He yelped and leaped sideways as Brooke exited the parking lot.

Checking her watch, Kattan said, "We need to hurry." It was ten a.m., which meant it was six p.m. in Al Arabic's main Dubai studio. With any luck, she would be able to broadcast a live report from the network's Washington studio in time for the network's most watched seven o'clock news hour.

As the van sped east on the I-66 expressway, Kattan scribbled out her script, and by the time she hurried into Al Arabic's bureau on Capitol Hill, she'd cleared her story with her editors and the government censors in the Dubai Media City compound, the hub for all broadcasts to the Arab world.

Kattan dashed into her dressing room, where she shed her western clothes for a modest, shapeless brown robe and drab hijab. She removed her makeup and with only seconds to spare, she mounted a stool behind a glass-and-chrome anchor desk next to the Al Arabic Washington bureau chief, Azim Basher, one of the network's most popular broadcasters.

When the live news broadcast returned from a commercial, Basher announced, "Ebio Kattan recently joined our Washington, D.C., bureau after reporting for us from Africa, and she has an exclusive follow-up story." Turning to address Kattan, he continued, "You first told us about this female American soldier nearly four months ago in one of our network's most watched documentaries."

The camera narrowed into a close-up of Kattan's face. "Yes, Azim," she said. "Last October, I reported that two Americans had avoided capture when Al-Shabaab fighters overran the American embassy in Mogadishu. Their names were Brooke Grant, a U.S. Marine, and Gunter Conner, who I revealed was the CIA station chief in Somalia."

Pictures of Brooke and Conner appeared on a monitor behind Kattan. "Gunter Conner was seriously wounded in Somalia during a confrontation with Al-Shabaab and was flown to a U.S. military hospital in Germany, where he was later assassinated by followers of an international masked figure known only as the Falcon. The other American—Brooke Grant—returned to the U.S. after preventing a suicide bombing in Mogadishu and freeing American hostages."

Kattan looked down at her notes, pausing for a second, before continuing. "Brooke Grant was in the news again when she helped protect President Sally Allworth during last week's attack. She tackled Fawzia Samatar, who had lit herself on fire and was running at the U.S. president. Fawzia's husband, Cumar, detonated a suicide belt when the president was fleeing." Footage of the mayhem outside the National Cathedral appeared. Those horrific images were replaced by jumpy footage captured by Kattan's lapel camera as she approached Brooke, Jennifer, and Miriam.

"Only hours ago, Major Brooke Grant refused to answer my questions when I attempted to interview her about a new fear gripping America—the fear of so-called homegrown terrorism by U.S. citizens who have sworn allegiance to jihadist organizations, such as ISIS."

Images of Brooke hurrying to her parked car now flashed on the screen. She could be heard saying, "I've got nothing to say to you!" Next came footage of Jennifer hiding under a shawl inside the Jaguar.

"The teenage girl covering her face is Jennifer Conner, the only surviving child of CIA agent Gunter Conner. Major Brooke Grant is now this girl's legal guardian. This teenager suffered brain damage nearly five years ago when a bomb hidden in their family car exploded in Cairo, killing her mother and brother."

The camera returned to a close-up of correspondent Kattan. "Major Brooke Grant became an orphan when her own parents were killed during the 9/11 attacks. Jennifer Conner became an orphan too." Kattan hesitated to let her viewers absorb the significance of what she'd just revealed and to add suspense to her closing comments. With the monitor behind her showing Brooke speeding backward in her Jaguar after nearly striking the camera crew, Kattan said, "Brooke Grant is in hiding because she is terrified that she and Jennifer will be the next victims of the Falcon who, sources tell me, has pledged to hunt them down and kill them even if they are in the United States. There is no place safe for them to hide."

PART TWO

A TRAITOR IN YOUR HOUSE

Et tu, Brute?

—William Shakespeare, *Julius Caesar*

CHAPTER TEN

Joint Chiefs of Staff Headquarters
The Pentagon
Arlington, Virginia

For a moment, Major Brooke Grant wondered if her uncle was ignoring her. He'd asked her to meet him in his Pentagon office for a noon lunch. Knowing that General Frank Grant abhorred tardiness and trying to make amends for appearing late at Decker Lake's funeral, Brooke had arrived at 11:40 a.m. for their meeting. That had been a half hour ago.

As she sat in his outer office, her mind wandered to when she'd visited the Pentagon as a child. General Grant hadn't been eager to have a ten-year-old tagging along even if it was Take Our Daughters Or Sons To Work Day. But Aunt Geraldine had insisted. The couple had agreed to raise Brooke after her parents were killed during the 9/11 attacks at the World Trade Center. General Grant already had two children, both boys, and while he had been comfortable fathering them, he had no idea how to raise a girl, especially one as clever and mischievous as Brooke had been.

On the day of her first Pentagon visit, General Grant had passed her off to an aide who, in turn, had handed her over to a Pentagon tour guide. For several hours, Brooke had walked every inch of the nearly seventeen miles of corridors in the pentagonal building. Hoping to impress her uncle, she had memorized much of the trivia that her guide had recounted. Even now, nineteen years later, she could remember the numbers: 3,705,793 square feet of office space inside the building, 9,000 parking spots, 23,000 employees, 4,200 clocks, 284 rest rooms. The Joint Chiefs even had their own separate zip code.

She'd never had a chance to regurgitate those statistics because her uncle, who had just earned his first star, had spent the entire day in meetings, leaving her to wait in his outer office, just as she was doing now.

Brooke had spent much of her youth trying to please him. She'd excelled academically, been a state-ranked swimmer, and entered the U.S. Naval Academy. Rather than winning accolades from her uncle, he had groused about the emerging role of women in the military and the fact that she'd chosen the Navy rather than the Army. He'd pressured her to enter the JAG Corps, but she'd chosen to become a Marine and longed for combat. Her uncle had overruled her wishes by having her assigned as a military attaché, first in Paris and then London. Only by a fluke had she ended up in Somalia, where she'd done what she'd always hoped to do: kill terrorists.

"General Grant is ready now," his secretary announced, shaking Brooke from her memories.

Every detail in his spacious office was masculine—royal blue carpet, heavy, dark wood furniture. The American flag and flags from each military branch lined one wall next to each service's official seal. General Grant had selected two portraits: General Dwight D. Eisenhower, the thirty-fourth president, five-star general, and Supreme Allied Commander, hung behind his ornate desk. The portrait that Grant could see at the opposite end of the room was a life-size painting of four-star general Colin L. Powell, the former chairman of the Joint Chiefs of Staff, National Security Advisor, and Secretary of State. Like Grant, he was black, and this was a matter of great pride to the general, although race was something that he never mentioned publicly.

When Brooke had lived with her parents in Tulsa, Oklahoma, her Baptist minister father had often let her tag along when he visited church members in their homes. She'd noticed then that most kept two pictures on display in their living rooms. One was of Jesus. The other was the Reverend Dr. Martin Luther King. In General Frank Grant's Washington, D.C., home, it was Jesus and General Powell.

"Major Grant," her uncle said when she entered. Whenever others were present, Brooke and her uncle observed military formality.

"Come have a seat with us," Grant said, nodding toward Lieutenant Colonel Gabe DeMoss, who was sitting next to General Grant at a conference table.

His secretary, who had escorted Brooke into the room, asked if the general wanted coffee served.

"No," he replied, answering for all three. "Major Grant and I will eat lunch in a few minutes, after Lieutenant Colonel DeMoss leaves. Tell the cook to keep it warm."

Brooke sat across from DeMoss with her uncle at the head of the table.

"Please continue your briefing," General Grant instructed DeMoss.

The deputy director for political-military affairs at the National Security Council smiled at Brooke and she returned it.

DeMoss struck her as the stereotypical male Marine—physically fit, shaved head, medium height, reasonably attractive. He wore a wedding ring, although Brooke had never heard him speak of his family. In the military, you were known by your rank, where you had been stationed, and what you had done, not by your spouse and kids unless you lived on base and they were an embarrassment. Brooke knew DeMoss was a lifer who'd enlisted straight from high school in a West Virginia backwater town. He'd fought in the first Iraqi war and done a stint in Afghanistan, where he'd been held prisoner and tortured for nine months by the Taliban before he'd escaped. He'd successfully ascended through a number of desk jobs at Marine Corps headquarters, graduated from college and earned a master's degree by attending night school, before being sent to work at the White House as General Grant's eyes and ears.

"Cumar and Fawzia Samatar were born into unassuming Somali immigrant families living in Minneapolis," DeMoss said. "Cumar had been working as an interpreter at the CIA before he committed suicide attacking the presidential motorcade. He had cleared a background check. That's embarrassing, but there's nothing in his past that would have raised our suspicions."

"Clearly, we haven't been asking the right questions," General Grant interjected.

"You raise an excellent point, General. Background investigators are not permitted to delve into an individual's religious beliefs, ask if they are practicing Muslims or what mosque they might attend. Unless a person volunteers that information to an investigator, it's considered outside our purview," DeMoss explained.

For the next several minutes, DeMoss provided them with details about when and where the couple met, when they were married, and when they had moved from Minnesota to Washington, D.C.

"If I may speak freely," Brooke said, pausing for her uncle to nod in approval, "most of what you've said about this couple has already been reported in the media."

"Yes, it has," DeMoss replied. "What hasn't been made public is that the FBI recovered a cell phone that Fawzia had been using before she burst into the sanctuary with her clothes on fire. The phone was recovered inside the janitorial closet where she'd been hiding."

"Tell Major Grant what else you have learned at the White House," General Grant said.

"When the FBI checked the phone's memory card, it showed that Fawzia had received a text message at exactly eleven hundred hours, sixteen minutes, fifty-two seconds," DeMoss reported. He removed a grainy black-and-white photograph from a yellow folder and slid it across the conference table to Brooke. She glanced at her uncle.

"He's already shown it to me, go ahead," General Grant said, waving his hand dismissively.

Brooke examined it.

"This photograph," DeMoss continued, "is an enlargement of a single frame captured from television footage at Decker Lake's funeral. Notice the time stamp in the photograph's right corner."

The image was marked 11:16:52. The photograph showed President Allworth as she was rising from her knees in front of Decker Lake's casket.

"The text message was sent to Fawzia's phone at the exact moment when the president was standing and about to walk from the casket to the pulpit to give her eulogy."

"What did the text message say?" Brooke asked.

"One word: *NOW.* Obviously, the text was signaling Fawzia, telling her the president was about to make her way to the pulpit."

DeMoss removed another photo, which he slid toward her. It showed Fawzia, with her clothing on fire, exiting the closet. The time stamp on it was 11:17:01, or nine seconds after the "now" text message had been sent.

"She received the text, unbolted the closet door, lit herself on fire, and ran at the president. Luckily, you stopped her."

"Do you have photographs of that?" General Grant asked.

"No, sir, but I could get them."

"That's not going to be necessary," Grant said. And then, in a moment of uncharacteristic humor, he added, "I'm familiar with Major Grant's tackling abilities from Fourth of July picnics when she used to knock down my boys."

DeMoss smiled and said, "I believe it's fair to assume—based on these photographs—that the person who sent the text was attending the service and sitting in the cathedral."

"You mentioned a television station was broadcasting the funeral. Maybe someone watching that live broadcast sent the text," Brooke said.

"The station had an eight-second delay, which is a common practice, which is also why the FBI is confident the 'now' text came from someone actually in the sanctuary attending Decker Lake's funeral."

"Any idea who sent it?" Brooke asked.

"The text was traced to a 'burner'—a throwaway phone."

"Where was it sold? I know many stores photograph customers as they're checking out. If they trace the serial number on the burner to a receipt, then they can—"

Her uncle interrupted her. "You don't need to tell the FBI how to do its job. It tracked down the source."

DeMoss looked at Grant.

"Go ahead and share that information with her too," the general said.

"The phone was one of two thousand burner phones sold in bulk to a specific organization. Unfortunately, that organization didn't keep track of who used each phone. It simply doled them out. So there's no way to identify the individual who actually used it."

"What organization?" Brooke asked.

"The president's reelection campaign."

A surprised look appeared on Brooke's face.

"It could have been stolen from the reelection committee, of course," DeMoss said, "or misplaced or taken by a staff member and sold on eBay to someone not connected to the reelection campaign."

General Grant lifted his hand a few inches from the table and waved it dismissively to his right, signaling that he had heard enough. "Thank you for your briefing, Colonel DeMoss."

Taking his cue, DeMoss rose from the table and said good-bye to Brooke as he exited.

After he was gone, General Grant said, "Brooke, that phone wasn't stolen, nor sold on eBay. Decker Lake's funeral was by invitation only and one of those invitees sent that text. The FBI and Secret Service have both told me that the phone was used by someone who they believe works in the White House." He hesitated and then said, "We have a traitor in our midst, and I'm worried that he or she is someone close to the president."

"Do they or you have any suspicions about who it could be?" she asked, trying to hide the anger and disappointment rising inside her at the thought that someone inside the White House had assisted two domestic terrorists trying to assassinate the president.

"We don't, but I'm conducting my own private investigation based on my own suspicions," he replied. "And I'm gradually narrowing it down. Brooke, I feel I'm close to identifying this Judas."

CHAPTER ELEVEN

The Oval Office
The White House
Washington, D.C.

Despite his stature, Chairman Thomas Stanton didn't have a government issued, lightly armored Cadillac at his disposal, which was the vehicle the federal government provided its upper-rung Washington bureaucrats for their personal safety. Members of Congress realized that images of them being chauffeured around Washington at taxpayers' expense in luxury cars wouldn't sit well with their constituents. They had to come up with their own alternatives. Stanton had a staff member ferry him around town so he could make phone calls or read in his car's rear seat.

As his driver neared the first Secret Service barricade outside the White House, Stanton glanced outside at the neoclassical home of the nation's president with a mixture of pride and envy. The pride came from knowing that the White House was the only private resident of a world leader that was open to public tours. It was the people's house, not its occupants'. That appealed to his Lincolnesque view of a government "of the people, by the people and for the people" even though Stanton knew that Lincoln had not originated that phrase when he uttered those famous lines in his Gettysburg Address. In one of the earliest English translations of the Holy Bible, printed in 1384, John Wycliffe had declared that the bible was not the property of the church but "This Bible is for the government of the people, for the people and by the people." It appeared that even presidents occasionally plagiarized.

Stanton's envy came from his disappointment in knowing he would never be president. He'd run for the nation's highest office the same year Sally Allworth had entered the race. Although Stanton had been viewed as the sure winner of their party's nomination—and should have been—he had found himself caught in an unexpected wave of anti-Washington voter sentiment that political consultant Decker Lake had helped foment for Allworth. This anger and the sense that the federal government had become ineffective and unresponsive crippled Stanton. Political historians would later compare it to the fervor that led to a farmer-frontier-worker political rebellion in 1828 against the Eastern establishment that had landed Andrew Jackson in the White House. Stanton had been painted as the ultimate Washington insider, a veteran legislator in a Congress that had disappointed voters for decades. In contrast, Sally Allworth had been the fresh-faced outsider. There was a Norman Rockwell purity to a woman who had never intended to seek office until her senator husband had collapsed dead. Reporters had cast her as a plain-speaking, earnest *Mr. Smith Goes to Washington* newcomer and—with Decker Lake behind the scenes subtly directing—portrayed Stanton as a relic, another old white man who cut deals in a smoke-filled back room. By the time Allworth claimed her first primary win, Stanton didn't need his half-glasses to read the writing on the wall. A party loyalist, Stanton had buried the hatchet and stumped for Allworth after she had secured their party's nomination. He'd drafted much of her foreign policy platform, including her position on fighting terrorism. They'd worked well together, but neither had any genuine affection for the other. Respect was expected, friendship was not, nor was it particularly wanted.

"Thank you, Mr. Chairman, for coming to see me," President Allworth proclaimed as soon as he entered the Oval Office. "Let's have a private chat." She nodded toward the two sofas in front of her desk near a rug embroidered with the Great Seal of the United States.

As soon as they were seated, Allworth addressed him by his first name, "Thomas, the two of us have always been able to speak candidly, which I greatly appreciate, so let's get right to it. I understand from my chief of staff that you intend to move forward with committee hearings about the embassy attack in Somalia."

"Ms. Harper and Director Grainger were not especially convincing in suggesting that I not hold them," Stanton replied. "As I'm certain they told you, my staff has obtained troubling information that suggests the CIA was warned at least four hours before the embassy was attacked but took no safeguards to protect our ambassador and staff."

"Yes, that's a very, very serious charge," Allworth said. The president paused for a moment—a subtle gesture intended to show Stanton that she understood the gravity of what he'd said. "Mallory is handling this for me," she continued, "and she has assured me that Director Grainger has a plausible explanation and has launched a thorough investigation."

Stanton and the president both knew that in Washington, leaders chose their words carefully, knowing that no matter how innocent a conversation may seem, it might be later used against them. The president's reference—"Mallory is handling this"—might sound as if it was merely a matter of the president delegating authority. But Stanton had a more suspicious interpretation. The president had a buffer—a possible scapegoat—in case events in Mogadishu blew up in her face. She could argue that she was unaware of any possible wrongdoing and her only fault had been to trust her chief of staff and the CIA director.

"If you are confident Director Grainger's probe will not find any mishaps, then I'm certain my committee will not find any either," Stanton said.

"Please do not misinterpret my reason for inviting you here to discuss this," Allworth replied. "If mistakes were made, I want to know them, and if someone in my administration acted improperly in any way, I will take the appropriate action. I am not opposed to you holding hearings."

"With all respect, Madam President, then why did you ask me here to discuss this?"

"Because two American terrorists just tried to murder me," All-worth said in a clearly irked tone. "Because two Americans attacked me in our nation's capital, the very heart of our democracy. The public is scared. Where will these radicals strike next? Who will they try to kill? Is it safe to go into a grocery store? Is it safe to send your children to an elementary school? What about your favorite bar or your church on Sunday? The objective of terrorism is to terrify, and these attacks on me inside the National Cathedral and on the streets outside it have made Americans feel vulnerable and unsafe. Certainly you understand that?"

"Yes, Madam President, I do."

Before he could continue, she said, "This is why I asked Mallory and Director Grainger to speak to you about delaying your hearings. It was not, and let me repeat that, it was not because I am concerned about what you might find. It is because holding hearings right now would further undermine the public's confidence in the government's ability to protect us from attack."

"Without being argumentative, let me suggest that hearings which showed no mistakes were made in Mogadishu might bolster confidence."

President Allworth shot Stanton a stern look. "Mr. Chairman, our people were taken hostage in Somalia. From what I've been told, that was because the local general there didn't protect our embassy—that his own troops turned on him—so we may have not done one thing wrong. But the fact that our people were held hostage and two of them were murdered and those murders were shown on the Internet—those facts alone are going to erode public confidence. We don't need a hearing right now rehashing that horrific incident. A hearing would play into the terrorists' hands by sparking more fear and terror. What difference will it make if you wait to conduct your hearings after Director Grainger has time to fully investigate what happened and there's some distance between those hearings and the embassy attack and attempts to murder me? Giving time for the public to regain confidence in our ability to protect our people doesn't seem like an unreasonable request."

CHAPTER TWELVE

Near the Somalia-Kenya border

The irony was not lost on the Falcon.

Speeding across an empty desert at night in a nation where half of its ten million residents survived on less than one U.S. dollar per day, he had excellent cell phone service.

Since the collapse of the twenty-two-year-old dictatorship of Mohamed Siad Barre in 1991, Somalia had been ravaged by what its few remaining poets called "the endless wars." U.S. foreign policy experts were more blunt, describing Somalia as "the most dangerous place in the world." It was ruled by anarchy and best known for piracy, kidnappings for ransom, harboring radical Islamists, corrupt leaders, more guns per resident than could be found in nearly any other nation, and widespread abuse by its citizens of a local drug called khat. Yet in this oasis of poverty, filth, depression, decay, and death, the Somali telecommunications industry flourished. It was the best in Africa.

The Falcon had watched Brooke Grant and her teenage protégée on the Al Arabic nightly newscast fleeing from reporter Ebio Kattan. He rarely missed watching the news and, like all narcissists, he'd been delighted when Kattan told viewers that he was responsible for the murder of the CIA's Gunter Conner in Germany and that he was now causing terror in America.

But there was another reason in addition to his ego for why he welcomed worldwide attention. He was waging two wars: one with terror, the other with publicity. Social media had made Major Brooke Grant a larger-than-life hero. She had outsmarted Al-Shabaab in Mogadishu and had helped kill its number two leader, Abdul Hafeez. The Al Arabic network had cast her as an avenger, taking revenge for her parents' death during 9/11. A popular Syrian blogger had compared her to Zenobia, an Arab warrior queen who had ruled the Palmyrene Empire (present-day Syria) in 267 after her husband and stepson had been murdered. Zenobia had been beloved by her subjects because she'd walked beside her foot soldiers rather than riding a stallion into battle. She'd spilled blood. So had Major Brooke Grant.

Like her, the Falcon had become a social media icon. He was described in the West as the world's master terrorist and in the Arab world revered by many as a faceless, ageless, unyielding sword of Allah.

The conflict between the United States and radical Islam now bore two human faces: hers and his. For this reason alone, he was obligated to kill her.

His contempt for Brooke ran deeper than their symbolic rivalry. Allah had created women to be lesser than men, and any female who challenged those divinely inspired roles disrespected Allah and deserved death.

The Falcon's cell phone rang. "Are you near?" a voice asked.

"Expect us in thirty minutes."

Shortly after midnight, the Falcon's four-vehicle motorcade entered the town of El Wak, a city of 16,000 that is divided by the Somalia and Kenya border. As was the case in many villages in Kenya's North Eastern Province, El Wak's residents were mostly Somalis. After passing through the slumbering hamlet, the convoy arrived at a walled estate about a mile outside the city's western edge.

Uniformed guards opened a heavy, motorized, ornate gate, allowing the vehicles to enter and continue forward to a Moroccan-style mansion where a dozen servants waited under a brightly lighted portico. The house's chief butler, a white man dressed in a white tunic, greeted the Falcon.

"Welcome to the home of Umoja Owiti," the butler declared in a heavy English accent. "Everything has been prepared for you and your fellow travelers. Please permit me to escort you inside to be personally welcomed by Mr. Umoja Owiti, the master of this estate, while the staff delivers your men to their sleeping quarters."

"Our vehicles?"

"The staff will park them out of sight in Mr. Owiti's private garage."

The Falcon followed the butler up four wide polished marble steps to the mansion's front entrance, where two armed guards in blue uniforms emblazoned with a bright gold insignia that contained the initials UO were stationed. The house's open foyer was three stories tall and had walls covered with gold leaf with shimmering black-and-white floor tiles.

"Sir, you might wish to remove your shoes," the butler said. "I can offer you silk slippers that are most comfortable, or if you would prefer, you may wish to walk barefoot."

The Falcon glanced down at the tiny sparkles around his feet.

"Each floor tile contains seventy-five slightly raised diamonds," the butler explained. "Mr. Owiti believes walking on diamonds helps increase blood flow in the feet. He will be barefoot."

The butler replaced his shoes with slippers.

A knee-high basin for foot washing was near the front doorway. The Falcon removed his shoes and a woman instantly appeared with a cloth and motioned him toward the basin. She washed and massaged his feet while on her knees, gently dried them, and then disappeared.

From the foyer, the butler led him through a series of hallways until they reached another pair of uniformed guards stationed outside two oversize ornately carved walnut doors. The room that the Falcon entered behind those doors was cavernous with a domed roof that rose from the center of the mansion. Water tumbled down from boulders stacked thirty feet high inside this massive chamber. The pool beneath the stone was big enough to accommodate eight adult bathers. Across from it was a larger-than-life statue of a Masai warrior made of black opal, which was more rare and expensive than diamonds. The Masai, a semi-nomadic tribe in southern Kenya, were feared fighters, and the muscular figure—dressed in a bloodred short skirt and flowing cape—clutched a gold-plated spear in his right hand and an oblong white shield in his left. He stared straight ahead. The Falcon gazed up at the dome ceiling and realized it was a programmable digital screen that was showing a cloudless African blue sky. The floor was cream-colored marble, cool to the touch. A half dozen settees, all covered with animal skins—giraffe, zebra, and leopard—were placed in a semicircle, facing a larger settee upholstered with the hide of a white rhino.

"*As-salamn Alaykum*," Umoja Owiti said, rising from the largest settee. He opened his arms as he stepped forward to embrace his hooded guest. "Please, come sit, eat some dates, you must be hungry."

Seeing the Falcon's bare feet, Owiti exclaimed, "You have walked across my floor of diamonds! A bit outlandish, but my African wife insisted our home pay homage to our continent's natural resources. Come, come and sit with me."

Owiti ordered his English butler to bring slippers for the Falcon. "We can't have you getting cold feet," he said, laughing. "I keep this room cooler than many of my guests desire. My love of air-conditioning is an unfortunate habit developed while living in America." Placing his hands on his watermelon-shaped belly, he added, "Another unfortunate gift from the West. Their foods are much too fattening." Owiti was a tall man with a round face and thick black glasses. He pointed at the domed ceiling above them.

"I can create any climate in this chamber," he bragged. "Even snow—and make it appear to be any time of the day that I wish." Picking up an iPad next to his settee, Owiti dimmed the ceiling until it became pitch black and there were only stars above them. Clearly pleased, he returned the scene to its noonday appearance. "I arrived this morning from a different time zone, so while it is currently after midnight outside, inside this chamber it is only a few minutes before noon."

"Tell me, my friend," the Falcon replied, "at what times do you pray in your computer-controlled world?"

In a slightly irritated tone, Owiti replied, "I pray five times daily, as required by the Holy Quran and, as you can see, Allah has blessed me."

Owiti was wearing white cotton slacks and a white collared shirt unbuttoned at the neck. He motioned toward a zebra-covered chaise near his own where trays of dates had been placed on knee-high tables.

"Would you prefer tea or coffee?" he asked.

"Neither."

Owiti pressed a button on an iPad and within moments, a woman brought him hot tea. "How do you eat and drink when you are wearing a mask?" the billionaire asked. "When you have sex with a woman, do you still hide your face? Is there no one you trust?"

"Allah sees my true face, as He does the faces and hearts of all men."

Owiti frowned and said, "You don't have to convince me of your piety." He nodded toward the oversize statue across the room from them. "Did you know my grandfather's people were Masai warriors? I will tell you a story. One day my grandfather saw a beautiful Somali woman and he took her and afterwards demanded she become one of his wives. She refused, so my grandfather threatened to kill her family. My grandmother was a Muslim who could read and one day my grandfather asked her about the Quran. Rather than teaching him how to read, she read to him every night, but she was a clever woman and because he was illiterate, my grandfather didn't realize she was inserting her own words into the holy book."

"That is blasphemy. Punishable by death," the Falcon said.

"Please," Owiti replied in a sarcastic tone. "Do not all men use the scriptures for their own purposes?" Continuing, he said, "My grandmother manipulated my grandfather. So you see the Masai blood of a warrior is in my veins, but so is the Somali blood of my wise manipulator, and the mixing of both makes me who I am."

The Falcon noted that he clearly enjoyed telling that story.

"Now let's talk business and why you have come to my home," Owiti said. "Tell me, did you encounter any soldiers from AMISOM near the border?" The billionaire was referring to troops from the African Union Mission to Somalia, a military force composed of soldiers sent by other African nations into Somalia to prop up its fragile, pro-Western government. A large percentage came from Kenya.

"No, they were snoring in their beds," the Falcon answered.

"I want to punish Kenya," Owiti declared. "The Americans will never fight us in Somalia after being embarrassed by what they call Black Hawk Down. They will use Ethiopians, who are believers in the Book of Lies, and Kenyans. The only way to reclaim Somalia is by driving out AMISOM."

"Yes, as you say, AMISOM is a puppet. The fingers inside belong to Americans. They are using their money to avoid spilling their own blood. I need your money to spill American blood on American soil," the Falcon said. "You are both a servant of Allah and a wealthy man, are you not?"

Owiti laughed. He often was described as the world's richest African. His first fortune had come from diamond and uranium mines. Later, he'd expanded into oil and natural gas production, telecommunication and Internet services, as well as traditional publishing. He owned businesses in Eastern Europe and had his toe in China. His Kenyan home was one of ten mansions scattered across the globe, including a multimillion-dollar Manhattan apartment overlooking Central Park. Each house came with a separate wife.

"Allah has smiled on me but I am a businessman as well as a

devout Muslim," Owiti replied, "and I trust the actions of men, not their rhetoric or dreams. Helping you will put my family, my fortune, and myself at great risk. What will I gain from taking these risks?"

"The glory of serving Allah," the Falcon replied.

Owiti took a sip from his drink without replying, making it clear by his silence that he expected more.

"You want to punish Kenya for supporting AMISOM," the Falcon continued. "I will do that for you. But that is nothing compared to how I will use your money to create chaos in America. A shrewd businessman should be clever enough to benefit financially from what I will do."

"Knowing in advance that another 9/11 attack is coming could be profitable."

"What I am planning eclipses the Twin Towers. With your financial assistance, I will destroy three of America's most important cities in one glorious act, striking a blow for Allah."

"You will destroy three cities simultaneously? An ambitious task, but ambition sometimes surpasses a man's ability."

"I am not a man who proposes the impossible. I have people in place in America, including one at the highest possible level. He tells me what the American president eats each morning, who she meets, and when she goes to bed at night."

"You have a spy inside the White House?"

"My friend, how else do you expect me to destroy it? If you help me, I will kill their president and destroy that city. I will wipe this abomination called Washington from earth's face. This is not a threat, it is a promise that I swear to you."

"And how will you accomplish this?" Owiti asked.

"I will share details of my plan with you, but not now. First, I will present you with a gift of blood. I will punish the Kenyans for supporting AMISOM. That should please you."

"Yes, it would greatly please me."

"Two hundred kilometers from here is the town of Mandera. My gift of blood to you will happen there. I will leave at first light. I already have men waiting there for me to join them."

"That is a seven-hour drive from here," Owiti said. "It will be faster and more comfortable for you in one of my helicopters. But it would be best if you landed outside the city. I do not want the Americans to discover my role. Now tell me more about your plan to destroy Washington."

"After Mandera," the Falcon replied, rising from the settee. "I must rest before morning prayers. Then I will fly to Mandera to instruct my men."

"Please, this is exciting to me. How many men are waiting in Mandera?"

"Six servants of Allah."

"Only six?"

"Allah will be with them. They will not fail."

"How many of them will be returning here with you on my helicopter after the attack?"

"None."

CHAPTER THIRTEEN

Umoja Owiti's compound
Outside El Wak

The four blades atop the Eurocopter EC175 were spinning idly when the Falcon boarded. Umoja Owiti had ordered his staff to paint over the aircraft's blue-and-gold exterior markings as a precaution even though he knew the chances of any governmental agency noticing the aircraft were slim. Neither Kenya nor its neighbors had radar equipment that reached into the lawless North Eastern Province along the Kenya-Somalia border where the levels of poverty, unemployment, and underdevelopment were among the highest in Africa and a major contributor to crime, insecurity, and alienation. Mandera, the province's largest city with 40,000 residents, was legally part of Kenya but was actually governed by local clans.

As soon as Owiti bid his guest good-bye, the helicopter headed north. It touched down a few miles outside the city where a Toyota pickup, six men, and a wooden crate had assembled. The Falcon instructed the pilots to wait for him as he exited to greet his men.

Now that he had arrived, the crate was opened and as the Falcon watched, each of the six men stepped forward, removed a suicide belt from the box, and strapped it around his waist. Next, each claimed an AK-47, the most prevalent assault rifle in the world.

"Today we will strike a blow against the sons of Zion, the worshippers of the Cross, and betrayers of Allah," the Falcon declared. "Today, you will teach the world that our enemies, who support

America, the head of infidelity and the symbol of aggression and tyranny in the world, will be punished by our Lord and Master, Allah, blessed be His name."

The men chanted in unison. *"Allahu Akbar! Allahu Akbar!"*

"Do not be deceived, my brothers," the Falcon continued. "America is leading a Crusader campaign to fight Islam. It is poking its head where it does not belong, bringing behind it an alliance of the Crusaders and their apostate agents. The head of the infidel's beast is America, but before we destroy it, we must remove its limbs."

"Allahu Akbar! Allahu Akbar! Allahu Akbar!"

The young men had formed a circle around the Falcon. Each man placed his arms on the shoulders of the man next to him and swayed as if they were football players in a huddle, all the while quietly repeating: *"Allahu Akbar. Allahu Akbar. Allahu Akbar."*

"The West will call you 'suicide bombers' because their media is controlled by Jews who by their birth are ignorant and liars."

"Allahu Akbar. Allahu Akbar."

"You are *fedayeen*. You will not kill yourselves today. That would be blasphemy. You will kill our enemies in battle and for your fidelity and sacrifice, Muhammad has promised you a vast reward in paradise."

"Allahu Akbar. Allahu Akbar."

"Whoso fighteth in the way of Allah," the Falcon said, quoting from the Quran, "be he slain or be he victorious, on him We shall bestow a vast reward."

"Allahu Akbar! Allahu Akbar!" The men's voices were growing louder as they became more excited.

"Let us remember the teachings of the Ayatollah Khomeini who said, 'the purest joy in Islam is to kill and be killed for Allah!'"

Next came another quote, this one from the Hadith, which is a collection of the teachings by the Prophet Muhammad.

"Nobody who enters Paradise will return to this world, even if he were offered everything on the surface of the earth, except the martyr who will desire to return to this world and be killed ten times for the sake of the great honor that has been bestowed upon him."

At this point, the men released their arms from each other and the Falcon stepped from one to the next, embracing each and handing him a red-and-white-checkered kaffiyeh, to cover his face.

"Allah be with you!" he declared.

The Falcon returned to the Eurocopter, while the men boarded the Toyota truck and sped toward Mandera.

Twenty minutes later, the terrorists reached the Technological Processes College campus, which consisted of five modest buildings inside a two-block area encircled by eight-foot-high mud walls. The college had only one street entrance, which was protected by two unarmed sentries. Both men were leaning with their backs against a wall in metal folding chairs, smoking Rooster brand cigarettes, the cheapest in Kenya, when the Toyota approached them. There was no gate at the entrance, no door, simply a gap between the walls under a corrugated metal canopy that contained the school's name.

When the Toyota reached the campus, its driver swerved off the street and drove directly into the opening between the mud walls, effectively blockading it. While he was doing this, an Al-Shabaab fighter riding in the truck's bed fired a burst from his AK-47, killing both of the startled guards and causing chickens wandering nearby to squawk and scatter.

Leaping from the vehicle, that same jihadist again fired his rifle, this time at the Toyota's front and back tires, turning it into even more of a barricade.

The sounds of gunfire and the sudden appearance of six gunmen racing into the campus courtyard caused an immediate panic. Students seated on the ground and strolling between their morning classes ran into the nearest school building—a four-story dormitory. Al-Shabaab had murdered 148 people during an attack at Garissa University College in 2015 and two years prior to that massacre had killed 67 and wounded 175 during a mass murder attack inside a Nairobi shopping mall.

The attack leader stood in the center of the dirt courtyard while his five comrades gave chase inside the dormitory. Within minutes, terrified students were being herded from the building back into the courtyard with their fingers clasped together behind their heads. Some two hundred students were soon forced to lay helpless on the ground—their clothing creating a patchwork of rainbow colors under the morning sun. The terrorists walked among them like shepherds controlling sheep.

"*Allahu Akbar!*" the leader shouted and then in Swahili, the official language of Kenya, he yelled, "Who here is Muslim?"

Having heard the terrorist praising Allah, all of the students immediately raised their hands.

"What? There are no Christians here?" the leader shouted in an incredulous voice. Reaching down, he grabbed the shoulder of a female student wearing a hijab and jerked her to her feet. "Are you a Muslim?"

The terrified woman answered: "Yes!"

Pressing the barrel of his AK-47 against her temple, he said, "Recite for me a verse from the Holy Quran."

"Allah and His angels send blessings on the Prophet."

Lowering his rifle, he said, "Sister, you may go."

But she didn't move.

"Leave!" he yelled. "Or I will shoot you!"

She glanced around, clearly frightened and uncertain what to do. Then she bolted toward the school's main gate, which was blocked by the Toyota. Everyone watched her running, unsure if the attackers would shoot her. But she reached the disabled truck and escaped out the opening by climbing over its hood and roof since there was no room on either side of it for her to pass through.

The Al-Shabaab terrorist ordered another student to stand. "Tell me a scripture," he ordered.

"Allah sends blessings on the Prophet," the man said, repeating exactly what he had heard the now freed woman proclaim.

"You think me a fool? A different one," the gunman demanded.

The student didn't reply and the gunman fired a single round into his head, spraying the students lying on the ground near them with blood and bits of brain. Several coeds screamed.

"Quiet!" he yelled.

His next target was a sobbing male, whom he ordered to stand. "Muslim?"

"Yes," the student answered in a shaky voice.

By now it had become obvious that having every Muslim student in the courtyard quote a different scripture would be impossible. The Christians hiding among them would simply repeat whatever verse they'd overheard.

"What separates Sunnis and Shiites?" the terrorist demanded.

"Sunnis followed Abu Dakr, the Prophet's advisor. Shiites followed Ali, the Prophet's cousin. This is the difference between them."

It was the correct answer, but rather than freeing the student, the gunman pointed his AK-47 at a woman lying close by.

"Muslim?"

The male student looked at her horrified face and then at the gunman threatening him. "I don't know her," the student said.

The gunman stepped back and fired, killing the male student, who fell dead.

"Any Muslim who is not with us is our enemy," the jihadist declared. "Do not act as if you don't know these infidels. If you betray your faith and your people, you will share their fate." He pointed his rifle at another male student and ordered him to stand.

"Are you a follower of the Cross?"

"No," the student replied. Without being asked, he hollered in a loud voice, "Allah has full knowledge of all things, chapter thirty-three, verse forty-one. *Allahu Akbar!*"

Convinced, the terrorist aimed his rifle at the same woman on the ground that he'd asked about earlier. "Is she a Muslim?"

"No, Christian," the student answered.

The gunman fired several shots into her. Now that he had found an informant, he began moving more quickly from student to student.

"Yes," the informant would declare. "No."

His declaration meant either freedom or death. Muslims being culled from the others were permitted to run toward the blocked gate, leaving the corpses of Christians behind. Two of the other terrorists plucked informants from their captors to assist them in identifying targets. The carnage continued. Fearing the inevitable, a Christian student leaped up and ran, only to be cut down by gunfire before reaching the Toyota.

More than two dozen students had been slaughtered when a Mandera policeman who'd arrived outside the walls and positioned himself near the Toyota fired at the Al-Shabaab leader overseeing the killings. His bullet hit the terrorist in his face. The Muslim informant assisting him froze as the terrorist's head literally exploded.

Before the policeman could fire again, the five remaining terrorists dropped to their knees as if they were praying. The Falcon had given them instructions. Do not fight or run when the police arrive. It was time for them to kill themselves.

Time seemed to slow in the courtyard. The students around the masked assailants began jumping up to escape, which made it difficult for the police now entering the courtyard to fire at the terrorists without risking hitting the fleeing students. In the midst of this confusion, the five assailants detonated their suicide vests.

The deafening *boom, boom, boom, boom* was followed by thousands of projectiles flying in every direction, maiming and killing anyone in their paths. Sounds of students crying in agony filled the blood-soaked courtyard.

A police car rammed into the back of the Toyota blocking the gate and pushed it into the courtyard, freeing the opening for police officers and an ambulance crew to enter. Pushing behind them were dozens of men and women who had heard about the slaughter and were related to students. Some were carrying hoes, picks, and machetes as weapons to fight the attackers.

As they raced between the wounded and dead, they discovered one of the terrorists was alive. His vest had not exploded and the students who'd jumped up around him had inadvertently protected him from the sprays of shrapnel from his comrade's vests.

He was shoved to the ground and about to be murdered when a policeman interceded. He warned that the vest wrapped around the terrorist's waist might still explode and that drove the angry mob away from the terrorist long enough for the police to take charge of him.

A military helicopter flew him to Nairobi for questioning and to make certain he was not killed by the families of those murdered.

CHAPTER FOURTEEN

U.S. Embassy
CIA station chief's office
Nairobi, Kenya

Darius Hall handed Walks Many Miles a thick binder.

"You'll need to read this," the Nairobi CIA station chief explained, "and then sign an affidavit." Hall pushed another document, this one only six pages long, toward Miles. "I'll have my administrative assistant witness your signature when you're ready."

"You're telling me that I can't talk to Yaasir Sharif, a terrorist responsible for massacring students at Mandera, until I read this binder and sign this affidavit?" Miles asked in a puzzled voice.

"Yep, regulations."

Miles opened the binder and read its title page. *Rules and Regulations for Detaining and Interrogating Terrorism Suspects*. Fanning through it, he said, "There's a hundred and fifty-eight pages. Is this some sort of joke—like college hazing—that you play on someone who just arrived in town?"

"I wish it were. But no, it isn't. Ever since the release of a Senate report back in 2014 that trashed the agency for using enhanced interrogation techniques—you know, sleep deprivation, waterboarding, slapping suspects, rectal infusion—all interrogations with enemy combatants must be done according to these guidelines. If you violate any one of the rules, you could end up in a federal pen."

"I understand why waterboarding and rectal infusion are no longer tolerated," Miles said. "People will say anything if they're being tortured. But what's wrong with refusing to allow someone to go to sleep? Wasn't that what broke Khalid Sheikh Mohammed, the 9/11 mastermind?"

"Ah, you've been reading about KSM. After the first time he'd been waterboarded, KSM realized his interrogators weren't going to drown him. They did it nearly three hundred times to him and never got him to talk. They watched him and he would count the seconds with his fingers, knowing that after ten seconds, they had to stop."

"But keeping him awake," Miles said, "that's when his own mind began torturing him."

"On page one hundred in the binder, you'll find a rule that requires each terrorist to receive a minimum of four hours of sleep during every twenty-four-hour period. If not, it's considered torture and is illegal. We can't do it."

"Al-Shabaab rapes women, sells children to sex traffickers, cuts off heads, and buries people up to their necks in the desert all in the name of Allah. Yet if we keep one of these pricks awake past his bedtime, we're in trouble."

"Trust me, these combatants know our rules better than we do," Hall warned. "I've had them laugh in my face. They aren't afraid of us. The first thing they demand is a copy of the Quran. Then they start telling me what sort of specialized food they can eat."

"Before coming here," Miles said, "I was told we got better and more accurate information if we developed a rapport with a suspect rather than torturing him."

"That's the current mind-set and I got no problem following it. We're under orders to find some commonality, gain their trust, convince them that it's in their best interest to help us by volunteering information."

"But you sound skeptical."

"It works when you're dealing with someone who is from a similar culture. Say the Germans. Remember stories of our guys and their guys singing 'Silent Night' at Christmastime in Bastogne and even back in the First World War when both sides declared a Christmas truce and sang Christmas carols. In those days, it wasn't difficult to imagine that the men killing each other on the battlefield might have been chums and shared a beer under different circumstances."

"You don't believe that's true now?"

"Muslims don't drink beer," Hall deadpanned. "The prisoner who you are going to interrogate believes Americans are the devil. You think he wants to become friends with Satan or drink a beer with him?"

Hall chuckled at his own comment and added, "I can tell you this. Yaasir Sharif isn't afraid of dying. He believes he's going to have sex with a bunch of virgins as soon as he's martyred."

"How can I convince him to tell me about the Falcon?" Miles asked. "I just flew in last night with my SAD team. I got a week, at most, to get intel from him."

Hall stepped from behind his desk, walked to a window in his office and turned a crank, opening it outward as much as he could since there were decorative iron bars around it. "Did you know it all started right here?" the fifty-seven-year-old station chief said, as he lighted a cigarette. "No one in America had even heard of Osama bin Laden or Al-Qaeda until August seventh, 1998. That's when suicide bombers drove trucks crammed with explosives into our embassies here in Nairobi and at Dar es Salaam, Tanzania. The bomb blast here killed two hundred and thirteen and wounded nearly four thousand. It was our radical Islamist wake-up call."

Hall took a long drag and continued. "We put bin Laden on the FBI's Most Wanted List after that. Bin Laden claimed he'd targeted our embassies because we'd sent troops into Somalia. Black Hawk Down. But that's not what our intelligence said."

Hall turned away from the window and looked at Miles. "According to our people, bin Laden was taking revenge against us because the agency had arranged the extradition and torture of four

Islamic radicals. His buddies. Do you see an irony now? Torture. The same issue you and I are discussing is what started all of this mess. We do it to them. They do it to us. We do it to them."

"My people, the Crow, believe you must move into the center of the circle if you wish to find peace and harmony."

"What the hell does that mean?"

"Philosophy. The difference between how white men and indigenous people view time and space."

Hall chuckled. "An Indian philosopher former Marine. Let me know if any of that helps you when you interrogate Yaasir Sharif."

"Based on the regulations you have given me to read, philosophy might be the only topic I can talk to him about."

"Sharif isn't afraid of us," Hall said solemnly. "He knows he's a goner anyway because Kenya is going to execute him for his role in the Mandera attack."

"I don't see how that will help me. You just said he isn't afraid of death. He's got virgins awaiting him in paradise."

"I'm going to make it help you. Do you remember General Abdullah Osman Saeed over in Mogadishu from your stint there?"

"That one-eared bastard is difficult to forget. He murdered an American contractor and he's a sadist," Miles replied. "How's he going to help me?"

"Yaasir Sharif knows he's going to die and he doesn't care, but I've learned that he has a wife, two daughters, and a son, and all of them live in Somalia. His parents are in Mogadishu too. The only relative who doesn't live there is a sister of his who is in the States. The general would be happy to slit the throats of everyone of his family members in Somalia if asked."

"Isn't slitting throats against the rules?" Miles asked, nodding at the thick binder of regulations now resting in his lap.

"If I spoke to General Saeed, you would not be threatening Sharif. You would not be violating any rules. You would be warning him about General Saeed. You would be telling him that you wanted to help save his family by intervening. Offering to help a combatant isn't against the rules."

Returning to his desk, Hall continued, "When you meet with Sharif, tell him that you've learned from Somali intelligence that General Saeed is planning on raping his wife, slitting her throat and the throats of his children and his parents in retaliation for the murders at the Mandera college. Sharif knows Saeed executes Al-Shabaab fighters and their entire families whenever he catches one. Then tell Sharif that the United States is willing to arrange for his wife, his children, and his parents to move to America where his sister lives. You offer him that carrot and then we'll see how much he hates the Great Satan. And oh, he speaks and understands English, so don't let him act as if he doesn't."

Glancing down at the binder, Miles said, "And the rules?"

"I'll keep them on the shelf for you to read when you get back."

An hour later after leaving Hall, Miles arrived at the Kamiti Maximum Security Prison in Nairobi. Growing up on the Crow reservation, Miles was familiar with poverty, but he'd never seen as barbaric conditions as what he observed while being escorted through the ancient prison. Before entering the interior cell blocks, he'd been given a paper mask to cover his nose and mouth to protect himself from tuberculosis, which was rampant, but that filter didn't block the stench of human excrement overflowing from communal troughs and the smells of decay and death. Starving inmates half dressed in soiled blue-striped uniforms were packed so tightly in cells that it would have been impossible for all of them to lie down on the grime-covered cement floors. He refused to make eye contact and kept a safe distance from the inmates who pressed against the cell bars, pleading for help. He didn't want to see the open sores on their faces nor risk being touched by their dirty, outstretched fingers.

Yaasir Sharif was brought into an interrogation room in leg irons and handcuffs. A bandage yellowed by sweat and puss was wrapped around his chest where he'd been wounded during fighting at Mandera. Miles had been in enough barroom brawls to recognize that the bruises on Sharif's face—his broken nose, swollen eyes, and cracked lips—had come after his capture.

When they were alone sitting across a metal table from each other, Miles said, "I'm an American. What can I do to help you?"

Sharif didn't answer.

"I know you are a deeply religious man; would you like me to bring you a copy of the Holy Quran?"

Sharif showed no reaction and remained silent.

During that first meeting, Miles did not mention anything about General Saeed.

The next day, Miles brought a copy of the Quran and food for Sharif, but he refused to take either and simply glared at his inquisitor. Once again, Miles didn't mention the threat to Sharif's family.

On the third day, Sharif didn't speak, but he did take the Quran with him. Miles considered that a good sign but still did not mention Somalia.

It was on the fourth day that Miles broached the subject. As before, Sharif had remained stoic during their sessions.

"You married?" Miles asked. When Sharif didn't answer, Miles said, "I've found the woman who I want to be my wife, but I'm not sure she would say yes if I asked her. You know, women in America are strong. Are you married?"

Sharif stared ahead at a wall without blinking. It was at this point that Miles let out a sigh. "Listen, I want to help you, but I can't if you don't want to help yourself."

On the fifth day, Miles arrived earlier than usual and when Sharif entered the room, he said, "Congratulations. You've won. You will go to your death and become a martyr knowing you didn't speak to me. I will not be coming back after today."

Yaasir Sharif spoke for the first time. "My family has been arrested in Somalia. General Saeed is threatening to rape and

butcher my wife and slit the throats of my children and my parents." He stared at Miles's face, searching for some clue that would
tell him if the American sitting across from him was aware and
behind the threats.

"I can get your family out of Somalia," Miles replied. "You will
die here. But I will intercede and move every one of them—your
wife, your children, and your parents—to America to live. They
do not have to die. Your children do not have to suffer. Your wife
doesn't need to be raped. Your parents don't have to have their
throats cut. I understand you have a sister living in the States. I can
get them safe passage there."

The mention of his sister caused Sharif to look at Miles even
more suspiciously. But in that same moment, Sharif realized that it
really didn't matter. His loved ones were in General Saeed's hands
and whether Miles and the CIA had arranged that or the general
was doing it completely on his own, the result would be the same.

"If you tell me about the Falcon, I promise you," Miles said, "I
will save them."

CHAPTER FIFTEEN

Ronald Reagan National Airport
Arlington, Virginia

Major Brooke Grant hit the speed dial on her cell phone as she hustled through the crowded airport terminal. When she'd spoken to Walks Many Miles in Kenya the day before, he'd complained that he still hadn't gotten any useful information from Yaasir Sharif. Today was his fifth day and final chance. Brooke let the number ring until it hit voice mail. The hands on her watch showed it was a few minutes before eight a.m. EDT, which meant it was nearly three p.m. in Nairobi. Miles was usually finished at the Kamiti prison by now. Perhaps Sharif was finally cooperating.

Glancing up from her phone, she noticed the TSA checkpoint was backed up. At least fifty passengers were waiting in the slow-moving line. Even worse, Al Arabic Washington correspondent Ebio Kattan was one of them. Avoiding Kattan was going to be difficult. Brooke decided to check a nearby airport display for a later flight that could still get her to Minneapolis before the White House task force's afternoon meeting.

"Major Grant," she heard a man say. "Cutting it a bit close, aren't you?"

Brooke found a smiling Representative Rudy Adeogo approaching her.

"Judging from that TSA line, both of us are," she replied. Nodding toward Ebio Kattan, she added, "I'd rather walk than be on the same plane as that reporter, but unfortunately, there are no other flights available today that will get us to Minneapolis in time for the meeting."

"And I really don't want you walking," he replied. "Follow me."

Adeogo led her around the line to where his media aide, Fatima Olol, was waiting with a TSA-uniformed employee.

"Come right this way, Congressman," the TSA official said.

"Major Grant is traveling with me," he explained. "She's part of our White House task force."

"Absolutely not a problem," the TSA official answered as he waved an electronic wand quickly around Adeogo's torso. "By law, we have to check everyone, including members of Congress, but we know your time is important so we certainly don't mind expediting the process by clearing you outside the line." He called over a female TSA worker who checked Brooke with the wand. Finding nothing suspicious, Adeogo and Brooke continued forward to the gate.

Brooke's phone rang as they walked and she answered it, hoping it was Miles.

"I'm hearing rumors about fraternization," a stern General Frank Grant said.

This was not a conversation Brooke wanted to have with her uncle, especially with Representative Adeogo, his press aide, and a TSA manager all within earshot.

"I'm about to board a flight," she whispered. "But you don't have to worry. Walks Many Miles is no longer a Marine. He's resigned from the Corps, which makes your concern a nonissue."

"Oh no, missy, we are going to have this conversation right now," Grant answered. "And it is anything but a nonissue. If word leaks out that you're dating him, the media will go wild."

Brooke stepped away from everyone. "No one in the media cares who I date. And you shouldn't either."

"You're being reckless and foolish. You and Miles are celebrities thanks to Somalia. You, in particular, given you stopped a burning woman from throwing herself on the president. The media will see this as a fairy-tale romance and then they'll turn against you."

"Turn against me? You're being paranoid."

"Brooke, stop for a moment and consider what will happen if some enterprising reporter begins digging into your past. Your last romance didn't turn out so well, did it?"

"I didn't know Jean-Paul Dufour was married when I was dating him."

"But he was, wasn't he? Once they start digging into your romantic life, a story about your London fling with a married French diplomat is bound to surface and it isn't going to reflect highly on you. You're on a White House task force now. You're a major in the Marine Corps. You're my niece. And now you and Sergeant Miles are—"

"Former sergeant," she interjected, correcting him.

"A sergeant who was under your command when you became involved. You need to end this right now. And, speaking as your uncle, I've got to ask: What do you possibly have in common with a Crow Indian who was raised on a Montana reservation? Hell, you've never even been to Montana."

"I wasn't aware visiting a man's home state was a prerequisite to dating him. And your reference about him being an Indian is racist."

"Don't you dare lecture me about racism."

"I'm sorry about that comment, but you're overstepping."

"You know what a battle buddy is, don't you?" he asked, ignoring her comment. "Don't confuse the bonds you make in the foxhole with romance. Are you prepared to give up your career and move to Montana to have this guy's kids on a reservation? Get real, Brooke!"

"Have you considered he will be the one who has to give up his career, and what makes you presume he wants to live on a reservation?" she snapped. "I have to board my flight."

She ended the call without saying good-bye. Glancing up from her phone, she saw Kattan approaching the gate. At that moment, Adeogo rejoined her.

"I asked the flight attendant to seat us together," he said. "I had them put you in a window seat next to me and added that we'd be working and would like our privacy. They've offered to let us board now, ahead of the others. I didn't think you'd want Ebio Kattan sticking a microphone under your nose."

"I don't think she'd dare. Our last encounter wasn't pretty."

"She's a reporter, she would dare," Adeogo said. "Unfortunately, neither of us can afford to show our true feelings at times. You must deal with Ebio Kattan and I must deal with Omar Nader at the OIN, who is also on our task force."

She was surprised by his candor. "I assumed the two of you were friends. I mean, you're both Muslims."

"Tell me, Major Grant, are you friends with every Protestant you meet?"

The gate attendant opened the door to the Jetway.

"I will tell you an Arab saying," Adeogo said as they walked down it toward the aircraft. "'Beware the levelheaded person if they are angry,' which means that you and I are much more dangerous when we finally become angry than those who are constantly ranting."

"My uncle calls that 'keeping your powder dry.'"

Once inside the jet, she slipped into a window seat, buckled her seat belt, and began reading a briefing report about Somali Americans born in Minneapolis who'd traveled to Africa to join Al-Shabaab and ISIS. Adeogo sat in the aisle seat.

When general boarding began, Ebio Kattan ducked through the door and immediately stopped to speak to them. "Congressman Adeogo, what a pleasure to see you and Major Grant, how fortunate for me that we are all on the same flight."

A flight attendant behind her said, "The congressman has work to do and we've got a plane to board. Please move to your seat."

"I'm hoping you'll have a minute to talk when we land," Kattan said to Adeogo, ignoring the attendant.

"I'll be speaking at a press conference inside the terminal as soon as we disembark," he replied.

"Yes, but I was hoping to catch you immediately outside the gate before everyone else. Maybe Major Grant will say a few words too."

"Miss, you need to move along," the attendant said. "People are waiting."

Brooke raised her hand and waved at Kattan dismissively.

After takeoff, Adeogo whispered, "I thought you controlled your temper very well with Ms. Kattan. I don't want to intrude, but I noticed you were having an intense telephone conversation before we boarded. I hope everything is fine now."

"Family matter," she said.

She returned to her reading, but had trouble concentrating.

Was it possible that she was making another mistake in falling for Walks Many Miles? Was her uncle correct in calling their romance a foxhole connection? She'd fallen deeply in love with Jean-Paul Dufour, and that had turned into a disaster. Where was her love affair with Miles headed?

CHAPTER SIXTEEN

General Grant's office
The Pentagon
Arlington, Virginia

Geneneral Frank Grant felt equally distracted after his telephone conversation with his niece. But he didn't have
time to ponder his thoughts. As soon as he'd put down his
phone, his National Security Council liaison, Lieutenant Colonel
Gabe DeMoss, entered his office.

"You asked to see me, sir," DeMoss said.

"Is there anything new from the SAD team that was dispatched
to Nairobi?"

"Nothing that I've been told," DeMoss answered. "Sir, I noticed
on your schedule this morning that you're meeting Director
Grainger. He would be the first to hear from the SAD team."
DeMoss glanced at his watch. "You need to be leaving now or you'll
be late."

"I want you to accompany me to Langley," Grant said.

"Sir, I have a meeting scheduled."

"Cancel it," Grant snapped. "I've learned a bit more about that
burner phone used in the assassination attempt on the president
and I want you there when I brief Grainger."

Within minutes, the two men were traveling north on Highway
110, a two-and-a-half-mile freeway built in the early 1940s, in part
to connect the Pentagon with the federal district. On some maps
the road was identified as the Jefferson Davis Highway, but that

name had fallen out of favor as part of a public campaign aimed at erasing everything from official landmarks that commemorated the Confederacy, especially the name of a secessionist president. The Potomac River was on their right and Arlington National Cemetery on their left.

About a quarter mile ahead of the general's government-provided Cadillac, a Ford F-150 truck turned on the same highway. The truck had been rented from a local home improvement store and had been fitted with a flatbed that could be raised and lowered. Large trucks and tour buses were banned from using Highway 110 after the 9/11 attacks because of the highway's proximity to the Pentagon, but pickup trucks like the F-150 were allowed. When it reached an interchange where Highways 110 and 50 connect with Interstate 66, the truck's driver pulled a lever that raised the vehicle's cargo bed. Cardboard boxes filled with thousands of roofing nails and stacks of two-by-four-inch pine boards slid onto the freeway. The two cars directly behind the truck slammed on their brakes, causing a chain reaction. Four cars rear-ended the vehicles in front of them.

"What's going on?" DeMoss asked Bill Lepinski, the general's driver, when their sedan came to a full stop.

"Looks like a major tie-up in both lanes," Lepinski replied. Because they were a dozen cars back from the blockage, they couldn't see the spilled debris. Lepinski opened the driver's door. "I'll go see what the holdup is."

From the rooftop of a high-rise apartment building less than a half mile away, the assassin known as Akbar watched Lepinski step from the Cadillac and thread his way through the stalled vehicles.

Akbar had been waiting patiently for this moment since before first light. He had selected this shooting spot weeks earlier after studying Google satellite images and inspecting each site. He had selected this apartment building at the northwest corner of the highway interchange because it was tall enough for him to clearly observe a section of Highway 110 for more than a mile. Although

he couldn't know exactly where the general's car would be forced
to stop, he knew General Grant would be in a kill zone as long as
the Cadillac was within a half mile of the highway interchange. His
Dragunov sniper's rifle, the most readily available to terrorists, was
most effective at 875 yards.

Akbar was lying prone on the building's white-painted roof
wearing a snow-colored camouflage poncho to conceal him from
any aircraft passing close to the building. Reagan National Airport was south of the Pentagon and pilots often followed a landing
course that followed the Potomac River near where he was hiding.

Snipers always had to compensate for distance and wind, but
Akbar also had needed to consider how his bullet would react when
it hit the Cadillac's glass. He'd scoured the Internet until he'd found
the bidding criteria that the federal government had posted when it
notified the public that it intended to buy dozens of lightly armored
sedans for use by government officials. The specifications had called
for an inch of bullet-resistant glass in all executive-level cars. That
inch was not nearly as thick as the glass in the two presidential
limousines—a reduction intended to help reduce the weight and
costs of the cars. Akbar felt confident that the 168-gram, solid copper, 7.62x54 mm NATO round that he had chambered would punch
through the window. But he wasn't certain if the path of the slug
would be altered by the glass, causing it to swerve and miss its target.

As he peered through the Dragunov's scope, he watched Lepinski
returning to the Cadillac, having learned the reason for the backup.
As the driver neared the car, Gabe DeMoss stepped from the right
side of the sedan. DeMoss momentarily glanced upward at the
high-rise where Akbar was hiding while surveying the scene. He
walked toward Lepinski, who gestured toward the cause of the road-
block. What happened next caused Akbar to begin praising Allah.

Having been briefed by Lepinski, DeMoss walked down the left
side of the Cadillac and opened the rear passenger door behind
its driver's seat. He opened the door because the one-inch-thick
bullet-resistant windows in the car doors could neither be raised nor

lowered, and he wanted to tell General Grant about the cargo spill that was causing their delay.

In that moment, Akbar had a shot.

He aimed the round between the gap that had been created by DeMoss when he opened the rear passenger door. From his perch, Akbar could see a sliver of General Grant sitting in the backseat. The assassin no longer had to worry about his bullet being deflected when it struck the vehicle's glass.

Marksmen often brag about head shots, but Akbar aimed at "center mass"—Grant's uniformed chest with its brightly colored award ribbons. His crosshairs were centered on the general's heart as he squeezed the Dragunov's trigger.

Akbar had correctly calculated the wind and distance. But he'd misgauged the bullet's spin, which influenced the round just enough for it to nick the edge of the Cadillac's reinforced doorframe, slightly altering the shot's trajectory. Rather than striking the general's heart, it struck Grant on the left side of his face, shattering his jaw. His head recoiled from the impact before his body flew forward.

Lieutenant Colonel DeMoss dropped to the pavement the moment he realized a sniper was shooting at them. But Akbar was already running across the rooftop, shedding his white poncho as he dashed down the building's stairway. His wife, Aludra, was waiting behind the wheel of a rental car at the building's ground exit, with its engine running.

She exited from the parking lot onto Highway 50 and drove west. Akbar had a second shooting to execute.

A medevac helicopter airlifted General Grant across the Potomac River to the George Washington University Hospital trauma center. Lieutenant Colonel DeMoss flew with him. As soon as they landed, DeMoss reached for his phone to telephone Brooke Grant. When she didn't answer her cell phone, he checked his watch and realized that she was still onboard a commercial jet flying to Minneapolis.

CHAPTER SEVENTEEN

A local coffee shop
Minneapolis, Minnesota

The executive director of the OIN, Omar Nader, invited Mary Margaret Delaney to join him for coffee at seven thirty a.m., about three hours before the commercial flight carrying Major Brooke Grant and Representative Rudy Adeogo was scheduled to land at the Minneapolis–St. Paul International Airport. He'd chosen the Alle Aamin Coffee Shop on Cedar Avenue in the Cedar-Riverside neighborhood of Minneapolis, home to most of the Twin Cities' Somali residents. When he arrived, his guest was already sitting at a corner table. Nader stopped to order at the counter before bringing her a cup of coffee and what looked like a pancake.

"This is *canjeero*," he said, placing the breakfast treat in front of her. "It is a type of Somali bread, and the coffee is called *qahwe*, which is coffee mixed with cardamom and cinnamon."

Delaney sipped the coffee. "It's not bad."

"Not bad?" he replied, sounding offended. "You Americans don't know good coffee, even with all of your fancy-sounding combinations ordered in a Starbucks. In my region of the world, coffee is sacred."

She broke off a piece of the *canjeero*, tasted it, and frowned.

"I prefer a scone," she said.

"No doubt a tribute to your Irish heritage." He glanced around the coffee shop and said, "I chose here so you could get a taste of

Somalia and also because it is unlikely anyone will recognize either of us, unless we bump into Leo Mezzrow."

"Who?"

"A local food critic," Nader replied, showing off his knowledge about the city. "At least no one in the media attending the White House task force meeting today will be coming here."

"You don't want to be seen talking with me."

"While I always enjoy your company, the topic of our meeting this morning is best discussed in private."

"The last time we met was in Washington during the presidential campaign."

"Ah, you remember."

"It's not every day someone arranges for their presidential political candidate to get five million dollars in contributions," she answered.

"Ms. Delaney, you know it would be against federal campaign laws for the OIN to contribute directly to a presidential candidate such as your former governor Coldridge."

"And that is why you rallied your 'citizen activists' and their PACs and Super PACs."

"When it comes to contributions, we simply follow the example of AIPAC," he replied. "The Jews have always understood the power of money. We only seek a level playing field."

"Giving my candidate five million dollars when you gave President Allworth's reelection twice that did not level our field," she replied with an edge of bitterness in her voice.

"Ah, Ms. Delaney. There's no point in holding a grudge in politics. The OIN hedged its bets by arranging generous donations through our members and their PACs for both campaigns. It wasn't personal. Besides, your candidate didn't lose because of a lack of money."

"Governor Coldridge lost because the White House ended the crisis in Somalia on the weekend before the election—a crisis that the president had created," Delaney replied.

Nader shrugged. "There is only so much a political handler, such as you, can control. Don't blame yourself."

"Oh, I don't. But I do remember who helped us and who didn't."

"Including Representative Rudy Adeogo?" he asked.

"What's this little tête-à-tête about?" she replied, ignoring his question for the moment. "Why did you ask to meet with me?"

"I've come to do you a favor."

Delaney took another sip of *qahwe*. Omar Nader and the OIN always had an agenda. They also had a reputation for rewarding friends and vehemently attacking enemies.

"A favor? What's in it for you?" she asked suspiciously.

"Ms. Delaney, I fear Washington has made you cynical. Perhaps my gesture springs only from the goodness in my heart."

"I stopped believing men acted from the goodness in their hearts after I developed breasts."

Nader was aware of Delaney's brash reputation, which he personally found amusing.

"My motivation? To be honest, I believe we share a mutual dislike," Nader said. "My sources tell me that Rudy Adeogo agreed to support your presidential candidate by appearing at a news conference about Somalia, but at the last moment he backed out. He betrayed you. That was a blow to your campaign, was it not?"

"Your sources? Do you mean the army of lobbyists and Washington snoops you pay?"

"What's the Washington cliché? Knowledge is power."

"Is there anyone in Washington who's not on your payroll besides me?"

His answer was a smug grin.

"Let's not be coy," he said. "I know you have been searching for information about Representative Rudy Adeogo—negative information."

He leaned forward and said in a low voice, "I am not a fan of Adeogo so you may speak freely."

Delaney tried another nibble of *canjeero*. She didn't trust Nader.

"Adeogo is the only Muslim in Congress," she said. "I would think you and the OIN would be strong allies of his."

"Let's just say the Minneapolis congressman is a bit too vocal and independent for our tastes."

"Was it his comments the other day about the need for Saudi Arabia and other Arab nations to do more when it comes to fighting extremists?"

"Yes, we would prefer that he would avoid making such statements."

"Or was it his comment about how Israel should be recognized as a legitimate nation?"

"Zionism always concerns us."

"There are more than forty thousand Jews living in Minneapolis," Delaney noted. "Adeogo is just playing to them. As you just noted, Jews have big pockets."

"And, I also said, so do we. It is not about money. He is naïve about Israel. We are disappointed in the congressman because he is choosing, as you Americans like to say, to not be a team player. He needs to be taught a lesson."

"Is there something more?"

Nader purposely took another long sip of the *qahwe* that he was drinking. "So you have sources in Washington too," he replied as he lowered his cup. "You have heard there is a personal matter between us, a personal grudge, but that is not germane to our conversation."

"When it is personal, it is always germane, especially in Washington."

"Perhaps another time, but for now, I am here to tell you that I have some information about him, some embarrassing information, that I'm willing to share under the right conditions."

"What can you possibly tell me about Adeogo that I don't already know?"

Nader drew a large envelope from a satchel and placed it between them. Delaney put aside her *canjeero* and reached for the packet, but before her hand touched it, Nader slapped his palm over the envelope, pinning it on the table.

"Before I allow you to look at the contents," he said, "you must give me your word that you will not disclose this information to anyone without my permission."

"It is your material," she replied. "I guess I can agree to that."

Lifting his hand, he waved his forefinger at her and said, "Not guess. You need to understand that if you read the contents of this envelope, you will be involving yourself in a situation that involves more than the two of us or even the OIN. It involves individuals who are not to be trifled with. Very serious people."

"What sort of serious people?"

"Serious people who have the ability to get information not available to the public."

She sat back in her seat, pulling back her hand. "Are you telling me that you have information in that envelope gathered by an intelligence service? Has a foreign intelligence service been spying on a member of Congress?"

"Let's just say the OIN has many influential members and some of them have access to useful intelligence information."

She slowly reached forward and retrieved the envelope. Inside it were two papers, which she read carefully before she glanced up. Checking the area around them to make certain no one could hear their conversation, she said, "If these documents are legitimate, Rudy Adeogo is finished as a congressman."

"No," Nader replied sternly in a low voice. "We are not going to use this information to destroy his political career. We want him to continue being a congressman."

"Then why show them to me?"

"We want to *control* him, not drive him out of office, Ms. Delaney. We want to turn him into our puppet."

"You don't need me to blackmail him."

"Yes, we do. Adeogo is an intelligent man. He knows the OIN would never make this information public because we would suffer too. Collateral damage. If we threatened him, Adeogo would know we were bluffing."

"Because you are fellow Muslims."

"Another of your American sayings seems appropriate: We would be shooting ourselves in our own foot." He looked into her green eyes. "I've heard Irish women with red hair and green eyes are volatile. Dangerous. As well as sexy."

"What you've heard is we can be crazy. But you can't trust clichés. Otherwise all Arabs would be bombers, belly dancers, or billionaires."

"Yes, yes, of course," he said, chuckling. "The point is that Adeogo will be afraid of you when he learns you have this information because he knows you hate him. He will not risk saying no to you and we can control him through you."

"What's in this for me?"

"The OIN can be extremely generous."

"How generous?"

"A yearly retainer for your services as a political consultant. Say in the six figures with a nice signing bonus."

"Make it high six figures."

"Agreed, but only if you are successful in controlling him. He is not so easy to manipulate."

"You let me worry about that. I can make him dance for you."

Nader glanced at his watch. "I have another meeting, but before I leave, I want to make certain we are absolutely clear. You may use this information to blackmail him, but you are not to make it public. We don't want a scandal, we want to muzzle him."

"Relax, I understand."

"Do you *understand*?" he asked in an intense voice.

"Yes, we are dealing with serious men."

"*Deadly* serious men. They do not play games. They reward those who serve them and..." He did not finish his sentence.

"If it is so risky, I'll expect that signing bonus to be very generous," Delaney said, tucking the envelope into her monogrammed satchel.

CHAPTER EIGHTEEN

Kamiti Prison
Nairobi, Kenya

Walks Many Miles checked his cell phone as soon as he exited the Kamiti Prison and saw that Brooke Grant had called. After listening to the message that she'd left, he checked the time and realized that Brooke was still on a flight traveling to her White House task force meeting in Minneapolis.

Although he knew that she wouldn't be able to answer his call, he placed it anyway.

"Brooke, I just got finished interrogating Yaasir Sharif. I finally got him to spill his guts and he told me that you and Jennifer have been targeted," Miles warned. "The Falcon has issued a fatwa against you both and a third person. I'm not certain who the third target is, but Sharif said it was someone high up in the U.S. military. I know you're still flying to your meeting so I'm going to ask Langley to patch me through to the FBI. We need to get you protection and someone out to your farmhouse to watch Jennifer."

He paused for a moment and then added, "I love you. Please, please take these threats seriously. I don't want to lose either of you."

The CIA and FBI have a well-documented history of rivalry and acrimony but within minutes after Miles finished briefing his CIA SAD supervisor, Miles found himself speaking to Wyatt Parker, the FBI's assistant director for counterterrorism.

"My boss just told me," Miles said in a concerned voice, "that someone shot General Grant less than an hour ago. I believe that shooting is linked to a fatwa issued by the Falcon, and there are two other Americans on his kill list—Major Brooke Grant and her ward, Jennifer Conner."

"I just got off the phone with Major Grant," Parker said reassuringly. "We had the airline connect us with her flight so we could tell her that her uncle had been shot. She should be safe on that plane and there's a private aircraft waiting to fly her back to Washington as soon as she lands in Minneapolis."

"That's great, but you need to send someone out to protect Jennifer Conner too. ASAP."

"I understand," Parker said.

"How's the general?" Miles asked. "No one at Langley seemed to know."

"He's currently in surgery and will be for some time. Critical condition. No one knows if he'll pull through."

"Do you know who shot him?"

"Not yet."

"My source here in Nairobi told me the Falcon wanted a high-ranking military official dead. I'm guessing General Grant is the third person named in the fatwa."

"That makes sense. I'll get word to Major Grant about the fatwa as soon as we're done speaking."

"I already left her a message on her cell phone," Miles said.

"You have her private cell number?"

"We're friends. Do you know where Major Grant's farmhouse is located? I can give you the address and directions. Jennifer Conner and her nanny, Miriam Okpara, should be there. A private security company is supposed to be protecting them but there's already been one security breach at her farm."

"What sort of breach?"

Miles quickly told Parker about how an intruder had managed

to appear outside Jennifer's bedroom window without setting off any alarms.

"I'll alert the security company and send two agents to check on things," Parker said. "If my people believe Jennifer and her nanny are in any immediate danger, they'll get her to someplace safe."

CHAPTER NINETEEN

Major Brooke Grant's farmhouse
Near Berryville, Virginia

At the same moment Walks Many Miles was speaking to the FBI's Wyatt Parker, a Dodge minivan approached the two security guards stationed at the highway turnoff that led to Major Brooke Grant's Victorian farmhouse. The woman driving the minivan lowered her window and asked: "Is this the road to where a Major Brooke Grant and a girl named Jennifer Conner live?"

Both guards noticed the driver was wearing a hijab and immediately became suspicious. The male security guard approached the minivan slowly while his female counterpart positioned herself at the front of the vehicle's passenger side where she rested her palm on the butt of her holstered Glock 22 pistol.

"Who are you?" the male guard asked when he reached the lowered driver's window.

"I'm from the doctor's office. They sent me to collect blood and urine samples from a Miss Jennifer Conner. They're routine tests we do because of the powerful medications she takes. This is my first time coming here. Is this the driveway to her house?"

As she spoke, the woman nodded at the winding gravel path in front of her vehicle that snaked its way up a tree-covered hill. From the highway entrance, she couldn't see the farmhouse.

"Lady, I'm not telling you anything until I see some identification.

Plus, I'll need to know the name of the doctor's office so I can call to verify that they sent you here."

"Are you doing this because I am wearing a hijab and am a Muslim?" she asked.

"Absolutely," he replied unapologetically. "The last time I checked, the only men and women who were Islamic terrorists were Muslims."

"That's profiling," she replied in an irritated voice.

"Yeah, so sue me. Do you have a driver's license?"

"Of course, it is in my purse and my purse is on the floor. Don't shoot me when I bend down to get it."

As he watched, she unbuckled her seat belt and leaned forward to retrieve her purse.

From the line of trees atop the hill about five hundred yards away, Akbar fired his Dragunov sniper's rifle. Because he had attached a suppressor to its barrel, the male security guard keeping a close eye on the woman driver didn't realize his coworker had been fatally shot in her head until she collapsed on the driveway at the front of the vehicle.

Akbar had shot her first because she had both of her hands free. The male guard was holding a clipboard and pen. Akbar fired again. This shot hit him in his throat, above the protective vest that he was wearing, severing his carotid artery.

Through his scope, Akbar watched his victim fall. "Aludra," he said quietly into the headset that he was wearing. "You can sit up now and drive to the house."

Aludra heard him through the earpiece under her hijab and sat upright in the minivan's seat.

Akbar said, "From where I am hiding, I can see another guard outside the house's front entrance. Drive up to the house now and I will kill him when he walks out to question you."

"The woman you just shot is blocking the road," Aludra replied. "I'll need to move her body."

"No! There's no time. Just drive over her. Others may be on the way here."

Aludra pressed down on the accelerator, causing the minivan to bolt forward over the woman's corpse.

The security guard stationed outside the farmhouse was sitting inside a Ford pickup parked near the front door chatting with his girlfriend on his cell phone when Aludra's minivan came up the hill. Because the farmhouse was set back from the highway entrance, he hadn't witnessed the two murders there.

"Hold on a second, babe," he said, lowering his cell phone and picking up a two-way radio.

"Hey, did you guys let a minivan pass without telling me it was coming?" he asked into the radio. When there was no response, he put down the microphone and spoke to his girlfriend.

"Got to go, honey, something screwy might be going down here."

He reached for an AR-14 semi-automatic rifle, opened the driver's door and positioned himself behind it. Using it as a shield, he pointed his assault rifle at the approaching van. Aludra smiled through the windshield and waved at him.

"I'm from the doctor's office," she hollered through the open driver's window when she stopped the minivan about a dozen feet in front of his truck. Thrusting her empty hands out the window, she added, "I'm alone and just a nurse."

The guard relaxed his grip on his rifle and stepped out from behind his truck's door.

It was an easy shot for Akbar. The guard dropped dead beside his truck. Aludra raced from the minivan to the house's unlocked front doors. She was holding a 9mm pistol in front of her.

The living room to Aludra's left and parlor on her right were empty, but she heard laughter coming from the rear of the farmhouse and picked up her pace as she rushed down a hallway toward the kitchen. Jennifer Conner and Miriam Okpara were sitting at a table having a snack of apple slices smeared with peanut butter.

Okpara was the first to see Aludra coming toward them with a raised pistol. Rising from her chair, Okpara said, "Don't you hurt this child!"

"Be quiet and sit down," Aludra returned, but the nanny remained standing. She was a tall woman, standing about five foot ten inches, and strong.

"What do you want with us?" she demanded.

Aludra appeared uncertain about what she was supposed to do next. "Be quiet and sit down," she stammered.

"No! You need to get out of this house now! Go!"

Okpara started to come around the rectangular table that separated her from Aludra but stopped when she saw a second figure running down the main hallway toward them.

"Get the girl," Akbar ordered as he slung his sniper's rifle over his shoulder and took the pistol that Aludra had been pointing at Okpara.

"You're not taking this girl," Okpara declared, stepping between Jennifer and Aludra, who had started to walk around the table. Okpara grabbed a paring knife from the table that she'd been using to cut apple slices. Its blade was only an inch long, but she raised it in front of her.

Aludra stopped, but Akbar didn't hesitate. He stepped past Aludra, pushing her aside and said, "Put that knife down or I will shoot you!"

"I'm not letting you abduct this child." Okpara lunged at him.

Akbar fired the pistol. The round pierced Okpara's right breast but it didn't stop her. She swung the knife upward, aiming at his neck, but Akbar flinched and the blade pierced his shoulder, barely missing his right collar bone. Their faces were now only inches apart. Akbar could feel the warmth of her breath and she could see the hatred in his eyes. He pushed the handgun against her chest and fired again. A look of intense pain swept across Okpara's face as she released the grip on the knife, leaving it impaled in his shoulder. In the final moments of her life, she turned so she could look at Jennifer, who was still seated at the table. Okpara tried to speak, but no words came out as she fell, hitting the kitchen table and then collapsing on the tile floor.

Jennifer's entire body began shaking.

"Stand up!" Akbar ordered as he pulled the paring knife from his shoulder and tossed it on the floor. It hit the tile and bounced against Okpara's lifeless body.

"Give me a piece of duct tape," Akbar told Aludra. She ripped off a four-inch piece of the tape that she had brought with her from the minivan. He gave her the pistol to hold, opened his shirt and slapped the tape on his puncture wound to stop the bleeding. Satisfied, he took back the pistol and shouted at Jennifer.

"I told you to stand up!"

Jennifer rose on shaking legs.

Aludra slipped around Akbar and peeled another strip of duct tape from the roll.

"Put your hands together," she ordered Jennifer.

As Aludra was binding the teen's wrists, Akbar said, "Put it on her mouth too so we don't have to listen to her."

"Her mouth?" Aludra asked. She glanced at Jennifer, who had started to cry. "Are you going to scream?" she asked her.

Jennifer shook her head, indicating no.

Glancing at Akbar, Aludra said, "I don't think we need to tape her mouth."

Akbar backhanded Aludra. Tucking the pistol in his waistband, he ripped a piece of tape from the roll and slapped it across Jennifer's lips. Akbar removed a second piece, grabbed Aludra's head, and put a piece of tape over her mouth too. "That will teach you to keep your mouth shut too."

CHAPTER TWENTY

The Madeleine Thackeray School for Girls
Potomac, Maryland

The Madeleine Thackeray School for Girls catered to wealthy and prominent Washingtonians and was known internationally as a gateway into the nation's most exclusive Ivy League universities for accomplished young women. Its campus was located north of D.C. in a curve of the Potomac River dotted with multimillion-dollar estates. The scenic area was ranked as the fourth most affluent community in the nation.

Eleven-year-old Cassy Adeogo was a day student who'd been offered a scholarship because she was the sort of African American the administration welcomed. Representative Rudy Adeogo's daughter was a focused high academic achiever, mature beyond her years, and a perfect fit for the school's diversity recruitment program.

Cassy had just changed from her school uniform into her brown horse riding breeches, tall black boots, and long-sleeved top in preparation for a ten o'clock riding lesson in the school's arena when a commercial van turned into the campus. Giant black ants and red termites were painted on the van's side panels along with the redundant motto: WE KILL BUGS REALLY DEAD. The FBI would later confirm that the van had been stolen from the parking lot of a nearby extermination business. The van parked near the double doors that led inside the riding arena and four men wearing black ski masks darted from it into the cavernous dirt-floored showground.

"Stop riding!" the leader of the intruders yelled, waving a pistol through the air.

The equitation class teacher calmly eyeballed the gunmen as the two student assistants near him and their half dozen charges brought their mounts to a standstill. "Ladies," the instructor said, "remain where you are while I ask why these men are interrupting us."

Because of widespread school shootings, the administration had held emergency drills but those practice runs had focused on steps that students in classrooms were supposed to take. No one had thought through how students on horseback should react if armed attackers burst into the arena. The instructor—an Englishman in his mid-sixties—nudged his steed toward the four men.

"Sir, what is your business here?" he asked.

The lead terrorist fired his handgun into the instructor's face. Students screamed as their instructor toppled from his horse, landing with a dull thump on the ground. His well-trained horse didn't flinch.

Pointing to the three black girls in the riding class, the gunman said, "You three take off your helmets. We only want Cassy Adeogo." As the girls slipped off their helmets, he quickly compared their faces to a snapshot of the Adeogo family that had been published in a Minnesota newspaper after Rudy Adeogo had been elected to Congress.

"You," he hollered, as soon as he recognized Cassy. "Get down." Two of the other intruders hurried toward her. For a second, Cassy thought about trying to flee on her horse, but decided that would be pointless since the arena openings used by the animals were closed. She slipped off her saddle.

The two men approached her, grabbed her thin arms, and led the eleven-year-old across the arena and outside through the double doors. They shoved her into the back of their panel van, and while one of them was busy binding Cassy's wrists and ankles with duct tape, his comrade started to return to the arena. At the same moment he reached its entrance, the school's director of security came speeding into the parking lot. He was coming to investigate reports of what had sounded like a gunshot.

"Captain Charlie," as the girls knew him, had spent twenty-five years working as a Washington, D.C., police officer before retiring and taking the head security job at the girls' school. Most days, he kept busy putting warnings (but never tickets) on cars parked illegally or ferreting out the occasional bag of marijuana that found its way onto campus. The school didn't allow him to carry a handgun because administrators felt it sent students and parents the wrong message—that the campus wasn't safe. But Captain Charlie kept a .357 Smith and Wesson revolver in the glove box of his campus vehicle, and when he spotted a gunman about to enter the riding arena, he grabbed it, leaped from his car, and began shooting.

His first round missed, but the next two shots struck their mark and the terrorist buckled and collapsed with his back resting against the arena's double metal doors. The former police officer moved toward the arena slowly with his pistol still pointed in front of him. When he reached the entrance, he bent down and felt the fallen attacker's neck for a pulse to make certain he was dead. Next, he peeked through the upper half of the doors, which had solid bottoms but were glass from the waist up. He could see two additional gunmen inside guarding eight students who had been forced to dismount and were standing in a line in front of their horses.

Captain Charlie dialed 911 on his cell phone and was about to explain what was happening when a bullet pierced his spinal cord. He'd been shot by the terrorist who had been inside the van duct-taping Cassy's wrists and ankles. He'd slipped unnoticed from the van when he'd heard gunfire.

Captain Charlie was still breathing but was now lying paralyzed next to the terrorist whom he had fatally shot moments earlier. Rushing forward from the van, his attacker fired two more rounds into the security director, killing him.

The gunman shoved both bodies out of the way, threw open the doors, and yelled a warning to his buddies. They reacted quickly. Turning, they began firing their weapons at the eight girls, who seemed immobilized by fear. All but one was cut down immediately. The girl who ran only made it ten feet from the others before she was murdered. The sound of the repeated gunfire spooked the horses. They ran in circles around their fallen riders.

Having gotten what they had come for, the three terrorists carried their dead jihadist to the van where they dumped his corpse next to a traumatized Cassy in the rear of the vehicle.

As the men fled from the school grounds, one of them checked the time. Their attack, the murders, and the abduction of the congressman's daughter had taken a total of seventeen minutes.

CHAPTER TWENTY-ONE

Terminal 1—Lindbergh
Minneapolis—St. Paul International Airport

The pilot's voice sounded stern as the arriving Washington, D.C., flight taxied to the gate at the Midwest's busiest airport.

"Two passengers need to disembark because of an emergency," he announced. "Please remain seated until they have deplaned and the flight attendants inform you that it is safe for you to leave your seats."

Craning her neck, Ebio Kattan glanced up the jet's aisle just in time to see Representative Rudy Adeogo and Major Brooke Grant hurrying from the plane. The reporter's cell phone buzzed. It was her producer at Al Arabic's Washington bureau.

"General Frank Grant, the chairman of the Joint Chiefs of Staff, has been shot," he informed her.

"His niece and Representative Adeogo just left the plane!" Kattan replied.

"Get footage of them. Now!"

Unbuckling her seat belt, Kattan darted into the aisle, startling those still seated near her. A flight attendant said, "Please remain seated." But Kattan ignored her and called to her cameraman. "We've got to go!" He stood, opened the bin above his seat, grabbed his camera, and followed Kattan. Neither bothered to take their carry-on luggage as they hurried down the aisle and literally shoved the flight attendant out of their way.

Kattan ran up the movable ramp into the terminal. But she didn't see Adeogo or Grant in the terminal. She paid no attention to a sign that welcomed visitors and explained that Terminal 1 was named after Charles Lindbergh, a Minnesota native who was the first American to fly solo nonstop across the Atlantic. Passengers walking toward her stepped clear as she and her cameraman hurried toward the main terminal. She still hadn't spotted Brooke or Adeogo by the time she reached the TSA security exit.

As Kattan had expected, reporters were waiting inside the main terminal for Adeogo to appear. They watched as she and her cameraman descended an escalator into the baggage claim area where Adeogo was supposed to hold a press conference.

"Where'd they go?" Kattan asked when she reached the reporters.

"They're still on the plane," one of them answered.

"I was on that plane and watched them get off."

The journalists swarmed around her.

"Did you interview them?" one asked.

"Did they say anything about General Grant being shot?" demanded another.

"No, they rushed off before I could get to them."

"Then where are they?" someone asked.

From the confused expression on Kattan's face, it was obvious she didn't know.

An airport security guard, followed by a middle-aged official dressed in a business suit, came through an unmarked door.

"Ladies and gentlemen," he said in a loud voice, "I've been sent to inform you that the congressman and Major Brooke Grant have boarded a private aircraft for a return flight to Washington, D.C. There will be no statement from either of them here this morning."

"What about the White House task force meeting?" a reporter called out. "Has it been cancelled?"

"You'll have to talk to someone else about that. All I can tell you is that they are on a private jet heading back to Reagan National."

The journalists immediately began calling their producers and editors on their cell phones. In the mist of their chatter, a camera-man yelled out: "FOX has something!"

There were no television screens mounted in the baggage area but the cameraman had FOX news streaming live on his cell phone.

A yellow ribbon across the base of the broadcast read: EXCLUSIVE BREAKING NEWS.

"Islamic terrorists have killed fourteen Americans in the Wash-ington, D.C., area and critically wounded the chairman of the Joint Chiefs of Staff in three separate attacks that appear to have been coordinated acts of terrorism," the FOX anchor proclaimed.

"An Islamic jihadist known to law enforcement as the Falcon uploaded a statement about the attacks on a website monitored by FOX News moments ago crediting his followers in the United States with carrying out the violence. Those attacks include the murder of eight teenage girls and their instructor at an elite Potomac, Mary-land, girl's school, and four others at a rural Virginia farmhouse. The Falcon also claimed he was responsible for the shooting of Joint Chiefs of Staff chairman General Frank Grant earlier this morning."

Images of a police SWAT team armed with assault rifles flashed on the screen. The officers had cordoned off the riding arena at the Madeleine Thackeray School for Girls.

"FOX News has confirmed that two girls have been abducted by terrorists during this morning's attacks." After pausing for a second to allow the gravity of his words to settle in, the anchor continued. "The girls have been identified as Cassy Adeogo, the eleven-year-old daughter of Minnesota U.S. Representative Rudy Adeogo, and Jennifer Conner, the fourteen-year-old daughter of a former CIA employee named Gunter Conner who was murdered late last year by Al-Shabaab terrorists. The congressman's daughter was kidnapped from the girl's school. Jennifer Conner was abducted from a Virginia farmhouse owned by Major Brooke Grant, the niece of the chairman of the Joint Chiefs of Staff, General Frank Grant, who was critically wounded earlier in the day. We expect

President Allworth to be making a statement about these horrific murders and the kidnappings within the hour."

A reporter standing next to Kattan said, "Hey, aren't you the Al Arabic reporter who was in Somalia with Brooke Grant when our embassy was attacked last year? You broke those stories about her and Gunter Conner. Tell us what you know about the Falcon. Why have terrorists kidnapped Conner's daughter?"

Another reporter said, "I saw your story—where you were chasing Major Grant and that girl in a parking lot."

Several reporters shoved microphones at Kattan and began filming her. But the Al Arabic correspondent had no interest in helping her competitors with background information. She spun away from the pack and hurried toward an escalator that would carry her up to the airline ticket counters.

"We're going back to Washington," she told her cameraman, who once again fell in behind her. "If necessary on a chartered flight."

Political consultant Mary Margaret Delaney had been quietly watching the ruckus in the baggage area and she now walked briskly toward the escalator. As it rose, she slipped forward until she was directly behind Kattan's cameraman.

By the time the trio reached the top step, Delaney was close enough to hear Kattan lecturing her cameraman. "The abduction of those two girls is the breaking story now. We've got to get to Adeogo in Washington. No use trying Grant. She'll never talk to me."

Delaney turned to her left while Kattan and the cameraman turned to their right in the direction of the ticket counters. Delaney had heard enough. She had come to the airport directly from her breakfast meeting with the OIN's Omar Nader. She had not come to confront Representative Adeogo nor to blackmail him. The airport was much too public a place for that scene. No, she had come simply because she had wanted to see him face-to-face. She had wanted him to realize that she was dogging him and she had come because she wanted to secretly feel the thrill of knowing that she had finally learned his secret and now had the power to destroy him.

As she watched Kattan walking away from her, Delaney thought, *You have no idea that you were only inches away from me and a real exclusive. You are scampering back to Washington, D.C., to chase a story when the documents in my bag contain evidence that could ruin Rudy Adeogo.*

Delaney smiled. *All in good time*, she thought. *All in good time.*

CHAPTER TWENTY-TWO

George Washington University Trauma Center
Downtown Washington, D.C.

Awaiting government car raced Major Brooke Grant from Reagan National Airport to the downtown university hospital where her uncle, General Frank Grant, had undergone nearly five hours of surgery. She found her aunt Geraldine sitting next to his bed in an ICU ward.

As she was hugging her aunt, the hospital's chief surgeon entered the room.

"Only single-digit millimeters separated the bullet from your uncle's spinal cord and main arteries," the doctor explained. "We almost lost him a couple times in surgery, but he's a real fighter."

General Grant's face was wrapped with bandages, a breathing tube was jutting from his mouth, and both of his meaty arms were attached to IVs. He was unconscious and completely unaware of the heroic efforts that the team of surgeons and battery of nurses had performed to keep him alive.

"We are not out of the woods yet," the surgeon continued. "There's always the threat of blood clots, but our biggest concern is swelling inside his brain."

"He was shot in the jaw, not the brain," Brooke said nervously.

"That's correct, but the general's brain was violently shaken by the gunshot when it shattered his jaw. Pressure is building inside his skull and there is no place for it to expand."

"What does that mean—no place to expand?" Brooke asked.

"The brain swells just like your thumb if you accidently strike it with a hammer. Pressure inside the skull is called intracranial pressure, or ICP, and we measure it in millimeters of mercury, which we refer to as mmHg. The ICP for an adult is seven to fifteen mmHg. Anything above twenty mmHg is worrisome, and there's a high risk at forty mmHg and above of permanent brain damage."

"We can't let that happen," Brooke said.

"That's why I'm going to take him back to surgery in a few minutes so we can insert an inner cranial brain pressure monitor to keep tabs on what is happening. We've already given him medication to help reduce the swelling. If that doesn't work, we'll insert a shunt or valve to release fluids from inside the skull to further reduce the pressure."

"What happens if you can't get the pressure down?" Brooke asked.

The surgeon glanced at Geraldine, who said, "Go ahead and tell us. We want the good and the bad."

"If the shunt or valve doesn't work, we'll remove a piece of his skull, because we can't let the pressure hit sixty mmHg. I'm afraid that amount of pressure would be fatal."

As the doctor spoke, two nurses arrived and wheeled the general out of the room toward a surgery suite.

"Doctor," Geraldine said as the surgeon was leaving, "I will be praying for God to guide your hands."

Brooke moved her chair next to her aunt's so they could hold hands while they prayed. When Brooke opened her eyes, she saw that Lieutenant Colonel Gabe DeMoss had entered the room. The White House liaison quickly recounted for Brooke how he and the general had been driving to CIA headquarters when a rented truck had dropped building materials onto the highway, intentionally stalling traffic so that a sniper could get a clear shot at the general.

"No one has been arrested," DeMoss explained. "But I was just informed by the FBI that agents believe the man who shot your uncle is also the same one who killed the three security guards at

your farmhouse. He didn't bother to take any of the spent shell cas-
ings with him after he shot your uncle and fired from the woods at
the farm. Clearly, he's not worried about leaving evidence behind."

"He had accomplices—beginning with the truck driver. What
have you learned about them, especially the ones that might have
helped him abduct Jennifer?" Brooke asked.

"The flatbed truck was rented from a local building supply store,
but the names on the agreement are fake. The FBI is reviewing video-
tapes from the store's security cameras. We're hoping they'll be able
to get a positive ID with facial recognition software. Clearly, the
attack at the girls' school and the one at your farm were done by
the same group of terrorists, but we haven't identified anyone yet."

Aunt Geraldine interrupted them. "The general's jaw was shattered so he won't be speaking anytime soon after he wakes up. He's
not going to like that one bit. He's going to be furious that Jennifer
has been abducted."

Brooke forced a smile. Geraldine Grant was oak-strong. As a
couple, the general and his wife of forty years seemed an odd match
physically. She was willowy while he was a bear of a man. He was
the highest-ranking military officer in the United States Armed
Forces. But inside the Grant household, she was clearly in charge.
Deeply religious, she held the unofficial honor of being the youngest participant in the Bloody Sunday March in 1965 when six hundred peaceful protestors crossed the Edmund Pettus Bridge over the
Alabama River outside Selma on their trek to Montgomery. State
troopers and local police had shot tear gas into the crowd and had
attacked marchers with nightsticks. Geraldine had only been nine
years old, but because of her small size, she'd looked much younger,
which her parents later theorized was what had saved her from a
vicious beating. Neither of them had been so lucky. Geraldine had
watched helplessly as two deputies knocked her parents to the pavement, struck them repeatedly with nightsticks, and dragged them
into a police wagon. Although Geraldine had been sobbing (she
later insisted it was because of the tear gas fired into the crowd),

she had continued marching through the melee until a sympathetic journalist had pulled her out of harm's way. Her resilience in continuing to protest that horrific morning had been a preview of the determined woman that she would later become.

"Brooke," Geraldine said, "being here with your uncle is my place. Yours is finding that child and getting that youngster home. You need to get going now."

DeMoss said, "President Allworth has asked to meet with you and Representative Adeogo. I said I would drive you to the White House."

"Honey," Geraldine said to Brooke, "you go with him now and don't you even think about going home tonight to your farmhouse. You're going to stay in your old bedroom."

"It would be much safer," DeMoss added. "The Pentagon has sent a protective detail there and has one here in the hospital."

"I'd like that, Auntie," Brooke replied, kissing her aunt's cheek. "What about you?"

"I'm not leaving your uncle's side. When he opens his eyes, my face is going to be the first that he sees—that he'll want to see. I'll be just fine now. You go see the president and tell her that I am praying for her and our country."

Brooke went directly from her uncle's room to speak to the ICU charge nurse. "When will they be bringing my uncle back here?" she asked.

"They're installing the monitor and taking a few more steps to help stabilize him."

"Can you check right now to see if the pressure level inside his skull is dropping?"

The nurse made a call.

"I'm sorry, Major Grant, but the doctor said it is still elevated."

"What's the number?"

"Thirty-nine."

Brooke fought back a feeling of panic rising within her. The surgeon had said anything forty or above could cause permanent brain damage. Before she could ask another question, someone touched her shoulder. It was her aunt Geraldine, who had stepped out into the hallway and spotted her. "Honey," Geraldine Grant said, "don't you worry about your uncle. He's a tough old bird. Besides, Jesus is with us. He isn't going to let anything happen to him that is not supposed to happen. Now go on."

CHAPTER TWENTY-THREE

The Oval Office
The White House
Washington, D.C.

I want to assure you that everything that can be done to locate and rescue your daughter, Cassy, and Jennifer Conner, is being done," President Sally Allworth said in a concerned voice as soon as Representative Rudy Adeogo, his wife, Dheeh, and Brooke Grant arrived.

In addition to the president and chief of staff Mallory Harper, the others in the Oval Office included CIA director Payton Grainger, the head of the Department of Homeland Security, the FBI director, and the FBI's counterterrorism chief.

"Agent Parker is in charge of locating your girls and finding the terrorists responsible," President Allworth said, introducing him.

The fifty-something Parker had a firm handshake and looked very much like a stereotypical FBI agent. He had a weight-lifter's build and was wearing a shiny Brooks Brothers two-piece suit

"Please give us an update," Allworth said.

"Thank you, Madam President," Parker replied. "We've established our command post in Reston, Virginia, where we have more than a hundred of our best agents pursuing leads and collecting evidence from three sites: the outside area where General Frank Grant was critically wounded, the Maryland girls' school in Potomac, and Major Grant's farmhouse in Virginia. Of course, we are also exchanging information with the CIA."

*　　*　　*

Brooke knew the CIA operated out of several buildings in Reston and she immediately assumed the FBI had established its command center in one of those CIA units. It was against the law for the spy agency to become involved in domestic operations, but the bureau needed its foreign expertise in dealing with the Falcon, so the two bureaucracies had joined forces out of necessity.

"Do you have any idea where they've taken our girls?" Brooke asked. Her question violated an unspoken but understood protocol in Washington that required underlings to wait until the highest ranking individual in the room was finished asking questions before speaking. In the Oval Office, that was the president, but Brooke didn't care. She wanted to know what was being done to find Jennifer, and President Allworth understood that angst and overlooked the faux pas.

"We have some promising leads, but nothing concrete," Parker replied.

"Agent Parker will be happy to answer your questions in more detail after our meeting here," the FBI director interjected, glancing at the president.

"Yes," Parker volunteered, "we'd like you to come to our command post. We need to interview you and Representative Adeogo and Mrs. Adeogo about your girls."

"I will be making a statement to the media," Allworth said, changing the subject. "Congressman, would you and Dheeh be willing to appear with me at a news conference? Major Grant, I'd like you there too, of course."

Parker looked startled and glanced at his boss. The president noticed and asked: "Agent Parker, is there something you would like to say?"

"Madam President, if I may offer a suggestion," Parker replied, clearly nervous. "It has been our experience in dealing with kidnappings that we need to be extremely careful about what is said during television or media appearances while the kidnap victims are still being held captive."

"Obviously," Mallory Harper said in a stern voice, joining the conversation, "the president is keenly aware of how sensitive this is and doesn't need to be reminded of the gravity of the situation. We will consult with your boss before we release any statements or hold a press conference. But you need to understand that it is imperative for the president to speak to the American people."

"The public is frightened," the president explained. "First, attempts were made to murder me at the National Cathedral and this morning, the chairman of the Joint Chiefs of Staff was critically wounded. Major Grant's farmhouse was attacked and a van full of terrorists drove onto the campus of an elite Potomac girls' school where they murdered eight children and two adults in cold blood before fleeing. Abroad, terrorists under the direction of this creature called the Falcon attacked a college campus, murdering dozens in Kenya. I can't remain quiet at a time such as this."

"The public expects the president to react," Harper said.

"As you are my commander in chief," Brooke volunteered, "I will do whatever is asked of me, but I personally have no interest in speaking to the media, especially while Jennifer is being held by these animals. The Falcon is trying to kill everyone I love and I'm not interested in giving him the satisfaction of knowing how deeply he is hurting my family and me."

"I'll defer to the FBI and its experts," Representative Adeogo said, glancing at Agent Parker. "If the FBI believes it will help our daughter by appearing at a press conference, then Dheeh and I will do it. I simply want Cassy home safe and unharmed."

"If I can make a suggestion," Director Grainger said, speaking for the first time during their meeting, "perhaps it would be better if the president were joined by the directors of the FBI and Homeland Security, rather than family members, at this point. To show a unified front and impress upon the public that a strong response is being made."

"That's a good suggestion," President Allworth said. "Mallory will arrange it. Let's schedule it for tomorrow afternoon so that our people can meet with Parker and his team to go over the language of what I will say." Alternating her eyes between the Adeogos and Brooke, she added in an earnest voice, "Rudy, Dheeh, and Major Grant, I want you to call me directly if you need my assistance and support as we get through these next few days together. I can only imagine how terrified you must feel and I want you to know that the American people are with you in their thoughts and prayers. I want to personally assure you that the terrorists responsible will be hunted down and punished regardless of how long it takes. They will pay the ultimate price. You have my word as president."

With that, the Adeogos and Brooke were escorted from the Oval Office accompanied by Agent Parker, who explained that two sedans were waiting outside the White House to drive them directly to the Reston office.

The trip northwest from downtown D.C. took about forty minutes. There was no identifying commercial sign outside the compound on Sunset Drive, no way of knowing it was leased by the CIA for use in combating terrorism. Even though Agent Parker was in the lead car, two guards stopped everyone and their vehicles. After their identities had been confirmed, they were allowed to enter the building. Parker directed his guests into a large conference area where he introduced them to a dozen agents overseeing the investigation. The Adeogos and Brooke were then taken into different offices to answer questions about Cassy and Jennifer. The Adeogos described Cassy's personality and habits. They theorized that their daughter had been targeted because her father was the only Muslim in Congress.

"They want to punish me," Adeogo said, "because I have been critical of their radical interpretation of Islam."

After three hours, Adeogo and Dheeh left the compound, but Brooke was still being interviewed by Parker. She patiently answered his questions about Jennifer, Gunter Conner, and the Falcon. Near the end of his questioning, Parker said, "I spoke earlier today to a friend of yours, a SAD team member named Walks Many Miles, who called the agency directly from Africa."

Brooke realized that she had forgotten to return Miles's call after hearing his message earlier on her cell phone. She had been too pre-occupied with the wounding of her uncle and Jennifer's kidnapping.

"May I ask how he is connected to all of this?" Parker said.

"He's a family friend. We were in Somalia together and now he's been sent to Africa to hunt down and kill the Falcon."

"The sooner, the better," Parker replied. "Thanks for your coop-eration. You'll need a ride. I'll have one of our female agents drive you to your aunt's house, which is where I've been told you will be staying. I'll let you know as soon as we hear anything."

"Whoa," Brooke snapped. "Now it's your turn to answer my questions."

For another half hour, she asked Parker about what he and his team had gleaned since the three attacks that morning. He was frustratingly evasive and she didn't learn anything new or helpful. Most of what he shared was information that she'd already heard from Lieutenant Colonel Gabe DeMoss at the hospital when visit-ing her uncle.

In an exasperated voice, she finally snapped, "You're not telling me anything I don't already know and I'm not going to sit on the sidelines here waiting for you to toss me scraps of information. I'm going to be part of your investigation. Jennifer is my responsibility, and I'm not leaving this up to you and your team."

Parker flashed a dismissive smile. "I certainly understand," he said, as if he were speaking to a child, "and I admire your determi-nation to help, but, Major, I can't allow it. We're good at what we do, so you'll just have to trust us. I can't have someone on the team with an emotional attachment to the two girls. It might become an encumbrance."

"Agent Parker," she replied in an unyielding voice, "don't assume because I am a woman or family member that I am incapable of keeping my feelings in check; and no one on your team knows as much about the Falcon and how he thinks and operates as I do."

"I'm certain you are correct, Major Grant, but the answer is still no. As I said, we will keep you informed."

"Like you just did?" she said in a scoffing voice. "I could have learned more watching the evening news."

She noticed a blue vein throbbing in his neck, but he kept a calm look on his face. Continuing, she said, "I thought I made it clear to you that the Falcon has a personal vendetta against me and my family, including my uncle."

"Oh, you made that perfectly clear. It's exactly why I can't allow you to be part of this investigation."

"I'm not asking you for permission to be on this team. I'm demanding it."

Parker narrowed his eyes, causing his caterpillar-like eyebrows to curve into half-moons. "No means no, Major Grant. There's no point in us arguing about this."

"If you push this," she replied sternly, "you'll lose."

Parker forced another grin. "Very well, Major, I'll speak to the director, but don't get your hopes up. I'm certain he'll agree with me."

"In that case, I'll call the president. And I'm sure she will agree with me. She told me that I could call her directly if there was anything that I needed from her, and I can be very persuasive."

For a moment, they stared at each other, as if they were schoolchildren trying to force the other to blink first.

He blinked.

Special Agent Parker was an ambitious man and he understood that this investigation would be a pivotal moment in his career. Having Brooke call the president to complain on the first day would not bode well for him with the FBI's director.

"Have it your way," he said reluctantly, "but if you are part of the team, that means you answer to me. Is that understood? You work for me."

"I look forward to working *with* you," she said as she turned and walked out of the command post office.

It was nearly midnight now, and when she exited, there was a chill in the night air. A driver delivered Brooke to the two-story brick colonial house in northern Virginia where she had spent her teenage years. It felt empty as she climbed the stairs to her former bedroom. Geraldine had hung eight-by-ten-inch photographs along the staircase wall and Brooke took a moment to glance at each one. Her cousins were in photos hanging near the bottom steps. All three boys had followed in General Grant's footsteps and were shown in their Army uniforms. When she reached the sixth step, she found her photograph on display. She was wearing her Marine dress uniform. One of the last events when their family had gathered together in this house had been the annual Army and Navy game. It had been Brooke against the rest of the Grant clan and she had gloated when a last-minute pass interception had won the game for Navy. At the top of the staircase, she discovered a new photo. It was of Jennifer, taken on the day that she and Brooke had moved into their Victorian farmhouse. Jennifer was squinting because Geraldine had insisted that she stand facing the sun so there would be "enough light for a good picture." But the child was clearly happy.

Where is she? Did she witness Miriam, her caregiver and best friend, being murdered?

Jennifer already had been through so much—her mother and brother killed by a car bomb, her father's murder by terrorists in Germany, and now she had been abducted.

Had Jennifer retreated back into the safety of her delusional world— a world that everyone had worked so hard to draw her from?

Despite her deeply religious upbringing as a preacher's daughter in Tulsa, Oklahoma, the buckle of the Bible Belt, Brooke had found herself with Job-like doubts after her parents were murdered during 9/11. Unless she was with her aunt, she rarely prayed. Yet at this moment, she felt compelled to shut her eyes and whisper aloud: "Please, God, please. Be with Jennifer. Protect her."

When Brooke entered her former bedroom, she called Walks Many Miles's cell phone. For some reason, the connection to Africa didn't work. After several attempts, she gave up and called her aunt at the hospital.

"How's Pooh Bear?" Brooke asked, using her pet name for her uncle.

"He's still in a coma but the swelling stopped," Geraldine said in an excited voice.

"How high did the pressure get?"

"The doctor said it started dropping when it reached thirty-nine. They don't believe he suffered any permanent brain damage, Brooke. I told you. Jesus is with us." Geraldine hesitated and then added, "He's with Jennifer too. I can feel it."

PART THREE

EVIL MASQUERADING AS PIETY

There are pretenders to piety as well as to courage.

—Molière, *Tartuffe*

CHAPTER TWENTY-FOUR

A Virginia cabin
Somewhere in the Appalachian Mountains

Everything was black. Jennifer could hear whimpering. Was this another of her delusions? No! This was real. A man and a woman had abducted her from her home. The man had put tape across her mouth but had removed it. The woman had insisted. She said the tape might cause her to choke. So he'd put a hood over her head that kept her from seeing who was crying now.

"Who's there?" Jennifer asked.

The whimpering stopped.

"It's me," a girl's voice whispered.

She was close by. "I'm Jennifer Conner. They've put a bag over my face so I can't see you. I can't move my hands or legs either."

"Me too," the voice replied. "I'm Cassy. Cassy Adeogo. They came to my school. A man murdered my teacher. I heard lots of shooting. I'm scared."

"How old are you?"

"Eleven, almost twelve. But I'm smart for my age. That's what my teachers tell everyone."

"I'm almost fifteen."

"What's your name?"

"Jennifer."

"My father tells me to pray whenever I'm scared. I'm going to pray now. You can pray with me if you want. *Aaoozobillahe minu-shaitanir rajeem.*"

"I don't know that prayer."

"It means 'In the name of Allah, the Gracious, the Merciful.'"

"You're Muslim."

"Yes, but I'm not like those terrorists on television. I'm a good Muslim. I don't believe in chopping off people's heads just because they aren't like us. In school, some of my friends are Jewish. Are you a Jew or are you Christian?"

"My mother was Muslim but not my father. I don't think he believed in God. All of my mother's relatives live in Egypt and they are Muslims. Maybe I'm half Muslim. I don't know because my family didn't really pray a lot. But I know it was Muslims who killed my mother and brother and my father. They're the evil Muslims."

"I'm sorry. I will pray for you," Cassy replied. "I can teach you if you want. I will ask Allah to tell the man and woman to release us."

"I hate them," Jennifer said. "I hope the police come and kill them."

"My father said it's wrong to hate your enemies."

"I don't have a father anymore because evil Muslims killed him. That is why I hate them."

"Who takes care of you if your family is dead? Did someone adopt you?"

"Major Brooke Grant is my guardian. She takes care of me. She and Miriam did, only the man murdered Miriam. She was my nanny. I will not pray for him. Brooke Grant is a Marine. She said Marines all stick together. They will come and kill the people holding us and save us. That's what Marines do."

When they heard the sound of a door opening, both stopped talking.

"What are you *gabars* talking about?" Akbar said.

"What's a *gabar*?" Jennifer replied.

"It's what my grandmother says," Cassy volunteered. "It's Somali."

"Cassy was praying for you," Jennifer said. "She was asking Allah to forgive you. But I hope God kills you."

Akbar jerked the black hood off Jennifer's head, surprising her.

"Watch your tongue, little *gabar*, or you could lose it," he threatened. "Don't think that I will pity you because you are a child."

He reached over and removed Cassy's hood too. "You both need a good beating. The Hadith tells us: 'Let your rod be hanging on them, as a warning and to chastise against neglect of their duties toward Allah.'"

Neither girl spoke. Neither wanted to be beaten. With their hoods removed, they could observe their surroundings. The girls were sitting in an empty room with one window and log walls. Someone had covered the window with white paper so you couldn't look out or in. A single lightbulb dangled from the ceiling. The girls were about a foot apart from each other on a cold linoleum floor with white and green specks. When their eyes met, they smiled at each other.

Akbar had knelt down so he could be eye-to-eye with them while he removed their hoods. He was still kneeling. Aludra was standing behind him watching.

"Please don't hit us," Cassy said. "We'll do what you tell us."

"You deserve a beating because your father is a hypocrite," Akbar said as he stood. Glancing at Jennifer, he added, "And you are worthless."

"She is half Muslim," Cassy said, defending her new friend.

"Why are you hurting us?" Jennifer asked.

"What I do is not your concern."

He handed the two hoods to Aludra. "Take them to the toilet in the next room, but if they disobey you, then leave them here to piss in their pants. I'll be back later, and when I come, I will beat them for being wicked."

He left them, shutting the door behind him.

"Are you Muslim?" Cassy asked.

"Yes," Aludra replied in a low voice.

"I'm a Muslim too, and I was taught that being a good Muslim meant you were kind and loving, not cruel to little girls," Cassy said.

"I will take you to the bathroom, one at a time," Aludra said. "This will be your only opportunity for several hours, so each of you should use the toilet."

"I need my medication," Jennifer said.

"Are you sick?" Cassy asked, clearly concerned.

"It's for my brain. It's broken. I have to take pills or I get confused really easily."

"We don't have any pills for you," Aludra said.

"Maybe you can get some for her," Cassy suggested.

"Enough talk about pills; do either of you wish to use the toilet?"

"I'd like to," Cassy said.

Aludra used a knife to cut the duct tape that had been wrapped around Cassy's riding boots, which she'd been wearing when she was kidnapped. Holding the knife in front of Cassy's face, she warned, "I'll cut you if you cause trouble."

"I just want to pee," the youngster replied.

Aludra removed the duct tape on Cassy's hands and helped her stand. Taking a firm grip on Cassy's right arm, Aludra led her out of the room to a nearby toilet. When they were finished, Aludra bound her wrists and ankles again with duct tape.

"Do you know a woman named Halgan who lives in Minneapolis?" Cassy asked.

"Why would you ask me that question?" Aludra replied.

"Because you look like her big sister. Her name is Halgan and she is a friend of my parents and I have been to her house and seen photographs of her sisters."

"Who I am doesn't matter. Now be quiet or I will tape both of your mouths."

"I was just asking. Halgan is beautiful. She's a nice woman from a good family. You and that man with you are Somali Americans, aren't you?"

"I told you to be quiet. Don't think talking to me will help you."

"Do you know Halgan?" Cassy persisted.

Aludra looked at the door to make certain it was closed and

Akbar couldn't hear her. Looking down at Cassy's face, she said, "She is my cousin."

"Then you are probably from Minneapolis too, right?" Cassy asked. "If you are, then you know who my father is and my mother, Dheeh. They're good Muslims."

"I warned you to be quiet or I'll tape your mouth. The man who is guarding you will beat all of us if he hears you talking to me."

"I saw him put tape on your mouth at the farmhouse when he got angry," Jennifer said, joining their conversation. "Please don't put the hoods back on us. We won't scream, and we've already seen both of your faces."

"Yes, we promise," Cassy said. "You wouldn't want your cousin Halgan to be hooded like this, would you?"

Aludra frowned at Cassy. "If I don't put the hoods on you, he will beat me." She put a hood over Cassy's head and then slipped the second over Jennifer's before standing to leave.

Neither Cassy nor Jennifer spoke for several moments.

"Do you really think she left or is she fooling us?" Cassy whispered.

"I don't know. But we'd better be quiet for a while."

After several more minutes, Cassy said, "I think she's really gone. There's something I need to tell you."

"Okay. If you think she is really gone."

"I was in my riding class when the men grabbed me, so I'm wearing riding boots that come to my knees."

"I don't understand."

"The duct tape is wrapped around my boots at my ankles to keep my legs together, but I think I can wiggle my feet out of the boots. If I can, then I can run for help."

CHAPTER TWENTY-FIVE

House Permanent Select Committee on Intelligence
U.S. Capitol Visitor Center
Washington, D.C.

Unless the chair hears an objection, this committee briefing will proceed with Representative Rudy Adeogo being listed in the official record as an invited guest of the Chairman," Representative Thomas Stanton announced. He nodded approvingly at Adeogo, who had been escorted inside the underground, secure hearing room to a chair at the back wall. From his seat, Adeogo could see the House committee's thirteen members from the majority party and nine from the minority. Their seats were elevated on two different levels, much like judges in a courtroom, with Stanton positioned in the middle of the highest row in the room's most prominent chair. "Please know that all of us are praying for the safe return of your daughter," Stanton added.

"Thank you for this courtesy," Adeogo replied. Because the committee often discussed classified materials, usually only its members were allowed to attend. Adeogo had asked Stanton for permission to sit in because both the FBI and CIA were scheduled to speak, and he wanted to hear what they were telling the committee about the terrorists who'd kidnapped his daughter.

"We'll now call our first witness," the Chairman announced, as CIA director Payton Grainger settled into a witness chair behind a small table before them. After explaining that this was an official briefing requested by the committee and swearing in Grainger,

Stanton said, "Mr. Director, thank you for joining us. Now please begin."

Fingering a remote, Grainger nodded toward a large television screen mounted on the left wall of the chamber. There was an identical screen on the right wall. A photograph appeared simultaneously on both.

"Many of you might recognize this man from news reports. He is African billionaire Umoja Owiti. Israeli intelligence has confirmed that Owiti met with the terrorist identified only as 'The Falcon' at Owiti's heavily guarded estate in Kenya the day before Al-Shabaab gunmen attacked the Mandera college." Grainger clicked the remote and a slide show of the carnage at the school appeared on the monitors.

"I hate calling this Islamic extremist 'The Falcon,'" Stanton said, interrupting Grainger. "It makes him sound as if he is some exotic figure."

"I agree, Mr. Chairman, and we've asked our Israeli friends to help us identify him by name because of their extensive sources in the Middle East. But they haven't been able to uncover his true identity. All we really know about him is that he is ruthless."

"What about the Saudis?" the Chairman asked. "Surely they know the face behind that mask."

"As you know from previous briefings, the Saudis are helpful when the information they share is mutually beneficial, but they claim ignorance when there is no direct benefit to them."

"Enough said. What's the connection between this billionaire and this murderer?"

"The overthrow of Muammar Gaddafi in Libya and execution of Saddam Hussein in Iraq left Iran as the biggest financial contributor to Islamic extremist groups. While we believe terrorists still reap millions each year from secret payments by Islamic nations, such as the Saudis, as a form of 'insurance' to keep the extremists from attacking them, their main source of income comes from exporting opium, kidnappings for ransom, and selling captured girls into sexual slavery."

A colorful pie chart appeared with estimates of each revenue source.

"We believe these groups' expenses are currently exceeding their income. The irony is that their expenses have increased because of their aggression and success. An estimated eight million individuals now live in territories controlled by radical extremists, and the ongoing cost of waging war in troubled Middle Eastern nations against their leaders and their Western allies and overseeing that controlled population has made it difficult for the Falcon and his supporters to adequately fund his operations. This is why he is seeking financial help from Owiti."

"Actually running governments rather than attacking them costs money," Stanton said, "is that what you are saying?"

"Exactly."

"Has there been any attempt to go after Mr. Owiti through the FAT Act?"

"We don't have enough evidence to charge him or freeze any of his Western assets under the Financial Anti-Terrorism Act," Grainger replied. "Mr. Owiti has a myriad of foreign-based holdings, including many in Africa, that are shell companies making his assets difficult to track and link to Islamic extremists. And, as a multibillionaire, he has lawyers on retainer from the best law firms in the U.S. and Europe. As you are aware, terrorists such as the Falcon prefer to deal in cash, oil, or contraband rather than relying on normal financial institutions for fund transfers. So we currently have no documentable evidence that Mr. Owiti has given a cent to the Falcon and nothing but the word of the Israelis that the two men have ever met face-to-face."

Grainger paused for a moment to see if the Chairman had another question. Stanton nodded at him to continue.

"We were able to learn from the SAD team that we sent to Nairobi that the Falcon is hoping to raise a considerable amount of money to finance a major attack on a U.S. city. We are not certain where this attack will happen or what form the attack will take.

Our ongoing fear is the Falcon is trying to raise enough cash to buy a nuclear device from the North Koreans, Pakistan, or Russia."

"Then I would strongly suggest that you find a way to stop Mr. Owiti from financing the Falcon," Stanton interjected.

"We are in discussion with our Israeli friends about options, but they are still unhappy about steps our nation took during the Obama administration to normalize relations with Iran. There are rumors that some Israelis believe another 9/11 attack in the U.S. might remind Americans of the threat that a nuclear Iran poses to them and the stability of the West."

"Mr. Director, even as a rumor, that is a serious accusation about our Israeli friends," Stanton said.

"As I said, it is a rumor and probably bluster, but it is an indicator of an underlying resentment being felt in Tel Aviv."

Grainger showed the committee another photo of Owiti on the television sets, this one taken in his Manhattan penthouse with several prominent New York officials, including the mayor.

"Mr. Owiti also has powerful friends who we assume are unaware of his dealings with the Falcon. While we cannot do much legally to stop Mr. Owiti," Grainger continued, "we can use him as bait— assuming that he meets again at his Kenya estate with the Falcon. Such a meeting could give us an opportunity to take decisive action against the Falcon."

"Care to elaborate?" Stanton asked.

"We're working on various scenarios that might create a favorable climate for Mr. Owiti to request another meeting with the Falcon, and if that were to happen and the Falcon were to expose himself, we could take steps to eliminate him."

"And what of Mr. Owiti?"

"That could be a problem if he became collateral damage, given his high profile and connections. As I said, we are speaking to the Israelis about options that might involve them rather than us."

During the next twenty minutes, Grainger answered questions from committee members, mostly about Owiti's business holdings and how helpful the Israeli intelligence service might be in killing the Falcon.

When everyone seemed satisfied, Grainger said, "Mr. Stanton, if there are no more questions, there's another matter that I need to discuss with the committee. It is related to the Falcon. But first, I'd like permission to show a video from YouTube." He chuckled and added, "It is not classified."

"Go ahead," Stanton said.

A staff member lowered the lights as the video began and voice of the video's narrator filled the chamber.

"This is a spider-tailed horned viper that is found only in western Iran," the narrator explained. "Notice that its skin is the identical color of its surroundings, making it nearly impossible for anyone to spot unless the viper is moving."

The film showed a snake that was nearly impossible to see in the rocky terrain. "What makes the spider-tailed horned viper unique is its tail. Instead of rattles like those found on rattlesnakes in North America, the horned viper appears to be dragging a large brown spider behind it."

On the screens, the viper twisted its tail, causing it to appear as if a large spider were darting back and forth on the rocks. From Grainger's vantage point, he could tell that Stanton and other committee members were shocked by how well hidden the snake was. One member asked a colleague to point out the snake because he had lost sight of it.

"In this desolate climate," the narrator continued, "insect-eating birds search for spiders." On the screen, an unsuspecting bird swooped down and grabbed the dancing spider in its beak. Suddenly, the viper's head emerged from the terrain, appearing as if from nowhere, stabbing its poisonous fangs into the bird, paralyzing it.

"That's an incredible nature film," Stanton said when the video ended and lights were turned back up. "But I'm not sure of its relevance to our committee."

"Our SAD team was able to interview the only Al-Shabaab fighter who was captured after the Mandera attack. He was taken to a Nairobi prison where our people interrogated him. Naturally, we followed all of the correct protocols."

"No enhanced interrogation techniques?"

"I can assure you of that, Mr. Chairman," Grainger said. "Our people were able to learn from this terrorist that the Falcon has successfully penetrated our government with a mole."

Grainger paused and then looked directly at the Chairman. "Someone in our government is helping these extremists."

"How trustworthy is this source of yours?" Stanton asked.

"Everything else he has told us has been authenticated."

"Did he say how high up in our government this reputed traitor is? Are we talking about some low-level clerk or lower-level manager?"

"Based on the information that we believe this individual has provided to the Falcon, we believe this source is not some low-level operative. It is someone higher up, much higher up."

"What sort of information are you basing your assessment on?"

"This source appears to have given information to the couple who attacked the president at Decker Lake's funeral. We believe this source provided a sniper with the location and time that General Grant was traveling on the Jefferson Davis Highway when he was shot. That information could only have come from someone highly placed inside our government."

No one spoke for several moments as the Chairman and committee members considered the gravity of what they'd just been told. It was clear that none of them had considered the idea of a radical Islamic mole inside our government.

Grainger said, "The FBI's assistant director of counterterrorism, Wyatt Parker, is handling the mole hunt and would be better able to answer your questions about it."

"Thank you, Director Grainger," Stanton replied. "We'll invite him in, but first you need to answer my earlier question. What was the point of showing us the YouTube snake video?"

"Mr. Chairman, we have learned from the captured Al-Shabaab terrorist in Kenya that the Falcon's code name for the mole is 'The Viper.'"

Chairman Stanton groaned. "What is it with these pseudonyms? Clearly these killers enjoy dressing themselves up with such monikers as 'The Falcon' and 'The Viper.' It turns my stomach."

"Forgive me for being so theatrical, Mr. Chairman, but when I learned that we had a mole hiding in our government who was calling himself the Viper, I had my people check for all possible clues, and one of them stumbled upon the Internet video. I showed it today because I felt it was a dramatic way to illustrate what we are facing."

"So we are the bird in the video?"

"I didn't mean to be so literal. We have a mole who has camouflaged himself to appear as if he is one of us. He is someone who is capable of hiding, luring us in, and then striking. Regardless of how we feel about the code name—Viper—this mole poses a real danger to all of us."

CHAPTER TWENTY-SIX

House Permanent Select Committee on Intelligence
Capitol Visitor Center
Washington, D.C.

O f the six million to ten million Muslims living in the United States," Special Agent Wyatt Parker said after being sworn in before the committee, "fewer than a hundred serve in elected positions in our nation such as mayors and police chiefs of major cities, in state legislators or in Congress. This includes Representative Adeogo."

"Special Agent Parker, you're not suggesting that the Minnesota congressman is this self-anointed Viper, are you?" Stanton said in a stern voice.

"Oh no, no, sir," Parker replied, clearly embarrassed. "I was simply providing the committee with a breakdown of Muslims who currently hold a public office."

"Can you tell us how many Muslims are employed by the federal government?"

"No, Mr. Chairman."

"Why not?"

"Because we don't know. We don't keep track of how many federal employees are Jewish, Christian, or Muslim. Some private organizations have broken down the religious affiliations of public officials, including members of Congress and the U.S. Supreme Court, but our government does not ask federal employees to reveal if they are religious and, if so, what faith they ascribe to."

Perspiration shimmered on Parker's bald head despite the windowless room's constant seventy-one-degree temperature. "Even if we did collect such data or attempt to discern employees' religious preferences, we suspect the Viper is keeping his religious affiliation secret. It's unlikely he belongs to a mosque, prays in public, or follows any of the identifiable religious instructions in the Quran that would make him easy to spot."

Using the television remote, Parker showed photos of Cumar and Fawzia Samatar on the committee room's two screens. "This is the couple who attacked the president, but both of them can be ruled out as being the Viper. Cumar Samatar did hold a federal job—he worked for the CIA as an interpreter—but he and his wife were already dead when the assassination attempt was made on General Grant and the two girls—Jennifer Conner and the congressman's daughter, Cassy Adeogo—were abducted."

"A few minutes ago, Director Grainger told us this mole is someone high up in our government, much higher than a low-level CIA interpreter. Do you agree?"

"Yes, for three reasons. First, we've found evidence that someone texted Fawzia Samatar while she was hiding in a National Cathedral janitorial closet. The text told her when to light herself on fire and attack the president, and it came from a burner phone that had been purchased by the president's reelection committee. We believe the Viper was one of the invited guests attending Decker Lake's funeral when he or she sent that text to Fawzia on that phone."

"Are you suggesting this traitor could be on the president's own White House staff?"

"We are not ruling out any possibility."

"What other evidence have you discovered?"

"The Viper clearly knew the route General Grant was taking when he left the Pentagon for the CIA. Again, this would require someone who was familiar with his schedule."

"And the third clue?"

"Major Brooke Grant employed a private security company to

protect her residence in rural Virginia. She shared the company's security information, such as how many motion detectors were being installed and their locations, with several federal agencies to ensure that this private firm was providing her and Jennifer Conner with the most up-to-date protection. We know that someone was able to elude all of that firm's safeguards and alarms and was about to break into the house to harm Jennifer Conner and Major Grant when the child woke up and screamed. The private security agency insists that this breach did not come from inside its organization, and interviews that we have conducted confirm that. It's likely someone inside our government who was privy to those security schematics leaked them to terrorists."

"Did the FBI have access to those plans?"

"Yes, we did."

"Agent Parker, you're cutting a wide swath here—from the White House to the FBI to the Pentagon. That's a lot of ground for one mole to cover. Is it possible there is a second or third traitor rather than one Viper?"

"We believe that is unlikely."

"Let me repeat what we've heard from you and Director Grainger. The CIA interrogated a source in Africa who claims a mole by the code name 'Viper' is operating inside our government providing help to the Falcon. You have no direct evidence that this mole exists, but based on circumstantial evidence and speculation, you agree that a mole has penetrated our government and is rather high up in it. This mole could be in the White House, your own agency, or the Pentagon. Does that sum it up?"

"Yes, sir. But that is more speculation than fact at this juncture."

"Let's move from speculation to what you do know for certain about these attacks, beginning with these two terrorists whose photos are on the monitors."

"Yes, sir. Both are from Minneapolis," Parker replied. "Both are Somali Americans. And we believe both were radicalized by a Somali American Imam who was from a Minneapolis mosque before recently moving to the Washington, D.C., area."

With the click of a remote, a new photo appeared on the television screens that showed a white-bearded, seventy-something Imam. "We consider Mohammad Al-Kader an Islamic radical because he is a strong proponent of Sharia law. The leaders of the Minnesota mosque where he was teaching asked him to leave after our field office in the Twin Cities traced money that he was generating to an international charity, which we believe has operated as a front for terrorist organizations. Cumar and Fawzia Samatar followed Al-Kader here from Minneapolis, and it's possible that Al-Kader may be involved somehow in helping the Viper or the Falcon."

"If the FBI knows this Imam is a radical, if we know he has raised money for terrorists, if you believe he might be helping the Viper or the Falcon, then why haven't you arrested him?"

"I wish it were that simple. He is an Imam, a religious leader, and he's very smart. The fact that he calls on his followers to donate money to international charities and those charities are later shown to be funding Islamic extremists isn't enough of a nexus for us to prosecute him. We are, however, investigating if we can revoke his citizenship on grounds that he was a close associate of Osama bin Laden."

"Did I hear you right just now? Did you say he was an associate of Osama bin Laden? Why in the hell is he still walking our streets?"

"Al-Kader's case is difficult and complicated," Parker answered, becoming even more uncomfortable.

"I believe this committee would like to hear about his case, regardless of how complicated it may be."

"Perhaps it would be helpful if I explained his personal history. Al-Kader was born in Afghanistan, but came here on a student visa in 1977. Two years later, we recruited him to raise money in the United States to help finance insurgent groups battling Soviet forces in Afghanistan. We decided to send him to Afghanistan in 1984 where he underwent training in an insurgent camp that we were helping fund. Our people were providing technical assistance.

From there, he joined Afghan mujahideen fighting the Soviets. That's when he became close with Osama bin Laden."

"Just so we're perfectly clear on the record here," Stanton said. "When you say *our* people, can we assume you are talking about either the CIA, the FBI, or both?"

"That's correct."

"So Al-Kader was recruited by the FBI, sent to Afghanistan by the CIA, trained there by the agency which then sent him to help fight the Soviets. We then asked him to buddy up with Osama bin Laden."

"That would be a fair interpretation of the facts. In 1989, when the Soviets retreated, Al-Kader applied for political asylum. You might remember that different factions were fighting among themselves for control of Afghanistan, and Al-Kader was on the outs with several of these groups because of his conservative religious beliefs. He wanted to become a U.S. citizen and because he had helped us, we green-lighted his application."

"His reward was American citizenship?"

"Yes, sir, in a manner of speaking."

"Was anyone aware that he was a radical Islamist?"

"Nearly everyone we recruited was, Mr. Chairman. We didn't hear much about him after that. He ended up in a mosque in Minneapolis and no one paid attention to what he was doing or saying until the Taliban seized control of Afghanistan in 1996. That's when we first began hearing reports that he was raising money for them."

"So this radical Imam is now working against us even though he is a U.S. citizen?"

"I suspect Al-Kader sees himself first as a devout Muslim, not a U.S. citizen, and he would argue that he never changed sides. He's always been fighting against anyone who opposes his rigid interpretation of Islam—whether it's the Soviets or us. We've put him on a no-fly list but, if I may speak candidly, Al-Kader has lawyered up. He's using his constitutional rights as a U.S. citizen to continue teaching his radical doctrine and his calls for the creation of a Sharia caliphate."

"You said Cumar and Fawzia Samatar followed him into our area. Had they popped up on your radar?"

"No, I'm afraid they hadn't. I'm afraid we are limited in our investigative abilities."

"What exactly does that mean? You knew this Imam was a radical. You knew he came here. I assume you know what mosque he's settled into. Aren't you monitoring him and identifying his followers?"

"Mr. Chairman, I'm certain you are aware that after the 9/11 attacks, then FBI director Robert Mueller instructed our field offices to 'count the mosques.' The bureau began infiltrating mosques and pinpointing which Imams support radical terrorism. This effort required us to relax our rules so we could proceed without first establishing probable cause. Our investigations enabled us to compile a fairly complete database—a 'Who's Who' of radical Imams and potential homegrown terrorists. But in 2008, the media, the American Civil Liberties Union and the Organization of Islamic Nations—the OIN—learned about what we were doing and immediately objected to our 'mosque outreach' program. This led to a series of highly publicized complaints and lawsuits, accusing us of violating the federal Privacy Act and the First Amendment rights of Muslim religious leaders and their congregants. Consequently, we were forced to dial back our intelligence gathering efforts and return to a pre-9/11 standard. We now engage in surveillance only after we have established clear probable cause that criminal wrongdoing is happening."

"In other words, the FBI has to wait until someone such as the Samatars commit a terrorist act before you can open a file on them."

"We must have probable cause, and that is difficult to obtain if we don't have access to a mosque, and we can't infiltrate the mosque under our new rules."

"Agent Parker, have you ever heard of the Aryan Brotherhood?"

"Yes, of course, Mr. Chairman," Parker replied. "It's a vicious prison gang."

"Isn't it true that the bureau routinely monitors and attempts to infiltrate that vicious gang with snitches to compile data about its members?"

"Yes, but I think you are comparing apples and oranges. The Aryan Brotherhood is a known criminal enterprise, a prison gang with tentacles out into the streets. It is not a religious group whose members might or might not be involved in radical causes."

"Apples and oranges? How do you know the Aryan Brotherhood is a criminal gang?"

"Because of its members' actions."

"Do you have to wait until one of them breaks the law to create a file on them?"

"No, sir."

"You have probable cause simply because of the group's past actions, is that what you're saying?" Stanton asked. Without waiting for an answer, he continued. "So explain to me how I am comparing apples and oranges? You can infiltrate an organization on the premise that its past criminal actions are prima facie evidence. But you can't infiltrate the mosque where Al-Kadar is an Imam even though you know he is preaching extremist views and generating funds for terrorists? Even now when you know two of his followers attempted to assassinate a sitting United States president?"

"As you know, Congressman, our Supreme Court is very protective of free speech and of freedom of religion. Al-Kadar understands this and uses our Constitution to his advantage. Inside his mosque, he is virtually untouchable."

"Okay, let's talk about the Samatars, these would-be assassins. Cumar Samatar, who threw himself against the presidential limousine, was employed as an interpreter at the CIA, wasn't he? How did he get hired?"

"Potential federal employees are not asked to disclose their personal religious beliefs or what mosque they might attend."

"You can't ask a potential employee if he is a Muslim?"

"The government can't discriminate based on an individual's religious or political beliefs."

"Just so I am certain I understand this, you can't ask someone if they are religious. You can't ask them if they attend a mosque. You can't ask them if they believe in imposing Sharia law."

"I had our human resources people discuss this with the Office of Personnel Management, which is responsible for establishing federal hiring guidelines. I'd like to read a synopsis of what I was told. 'Any question direct or that an applicant could surmise is attempting to discover religious beliefs or affiliation are strictly prohibited. If a potential employer is shying away from hiring someone because they suspect their religious affiliation will require them to take certain days off, for instance, they could ask if an individual would be able to regularly and consistently meet the required work schedule for a specific position. But they would be in violation if they revealed that they were concerned about the potential employee missing work because of his religious beliefs.' The Equal Employment Opportunity Act severely limits such questioning. For example, federal hiring managers are prohibited from asking such rudimentary questions as where an applicant currently resides because that could be seen as being 'discriminatory hiring' if they are refused a job and believe it was because of their residence."

"Wait a second," Stanton said, interrupting. "You can't even ask where a person lives because that might be discriminatory?"

"It sounds crazy, but if two applications are under consideration and the one lives in an affluent area and that person gets the job, the other one can claim discrimination."

"Do those same rules apply to the CIA?"

"I'm not totally familiar with what the agency can and can't ask its potential employees. But I've been told that questions about an individual's religious beliefs cannot be asked during employment interviews or background checks. Cumar Samatar was a U.S. citizen, so his rights to privacy and his religious beliefs were protected, as are the rights of every Muslim who applies for a federal job. Questions about their religious beliefs cannot be asked."

For another hour, Parker answered questions until the hearing ended. Afterward, Chairman Stanton walked from the chairman's seat to where Representative Rudy Adeogo was sitting and invited him into his private committee office.

"As you are aware," Stanton said, "today's hearings were closed to everyone but committee members and you. How would you react as a member of Congress if I decided to conduct a series of public hearings about these same issues, excluding any mention of the Viper?"

"What specific issues would you include?" Adeogo asked. "Your committee covered many topics this morning."

"I'm talking about holding public, televised hearings that would examine if and when our national security interests should override religious safeguards. Hearings that would investigate whether we are handcuffing federal law enforcement agencies by not allowing them to infiltrate mosques known to house radical Imams, such as Al-Kader. Hearings to determine if we should allow federal agencies to ask if a potential employee is a Muslim and, if so, if he or she believes in Sharia law or supports the creation of a caliphate."

"It would be easy for those hearings to be viewed as an attack on the Muslim religion and its adherents."

"I agree, and I don't wish to persecute Muslims or any other religious faith. But I do want to protect our nation against radical religious extremists who are using our own laws and political correctness to their advantage. Unfortunately, all of those extremists are Muslims, so where do we draw the line between protecting ourselves and protecting their rights to privacy?"

"Omar Nader and the OIN will *not* see this as a debate about political correctness. They will accuse you of being on a witch hunt."

"Which is why I am asking if you would support me. Having the only Muslim in Congress stating in public that we need to take a serious look at these potentially explosive subjects would give the hearings objectivity and credibility."

Adeogo spent a few moments quietly considering what Stanton was proposing. "Mr. Chairman, aren't you already planning on conducting public hearings about the embassy attack last year in Somalia?" he asked.

"Yes, up until this moment, that was a priority to me. I'm certain you've heard rumors that the CIA and possibly the White House knew an attack in Mogadishu at our embassy was imminent but didn't react."

"You must understand, Mr. Chairman, at this moment, my priority is rescuing my daughter, Cassy, and freeing Jennifer Conner. I would prefer that the FBI and the CIA remain focused on working together to save both girls rather than being distracted by hearings that might require them to defend their actions in Africa. I'm also concerned about holding investigative hearings about possible incompetence when our president has been attacked, the chairman of the Joint Chiefs of Staff has been critically wounded, and my daughter and Jennifer Conner have been abducted. The American people might view an investigation into possible errors made in Somalia as giving comfort to our enemies."

Stanton had not expected Adeogo to bring up the committee's intention to investigate the Somalia debacle.

"May I suggest that you postpone those committee hearings until a more appropriate time," Adeogo said. "If you did that, I would be willing to support your new idea."

"You would state publicly that we need to explore whether political correctness and laws about religious freedom are endangering our national security?" the Chairman asked.

"Yes, I would be willing to support hearings that would examine issues about religious freedom. My goal is the same as yours—to find better ways to identify and root out homegrown extremists. You must understand that no one is more offended than the Muslim community by what these radical Islamists are doing."

Stanton took a moment to consider Adeogo's recommendation.

Something in his gut was troubling him. He knew the CIA opposed hearings about the embassy attack because Director Grainger didn't want the public to discover that the NSA had warned his agency that an attack was imminent, yet it did nothing to prevent it. The Chairman also had heard whispers that Mallory Harper and the White House didn't want his committee investigating the Somalia hostage crisis because of a possible embarrassing payoff scandal. There were rumors on the Internet that President Allworth had agreed to secretly pay Al-Shabaab a multimillion-dollar ransom even though it was U.S. policy not to negotiate with terrorists. What Stanton didn't know was if Adeogo also had an undisclosed ulterior motive for not wanting those hearings to be held. *What secret could he be hiding? Did he have some personal reason for not wanting the committee to investigate the events in Somalia?*

"I will not abandon my decision to hold public hearings about the events that occurred in Mogadishu," Stanton said. "However, I believe the points you've raised about timing are valid. So I will put those hearings on hold for the moment and instead have this committee conduct hearings on whether our intelligence community and law enforcement need more freedom to investigate religious leaders and groups that are clearly hostile to our government. Is that good enough for you?"

"Yes, Mr. Chairman, I can support those hearings, but please understand that I will not issue any statements about these issues until after my daughter is rescued. I can't risk saying or doing anything in public that might put my child's life in greater jeopardy."

"Understood," Stanton replied. "I don't need you to speak out immediately, but knowing you will eventually be at my side will be useful when the OIN and its attack dog, Omar Nader, start demanding my head."

CHAPTER TWENTY-SEVEN

En route to El Wak
Eastern Kenya, border with Somalia

S he didn't cheat on *me*," Ironman insisted. "It was some dude I met in a bar."

Walks Many Miles was listening to Ironman through an earpiece inside a helicopter carrying their six-member SAD team to a drop-off point near the El Wak home of African billionaire Umoja Owiti. Israeli intelligence had notified Langley that the Falcon was about to visit there again, and the agency wanted "eyes on the ground."

Miles, who was known inside the team as "the Chief," was sitting between two soldiers nicknamed Ironman and Pyro. They were facing Reaper, Merc, and Ghost inside the Mi-8TV ZS-RUB helicopter, a Soviet-built twin-turbine aircraft popular in Africa and much less likely than a U.S. helicopter to draw fire from Al-Shabaab or Boko Haram extremists.

"Okay, Ironman, tell us what happened to your *friend*?" Merc said, making it clear from his pronunciation of "friend" that he still believed Ironman was talking about himself.

"This guy gets engaged to a real looker," Ironman said.

"Hooker?" Merc asked, interrupting. "Because if she was a hooker, then this story definitely is about you." Thrusting his hips upward from his seat, he broke into a falsetto: "Oh, Ironman! Oh, baby, oh, baby. What? But it's only been five seconds!"

Everyone but Ironman laughed.

"You want to hear my story or not?" Ironman demanded.

"Your story?" Pyro declared. "So it is about a girl who dumped you."

"No, it was a friend," Ironman declared, clearly frustrated. "Now shut up and listen. This guy gets engaged, right, and the bride's parents are so happy they mortgage their house to pay for their little girl's wedding. Everything goes well, until the reception. After the best man gives his toast, the groom stands and thanks everyone, especially his in-laws for taking out a second mortgage so their little princess can have a dream wedding. Then the groom announces that his new bride cheated with his best man on the night before the wedding."

"That's cold," Merc said, interrupting again.

"So the groom tosses his champagne toast into his bride's face and files for an annulment the next morning. He got his revenge by totally humiliating her in front of all their friends and by sticking her parents with a huge bill."

"Serves her right," Pyro said.

"Great story," Walks Many Miles said, joining their conversation for the first time. "Too bad none of it's true. It's an urban legend."

"No way," Ironman said. "I heard this directly from the guy it happened to."

"A guy you met in a bar. A guy who probably got you to pay for a couple of drinks out of sympathy and in return for him telling you that story. You're an idiot for believing him. Go ahead and Google it," Miles replied. "You'll find versions where the groom puts photographs under all of the chairs at the reception of his bride and the best man having sex for people to see. It never happened."

"The Chief is right. It's got to be fake," Pyro said, "because a Marine would never cheat with another Marine's fiancée the night before their wedding. *Ooh rah.* Bros before hoes."

"Okay, I remember now," Ironman said, grinning. "The guy who told me this—he was in the Army."

"Then it's probably true," Merc declared, "because a grunt will sleep with anything."

Walks Many Miles was still chuckling when a brilliant flash blinded him. The explosion slammed the back of his skull against the helicopter's fuselage. That initial concussive blast was followed microseconds later by air being sucked backward to fill the atmospheric void the explosion had created. Miles's body snapped forward against the safety harness holding him. The air in his lungs was sucked out. As Miles watched helplessly, Ironman's safety straps broke and his body flew from his seat at the same instance the end of the helicopter came apart. Ironman disappeared out the opening into the morning air as the main body of the aircraft began spinning downward out of control.

In the moment before he blacked out, Miles had two thoughts. The helicopter's tail boom had been hit by an RPG.

And he was going to die.

Miles wasn't certain how long he'd been unconscious when he awoke. Helicopter parts were littered around him. He was still secured to his jump seat, which was attached to a section of the helicopter's fuselage. It had busted loose from the main cabin, catapulting him free from the crash, much like a jet pilot ejecting in his seat from a cockpit. Freeing himself, he tried to stand, but his knees buckled and he toppled face-first onto the sand. Miles steadied himself and surveyed his surroundings. The first body he saw was Pyro, who had been thrown from the aircraft. Miles crawled to him. Pyro's neck was broken. He was dead. Managing to stand, Miles checked the rest of the team. He found Ghost, Reaper, and Merc dead inside what was left of the helicopter. The aircraft's two pilots, who were still buckled in their harnesses in the cockpit, also were dead. Ironman was nowhere in sight. In what clearly was a fluke, Miles was the lone survivor.

Most likely the throbbing pain in his right side was from cracked ribs. He wasn't certain how many were broken, but that seemed to be the extent of his injuries. *Now what?*

Whoever had shot down the helicopter would be coming. He needed a plan. None of the SAD team members was wearing a dog tag, but the two pilots were, so Miles took them. He also collected Pyro's P226 Sig Sauer handgun from its holster as a backup weapon and retrieved additional ammunition and two canteens. He looked for a rifle but couldn't find any of the team's other weapons.

He would not be able to outrun the terrorists who would be coming like vultures eager to pick over the remains. He looked for a place to hide. The terrain was flat and sandy with only ubiquitous *Acacia karroo* thornbushes for cover. He chose a bush about fifty yards away and used his shirt to sweep over his tracks as he walked to it. A piece of metal from the helicopter's underbelly had landed against the bush. It was rectangular and large, approximately six feet by four feet. With adrenaline fueling him, Miles tugged and pushed until he'd positioned it against the bush much like a lean-to shelter. He left enough room between the ground and the metal covering for him to slide between them on his stomach. His cracked ribs made him grimace but he had no choice but to lie on his chest. He needed to look from his hiding spot at the crash site and he couldn't have done that on his back. He shoved sand in front of the opening near his face, leaving only enough space so that he could peer out from under the lean-to covering. He drew Pyro's Sig Sauer.

Miles didn't wait long. The first sound was the noise of approaching vehicles. Two Land Rovers arrived, but the five men who emerged from them were not Islamic terrorists. They were wearing uniforms with insignias that identified them as being security guards for Umoja Owiti Enterprises. Four of them went directly to check on the dead Americans while the fifth spoke into a satellite phone.

The guards stripped the bodies of their handguns and holsters and rifled through their pockets, taking whatever valuables they could find. They tossed the holstered pistols on the ground at the feet of their supervisor at the same moment he completed his phone call.

Miles watched him bend down, examine the pistols, and suddenly bolt upright. In an excited voice, he began barking orders as his men unslung their AK-47 assault rifles.

Miles realized he had made a mistake by taking Pyro's pistol. All of the holsters had snaps over the guns' hammers securing them in place. Counting the two pilots, there were six bodies at the crash site and each man had been wearing a holster, but there were only five handguns. There could be only two explanations. Either one man had unsnapped his weapon and it had been lost during the crash or someone had survived and removed the weapon before Owiti's guards had arrived.

The men formed a circle around the crashed aircraft and methodically began marching out from that epicenter. One of them was aimed directly toward the bush and metal debris under which Miles was hiding. If the approaching security guard bent down and peeked underneath the metal covering, Miles would have no choice but to shoot him in his face. But that pistol shot would reveal his position and he would be trapped. The sheet metal hiding him was too heavy for Miles to throw off. He would have to crawl from beneath it after shooting the guard, and that would make him an easy target.

In what he believed might be the last moments of his life, Miles thought about Brooke Grant and the love that he felt for her and Jennifer. He had never planned on dying in an African desert, but how many men plan their deaths or see them coming? Only a short time ago, he had been laughing with his teammates. Now they were dead and he faced their fate. He tightened his grip on the trigger.

As Miles had anticipated, the approaching Owiti guard stopped when he reached the metal lean-to and bush. The man's black-laced boots were mere inches from Miles's face and pistol. Miles readied himself mentally for what was to come. That's when he heard a splashing noise. It took him a second to understand what was happening. Rather than bending down to check under the metal, the security guard had unzipped his trousers and was urinating on the debris. When he finished, he stepped around it and continued walking away from the crash. Miles was safe. At least for the moment.

As he continued to look out from under his make-do hiding place, Miles heard the sound of additional vehicles approaching the crash site. Three pickup trucks arrived. The men disembarking from them wore kaffiyehs on their heads. Miles wasn't certain if they were from Boko Haram or Al-Shabaab, but he knew they were Islamic terrorists because the trucks were decorated with the black flag of jihadism, a black banner with a white *shahada* (Islamic creed) printed on it. As he watched, the security guard in charge pointed into the air where the helicopter had been traveling when it was hit and then pointed in the direction of Umoja Owiti's compound. Miles understood what was being said even though he couldn't understand the dialect they were speaking. It had been the billionaire's security guards who had fired the fatal RPG downing the helicopter, not the Islamic terrorists whom the guard had called to the crash site.

The security guard in charge hollered to his men, who returned to the crash site and boarded the Land Rovers. As those vehicles were driving away, the newly arrived terrorists scooped up the pistols and holsters from the ground and began stripping the dead soldiers and anything useful from the wreckage. They carried the six corpses out onto the sand where they lined them up in front of the cockpit for photographs. One fighter held his rifle above his head as he planted his boot on Ghost's chest. Miles felt the anger building up inside him, but knew there was nothing he could do but watch. Satisfied with their souvenirs, the terrorists tossed the bodies into the back of a pickup truck. Even dead, they would be worth ransoming.

One of them lifted binoculars to his eyes and turned in a circle studying the desert. He skipped over the lean-to hiding Miles. Having not seen anyone running from the wreckage, the terrorists left one man behind while the others boarded their trucks and drove southwest. They were traveling in the direction that the helicopter had come from and Miles assumed they were retracing that flight path on the assumption that the missing American would be retracing the route to wherever the flight had originated.

Miles studied the lone sentry as he took cover in a shaded area at the base of the helicopter's cockpit. Squatting down, the man rested his AK-47 across his thighs and pulled a white packet from his clothing. Miles couldn't see what his enemy was removing from it but when he raised his fingers to his lips, Miles understood. The sentry was chewing khat, the amphetamine-like buds and leaves of the drought-tolerant *Catha edulis* evergreen shrub. Everyone's favorite Somali high.

March in Kenya was one of its hottest months and Miles's metal hiding spot quickly began to make him feel as if he were inside an oven. His broken ribs made every breath painful. While Miles could see the squatting sentry, firing the pistol at him with any accuracy would be difficult from his prone vantage point. Miles couldn't risk shooting and missing. Digging the toes of his boots into the sand, he propelled himself forward, head first, from under the lean-to shelter.

The security guard spotted him. Perhaps it was because he was startled. Perhaps it was the numbing effect of the khat. No matter. By the time the terrorist stood and aimed his assault rifle, Miles had slipped far enough out from under the metal covering to rise up onto his knees. He aimed the Sig Sauer handgun.

Now panicked, the terrorist began firing without taking aim, a common mistake with a weapon capable of firing bursts of rounds. Miles didn't duck or flinch. Seemingly oblivious to the slugs ripping the air, bush, and sand near him, he focused on his target, paused his breathing when his lungs were full of oxygen, and squeezed the trigger. *Pop. Pop.* Two rounds. Check the target. Re-aim. Fire two more. His training had taken charge over his emotions.

The terrorist stumbled backward still firing his rifle. He hit the ground on his back and didn't move.

Leaping to his feet, Miles bolted toward his target, firing another two-round report. When he reached the gunman, the man's eyes were fluttering, blood was flowing from his mouth. Miles fired a final shot into the terrorist's face.

Moving quickly, he claimed the sentry's AK-47 and retrieved an additional forty-round magazine from the dead fighter's clothing. He was hoping to find a satellite phone, but the only other item in the man's vest was his packet of khat. Miles took it too. It might prove useful easing the pain in his rib cage.

Hurrying into the cockpit, Miles checked the helicopter's instrument panel. The communication equipment had been stripped away.

It had been nearly three hours now since the crash. Miles had no idea if a rescue team had been sent or would be. But he felt certain news of the crash would spread to El Wak, a city where every scrap of metal was considered precious. Its residents would be drawn like flies to the leftovers. He could wait and see if they would help rescue him. But that was risky. It might be more profitable for them to tip off their billionaire neighbor or capture him for Boko Haram or Al-Shabaab, knowing that both would pay a reward.

There was only one major highway that passed through El Wak and it was north of the crash site. Umoja Owiti's security guards and terrorists would have traveled on the Isiolo Mandera highway before veering off to reach the helicopter crash. He could follow their tracks north to the highway. But what would he do after he reached that roadway?

Swinging the AK-47 over his shoulder, he began walking north. *One step at a time*, he told himself. There would be phones in El Wak.

As he walked, another thought came to him. The SAD team helicopter had been flying over miles of desert primarily populated by lizards, snakes, and spiders. How was it that the African billionaire Umoja Owiti's security guards had known where to position themselves to shoot down a helicopter with an RPG? They would have needed to know its flight plan. In Kenya, only the six members of the SAD team and two pilots had known the route, and all of them except him were dead.

He reached a chilling conclusion. Someone in Washington, D.C., who was aware of the secret mission had betrayed them.

CHAPTER TWENTY-EIGHT

A Virginia cabin
Somewhere in the Appalachian Mountains

Jennifer Conner heard a woman scream, but she needed to make certain it wasn't her own brain playing tricks on her.

"Cassy?" she whispered.

"Yes," her fellow captive replied. "I hear it too. He's beating her."

As they listened with their heads covered by hoods, a door opened followed by a loud slap, like someone smacking their open palm against a tabletop.

Cassy yelped.

Another slap.

Jennifer's hood was ripped off.

"You're next!" Akbar threatened.

Jennifer could see him now. He was standing in between them. A black leather belt was dangling from Akbar's right hand. He'd looped the belt in half by grasping its tip and metal buckle together. Lifting it to his shoulder, Akbar brought it down hard, striking Cassy across her shoulders. He'd already removed her hood but Jennifer couldn't see the eleven-year-old's face because Cassy had curled her body into a fetal position on the floor and was covering her cheeks and eyes with her bound wrists.

Another cruel whip across Cassy's back caused her to scream. Akbar raised his belt again and brought it down with such force that the belt's tip flew loose from his grasp. Now in a frenzy, he didn't bother to re-loop the belt. He continued swinging it like a whip, striking her again and again.

"Stop!" Jennifer yelled.

Turning his face away from Cassy, Akbar said, "Now, it's your turn!"

He swung, hitting her buttocks with the leather. As he pulled back his hand, she readied herself for another blow, instinctively tucking her knees against her chest as she lay on her side. She raised her duct-taped wrists over her face just as Cassy had done.

This time when he struck her, she did not scream. She was no longer on the floor in the cabin. She'd withdrawn inside the mansion in her mind. He struck her again. But she had entered a room with a window that looked out onto a happy place beyond the glass. A unicorn, bright blue with a pretty pink horn, was prancing next to a waterfall and pool of clear water.

Crack. He struck again. *Slap.* Another hit. Jennifer was focused on the unicorn. It turned its head, glancing up from the pool, and winked at her before it opened its magnificent feathered wings and with a single leap left the ground, gracefully soaring higher and higher, until the unicorn disappeared in pillow-shaped clouds.

Jennifer heard Cassy sobbing.

She left the room inside her mind where she was hiding, exited the mansion, and opened her eyes. The two girls were alone. Akbar was gone.

"No one ever hurt me like that," Cassy said. "I'm not brave like you are."

"I wasn't here."

Jennifer told Cassy about the mansion. She told her about the room. The one with the window. The one with the blue unicorn and his pink horn and his wings, and when she finished, Cassy had stopped crying.

"I wish I could see your unicorn," Cassy said.

"Let's give him a name," Jennifer replied. "If we give him a name maybe he'll come back and I can introduce you to him."

"But he's not real. He's imaginary."

Jennifer didn't respond.

"There's nothing wrong with having an imaginary friend," Cassy said. "I had one when I was little. Her name was Kat, like Kit-Kat, and she was my very best friend. BFF. We'd drink tea in the afternoons and I told her all of my secrets."

"What happened to her?" Jennifer asked.

"She went away."

The door opened and both of them immediately raised their hands over their faces and tucked their knees into their chests. But it was Aludra. Her eyes were puffy and her lips swollen.

"Come use the toilet," she said. "You need to clean yourselves."

"He beat you too, didn't he?" Cassy said.

"Do you need to use the toilet or not?" Aludra snapped.

"My father has never hit my mother or me," Cassy said.

"You're a child. You don't know."

"I do know. My grandfather used to hit my grandmother. All the time. My father hated it and when he got old enough, he ordered him to stop. He said it was wrong."

"No, it was your father who was wrong for interfering and not respecting your grandfather. It is allowed," Aludra said. "It's written in the Hadith."

"What's that?" Jennifer asked, joining their conversation.

"A holy book," Cassy said.

"The teachings of the Prophet," Aludra replied.

"I've never heard about it."

"A woman came to the Prophet and begged him to stop her husband from beating her. He did not admonish her husband, but ordered her to return to him and submit to his wishes. That is what is written in the Hadith."

"My father says some stories are more important than other ones," Cassy replied.

Aludra raised her hand to slap Cassy but then changed her mind. "Do not disrespect the teachings of the Prophet," she lectured. "Do you need to use the toilet or not?"

"Yes," Jennifer said. "I need to go."

Aludra cut through the duct tape on her legs and wrists, freeing her. "Come on," she ordered.

When Jennifer finished, Aludra used duct tape to bind the teen's ankles and wrists again.

"What about you?" she asked Cassy.

"I need to wash before I pray," she replied. Aludra cut through the tape but Cassy stumbled when she tried to stand. Aldura took her arm and helped her into the bathroom. After Cassy finished using the toilet, she moved to the sink. Cupping her hands under the faucet, she splashed water over her eyes and cheeks.

"Lift up your blouse," Aludra ordered. Cassy was standing in front of Aludra facing a mirror over the sink.

Cassy looked at the older woman's reflection and raised her shirt. Cassy's back was a roadmap of red marks and swollen skin. Aludra undid the cap from a tube of ointment.

"This will help," Aludra said. She gently rubbed the cream on Cassy's back.

"Why did he do this?" Cassy asked. "We didn't do anything."

"He hit you harder than the other girl," Aludra said, ignoring her question. "It's because you are one of us."

"But I'm not like him or you."

Aludra took her hands away from Cassy's shoulders. "You are a Muslim. You have an obligation."

"Your cousin, Halgan, is one of the kindest persons I know," Cassy said. "Would you let him beat her with his belt?"

CHAPTER TWENTY-NINE

Al Arabic newsroom
Northwest Washington, D.C.

Reporting live from Al Arabic's Washington studio, Ebio Kattan warned viewers that the footage they were about to be shown contained a threat so disturbing that children should be taken from the room.

"Followers of Allah, glory be to His name, heed my declaration," the Falcon declared moments later on a video that had been e-mailed to Kattan. His black eyes stared through a narrow slit in his black ski mask. "Rise up and join us! This is not the work of one, two, or three people. All Muslims are responsible for carrying on jihad until we establish the Islamic state under Sharia law. Fight the infidels or face their fate."

For several more seconds he continued his rant until his image was replaced on the screen by footage that Akbar had taken of Cassy Adeogo and Jennifer Conner as hostages. A close-up angle showed Cassy whimpering after being beaten. As the camera drew back, Jennifer was shown, bound with duct tape, immobile on a tile floor as if she were in a trance.

"America must release two dozen of our brothers from prison or I will remove the heads of these daughters of the damned!" the Falcon threatened before he ended his message by praising Allah.

Reappearing on the television screen, a clearly excited Kattan breathlessly announced, "The Falcon did not set a deadline in this exclusive message that was e-mailed directly to me. He did not disclose when the United States must free two dozen prisoners currently being held at Gitmo—a U.S. military prison in Cuba. We will broadcast his next message as soon as I receive it."

Brooke Grant watched the Falcon's threat on a wall of television monitors while standing next to Special Agent Wyatt Parker inside the Reston command post.

The image of Jennifer lying helplessly on the floor after being beaten caused her eyes to swell with tears, but she fought to control the fury that filled her body, knowing that showing her emotions would be counterproductive—especially in Agent Parker's presence. In as calm a voice as she could muster, she said, "This idea of yours, Agent Parker, isn't going to work."

Parker ignored her as they watched the Al Arabic network switch from showing Ebio Kattan inside its Washington studio to a reporter stationed outside Representative Rudy Adeogo's house in the Tacoma Park neighborhood of D.C.

"We are expecting Representative Rudy Adeogo to make a statement any moment now," the reporter announced.

Parker turned his head and glanced at Brooke. "Your enthusiastic support is most appreciated," he said in a sarcastic voice.

"I'm just being frank," she replied. "I'm familiar with the bureau's Behavioral Change Stairway Model for high-stakes hostage negotiations. I know about the five steps—active listening, empathy, developing rapport, gaining influence, and ultimately achieving behavioral change. But you can't apply those hostage negotiation techniques to a religious fanatic like the Falcon. You can't have empathy with him, develop rapport, and you will never change his mind."

"Major Grant," Parker said, "how many hostage negotiations have you personally handled?" Without waiting for her reply, he said, "Let the experts handle this." He noticed the tears in her eyes and was about to say something about her emotions, but stopped himself.

"The Falcon is not interested in negotiating," Brooke said. "The only chance we have of saving Jennifer and Cassy is by finding out where he is holding them and sending in a team."

"There's a reason why the Falcon didn't give us a deadline for releasing prisoners," Parker countered. "He knows it's an unrealistic demand. It's bluster. He'll come back with a more reasonable demand as long as we don't challenge his authority. We need to stick to the plan and establish empathy and develop trust."

"You aren't listening. You can't trust a rattlesnake. The only way to negotiate with the Falcon is by putting a bullet in his head. I learned that lesson dealing with his protégé in Somalia."

"Really, Major Grant? A bullet to the head," Parker said flippantly.

He returned his gaze to the television monitors where Representative Adeogo and Dheeh were now being shown stepping onto the front porch of their white brick rented home.

"I would like to read a brief statement," Adeogo explained as reporters clustered around. While his voice sounded calm, his hands were quivering as he read from a sheet of paper. Photographers jostled for position while television camera crews zoomed in. The front yard of the house was overrun with the media.

"Cassy," he began, "your mummy and daddy love you and are doing everything we can to bring you home. Be brave. Listen to the people who are holding you." He looked up with teary eyes and was met by a chorus of clicking cameras. Not wishing to misspeak, he returned to the written text that Agent Parker had personally approved. "I would like to speak to the men holding you. Our daughter and Jennifer Conner have no control over the actions of the U.S. government. These girls are innocent children. You, the caliph, can grant amnesty. We acknowledge your love and devotion to Allah, the Merciful, and we would ask you to use your authority to spare our children's lives. We urge you to follow the example set by the Prophet Muhammad, who protected people of the Book. We ask that you follow the Prophet's example in caring and protecting children. Just as Allah shows all of us mercy, we plead that you will show us mercy."

He folded the paper.

Reporters began shouting, but neither Adeogo nor Dheeh acknowledged them as they retreated into their home.

"Perfect," Parker said. "Having a U.S. congressman be respectful and acknowledging that the Falcon is clearly in control is going to feed his ego and buy us time. Citing Allah's mercy was pivotal. I feel confident the Falcon will bite and get word to us about how we can negotiate an end to this."

Brooke was about to utter a one-word profane response, but caught herself when the scene on the television monitors shifted to the White House. President Sally Allworth was about to deliver a national statement.

"Our nation has once again come under assault by terrorists," the president said. "We've all heard it said, 'One man's terrorist is another man's freedom fighter.' That's a catchy phrase, but it is misleading."

The president was sitting behind her desk in the Oval Office with her hands calmly folded in front of her. "Freedom fighters do not need to terrorize a population into submission. Freedom fighters target the military forces and the organized instruments of repression keeping dictatorial regimes in power. Freedom fighters struggle to liberate their citizens from oppression and to establish a form of government that reflects the will of the people. Now, this is not to say that those who are fighting for freedom are perfect or that we should ignore problems arising from passion and conflict. Nevertheless, one has to be blind, ignorant, or simply unwilling to see the truth if he or she is unable to distinguish between those I just described and terrorists."

Raising her voice slightly, she continued: "*Terrorists* intentionally kill or maim unarmed civilians, often women and children, often third parties who are not in any way part of a dictatorial regime.

Terrorists are always the enemies of democracy. And today we are dealing with the acts of terrorists, not religious devotees fighting for some noble cause. We are dealing with common criminals and cold-blooded murderers."

Allworth paused, but did not shift her gaze from looking directly into the camera, while reading from a teleprompter. "This time these despicable killers have targeted children, the most vulnerable of our citizens. They consider them bargaining chips. Is there anything more heinous and repulsive than using innocent children as pawns? All of us are praying for the safe return of little Cassy Adeogo. All of us are praying for her parents, Representative Rudy and Dheeh Adeogo, and for Jennifer Conner whose short life already has seen several lifetimes of death and tragedy."

Slowing her speech to make her words sound more sympathetic, she said, "We are praying for them as a nation, one unified people whether we are Muslims, Christians, Jews, or adherents to other faiths. We are unified in praying on behalf of all civilized people, who respect the diversity that makes our world unique and a wonderful place created by a loving God, no matter what name that God is called or how that deity is worshiped."

The tone of her voice shifted again, this time to one of steely determination. "To those terrorists holding our children, let me be clear. The complicated and heartrending issues that perplex mankind are no excuse for violent, inhumane attacks, nor do they excuse not taking aggressive action against those who deliberately slaughter innocent people. We will not tolerate your barbaric tactics. We will not lower our resolve to placate you. We will not succumb to your bullying and threats. Each and every one of you will be held accountable for your actions. You will be exposed as the frauds and cowards that you are and you will be punished. We will not excuse your actions and neither will our creator when you stand before Him on judgment day. You will pay the ultimate price for your actions. We will hunt you down and we will kill you."

She had cribbed her speech from one given by Ronald Reagan.

Inside the Reston command post, Brooke turned to look at Parker. "Obviously, the White House didn't get your memo about appeasing the Falcon so you could develop empathy and rapport with him."

Ignoring her jab, Parker continued staring straight ahead at the television screens.

Chief of Staff Mallory Harper appeared inside the White House briefing room behind a bouquet of microphones answering reporters' questions.

"Will the president free two dozen prisoners being held at Guantanamo?"

"The president will confer with her cabinet and consider all options."

"Does that mean she will meet the Falcon's demands?"

"It means exactly what I said. The president will confer with her cabinet and consider all options."

"You're not answering my question. Our country doesn't negotiate with terrorists or ransom hostages. Is the president going to change that policy and release those terrorists in exchange for those two girls' lives?"

"You can ask the same question a dozen times," Harper replied, "and I will still give you the same answer. The president will confer with her cabinet and will consider all options."

"So you're saying that the president might release them?"

Harper smiled and walked away from the podium.

Instantly, the television networks began broadcasting live discussions inside their studios with Middle Eastern scholars and retired FBI hostage negotiators. Brooke noticed one guest who seemed to slide from one monitor to the next, appearing on every network.

"Islam means the religion of peace," Omar Nader assured viewers. "The aim of Islam is to establish peace between man and Allah, the Creator of all; between man and man; and between man and the rest of Allah's creations. In the Holy Quran, God deals with the issue of terrorism by teaching Muslims *never* to become terrorists.

Two of the Prophet's earliest teachings are: '*Al-Fitnatu ashad-du minal qatl*'—meaning that in the sight of Allah, 'persecution, or making people constantly fear for their lives, is much worse than killing.' And also: '*Là ikrâha fid-dîn*'—'There shall be no compulsion in religion,' that is to say, that no one has the right to force others into complying with their demands or compelling others to follow their line of thinking."

Continuing in a soothing voice, Nader said, "Your president called these people criminals and that is accurate. They do not represent our religion or our people. They are fanatic criminals."

Parker had seen enough. "Major Grant, let's go into my office. I have some fresh intel to share with you."

He walked directly to a locked file cabinet where he retrieved a red folder. "Early this morning, we got a positive DNA match from the blood recovered from the paring knife—the one found in your kitchen lying next to the body of the victim there."

"Her name was Miriam Okpara," Brooke said.

"As we suspected, the victim, ur, Ms. Okpara, stabbed one of the kidnappers who abducted Jennifer." Parker handed her a photograph of a man. "He goes by the single name Akbar but his full name is Ahmadullah Aba-Jihaad. It's his DNA on the paring knife."

Brooke studied the lean, hollow face in the picture. "How'd you happen to have his DNA?"

"Because Akbar, aka Ahmadullah Aba-Jihaad, was once a prisoner at Gitmo. He was captured in Afghanistan in 2002 but was released after five years when he signed an agreement stating he would no longer take up arms against the U.S."

"He signed a paper, an agreement, and we let him go?"

"About thirty percent of the Gitmo prisoners who we have released have returned to fight against the U.S. In Akbar's case, we released him to Yemen, where he subsequently vanished. It appears he and a woman named Aludra used falsified papers and names to re-enter our country. We've tracked them to the same northern Virginia mosque that Cumar and Fawzia Samatar attended. A radical Imam named Mohammad Al-Kader has developed a following there and, we suspect, could be involved in various plots against the U.S."

Parker slipped another sheet of paper from a folder. "We believe Akbar also is responsible for shooting your uncle." He handed her a grainy image from a security camera. "This was taken at the checkout counter inside the local rental agency where two men and a woman secured a flatbed truck. They used that rented truck to dump building supplies on the Jefferson Davis Highway to block traffic, as you already know."

Brooke studied the two men and the woman photographed by the security cam.

"Facial recognition software identified Akbar based on mug shots of him at Gitmo," Parker continued. "We believe the woman is Aludra, but we haven't been able to identify the other man."

"So there's no question that Akbar is one of the kidnappers based on his DNA being on the paring knife and his picture at the rental counter. What evidence do you have that he shot my uncle?"

"It's circumstantial at this point but credible. Akbar was trained as a sniper by the Iranians before he was captured. Here's the scenario as we see it. The unidentified man at the rental counter was responsible for dumping the truck's payload on the highway, blocking traffic so Akbar could fire from the roof of a nearby apartment building. Someone, possibly Aludra, drove the getaway car, but rather than fleeing, she and Akbar took either Highway 50 or Interstate 66 out to your farmhouse, where Akbar murdered Ms. Okpara and abducted Jennifer while a different team of terrorists attacked the boarding school where they kidnapped Cassy Adeogo."

"Do you think Akbar was fatally wounded when he was stabbed?" Brooke asked.

Parker shrugged. "Not sure, but I'm guessing she stuck him once and didn't hit any arteries because of the lack of blood splatter in your kitchen. Nothing on the floor or walls or her clothing. Probably a non-incapacitating jab at best. But we can't be sure."

"What about the others involved in this? What about the driver of the flatbed truck and the men who murdered those students, their riding instructor, and the security guard at the girls' school?"

"We believe Akbar and Aludra had at least five accomplices, but we haven't been able to identify them yet. We suspect, however, that they are all tied in some way to the mosque where Al-Kader is the Imam. As you know, we recovered an abandoned van that had been stolen from an exterminator company—the one used during the attack at the girls' school in Potomac. It had blood inside that didn't match Cassy Adeogo's, based on her medical records, but we haven't been able to match it to anyone in our DNA database. That suggests one of the terrorists was wounded or killed. But no one showed up at area hospitals with a suspicious wound, and we've not found any bodies."

"Fingerprints?"

"There were no fingerprints found."

A knock on the door interrupted them. Parker waved in one of his command post team members.

"The agency has informed us that a helicopter carrying a six-man SAD team was shot down in Kenya near the Somali border earlier today—they are seven hours ahead of us," the agent said. "Al-Shabaab is claiming credit for downing the helicopter with an RPG and moments ago posted photographs of six dead Americans on the Internet. Counting the two pilots, there were eight men on that helicopter, so there are two Americans still unaccounted for."

Brooke felt her pulse quickening. "Do you know those two men's names? Have they been taken prisoner?"

"If Al-Shabaab captured them," he answered, "they would have posted video of them. They're always proud to show off their prisoners. The agency doesn't know if they're dead or survived, only that they are missing."

"My guess is the terrorists simply haven't recovered their bodies yet," Parker said in a grim voice. "The odds of surviving when a helicopter is blown out of the air by an RPG are extremely slim."

"The agency sent us the names of the six dead based on the Al-Shabaab video," the team manager said. He handed Parker a printout. Parker scanned it quickly and then held it out for Brooke.

She reached for it and immediately began looking for Walks Many Miles's name. He was listed as being "Missing/Unaccounted For."

"I noticed your friend, Walks Many Miles, is on that list," Parker said.

"Yes, he is," she replied, handing the sheet back to him.

"I'm sorry," he said. He was watching her closely to see how she would respond.

"I wouldn't be in a rush to bury him," she said. "Walks Many Miles is a survivor."

CHAPTER THIRTY

Outside Rudy Adeogo's home
Tacoma Park neighborhood of Washington, D.C.

Mary Margaret Delaney weaved through the reporters camped on the closed-off street outside Representative Rudy Adeogo's house. The D.C. Police Department had strung bright yellow *Do Not Cross* tape around the property's edge to keep the media from overflowing onto the front yard and peeking through windows.

Without breaking her stride, Delaney ducked under the tape and marched toward the front doorway where two police officers were stationed. One of them hurried down the porch's three concrete steps to intercept her as curious journalists watched.

"Ma'am, you need to move back to the other side of the tape right now!" the approaching officer warned.

"I'm not a reporter," Delaney replied.

"Ma'am, move behind the yellow tape or I'll arrest you for trespassing."

"Listen, I'm not some publicity seeker or a mental case. The congressman knows me and I need you to take him my card and show him the note that I've written on its back."

She jabbed her card toward him as if it were a knife. He read it, flipped it over, and examined the handwritten note. *I know the truth about George, your brother.*

"Just show it to him," Delaney said as she turned and walked back to the street to wait.

"Who are you?" a reporter asked when she joined the media throng.

Delaney ignored him and watched the officer return to the porch where he showed her card to his partner. That officer read it and then spoke into a two-way radio.

For several minutes nothing happened and Delaney thought her request would be ignored. She was about to cross under the tape barricade again when the house's front door opened and a man in a dark business suit wearing a flesh-colored earpiece came outside to examine her card. One of the officers raised his hand and pointed at Delaney. The man, who Delaney assumed was an FBI agent, stepped back into the house, taking her card with him.

Ten minutes passed and the reporters who'd been curious about Delaney returned to what they had been doing before she'd arrived. At that point, the FBI agent reappeared and said something to the D.C. policeman who had first intercepted Delaney. He strolled from the porch to the street where she was standing.

"Come with me," he said, lifting the tape barrier for her to slip underneath.

Suddenly, the reporters became interested again. Several took photos of her on their cell phones and sent them to their editors to find out if anyone recognized her. Within seconds word spread through the pack that Delaney was the Washington political consultant who had helped run defeated presidential candidate Timothy Coldridge's campaign. As she was climbing the front porch steps, one of them yelled: "Hey, Delaney, why are you here?"

She didn't respond and instead walked through the door into the house's large foyer, where three FBI agents were waiting for her.

"Does your note have anything to do with the abduction of Cassy Adeogo?" one asked.

"Heavens, no. This is a private matter between the congressman and me."

"What does your note mean: 'I know the truth about George, your brother'?"

"I said this was private, but if Representative Adeogo wishes to explain it, that's his prerogative. Now please show him my card because he will want to speak to me."

The agent studied her for a moment and then told her to wait in the entryway. Still holding her card, he climbed a carpeted staircase to the second floor.

It was obvious to Delaney as she glanced around the house that Representative Adeogo and his wife, Dheeh, had rented the place furnished. An English grandfather clock was tucked into one corner of the foyer but its pendulum was not moving and its hands were stopped at six o'clock. It either was broken or the Adeogos didn't enjoy listening to its loud ticking and hourly strikes. Delaney doubted the couple had chosen the foyer's artwork, which consisted of two framed prints that showed English foxhunters surrounded by their hounds.

No one spoke to her. After several minutes, the agent who'd taken her card upstairs returned and said, "The congressman will speak to you privately in his study. Follow me."

He turned to his right and slid open two wooden pocket doors. Adeogo's study was lined with floor-to-ceiling mahogany bookcases. The carpet was dark blue. There was a photograph of Dheeh and Cassy on his large executive desk, but otherwise the room was empty of any personal touches. Delaney sat down in a high-backed red leather chair and felt smug.

Adeogo did not utter a word when he entered his study. It wasn't until after he closed the pocket doors that he spoke, and when he did, his voice was quiet but filled with contempt.

"You dare to come here," he hissed, "to come into my home—to come into my house when my daughter is being held captive—to come into my house with my wife upstairs?"

His eyes were red, as if he had been crying, but they were filled with anger now, and she felt no pity for him.

"I have finally discovered your family secret," she replied triumphantly. "I know your brother's identity."

Adeogo's hands turned into fists, and for a moment it looked as if he might assault her, but he slowly opened his palms and walked to the front of his desk. Leaning against it, he crossed his arms as if he were a teacher facing an unruly student sitting before him.

"And what do you think you know?" he asked her.

"I have two legal documents. One is your younger brother, George Adeogo's birth certificate."

The congressman shrugged. "Anyone can get a copy of a birth certificate, and it's no secret that I had a younger brother."

"Which makes my second document even more valuable. It is a sealed juvenile court record that describes his arrest."

"If it is a sealed juvenile record, how did you acquire it?"

"That doesn't matter, and neither does the petty crime that your brother committed as a teenager. It is the conversation between your brother and the judge that's important."

Adeogo tried to appear nonchalant. "You're wasting my time," he said.

"According to the juvenile court transcript, your brother informed the judge that he no longer answered to his slave name— the name on his birth certificate: George Adeogo. He insisted the judge address him by his Muslim name—*Abdul Hafeez.*"

Despite his best efforts to conceal his emotions, Adeogo flinched. Delaney had learned the painful truth from his family's past. George Adeogo was Abdul Hafeez, the Al-Shabaab terrorist who had executed a Canadian NGO worker in Pakistan and later led the successful attack on the U.S. embassy in Mogadishu. His youngest brother was the much-hated terrorist who had chopped off the hands of an American diplomat before executing him and another State Department hostage while being filmed for an Internet video.

"You knew your brother was wanted by the U.S. government for acts of terrorism and murder, but you didn't lift a finger to help our country catch him. You knew he was the second-in-command of Al-Shabaab working directly for the Falcon."

"What do you want?" Adeogo asked in a quiet voice.

But Delaney wasn't finished gloating. "How do you think most Americans would react if they were told that the brother of a United States representative was a cold-blooded, radical Islamic murderer who'd pledged to destroy our nation? Would they trust you after you have been so deceptive? Or would voters want to impeach you and federal prosecutors charge you with criminally conspiring with an enemy of our country? What would happen if I walked outside right now and told the reporters watching your house that Abdul Hafeez was your brother?"

"Why have you come here to tell me this now?"

She rose triumphantly from her chair and walked toward him until they were so close that their faces were only inches apart. "You betrayed me during Coldridge's presidential campaign," she whispered. "You agreed to help us and then you betrayed us. You slept with me and then you humiliated me."

"Is this what your hatred is about? You're a scorned woman?"

Delaney tittered. "Scorned but not defeated."

"You will expose me," he said, "at the very same time my daughter is being held hostage by terrorists? You will throw even more pain into my life."

"Oh no, sharing your secret now would be too quick and not painful enough. With this information, I now own you. I have clients who will pay me large sums of money when I tell them that I have you dancing on my strings. You are going to be my personal stooge."

"And if I don't go along with your demands?"

"Do you really have a choice?" Delaney asked. "Because if you don't do what I say, I will tell the world about your brother and you will be ruined politically, possibly even arrested. You and your precious little wife will be despised regardless of where you go."

She reached out with her right hand and gently caressed his cheek with her open palm, turning what normally would be an act of affection into one of pure mockery.

"Poor little Rudy," she said. "What a naïve man to think you could come to Washington—into my house—and betray me."

CHAPTER THIRTY-ONE

George Washington University Hospital
Washington, D.C.

Major Brooke Grant saw the shadow moving on her left as she exited the Whitehurst Freeway toward Pennsylvania Avenue. It was almost dawn and she was on her way to visit her uncle Frank after an all-night session at the Reston command post. A loud thump caused her to brake her Jaguar XF. She'd smacked something. A cat? On earlier trips, she'd spotted strays ducking in and out of the bushes between the freeway and 26th Street N.W.

Flipping on the hazard lights, she stopped in the middle of the road to investigate. The frustrated commuter behind her immediately honked his horn as he became the first in a four-car backup. Brooke spotted the smashed animal on the pavement close to her front tire but it wasn't a cat. It was a squirrel and it was dead.

Brooke's eyes were puffy when she reached the hospital's ICU ward, where her aunt Geraldine had spent the night in a chair next to her husband's bed.

"What's wrong, honey?" Geraldine asked. "You've been crying."

"I hit a squirrel," Brooke replied.

Geraldine hugged her and whispered, "You know all this emotion isn't about some mangy old squirrel."

Her aunt was right. Brooke had fatally shot three men and killed another with a knife in Somalia. None of those deaths had caused her to tear up. But now she began to blubber.

"It's about your uncle, and Jennifer, and that other girl," Geraldine said.

"Someone else too," Brooke explained. "Walks Many Miles is missing in Kenya. A helicopter that he was riding in was shot down. I'm afraid, Auntie. I'm afraid about Uncle Frank and Jennifer and now he's missing too."

"Honey, you're human. But sweetie, being scared and worried is a complete waste of time and energy. Worry doesn't accomplish anything but rob today of its joy. You need to stay focused and keep doing what you're doing. You need to find Jennifer."

"How can you not be worried about Uncle Frank lying in bed in a coma?" Brooke asked, looking at her unresponsive uncle in his bed. "What if he doesn't wake up? What if he wakes up and his mind is gone or he can't walk or even talk?"

"Don't you even say those things! You got to think positive. Your Jennifer is going to be rescued and your uncle Frank is going to wake up and smile and be fine. And your Indian friend is going to show up in Africa. Now you tell me something. How is me sitting here worrying and crying about all this—how is that going to change the outcome? Do you think if I sit here blubbering about your uncle, it's going to help him wake sooner? Now praying, that will help. But all I can do is be grateful that your uncle didn't die on that highway and be grateful that when I opened my eyes this morning, he was still with me, and what happens tomorrow, well, that's between your uncle and the good Lord, but me crying isn't going to do any good."

"Auntie," Brooke said, "you're the strongest woman I know, but I'm not that strong and I don't have your faith. I'm angry at God. Angry that He's allowing this, that He's allowing bad people to hurt good people, people who I love."

"And what would you have God do? Send a lightning bolt to strike them dead?"

"Yes, that would be a great start. I wish He'd kill every last terrorist out there, beginning with the Falcon. I wish He'd wipe them off the face of the earth. We don't need them here."

Geraldine let out a sigh. "Your father and mother taught you better."

"And both of them were murdered by terrorists."

"Don't misunderstand me, child. There is evil in this world. That is what your parents and your uncle and you have dedicated your lives to fight against. But that evil isn't God's fault. He's not behind it."

"Auntie, I don't believe there is a devil who takes control of people's hearts and minds."

"It isn't the devil, Brooke, it's called free will. God gives you a choice because He knows true love can only happen when someone chooses to love someone else, and that includes us loving Him. If God sent down that lightning bolt, you wouldn't love Him because of who He is. You'd love Him because you were afraid of Him and that's not love, that's fear and intimidation. And if He saved your uncle's life, I would love Him because He did that. But that's like buying love. No, I have to love God unconditionally and be thankful for each day without putting conditions on that love. What happens happens and we should be grateful that God created us and gives us the time that we have with each other—whether tomorrow comes or it doesn't."

Brooke shook her head and said, "I'm not grateful. I'm angry."

"Well, you need to pull yourself together then," Geraldine replied. "You need to stop your boo-hooing and feeling sorry for yourself because that isn't going to help your uncle, Jennifer, or your fella."

Brooke stepped over to the bed and touched her uncle's hand. It felt cold. His face was still heavily bandaged, he was intubated, and there seemed to be more IV tubes in both of his arms than before. "I can sit here awhile, Auntie," she volunteered, "if you want to go home and rest or take a shower."

"Me? Now you know I'm not leaving your uncle's bed here. When he opens his eyes, he isn't going to care one hoot if I've had a shower and am rested."

"Can I bring you anything?"

"I could use my morning coffee. Black without anything."

"I remember," Brooke said. "I used to smell it first thing in the morning."

"Your mommy and daddy were never coffee drinkers. But me and that old man in the bed there, we drank gallons of it and sometimes on weekends, he'd add a bit of something-something to it."

"Your coffee?"

"A bit of Irish whiskey. Your uncle, he likes to be all gruff and stern, but he's got a playful side too. He just don't show it much, especially to you. He never did understand how to raise a girl."

"Gruff? You just gave me a lecture telling me to stop crying."

"Did I?" she said, smiling. "Well, I guess I was channeling him. Now you hurry downstairs. They have a Starbucks in the lobby there."

"I'll ask if they can add a shot of whiskey."

"Oh, you're being a little snip! And I'm glad. I like this Brooke better than the one who walked in here crying!"

The GWU hospital lobby was moon-shaped with a Starbucks to Brooke's right when she exited the elevators from the ICU. The coffee shop was at one end of a spacious seating area with chairs and tables. At the opposite end was a full-service cafeteria where hospital cooks were flipping pancakes and frying bacon. Brooke had just gotten into line at the Starbucks counter when Lieutenant Colonel Gabe DeMoss appeared.

"Good morning," he said cheerfully. "I was hoping I'd bump into you here."

"I'm just getting coffee to take upstairs to my aunt," Brooke explained.

"You should have more than coffee. This hospital has a really good breakfast selection. Come with me and I'll introduce you to a delicious egg sandwich that the short order cook makes. Besides, I'd like to speak to you privately."

Brooke stepped away from the Starbucks line and followed

DeMoss through the dining hall into the cafeteria where she chose a medley of mixed fruit in a plastic cup while he chatted with the short order cook working at a grease-covered grill.

"It would be more private if we ate in the outside courtyard," DeMoss said after they'd paid the cashier. "It's not that cold this morning but cold enough that we'll be the only ones sitting there."

A glass door led to a patio area. From their metal seats, she could see a steady stream of commuters emerging from the nearby Foggy Bottom Metro subway stop going to work.

"How's the sandwich?" she asked.

"Delicious. Usually, I'll have a bagel, but the ones they sell here are store bought. I spent time in Manhattan so I'm a bit of a bagel elitist."

Brooke was only half listening as she poked a plastic fork into a green melon cube. She was thinking about Jennifer and Walks Many Miles. Despite her aunt's lecture, she remained worried.

"Let's talk about your uncle and why he was a target," DeMoss said.

"He was shot because the Falcon has promised to murder everyone I love. He's out for revenge, and I've put everyone I care about in harm's way."

"It's not only you. I believe General Grant was shot because he was zeroing in on the identity of the mole who everyone is calling the Viper. Did your uncle tell you anything in private about the mole when you had lunch with him after the president was attacked at the National Cathedral?"

"You mean after you finished telling us during your briefing that Fawzia Samatar had gotten a text while hiding in the closet?"

"Yes, a text sent to her on a burner phone by someone at the funeral." DeMoss flashed a smile and added, "Ironic, right? A burner phone used to text a message to a woman who commits self-immolation."

Brooke didn't find that funny. Ignoring his comment, she said, "You told us the burner phone had been bought by President

Allworth's reelection campaign and had been used by someone who probably worked inside the White House."

"That's right. Did your uncle mention a specific name—someone inside the White House who he suspected of being the Viper?"

"No. No names."

"He didn't tell you who he thought might have used that phone to send that text?"

"Wouldn't he have told you if he knew a name?" she asked in a puzzled voice.

"Yes, probably, but I got the feeling that morning that he was holding something back from me. I believe he had a specific name, but he didn't tell it to me before he got shot."

"He? How do you know the Viper isn't a woman?"

"You're right. It could be a woman."

"I wish my uncle had told me a name. If I knew who the Viper was, he or she would be dead right now. That traitor is responsible for Jennifer and Cassy being abducted and the murders of those poor girls at school and Jennifer's nanny, who happened to be a very good friend of mine. I'll have no trouble pulling the trigger."

"Are you any closer to finding Jennifer and Representative Adeogo's daughter?" DeMoss asked in a concerned voice. "The NSC is receiving daily reports, but if someone in the White House is under suspicion, those reports might be heavily edited."

"I'm not aware of anyone holding back information from the White House or NSC."

"Well, there hasn't been much in the reports that I'm being shown."

"That's because no one has much to report. Most of the tips that we have gotten about the girls have been dead ends."

"Helpful citizens and crackpots," he said, taking another bite of his egg sandwich. Brooke had eaten only about a third of her fruit cup. She hadn't had much of an appetite since Jennifer's abduction. She pushed it aside.

"We received a lot of tips yesterday after Representative Adeogo made his emotional appeal on national television," she said. "But none of them has led anywhere."

"I assumed that press conference was scripted by Wyatt Parker. It was a page right out of the FBI's hostage negotiator's handbook."

"Parker doesn't think outside the box and neither do the agents working for him."

"You probably don't move up the FBI chain of command by taking risks," DeMoss said. "You sound disappointed in him."

"Frustrated would be a better description. There are two different teams reporting to Parker. One is focused exclusively on finding Jennifer and Cassy. That's almost exclusively FBI agents. The other is hunting for the Viper and is a collaborative effort with the CIA and Homeland Security. Neither are being aggressive enough for me."

"And you're being briefed by both teams?"

"I'm working side-by-side with Parker and see everything that he sees, but my main focus is finding the girls."

"And you disapprove of what Parker is doing?"

"I don't think Parker feels the same urgency I do."

"Any chance he's hiding information from you?"

"No, why would he? I attend all of the Viper briefings and read all of the incoming intel. He'd better not be keeping information from me."

"How about from the White House and NSC?"

"You already asked me if Parker is censoring his reports to the White House. I don't know of any decision to keep information from the White House and NSC and don't know why he would."

"Good," DeMoss said, adding, "the latest material I received from Parker was about the SAD team being shot down in Kenya."

"Then you're current. Parker's team is trying to determine if it was a fluke that terrorists happened to be in the area when the SAD team flew over them or if the team's helicopter was specifically targeted because the Viper knew about the mission and sent word to the Falcon." Brooke hesitated to think for a moment and then asked, "Did the reports that Parker sent to the White House and NSC contain detailed information about the SAD team?"

"I don't recall how detailed those reports were. I do remember that your friend Walks Many Miles was one of the SAD team members who was listed as being part of that mission. I'm certain you are worried about him. Your uncle told me Miles quit the Marines so he could date you."

Brooke was surprised. Her uncle was not a gossip. "I didn't realize my uncle discussed personal matters about me with you."

DeMoss grinned like a schoolboy. "Having a Marine quit the Corps—that's quite a compliment."

She averted her eyes. She didn't feel comfortable speaking to him about her personal relationships. Moments of stress and tragedy often made casual acquaintances feel a familiarity with each other forged by empathy, which she understood. But she didn't know much about DeMoss's personal life and only a few details about his military career. She knew DeMoss had been decorated in Iraq and had been taken prisoner by the Taliban later in Afghanistan. She knew he was considered a promising up-and-comer, hence his appointment to the NSC. But he was a lieutenant colonel and she was a major, so there had been no personal familiarization between them.

"I have some information that Special Agent Parker might not have shared with you, assuming he knows it," DeMoss said. "Al-Shabaab has contacted the State Department. They're demanding one million dollars for the return of each body that was recovered from the SAD helicopter crash. If either the government or the men's families refuse to pay, they will desecrate the corpses and post videos of them on the Internet."

"And these animals claim to be pious Muslims," she said bitterly.

"If I remember correctly, during the Somalia embassy crisis you referred to one of them as a flea feeding on a camel turd." He chuckled.

"How'd you hear that?"

"You were wearing a microphone that was connected with Langley, the Pentagon, and White House at the time, remember? When we heard about that description at the NSC, it made the rounds."

"I didn't realize the NSC knew about that conversation."

"You'd be surprised at what we have at our fingertips. There's not much we can't access."

"I'm afraid my comment wasn't very diplomatic. I tend to be blunt when I am angry."

"I thought it was spot on." He grinned but quickly turned serious. "In addition to Miles, the other missing SAD team member has been identified as Jason Angel, who was known by his buddies as Ironman. He apparently was thrown from the helicopter when it was struck by an RPG."

"How do you know that?"

"Al-Shabaab posted a photo of his body less than an hour ago and the CIA identified him in an intel bulletin sent to the White House. It came from Director Grainger personally so Parker and his teams might not have gotten word yet."

"That troubles me."

"Angel's death?"

"Yes, but also that Grainger bypassed us. How many other reports are being circulated without us knowing? No wonder the Viper can learn what we're doing. We need to compartmentalize information and keep tighter controls on what is being shared."

"You're right," he said. "I'll mention that to my superiors." DeMoss took a last bite of his egg sandwich, and when he finished chewing, he said, "Did you know all of the SAD team members on that crashed helicopter had nicknames, such as Ironman?"

"Everyone uses nicknames because they don't want terrorists to know anything about their personal lives and families back home if they overhear them talking," Brooke said.

"Do you know Miles's nickname?" he asked her.

"Yeah, he mentioned it to me and it wasn't overly creative. His buddies called him 'The Chief.'"

DeMoss nodded. "When I was in Iraq, I was called Banjo."

"Because you play the banjo, I assume."

"No, I don't play any musical instruments. It's because of the movie *Deliverance*."

"I've never seen it."

"There's a scene in the movie called 'Dueling Banjos,' where an inbred kid from the backwoods and a city slicker with a guitar go head-to-head. I'm from West Virginia so I got tagged Banjo. What was your nickname in Somalia?"

"I wasn't part of the guys—the Marine embassy guards there—I was a liaison officer. If I had a nickname, they didn't share it with me." Actually, Miles had later told Brooke that the Marine guards in Somalia had nicknamed her "Legs," but none of them had dared use that sexist term around her, even though they meant it as a compliment. She didn't see any need to share that information with DeMoss.

"I believe," he said, "there are two possibilities of what happened to Miles. He either got blown out of the aircraft like Ironman, and his body has not been found and may never be. Or, he somehow survived and has managed to evade capture."

"If he'd been captured," Brooke said, "Al-Shabaab would have posted video of him."

"Exactly, the problem is that our people can't send in a rescue team because we don't know where Miles is or even if he survived. And it's not safe to send another helicopter into hostile territory to search for him. If Miles did survive that crash and is still alive, he's completely on his own."

CHAPTER THIRTY-TWO

Near the border city of El Wak
Northeastern Kenya desert

Walks Many Miles followed the tire tracks leading away from the helicopter crash toward the Isiolo Mandera highway, the main route that snaked up Kenya's northeastern border into Ethiopia and Somalia. Without those tracks directing him, he might have spent days wandering in the sameness of the African terrain. About a thousand yards from the crash, the tracks vanished on a patch of wind-swept landscape that had turned raw and hard.

After walking for an hour, Miles looked for a shady spot to escape the blistering afternoon sun. There were fewer *Acacia karroo* bushes here, but he spotted a lone tree stubbornly growing from a crack in the dried earth. The Kenyans called it a "toothbrush tree," so named because natives used its twigs to brush teeth and gums. Its bark suppressed bacteria growth and plaque. It was an oddly shaped evergreen, resembling a bush more than a tree, with its branches hovering close to the ground as if the sun had beaten them down. The Al-Shabaab fighters would be returning soon to retrieve the sentry whom they'd left behind. Discovering him dead would lead to both outrage and a manhunt. The tree would provide Miles with much needed shade and a hiding spot.

Miles noticed a baseball bat–sized branch that had broken from the tree and was lying on the ground. He swung it against the toothbrush tree and then swept it under its branches. A half dozen scorpions scampered into the sunlight. The venom in most scorpions was not powerful enough to kill a man, but these were death-stalker scorpions, commonly found in Ethiopia and Somalia, and their stings could be fatal to the elderly or small children. If bitten, Miles would survive, but he would be in incapacitating pain for several days—something he couldn't afford.

After again sweeping the branch under the lowest limbs to scatter insects, he crawled under the foliage. His cracked ribs were even more painful as he lay on his back. He put a pinch of the khat between his teeth.

Being raised on the Crow reservation, southeast of Billings, Montana, and northwest of Sheridan, Wyoming, Miles had often purified himself by spending time in a sweat lodge. In comparison, the desert heat that he was now feeling seemed mild. He felt sleepy and the khat made him relax. His mind wandered and he found himself thinking of his grandfather. The old man had been a powerful force in Miles's life. In the 1960s, his grandfather had been an activist in the emerging American Indian Movement and had occupied Alcatraz Island with other native people. By age forty, he'd become the subject of a rather thick FBI file. But now at age seventy-two, he was a respected professor at Big Horn College, where he taught tribal history.

Miles idolized his grandfather and had wondered how such a powerful figure had fathered an abusive, alcoholic son who had cared only about himself and had never wanted a son of his own. Cirrhosis of the liver had killed Miles's father. Alcohol, introduced by the white man, had killed more Crow than bullets, his grandfather had told him. Neither Miles nor his grandfather had wept at the funeral.

From his grandfather Miles had learned how to mask his emotions. His grandfather was well liked by whites off the reservation and at educational conferences. But Miles knew his grandfather privately felt only contempt for whites. Associating with them was a necessary evil. His grandfather's mantra, which he often told Miles,

came from a quote attributed to Plenty Coups, the last of the great
Crow chiefs. "With what the white man knows, he can oppress us.
If we learn what he knows, then he can never oppress us again."

His grandfather had wanted Miles to do well in school. But he'd
never been a good student. Books had not interested him. He had
little interest in reading about what others had done or seen. He
wanted to learn and see for himself.

The khat reminded him of another important moment in his
childhood. Many of his peers had abandoned the old ways, but
Miles's grandfather had insisted that his grandson abide by the
traditions that made him a Crow. At puberty, Miles had been
driven by his grandfather past the site of the Battle of the Little Big
Horn where Lakota, Cheyenne, and Arapaho had defeated General
George Armstrong Custer. They had stopped in the mouth of a
canyon at the base of the mountains. Despite his tender age, Miles
had been left alone for four days. Among the meager supplies that
his grandfather had given him was peyote to help him have a dream
during which he would come to understand his purpose in life.
The first night, Miles had chewed it and fallen asleep without any
effect. By the third night, he'd decided that he was immune to the
hallucinogen and that talk of visions and visits by spirits was nothing but tribal folklore. But on the last night, Miles had fallen into
a trance, no doubt helped by his hungry belly and exhaustion, and
during a dream a talking coyote had visited him. When his grandfather had come to fetch him, Miles had told the old man about
the coyote, and that had pleased his grandfather because among
the Crow, it was Old Man Coyote who had created the earth, the
first man, and the first woman. A visit from the coyote was a good
omen. But Miles had not told his grandfather, nor anyone else,
what the coyote had told him about his future. After his vision
quest experience, Miles stopped using his white name—Jonathan
Walks Many Miles—and insisted on being called only by his native
surname.

As he drifted off to sleep under the toothbrush tree's branches in the African heat, Miles found himself feeling strangely optimistic. He was alone and being hunted by terrorists in the African desert. He was a man on foot. What better name to have than Walks Many Miles?

Miles had been asleep about two hours when he was awakened by the sounds of gunfire. Peeking from under the branches, he saw the same three pickup trucks that he'd observed earlier at the helicopter crash site. It was the Al-Shabaab terrorists about five hundred yards away from his hiding spot under the tree. He guessed the gunmen had returned to the crash site, discovered their dead comrade, and now were searching the area for him. Instead of finding Miles, they had come upon an old man tending a herd of goats. As Miles watched, one of the terrorists drew a pistol and struck the man across his face. The blow knocked him to the ground, but he pushed himself up onto his knees and then stood. The gunman struck him again, causing the man to again hit the desert, and this time when he tried to stand, another gunman kicked him several times until he stopped moving. Apparently satisfied, one of the gunmen fired his pistol, killing a nearby goat before the gang boarded their trucks and continued their search.

Miles watched the man slowly rise to his knees and then fall back against the hardscape. Several moments later, he rose again and this time, he managed to stand. Holding his side, the man inspected the dead goat while the other animals in the herd milled around, oblivious. The man tried to lift the carcass but couldn't hoist it to his shoulders. When he tried again, he stumbled back and again collapsed. It took him longer to stand and when he did, he began dragging the goat by its legs, but after traveling less than fifty yards, he fell.

Miles watched for several moments as the animals walked around the fallen herder. All of Miles's instincts told him to ignore what he was seeing and to slip away. He had enough problems of his own. But there was something about the man's determination and unwillingness to leave the dead goat behind that he admired. Although the fallen man was a stranger, Miles felt obligated to help. He crept from under the branches of the toothbrush tree and approached the herder cautiously while cradling the AK-47 in his arms.

The goats cleared a path when he reached the fallen man. The herder appeared to be as old as Miles's grandfather, but Miles knew that African nomads often seemed much older than they were due to their harsh living conditions. He was bony and had weathered, leather-like skin. His lips and cheeks were puffy from being pistol-whipped, and he seemed defeated, but there was no fear in his eyes.

"*No gattee hindeemin,*" the herder said.

"Do you speak English?" Miles replied.

"*No gattee hindeemin,*" he repeated.

Miles offered him a drink from his canteen, which the man gulped down. The herder touched his rib cage where he'd been kicked and moaned. Miles assumed the beating had cracked the old man's ribs, but it didn't appear he had suffered a punctured lung or other internal damage.

"Phone?" Miles said. He raised his hand to his right ear as if he was talking on a cell phone.

"*No gattee hindeemin,*" the herder repeated.

Miles shook his head and again said "Phone," only this time louder, as if that would help the man understand. It didn't.

"Can you stand? Walk?" Miles asked. He moved two fingers on his right hand to imitate legs moving.

The herder reached up to grasp Miles's shoulder. With Miles's help, he stood and pointed his hand to the north.

The herder was still holding onto Miles as a crutch, but when Miles began walking, the old man stopped and began jabbing a finger at the dead goat.

"You got to be kidding me," Miles responded. He shook his head, indicating no.

The old man released his grip on Miles shoulder. He was not going to leave the dead goat behind.

"I should've stayed under that tree," Miles complained.

"*No gattee hindeemin*," the herder said.

"Yeah, I heard you the first time. *No gattee hindeemin*," Miles repeated. "Whatever the hell that means."

Shaking his head in disgust, Miles said, "I can't believe I'm doing this." Bending down, he grabbed the goat's front and back legs and lifted the dead animal onto his shoulders. The old man steadied himself by taking hold of Miles's upper arm.

"I'm not carrying this goat far," Miles declared, as he and the old man began walking. The other goats fell into step behind them. If the terrorists returned, Miles was sure that both of them would be killed. As they marched, Miles quietly rebuked himself. It would have been smarter for him to have remained under the tree until nightfall. He should not have shown his face to a stranger. And he should not be carrying a forty-pound dead goat across the African desert with a crippled old man clinging to him, especially since both of them had cracked ribs.

But he also knew that he had no choice.

More than twenty years earlier, a coyote had spoken to him in his peyote-induced vision. In his dream, Miles had been wandering in a strange land far from the reservation, lost, hungry, thirsty, and alone. The ground had been burning his naked feet and the sun had scorched his skin. The coyote had told him that he would encounter a stranger. Miles felt a sense of déjà vu. Either that, or it was the khat.

PART FOUR

PERSEVERANCE

No one saves us but ourselves. No one can and no
one may. We ourselves must walk the path.

—Buddha

CHAPTER THIRTY-THREE

Studio A
Capitol Visitor Center
Washington, D.C.

P olitical correctness and overregulation are keeping the FBI and U.S. law enforcement agencies from identifying Islamic extremists living in the United States," Representative Thomas Stanton announced. "Our own government is handcuffing our efforts and putting us in danger."

Reporters crammed into the congressional studio were eager to begin asking questions, but Stanton was just getting started.

"We all know what happened in Paris years ago when the government there allowed radical Imams to spew their hatred of democracy in more than three dozen mosques in the City of Light. France allowed jihadists to recruit converts on French soil and the result was bloodshed and mayhem. As chairman of the House Permanent Select Committee on Intelligence, I have decided to hold investigative hearings to determine if the FBI should be given authority to infiltrate mosques that are known breeding grounds for radical Islamic terrorists. We need to know if our nation's efforts to identify radical Imams, who spew their anti-U.S. rhetoric and encourage their devotees to take up arms against us here on our own soil, are being undermined."

With a concerned look on his face, Stanton peered directly into the camera and continued. "I am speaking about radicals such as Mohammad Al-Kader, an Afghanistan-born Imam who was expelled from a Minneapolis mosque by his fellow Imams after they learned he was raising funds for an international charity believed to be a front for Al-Qaeda. Al-Kader was a known associate of Osama bin Laden, and his teachings show that he is a strong proponent of Sharia law, which is undemocratic in its nature and much more than that in its practice. The couple who died while attempting to assassinate President Allworth at the National Cathedral followed Al-Kader to the Washington, D.C., area. They believed in Sharia law and his radical interpretation of it. They are dead, yet he continues to spout rhetoric that is clearly anti-American and anti-democratic in a Washington suburban mosque.

"I intend to subpoena Al-Kader, who is a U.S. citizen, to testify before my committee. I intend to question him about his anti-American teachings. My committee's hearings also will investigate if Islamic radicals have successfully infiltrated the ranks of our federal government. Are these extremists lying in wait as sleeper agents ready to unleash an attack if summoned? The recent attempt on the president's life at the National Cathedral here in Washington, D.C., by Cumar Samatar, who worked for the CIA as an interpreter, should be a wake-up call. We cannot let our timidity and political correctness prevent us from identifying and tracking down radicals who have embedded themselves in our communities and possibly inside our own government."

Omar Nader watched Stanton's Capitol Hill news conference from the plush Washington offices of the Organization of Islamic Nations on K Street and immediately began telephoning Congressional leaders who were obligated to the OIN, largely because of its generous campaign contributions. Within two hours, four House members appeared at a hastily arranged press conference in Studio A to denounce Stanton and his call for committee oversight hearings.

"The Chairman's insinuation that Muslims employed by the federal government are sleeper agents is outrageous!" the first congressman exclaimed. "The Chairman's *Islamophobic* words are the same old hate speech in a new wrapper. Has the Chairman forgotten our nation's shameful past? Does he not recall the fearmongering of McCarthyism? This time the target is Muslims rather than innocent citizens who were smeared as Communists. This time the target is Muslims rather than innocent Japanese who were unfairly interned during World War Two. It is during times of alarm when our core values matter most and we should not abandon them because of fearmongering and hate speech."

The next House member to face reporters was equally peeved. "In the years since the terrorist attacks of 2001, hate crimes against American Muslims have mushroomed. American Muslims get the kind of treatment once reserved for blacks and Jews, both dehumanized groups that were the victims of racial and ethnic prejudice and violence. I am deeply saddened that a respected and high-ranking member of the House of Representatives would stoop to such a low level. Chairman Stanton has embarrassed all of us by calling for these hearings."

Next up to the microphone was a congresswoman. "Representative Stanton has portrayed Arabs and Muslims as villains and enemies when, in fact, theologically Islam is no more violent or less violent than Christianity or any other monotheistic religion. There certainly is no need for these anti-Muslim hearings and Chairman Stanton owes the Muslim community a public apology."

It was the final speaker who lobbed the biggest bomb. "Today, we are calling for Representative Stanton to not only rescind his call for these unnecessary and mean-spirited hearings, we are demanding—not asking, but demanding—that he relinquish the chairmanship of the House Permanent Select Committee on Intelligence. His call for anti-Muslim hearings shows that he is no longer fit to serve as chairman of a congressional committee. If Chairman Stanton does not step down voluntarily, we will certainly be working to accomplish his removal."

As soon as the four House members were done on Capitol Hill,

Omar Nader held a separate news conference across town in the lobby of the OIN headquarters. "Chairman Thomas Stanton's words and actions leave the OIN no choice but to put his name to our list of American Islamophobic Individuals," Nader declared in a sober voice. "We join in the call for his resignation as chairman of the Intelligence Committee."

A Harvard University–trained Muslim lawyer employed by an OIN-funded, Washington-based think tank joined Nader at the podium of his news conference.

"In 2010," the attorney said, "we saw an example of toxic hate against American Muslims when plans were announced for an Islamic cultural center in lower Manhattan. Opponents wanted to stop the expansion of Islamic places of worship in a nation that was created by Pilgrims seeking religious freedom. Now, Chairman Stanton is trying to invade our mosques and is smearing the reputations of American Muslims who are employed by our government. This is scurrilous conduct. Let me ask you a simple question. If Stanton is successful in sending federal agents into our houses of worship to monitor what Imams teach, what religion will be next? Methodist? Baptist? Catholic? What other Constitutional rights will fall after religious freedom is no longer tolerated?"

Omar Nader was pleased after his press conference ended. He had moved quickly to challenge Stanton's call for hearings. But Nader knew this was only the first round, and he suspected Stanton's efforts would be embraced by a substantial number of Americans who were afraid of homegrown terrorism. From OIN poll data, Nader knew there was a looming fear and mistrust of Muslims simmering just under the surface. To counter it, he would need to change public opinion. He would need to reassure the public that they had nothing to fear but fear itself. Omar Nader prided himself on thinking big, and his first thought was about White House Chief of Staff Mallory Harper and President Sally Allworth. Getting the president to condemn Stanton's call for congressional hearings would be a major coup, and Nader felt optimistic about his chances. His last White House meeting with the president had gone well.

In addition to using influential thought-leaders to attack Stanton, Nader would launch a public campaign to win the hearts and minds of the public by putting the OIN's vast wealth to work. He began jotting down ideas: a national conference to promote religious tolerance, a public service announcement campaign about diversity, prizes for high school essays about religious freedom, seminars on college campuses about prejudice.

While Nader was considering his next step, his private cell phone rang, and he knew from the caller ID that it was Mary Margaret Delaney.

"I hope you have good news to share," he said when he answered her call.

"Thanks to you," she replied, "I now own Rudy Adeogo."

"Then congratulations are in order."

"I confronted him yesterday at his home. He's my puppet now, and Chairman Stanton's call for investigative hearings is a perfect opportunity for you to begin putting Adeogo to use."

Nader snickered. "You're correct. Having the only Muslim member of Congress condemning Chairman Stanton's actions will help us."

"Aren't you forgetting something?" Delaney asked.

"Ah yes, a contract for your services. I believe we agreed on six figures."

"Considering the importance now of having Adeogo attack Chairman Stanton's actions, I think we need to increase your initial offer."

"With as much pleasure as you will take in controlling Adeogo, you should be doing this without charge," Nader replied. "Are you now trying to take advantage of me?"

"It's not personal, remember. Isn't that what you told me in Minneapolis when I complained about the OIN arranging donations for both presidential candidates in the last election? You were just hedging your bets. Now the tables are turned. I have a commodity and Stanton's actions have made that commodity worth more."

"I will speak to my superiors, but be careful, Ms. Delaney. Do not push too hard or you may not like the response."

It was eleven p.m. when Nader was finally ready to leave his OIN office, and as he was reaching for his overcoat and about to switch off the lights, he noticed Al Arabic correspondent Ebio Kattan appear on one of a dozen television monitors near his desk that he never switched off.

"We've just been told," Kattan announced, "that U.S. Representative Rudy Adeogo will be making a public statement outside his Washington, D.C., home any moment now."

All of the other major television networks began showing the same scene: reporters gathered behind the yellow tape outside the congressman's Tacoma Park house waiting for him to appear. Within seconds, Representative Adeogo and Dheeh emerged and walked from the doorway across the front yard to where the media were corralled.

Under the glare of television lights, Adeogo said, "Dheeh and I want to thank all of you who are praying for the safe release of our daughter, Cassy, and also for Jennifer Conner. Once again, we appeal to those holding these innocent schoolgirls—in the name of Allah, the giver of all mercy—please release them unharmed."

Visibly nervous, he hesitated, glanced sideways at Dheeh who was standing beside him tightly holding his hand, and then continued. "Many Muslim families have found themselves divided by disagreements about our beloved religion and how best each of us can serve Allah. For American Muslims, this is much like your Civil War when Northern and Southern families found themselves with sons fighting on separate sides. It is heart wrenching. This unfortunate division has occurred within my own extended family. I have always strived to keep my parents and siblings out of the news.

Seeking public service is my choice, and I respected their rights to privacy. I did not wish to drag them into a national spotlight."

His voice began to quiver. "However, I can no longer protect them from scrutiny. I have, or had, a younger brother named George Adeogo. He is deceased. Some of you have written that he died as a teenager in an automobile accident. I must now correct these erroneous reports."

Glancing down at his feet for a moment, as if he were ashamed, Adeogo said, "My brother George Adeogo was deeply troubled as a teenager. Like many Somali American teenagers who feel lost, he joined a street gang in Minneapolis. My parents took him to our mosque and asked the religious leaders there to counsel him, which they did. My brother underwent a transformation. He went from being a street tough to becoming a deeply religious young man."

Adeogo raised his eyes so that he now was looking directly into the cameras broadcasting his image. "Sadly, through the Internet, my brother became enthralled with jihad, especially after he saw fighters in Iraq battling U.S. soldiers. My brother George became radicalized and, against our family's wishes and my counseling and instruction, he decided to travel secretly to Somalia to participate in the fighting there. This was a tremendous embarrassment to my parents, my siblings, and especially to me. For this reason, the story that George Adeogo had died in an auto accident became my family's way to conceal the shame that all of us felt because of my brother's misguided actions. I cannot and will not blame my parents and siblings for wanting to hide George's radicalization. By remaining silent and not correcting the record, I also endorsed this fabrication."

Adeogo's eyes suddenly filled with tears. "The truth always surfaces, and today, the truth about my brother needs to be exposed and explained to the American people. My brother George Adeogo changed his name when he was a teenager. He began calling himself Abdul Hafeez."

As Adeogo watched, stunned looks appeared on the faces of the reporters witnessing his impromptu news conference.

"Yes, I am speaking about the same Abdul Hafeez who led an attack on the U.S. embassy in Mogadishu and who murdered two U.S. diplomats there," he continued in an apologetic voice. "George Adeogo was my youngest brother. I remember him as a sweet and impressionable young boy. When he became Abdul Hafeez, he stopped being my brother. He became a murderer who fell victim to corrupt teachings. On behalf of my family and myself, I want to apologize to the American public for his actions and the suffering that he caused. I ask for your understanding and forgiveness. While I cannot change the past, Dheeh and I are also victims of the horror that he encouraged. Our daughter was targeted and abducted, we believe, because Al-Shabaab wants to punish us for distancing ourselves from Abdul Hafeez. Please continue to pray for me, my family, and our daughter, and please forgive us for the terrible wrongs that he committed."

Reporters shouted questions, but Adeogo and Dheeh quietly returned to the safety of their house.

"This is absolutely stunning news," Ebio Kattan proclaimed, when she reappeared on the television screen. "The only Muslim elected to the U.S. Congress has just revealed his youngest brother was one of the most hated men in America—Abdul Hafeez, a high-ranking member of Al-Shabaab who declared war against his own country. So who was Abdul Hafeez?"

In a somber voice, Kattan warned viewers that Al Arabic was about to broadcast video that was so disturbing it was not suitable for children. "I will wait fifteen seconds before continuing if you wish to remove them from the room." The image of Kattan seated behind a news anchor desk without uttering a word added even more drama to the broadcast. When the fifteen seconds elapsed, she announced, "The figure you are about to see was identified as Abdul Hafeez by U.S. intelligence officials based on voice recordings."

Video of a masked man dressed in black filled the screen. He was clutching a long knife while standing over an American diplomat who was being pinned to the floor by two other masked jihadists. The hostage's outstretched hands had been forced onto a cement block before him. As Hafeez brought down the knife, the network used pixels to hide the amputation of the man's hands but did not mute his screams.

When the camera returned to Kattan, she was holding an eight-by-ten-inch photograph of Hafeez with his arm around the shoulder of his older brother, Rudy, which had been taken when they were youngsters.

"Representative Adeogo's office has released a family photograph that shows Rudy Adeogo and his younger brother George—who the congressman has just acknowledged was Abdul Hafeez. This photo was taken several years before Hafeez traveled to Somalia and before Rudy Adeogo was elected last year to the U.S. Congress. It shows both men as young, carefree boys. The brothers severed all contact after Hafeez joined Al-Shabaab."

Inside his OIN office, Omar Nader muted the television and hurriedly dialed Mary Margaret Delaney's cell phone.

"Do you call this controlling Rudy Adeogo?" Nader demanded, barely able to control his anger. "He has told everyone about his brother! Now Americans will think that every Muslim has someone in their family who is a terrorist."

"How was I supposed to know he'd go on national television and confess?"

"You should've known! You pushed him too hard. You went to his house rather than talking to him discreetly. Reporters saw you at his house, didn't they?" Nader snapped. "Now those same reporters are going to be suspicious of why he made his announcement. Some of them will remember your visit. They may see a link, a connection. I told you the OIN cannot be tied to any of this." There was genuine fear in Nader's voice. "It would ruin me and the OIN if the word leaked out that we gave you documents so you could blackmail Adeogo. You have put the OIN and me personally in grave danger."

"Calm down," Delaney replied. "Adeogo doesn't know how I got his brother's records."

"How do you know that Adeogo will not make another public statement? How do you know that he will not tell the world that you tried to blackmail him?"

"You're overreacting. He's not going to say anything and as long as you and I keep our mouths shut, no one will trace this information back to the OIN and your sources."

"You can't guarantee this, given that he's just told everyone about his brother. I cannot have your actions traced back to the OIN."

Neither of them spoke for a moment, and then Delaney said, "Listen, I did what you asked me to do, which means that the OIN still owes me a retainer fee. You understand that, don't you?"

Nader couldn't believe her gall. He felt as if he were about to explode. But he calmed himself and hid his outrage when he replied. "Yes, I understand."

When he ended the call, Nader felt physically ill. Circumstances had shifted under his feet. He'd provided the damning information about Adeogo's family to Delaney thinking that together they could manipulate the congressman. But Rudy Adeogo had outed himself and now, with Chairman Stanton raising questions about the loyalty of Muslim Americans, Adeogo's confession would only feed mass Islamophobia. Nader had miscalculated. He'd made a major blunder.

His private cell phone rang and when he saw on the caller ID that it was coming from Saudi Arabia, his hand began to tremble. He answered it.

"Yes," Nader said obediently into the phone receiver. He listened without comment and when the caller finished speaking, Nader said softly, "I agree that she is a problem. I will handle her."

CHAPTER THIRTY-FOUR

Mountaintop, Virginia
Allegheny Mountains

Aludra needed to act quickly. Akbar was pumping gas and had sent her alone into a general store, the only grocery in this tiny crossroads town.

The store itself was more than a hundred years old and still displayed its groceries, dry goods, and hunting and fishing supplies much as they'd always been shown. It was not the store's supplies or the plaques on the walls warning customers to "Be nice or leave!" or "Our Credit Manager is Helen Waite. Want Credit? Go to Helen Waite" that interested Aludra. Near a public restroom at the rear of the building was a pay phone.

Aludra had memorized a hotline tip number the night before when it had been shown at the bottom of the screen during a newscast about the abduction of Jennifer Conner and Cassy Adeogo. That number had appeared under a mug shot of Akbar which U.S. officials had taken when he'd been a prisoner at Gitmo. Thankfully, they had not shown her photograph—assuming they had one of her in their records. There was a $500,000 reward for any information that helped lead to his capture.

Before today, Akbar had always insisted that Aludra stay behind with their two hostages at the cabin in southwestern Virginia near the state line whenever they needed supplies. But because of last night's broadcast, he had become wary of being seen in public.

He'd remained outside the store at the gas pump wearing large sun-glasses, a baseball cap, and hooded sweatshirt.

Akbar had permitted her to dress in western clothes without wearing a hijab. She was supposed to blend in, like any other trav-eler who'd stopped to buy locally raised buffalo meat or ask about the area's colorful history. It had once been home to Cherokee Indi-ans who used red clay from nearby rivers to make pottery and also donned it as war paint.

Aludra, a short and pudgy woman with dramatic dark eyes, a strong chin, and beautiful caramel colored skin, hurried to the pay phone near the store's restroom but realized when she lifted its receiver that she needed to deposit a coin in order to make a call, even though it was an 800 number. She didn't have change, so she returned to the cashier near the front door.

"I'd like change for a phone call," she explained, handing the clerk a crumpled dollar bill that she had kept hidden from Akbar.

"We're probably the only folks around who still have a pay phone," the older woman replied, taking her money. "Everyone has cell phones now. Even my grandkids, and they're not even ten years old yet. But it's hard sometimes to get signals here in the moun-tains, so people come in to use our landline."

Aludra glanced through the store's front windows outside where she could see Akbar still standing at the gas pump. She needed to hurry. The clerk followed her eyes outside.

"Your husband waiting, dear?" she asked.

"Yes."

"You should tell him to come inside and look around. We got lots of man things in here, like bait and lures, and stuff you don't see in most stores anymore, like a pickle barrel."

"A what?"

"A barrel full of pickles and you pick out whichever pickles you want to pick? Try saying that seven times." She chuckled. "Does he hunt or fish at all?"

Aludra scooped up the change. "After I make my call, I will tell him about the pickles."

She walked to the phone and dialed the hotline number. The person who answered was skeptical when Aludra first asked to speak to Major Brooke Grant whom she'd seen being interviewed on television. Only after Aludra had correctly described what Jennifer Conner had been wearing when she'd been abducted did he agree to immediately connect her to Brooke.

Even so, it took several moments for Brooke to come on the line, ratcheting up Aludra's stress. She couldn't risk having Akbar come inside the store looking for her. If he saw her using the phone, he would know she was betraying him and kill her and the chatty clerk. He had a pistol under his sweatshirt and an assault rifle under a blanket in the backseat of the car.

"Is this Aludra Aba-Jihaad?" Brooke asked the moment she came on the line.

Aludra knew the FBI had identified her, but hearing her name was unsettling. "That is not my last name, but I am Aludra. I did not take Akbar's name when I was forced to marry him."

"Where are Jennifer and Cassy?"

"In the basement of a cabin."

"What cabin?"

"It's named Perfect Hideaway. Look on the Internet. VRBO. Mountaintop, Virginia. Only Akbar and I are there with them. But you must come now. Tomorrow will be too late."

"Why? Is Akbar going to kill them?" Brooke asked, in an alarmed voice.

"No. He beats them. But yes."

"I'm confused. Yes, he's going to kill them?"

"No, rape them. He can't behead them until he gets an order."

"Rape? They're children!" Brooke exclaimed. "Who's giving him orders?"

"A man in Washington. I have to go. I can't talk now. He will kill me if he catches me."

"Wait, why are you helping us?"

"I want out. I want to be rid of him. An American prison is better than being his wife. He is an animal who rapes and beats me."

"Here is my cell phone number," Brooke said, telling her the digits.

Aludra had been keeping an eye on the grocery store's front door, and she hung up the phone at the exact moment Akbar came through it, causing a tiny bell on the doorframe to ring.

Forcing a smile, she hurried toward him. "I've taken too long but I needed the toilet," she said.

He looked at the back of the store at a sign. REST ROOM. But she couldn't tell from his eyes if he'd noticed the pay phone outside it.

"Where are the groceries?" he asked.

Aludra felt a renewed sense of panic. She couldn't risk having the talkative clerk asking her about her phone call in front of him.

"Akbar," she said, her voice a whisper, "you don't want the woman at the cash register to recognize you. You must return to the car."

He studied her face before handing her twenty dollars and exiting the store.

She quickly gathered up the supplies they needed and took them to the checkout counter.

"Did you get that call made, dear?" the clerk asked.

"Yes, to my sister. We are going to visit her at the Virginia Technological University. We've always wanted to see the mountains so we are driving through them to Blacksburg."

It was a plausible explanation that she and Akbar had devised in case anyone questioned why they were in this remote area.

"My daughter went to Radford," the clerk volunteered while slipping the groceries into thin plastic bags. "It's right next door to Tech. It's a lovely drive from here to there."

"Thank you," Aludra said. "I like your store. It's quaint."

"Honey, it's old, just like me," the clerk replied. "Nothing quaint about that."

Aludra was opening the door to leave when the clerk called after her. "Hey, you forgot about the pickles. When your husband came in. You were supposed to tell him about the pickle barrel."

"Yes, how many pickles can you pick." She forced a laugh.

Akbar was waiting with the car engine running. "What did you say to that woman?" he demanded.

"Nothing. She wanted me to tell you about pickles."

"Pickles?"

"Foolish woman talk."

"Why didn't you wait to use the toilet at the cabin?" he asked suspiciously.

She removed a box of tampons from the grocery bag. "This is allowed," she said, referring to an edict by their Imam that permitted women to use them. Her explanation quieted him.

For the next twenty minutes they drove in silence until they reached a cabin in a heavily wooded area. Aludra had rented the cabin online on VRBO, and it was appropriately called the Perfect Hideaway. It was a newly constructed log cabin that was built on three levels. Jennifer and Cassy were bound with duct tape in an unfinished storage room on the cabin's ground floor. A wraparound porch surrounded the main floor, which contained the kitchen and a great room with a huge river rock fireplace. The cabin's owners had mounted a bear's head over the mantle. In a framed letter posted for renters, the owner explained that he had killed the bear about a mile from the cabin while bow hunting. An open staircase led to two upstairs bedrooms. The cabin was built into the mountainside so that three of its ground-level walls were covered with earth. The one that wasn't contained a double glass door that looked out onto a clearing to the immediate west of the cabin.

As the couple neared the cabin on its gravel road, Akbar suddenly stopped, jammed the car's transmission into park, and reached back into the rear seat for his assault rifle. The house's front door was wide open.

*   *   *

The moment Brooke finished speaking to Aludra over the phone, she hurried into Wyatt Parker's office inside the Reston command post and together they found the location of the Perfect Hideaway rental cabin on VRBO. Parker passed that address to the FBI's elite Hostage Rescue Team in Quantico, Virginia.

"I'm going there with them," Brooke declared.

"No, you're not," Parker replied. "I'll get us a separate chopper. You would be in their way, just as I would. We must let them do their jobs."

Brooke knew he was right but she didn't like it. The special agents selected as HRT tactical "operators" were among the most highly trained in the country. They were capable of launching a rescue anywhere in the United States within four hours. It would not take them that long to reach the Perfect Hideaway cabin, which was tucked between Potts Mountain and Peters Mountain, about 250 miles southwest from the Washington, D.C., area.

"HRT's motto is *servare vitas*," Parker said reassuringly, as he and Brooke drove to nearby Dulles International Airport to a waiting FBI helicopter. "That's Latin for 'to save lives.'"

Brooke was familiar with the HRT motto, but her mind was on other matters. She was thinking about Jennifer and Cassy, and what Aludra had told her. *What kind of man raped young girls and then wrapped himself in religious purity?*

As they neared the helicopter, she thought of a story that she'd heard about the origins of the FBI's HRT. Legend had it that former FBI director William H. Webster had embraced the HRT concept after witnessing a rescue demonstration by the Delta Force, the military's most elite special force. Webster had noticed during the show that the anti-terrorism operatives didn't carry handcuffs and had asked why. "We put two rounds in their forehead," a team member quipped. "The dead don't need handcuffs."

Brooke liked that approach.

Once airborne, Brooke and Parker listened through headphones to the FBI base commander directing the HRT. The rescue plan was straightforward. The HRT's specially equipped helicopter would hover over the trees far enough away from the cabin that it would not be detected but close enough so that rescuers could fast rope down into the woods and quickly hike there. They would surprise and neutralize Akbar and rescue the two girls. No one believed Akbar would surrender. There would be no need for handcuffs.

With his finger on the trigger of his assault rifle, Akbar entered the Perfect Hideaway cabin and moved cautiously from room to room before he returned to the front porch and waved to Aludra to come inside from the car with their groceries.

"One of the girls has escaped," he hollered angrily as Aludra climbed the front steps. "She can't be far. I'm going to find her." He left the porch, heading in the direction of the clearing to the southwest of the cabin as Aludra hurried inside, depositing the bags of groceries on the kitchen table. She rushed down a flight of stairs to the ground floor and into the storage room where she found Jennifer Conner lying on the tile floor still bound with duct tape.

"How did she escape?" Aludra asked the teen.

Jennifer didn't answer.

Aludra noticed Cassy's black riding boots lying nearby. They were still tied together with duct tape at the ankle, which meant that Cassy had slipped her feet from inside them.

"She couldn't break the tape you put on her wrists," Jennifer said quietly. "She went upstairs to get a knife and must have heard your car."

"Akbar will catch her, and when he does, he will hurt her bad. He will beat all of us."

"He's a bad man, but you aren't. Can you help me escape?"

"We wouldn't get far. You must be patient."

Neither Jennifer nor Cassy had been wearing hoods when Akbar and Aludra had left earlier to get groceries, but now Aludra placed a hood over Jennifer's face.

"This is best," she said. Dropping her voice to a whisper, she added, "The FBI is coming and they will know you are a hostage if you are wearing a hood. Just be quiet and wait."

"The FBI is coming!" Jennifer exclaimed.

"Sshh. You must be quiet. I spoke to your Brooke Grant. She will send someone, but you must be quiet. He will kill us if he knows they are coming to rescue you."

The HRT sniper secured a shooting position in the tree line about thirty yards southwest of the cabin at the edge of a clearing and watched with his spotter while their fellow operatives closed in on their target. It was mid-morning, the sky was clear, and anyone inside the Perfect Hideaway looking out of its windows could have seen them. But there were no visible signs of movement. Nor were there any cars parked outside the cabin on the gravel driveway.

The team reached the wraparound porch without incident, moving quickly to the cabin's front entrance where the team's "breacher" fired a twelve-gauge shotgun into the middle hinge of the front door. He fired at the top and bottom hinges next. Each blast contained nine .30-caliber balls that easily busted the hinges free. After kicking in the door, the breacher spun out of the way to give another HRT gunman a clear shot at anyone inside. A third team member simultaneously pitched flash-bangs into the main living area. They exploded, causing a tremendous noise, blinding flash, and a shock wave designed to disorient and confuse. In less than a minute, the team had gone through the entire cabin and determined that it was vacant.

"We missed them, but not by much," the HRT leader explained when a clearly disappointed Brooke and Parker arrived. "Two bags of groceries were on the kitchen table and the time stamp on the receipt showed they'd been purchased less than two hours before we got here."

"Roadblocks?" Brooke asked.

"There is no local police department in this area," the leader said, "but I've notified state troopers here and across the state line in West Virginia. I told them to be looking for a Somali American couple traveling with one white and one black girl."

Suddenly, the team leader pressed his right hand against the earpiece that he was wearing to better hear what was being said. Brooke and Parker, who were standing with him on the wraparound porch, were not wearing earpieces, so they had no idea what he was being told.

"I see them now," the team leader replied into a thin microphone near his mouth. He raised his right hand and pointed away from the cabin. Brooke and Parker, who were facing him, turned so they could see southwest where he was pointing. Across the clearing, an HRT operative emerged from the trees holding Cassy's hand.

Brooke darted down the porch steps and bolted across the clearing toward them. "Is Jennifer with you?" she yelled.

Cassy threw her arms around Brooke, the only woman in the rescue party, and began crying.

"They got her," the eleven year-old said, her words coming out in gulps because of her sobs.

"I'm Jennifer's guardian. Are you okay?" Brooke asked. "All of these men have first aid training."

"She's dehydrated but otherwise seems physically fine," the HRT operative who had brought her from the woods said. "She's one tough little girl."

"That bad man hit me and Jennifer with a belt, but I'm okay."

"We need to get her to a hospital and then to her mom and dad," Parker said when he joined them in the clearing.

"I don't want to go inside there," Cassy said, nodding toward the cabin.

"You don't have to," Brooke said. "Have you had a helicopter ride?" Brooke was on her knees so that she was face-to-face with Cassy.

"No."

"We flew down here in one just to get you," Brooke said. "It's parked close by." She took Cassy's hand and began walking with her and Parker toward the chopper, which was parked on a wide spot that was part of the gravel driveway. When they reached it, Brooke buckled Cassy into the passenger seat next to hers and said, "You're safe now. Before we take off, can you tell us how you escaped?" She was still holding the girl's hand.

"The man and woman watching us left this morning. I knew they both were gone."

"How did you know that?" Parker asked. He'd taken a seat directly across from them after closing the helicopter's door.

"Their car was parked outside the room where we were being held. When I heard two sounds—two car doors closing—I knew both of them were leaving."

"That was really clever, Cassy," Brooke said, squeezing her hand. "And you are one very brave young lady."

"I'm sorry I couldn't help Jennifer," the teen said. "My hands were tied with tape." An HRT operator had freed her wrists when he'd spotted her hiding in the woods. "I couldn't get it off and couldn't get the tape off her hands either."

"I'm just glad you're safe," Brooke said in a reassuring voice. She'd noticed earlier that Cassy wasn't wearing any shoes.

"That man taped my riding boots together. But I managed to slip out of them. They were too big for me when my mom bought them. She said I was growing so fast I would grow into them."

Brooke smiled. "We'll need to thank your mom for those boots."

"I couldn't get the tape off my arms or Jennifer's, so I went upstairs to get a knife in the kitchen. I told Jennifer I'd be right back, but when I got upstairs I heard the car coming, so I ran out the door as fast as I could until I was in the woods."

"Did you see the man and woman? Akbar and Aludra?"

"Yes, I watched them from behind the trees. I was scared and didn't know where to hide. When they parked the car, the man came out with a gun and went inside the house. I was afraid he was going to shoot Jennifer, but I didn't hear a gunshot. He came out and called the woman, who carried in two plastic bags. While she was doing that, he started walking away from the cabin. He was coming right toward me and I was really scared. I wanted to run, but I was so scared my legs wouldn't move. I just stood there. Frozen. But then he stopped before he reached the woods and saw me."

"Why? Why did he stop, Cassy?" Brooke asked.

"He got a phone call."

"A phone call?"

"He had to answer his funny-looking old phone. It had a big antenna like the phones my grandparents used to have at their house in Minneapolis."

"It was probably a satellite phone," Parker volunteered. "They have big antennas."

"What happened next?" Brooke asked.

"The man talked into the phone to whoever called him and when he finished, he turned around and ran back to the cabin. The next thing I saw was him bringing Jennifer outside. Her hands were still tied with tape and she had a hood on her head so the woman was helping her and they all got into their car and left. I didn't know what to do, so I just stayed in the woods watching the cabin and the next thing I saw was the soldiers crossing the field to the house and then one of them came up behind me and told me I was being rescued. And then he brought me out to you."

Brooke glanced over at Parker. "She said Akbar got a phone call. That means someone warned him we were coming. That's why he didn't keep looking for Cassy in the woods. He knew we were on our way, so he ran back inside and got Jennifer."

"This is important," Parker said to Cassy. "Do you know what model of car they left in?"

"It was a Chevrolet, a black Chevrolet. I have an uncle who has one like it. A Malibu. I knew you would want to know and I looked at the license plate too. The first three letters were KWB. I know the numbers too." She told him, and Parker immediately picked up a pair of headphones in the helicopter and spoke to the HRT commander in Quantico.

Brooke leaned sideways and kissed Cassy on her forehead.

"You did fabulous," she told her as the pilot started the helicopter's engine.

"I'm sorry I couldn't save Jennifer," Cassy said, as the aircraft began to lift off. She began to cry.

"Me too," Brooke replied. "But you're safe and your mother and daddy will be waiting for you at the hospital."

"I hope he doesn't hurt Jennifer," Cassy said. "He's a bad man. My father told me it is wrong to hate people who hurt you. He said we have to pray for them. But I want him dead."

"Yes, me too."

CHAPTER THIRTY-FIVE

Near the border city of El Wak
Northeastern Kenya desert

Surrounded by goats and carrying a dead one across his shoulders, Walks Many Miles helped the old herder cross the desert for about an hour before they came to a hut made of sticks, pieces of scrap metal, and tattered strips of canvas. As they approached it, the herder released his grip on Miles's arm and made his way painfully forward to a rickety pen, calling his animals to follow him.

Miles dumped the carcass on the ground and listened as the old man yelled out what sounded like a name. A woman wearing a bright yellow headscarf and ankle-length blue-and-red-striped dress emerged from the hut. She was about the same age as Miles. She eyed him suspiciously as she hurriedly spoke to the herder in a dialect foreign to the American.

The woman helped the herder close the pen's gate and took his arm as the two of them walked toward the hut's entrance. The goat herder waved his hand, motioning Miles to join them inside.

Miles was surprised at how large the interior of the hut's dome-shaped room was and how much cooler the temperature became under the covering. The woman brought the old man a clay cup of goat's milk and offered one to Miles as both of the men sat on threadbare rugs. She'd heated the milk and added spice to it.

Miles listened as the herder spoke rapidly, apparently explaining to the woman how Al-Shabaab terrorists had accosted him and killed his goat. As he spoke, he nodded at Miles and when he finished, the woman parted the hut's fabric door flap and disappeared outside. Worried that she might be on her way to tell someone about his arrival, Miles followed her outside. He found her butchering the dead goat and realized he had carried home their dinner. Returning inside the hut, he sat on the floor and watched as the old man rubbed salve on his chest. When the herder finished, he scooted toward Miles with a handful of blackish goop clutched in his bony fingers. Miles shook his head. "Thank you, but no thanks. I got busted ribs and that isn't going to help them."

The old man looked puzzled and again signaled with his hand, indicating that Miles should lift his shirt. Reluctantly, Miles complied, and the herder rubbed the black concoction onto his chest and sides. To Miles's surprise, the pain eased, causing him to wonder what analgesic the sticky substance contained. The old man fetched another cup of milk for himself and Miles. They drank it in awkward silence, occasionally grinning at each other.

Outside, the woman was cooking several pieces of goat meat over a fire. She'd already skinned the animal and scraped its bones, which she then boiled in a clay pot, making bone soup.

When she rejoined the men in the tent, she served them soup, meat, and wild berries. Miles found the meal more delicious and satisfying than the energy bars and prepackaged food in his field ration.

By the time they finished eating, it was dark, and now somewhat rested and refueled, Miles decided to leave. Unfortunately, he wasn't exactly certain where he was.

"El Wak," he said, as the three of them sat in a semicircle around a tiny clay pot that contained some sort of flammable oil and was being burned as a lamp inside the hut. "Me go El Wak now."

The old man said something to the woman, who replied, and from the sharpness of their conversation, it sounded to Miles as if they were arguing.

Miles rose to his feet. He would use the stars to guide him east to where he assumed the highway was located.

"Don't leave," the woman said.

"You speak English?" he asked, clearly startled.

"My late husband taught me. He was a missionary in Mandera before he was murdered. But my father does not understand or speak it."

"I know," Miles said, smiling. "All he kept saying when I found him was the same phrase. I heard it so many times, I memorized it: *'No gattee hindeemin.'*"

"It is Cushitic. He was asking you to not leave him or his goats behind."

"How old is he?" Miles asked.

"Sixty," she replied.

Miles had guessed the herder was in his late seventies, possibly even older than that.

"Will you ask my age too?" she said.

"No, ma'am, but I'll ask your name."

"Hani, a Somali name that means 'happy.' My mother was Somali. My father married outside his clan. I am their only child and I married a Kenyan missionary from the south. We are a family of outsiders, which is why we live alone and are not protected by a clan. It is why those men beat my father."

"Did those men kill your husband?"

"He was murdered three years ago because he was a Coptic Christian."

"By Al-Shabaab?"

She shrugged. "Al-Shabaab, Al-Qaeda, Boko Haram, they all eat from the same plate. Who can be sure today what they call themselves?"

"But they spared you, why?"

"My husband knew how dangerous it was for me. He told everyone I was his cook. I was never baptized and am still a Muslim, like my father. But I had to leave Mandera after he was murdered. It was where I was studying to be a teacher, and that made me a target. They do not like women to be educated."

Her father said something and she spoke bluntly to him.

"What did he just tell you?" Miles asked.

"He wants one of your guns. He wants to have a weapon to shoot the men who killed his goat. He is willing to give you two of his best goats for your rifle."

"Unless I can ride them out of here, I've got no use for them," Miles said, grinning. "But I do have use for my weapons."

"What is your name?" she asked.

"Walks Many Miles."

"That is not an American name."

"It is the name of a first American. I'm Indian."

She let her eyes linger for a moment on his face. "Like the ones in movies?" she asked.

"No, those were white people painted to look like Indians. I'm the genuine thing."

"My father says he saw the helicopter you were riding in when it was shot down. He was not far from where it crashed. He said he saw you and the men chasing you."

"I need to use a phone," he replied. Glancing around their sparsely furnished hut, he added, "I don't suppose you have one handy."

"There are phones in El Wak, but it is a tiny village and going there would be dangerous for you. Al-Shabaab controls it, along with a rich man who has his own private army and lives outside the town."

"Yes, I know. He's the billionaire Umoja Owiti. Do you know where he lives?"

"In a big house not far from where my father takes his goats to graze because there is water there. My father could guide you there, but this man is friends with Al-Shabaab. It would not be safe."

"How do you know Umoja Owiti is friends with Al-Shabaab?"

"Because he welcomes Al-Shabaab into his house. His soldiers allow my father to graze his goats near the house except when several black trucks come to the compound. My father is always warned the day before to stay away and is not allowed to come close to the house with his goats until those cars are gone several days later."

A visit by the Falcon, Miles thought. That had to be the reason why the goat herder was told to stay away. The SAD team had been sent to watch the Umoja Owiti estate. Israeli intelligence had sent word that the Falcon was supposed to return there sometime during a five-day period. Once the team had confirmed his arrival, Langley would decide how best to capture or, more likely, kill him.

"I will give your father this rifle and ammunition," Miles said, slapping the butt of the AK-47 next to him, "in return for two favors."

"My father will be killed if he has a gun," she replied. "I will not tell him your offer."

But the old man, who'd been watching them intently, had seen Miles touch the rifle and instantly understood that it was being discussed. He spoke rapidly to his daughter, who again argued with him. Finally, the old herder shook his fist at her.

"He has told me that he will agree to your demands whatever they are. He has told me I am a bad daughter for arguing with him. He says we can use the rifle to protect ourselves from the men who beat him."

The old man spoke again. "He wants to know what you want for the rifle," Hani said. "What are the two favors?"

"I need you to walk into town and make a phone call," Miles replied. "You speak English. Call a number and tell them I am alive and I will let them know when I need them to send help. Could you make a call like that without putting yourself in danger?"

"Everyone who lives here is in danger. What else?"

"I want your father to take me with him and his goats to graze near the house of Umoja Owiti. I want to see it."

She relayed his demands to the old man and said, "He's not sure. He's worried they will kill us if they discover that we helped you. He will give you an answer tomorrow."

The next morning, the herder nudged him awake before sunrise and handed him a bundle of clothes. The pants were several sizes too big as was the white buttoned shirt. The old man nodded approvingly when he saw how huge they hung on Miles. In the oversize garments, he appeared thinner. Several holes in the shirt's back panel had been mended, causing Miles to assume that Hani's Coptic missionary husband had been wearing the clothing when he was murdered. He tucked both of his pistols under the billowing shirt and stepped outside the hut. Hani already had made a fire and was heating milk for them.

"Good morning," he said, taking a cup from her. "Can I assume your father is willing to take me since I am now wearing these clothes?"

"He will take you to the house and I will walk into El Wak and make the call," she said. "In return, you will give him your rifle and bullets."

"Let's hold off on that phone call. I want to see the house first."

She placed another branch on the fire while her father emerged from the hut carrying a long piece of black cloth. "Are you finished with your milk?" she asked Miles. He handed her his empty cup and she poked a small burning stick inside it which she rubbed against the inside of the clay cup, sanitizing it, since water could not be wasted on washing dishes. Next, she took the long piece of fabric from her father and began wrapping it around Miles's neck and head until only his eyes peeked through a slit.

"Now you look like a poor herder," she declared.

Using a walking stick to support himself, the old man opened the pen's gate, freeing the goats to walk with them. He and Miles herded the animals north, away from the hut.

Traveling with goats was mind-numbingly slow as they inched forward at their own pace despite Miles's prompting. By the time they reached a slight incline, they'd been walking for nearly two hours, and the sun was rising.

The old man nodded toward a walled compound, causing

Miles to turn his attention away from the meandering goats. A massive white dome rose from the center of Umoja Owiti's main house, which had been built in the center of his expansive estate. A ten-foot-tall wall made of dried mud and painted white protected the grounds. The landscape outside of the compound was largely barren, but on the other side of the wall, Miles could see the tops of palm trees.

The herder gently prodded the goats toward the estate but stopped fifty yards outside the wall. While the goats searched for food, Miles sat next to the herder on a windblown stone and studied his target. The main gate had four sentries posted outside its metal doors. They were armed with assault rifles.

By noon, the goats had made their way to within ten yards of the mud walls. Miles had watched the comings and goings at the main entrance but had not seen anything that seemed out of the ordinary. Occasionally, a Land Rover from inside would emerge only to return later, presumably after running an errand into town. The afternoon warmth made Miles drowsy, and he fought to stay awake. His headscarf helped cool him, and when a sudden burst of wind sent sand flying, he was happy that his disguise was functional. His mind wandered. He thought of Brooke and wondered if she knew by some psychic bonding between them that he had not died during the helicopter crash nor had he been captured. Was she thinking about him? He had no way of knowing about the attack on the girls' school and Jennifer's abduction. Instead, he envisioned Brooke and Jennifer at the farmhouse waiting eagerly for him to return.

Miles snapped awake when a Land Rover exited from the front gate and drove off the road that led to El Wak toward them. Miles casually slipped his hand under his baggy shirt where his pistols were being held in place by a piece of rope holding up his oversize pants.

The two security guards riding in the vehicle were dressed in the same Owiti company uniforms that Miles had first seen at the helicopter crash site. When their vehicle neared the old man, the passenger lowered his window and hollered out to him.

The goat herder bowed his head obediently and raised his right arm in a gesture that Miles took to mean that he understood the man's command. The driver began a U-turn to return to the main gate, and as he did, the Land Rover passed close by Miles and the guard seated in the passenger seat stared out at him.

If the men stopped to question him, he wouldn't understand their orders and he would have no choice but to draw his pistols and kill them. *Then what?*

Miles lowered his eyes in submission as the Land Rover continued its turn without stopping and made its way back to the gated entrance.

There was no point in asking the herder what the security guard had told him without Hani being there to interpret. When they finally collected the goats and made the arduous trip back to the hut and pens, it was turning dark. They found her squatting over a fire preparing dinner.

As he moved toward the fire to greet her, Miles noticed that Hani's eyes were puffy and one was black.

"What happened?" he asked.

She ignored his question and lifted her headscarf to cover what appeared to be bruises on her face. The herder also noticed and spoke to her in a harsh voice. Hani retired from the outside fire to the hut. The old man poured them milk from a pot resting on a stone next to the hot coals, and when they squatted near the campfire, he pointed at Miles's waist.

Miles drew one of his pistols from its hiding place, removed its metal ammunition clip, pulled back the slide so he could empty the gun's chambered round, and handed the now unloaded pistol to the old man, who snatched it from his grasp.

As Miles watched, the goat herder expertly disassembled the handgun before reassembling it and returning it to Miles in a move meant to demonstrate his expertise.

Leaving the herder by the fire, Miles reloaded the weapon, tucked it back under his shirt, and walked to the hut's door flap.

"May I come inside?" he asked.

She did not reply, so he lifted the door covering and stepped inside.

"Are you okay?" he asked. "What happened to you while we were gone?"

"It is not of your concern."

For an awkward moment neither spoke, and then he said, "Two security guards came out of Umoja Owiti's estate this afternoon and said something to your father."

"Yes, he told me when you first returned with the goats."

"What did they say to him?"

"They said he could graze his goats tomorrow but he could not come the day after that. If he did, they will kill his goats."

Miles glanced again at her puffy face, which was illuminated by the oil lamp.

"Was it Al-Shabaab who hurt you?" he asked.

She pulled away from the flickering light. He wanted to say something comforting to her, but he didn't know what to say, so he left her alone in the hut. Outside its entrance, he counted his paces until he had walked to a sandy spot about fifteen feet from the hut's entrance. Dropping to his knees, he began digging with his knife until its metal blade struck metal. Using his hands now, he unearthed the AK-47 and extra ammunition that he had hidden there that morning before leaving with the old man and goats.

Returning to the campfire, he handed the assault rifle to the goat herder, who immediately began breaking it down, cleaning it.

It was time, Miles decided, to even the playing field.

CHAPTER THIRTY-SIX

Chief of Staff Mallory Harper's office
The White House
Washington, D.C.

Omar Nader telephoned Mallory Harper's office and asked for an appointment to see her. The matter was private and urgent, he told her secretary. Within an hour, the secretary returned his nine a.m. call. Harper could see him at one p.m.

It was only a ten-minute walk from the OIN headquarters on K Street to the White House, but Nader left his office at twelve thirty, knowing it would take time for the Secret Service to clear him at the White House's front gate, even though Harper's secretary had supplied them with his Saudi Arabian diplomatic passport number and he'd been admitted as a visitor on earlier occasions.

As he approached Lafayette Park, across from the White House, Nader thought about what he hoped to accomplish during their face-to-face. His goal was to seek Harper's help in stopping Representative Thomas Edgar Stanton from investigating Muslim mosques and Imams. Nader had heard from well-placed sources that Harper wasn't personally fond of Stanton.

Derailing the hearings would not be simple or easy. Chairman Stanton had lots of friends in Congress, having accumulated plenty of political IOUs during his many years in office. He also belonged to the same political party as President Allworth, and that prevented Harper from launching any overt actions against him.

Nader thought he knew why Harper disliked Stanton. She

could not control him. Nearly all senators and House members had the same Achilles' heel. Once elected, they wanted desperately to remain in office. This made them easy for a president to manipulate. All it took in most instances was the offer of a piece of prime federal pork to serve voters back home—a fish hatchery, a regional office for some federal agency, or funding for a legislator's pet project. If those goodies were not enough to make an elected leader in Congress dance, the White House could crack a whip. Delaying the appointment of a federal judge, holding back the release of block grant funding, or killing a legislator's pet bill were all threats that only the foolhardy ignored.

Unfortunately for Harper and the White House, Representative Stanton was not easily cajoled. Even worse, he could fight back. The Chairman could tie up legislation that the White House wanted passed. As an incumbent, Stanton also appeared to be unbeatable. His approval rating in his South Carolina district was the highest in Congress.

Even without his strong voter base and his influential connections, Stanton would have been difficult for any president to manipulate. He paid little attention to what his pollsters or his political party bosses said. Stanton genuinely believed that he knew what was best for the nation and that made him unpredictable. The White House could never be a hundred percent certain what he might do.

Stanton's call for investigative hearings had unleashed a new wave of anti-Muslim rhetoric. All Muslims were being typecast as terrorists, and Islam in general was being defamed. Stanton had to be stopped and also punished before this wave became a typhoon.

By the time Nader entered the White House grounds, he'd decided the best way to get Harper's help would be by appealing to her vanity. He arrived five minutes before his one p.m. appointment. Thirty minutes later, he was escorted into Harper's office. She offered no apology for making him wait. After they exchanged niceties, Nader made his pitch.

"I've come to ask you for advice about a political matter. It's about Chairman Stanton. The OIN and I, personally, are distressed about the anti-Muslim feelings that he is generating. He is promoting fearmongering, and his call for law enforcement to become more aggressive in infiltrating mosques and censoring Imams is blatant profiling and a threat to religious freedom."

"I may agree," Harper replied, "but like it or not, Chairman Stanton's call for hearings has struck a nerve with many Americans. They are afraid of homegrown terrorism, and polls show a large number of them believe that political correctness has gotten out of hand. The recent attacks here in Washington haven't helped your cause."

"If Stanton goes forward with committee hearings, he is going to further alarm and inflame the public. What will happen next? Will Muslims be gathered up into internment camps like your country gathered up the Japanese? Will mosques be closed, Imams arrested? Will Muslims be deported or not allowed to enter your country? Stanton is dangerous, which is why I need your guidance."

"Why are you asking me for advice?"

Nader glanced around her office. Hanging on its walls were photographs of Harper posing with President Allworth, various Washington power brokers, and international leaders. "Isn't it obvious? You are the top of the mountain. You understand American politics and, despite my best efforts to educate myself, I come from a nation ruled by a king and royal family. None of us is as skilled as you are at dealing civilly with political opponents."

"In a monarchy you simply arrest them or worse."

"You must admit," Nader said with a smile, "prison and death are effective deterrents. But I do not think you and President Allworth have that luxury with Representative Stanton."

"You do realize that Stanton and the president belong to the same party, don't you?"

"Of course, but that should not keep the president from defending America's core values. I would like to offer the president an opportunity to do exactly that."

"What type of opportunity?"

"The OIN will soon announce plans for a million-man Muslim march on Washington. We will be calling on all Muslims to come to show their support for religious freedom and tolerance. And we would like the president to support our march."

"As long as it is nonviolent, I am fairly certain she will be open to releasing a statement."

"We are hoping for more than a mere statement. We would like the president to speak at our rally about the importance of religious freedom."

"The president would need to know more details before committing to a speech. But your chances of getting her to attend would be better if you didn't bill this as a Muslim march, but rather as a march for all faiths. You could include Christians, Jews, and other faiths."

Nader shook his head in amazement. "You see, this is why I have come seeking your advice. That is a brilliant idea. Consider it done."

"I'm not clear how a march will solve your problem with Chairman Stanton," Harper said.

"We are trying to shame and embarrass him. I'm certain you have heard that we put him on our list of Islamophobic Americans."

"And that probably made him more popular, not less."

"You see my frustration then," Nader replied. "Perhaps, you can offer me some better ideas—unofficially, of course."

Mallory Harper studied the seasoned diplomat sitting across from her cluttered desk. She did not believe Omar Nader was as naïve as he was pretending. Rather, he was probing. He was trying to learn if she, and more importantly the president, would be willing to help the OIN go after Stanton.

What Nader had no way of knowing was that Mallory Harper was just as eager to destroy the Chairman as was the OIN. Her interest in ridding herself of Stanton went beyond her personal disdain for him. The Chairman still intended to conduct hearings in the future about the Somalia embassy debacle—hearings that would badly embarrass the president.

Harper lowered her voice to a whisper. "Unofficially," she said, "I will offer you some advice." Pushing back in her chair, she turned sideways so she was now facing her computer. Typing quickly on its keyboard, she explained, "I'm going to assume that you haven't seen an interview that Chairman Stanton gave after his press conference to a reporter from his home district. The interview was for a cable television show on a local access channel. No one ever watches these shows, but stations are obligated by their licenses to provide a certain amount of free programming to the locals."

"You are correct, I am not aware of this."

Having found what she was after, Harper turned her computer screen so he could watch the interview from where he was sitting. The reporter questioning Stanton looked as if he were still in high school.

"What you're doing doesn't seem any different from Senator Joseph McCarthy's claim in the 1950s that communists were infiltrating the federal government—those charges turned out to be nothing but fearmongering and hate speech that destroyed lives and Hollywood careers."

"Young man," Stanton said, clearly irked, "you need to take another look at your history books. It was the House Committee on Un-American Activities that blacklisted hundreds of actors, writers, and directors after World War Two because they were suspected of being communists, not Senator Joe McCarthy."

"But that committee and McCarthy both engaged in false accusations and smearing innocent Americans. That's what McCarthyism is," the reporter replied, standing his ground.

It was Stanton's next statement that Harper wanted Nader to hear. Rather than condemning the much-shamed Wisconsin Republican senator, Stanton said: "It's Joe McCarthy who has been falsely smeared by history. The Soviet Union was planting sleeper agents inside our government—in the highest levels of power. What

McCarthy was warning the American people about was real. He got in trouble because he was bombastic and that actually aided the Reds."

Harper turned off the interview being shown on her computer and turned back in her chair so she could face Nader. "Joe McCarthy," she said, "is one of the most vilified politicians in American history. McCarthyism is synonymous with irresponsibility and hyperbole. Stanton has handed you his own head on a platter. All you need to do is shift the public debate away from Muslims and onto him."

She could tell from the intense look on Nader's face that he was eager to hear more, so she continued. "Some ten to twelve thousand Americans lost their jobs during the height of McCarthyism because they were accused of being communists. More than three hundred Hollywood movie stars were blacklisted. It is considered one of the darkest periods politically in U.S. history. And yet you have Stanton on a video defending McCarthy, no, applauding him. Do you understand how that could be interpreted? We live in a twenty-four-hour news cycle. We live in an age of social media. Imagine the political fallout if someone posted a montage on the Internet of what Stanton is saying today interspersed with Joe McCarthy's rants."

Harper wasn't yet done. "Do you know who the most offended Americans were by McCarthyism? It was the media. Edward R. Murrow, a pioneer television journalist, went on the air exposing McCarthy. His broadcasts led to his censure and ultimately to public opinion turning against him. Murrow's actions are considered one of the greatest moments in the history of journalism. It's time you put Stanton on trial for attacking the country's core values of fairness, honesty, religious freedom, and freedom of speech." She paused for a moment to catch her breath and then said, "You need to understand that Thomas Stanton has always enjoyed an excellent relationship with the media. They have never put him through the meat grinder. He's always been loved. Exposing him as a political reincarnation of Joe McCarthy and the embodiment of McCarthyism will devastate him." She sat back in her chair, having finished her soliloquy, but then added, "Unofficially speaking."

"Would the OIN have a friend or foe in the White House if someone took that anonymous unofficial advice?"

"I believe the president would feel that she didn't have a dog in the fight. Chairman Stanton would need to defend himself," Harper replied. "But if you decide to launch a crusade against him, you need to go all in. You don't want Stanton coming back at you at some later point."

"I'm not certain that I know what 'all in' means in this context."

"I will assume the OIN will be actively supporting his opponent when Stanton runs for reelection. Is that correct?"

Now Nader understood. While she had posed her remark as a question, it was clearly a recommendation.

"If you are aware of a viable candidate," he replied, "the OIN would be grateful to hear his name."

"Mr. Nader, as you pointed out earlier, Chairman Stanton is a member of the president's party. No one in our party would dare challenge him in a primary because he is so popular and it would be unprofessional of me to help the other side field a candidate. But I believe the last person from the opposition to challenge him was a college professor from Smithville University. Are you familiar with that school?"

"Unfortunately, I'm embarrassed to say I am not."

"It's in the heart of South Carolina's Third Congressional District, which Stanton represents. You probably missed it because Smithville University is a small private Christian university supported by the South Carolina Baptist Convention. Although it is very highly ranked for its academics, it remains a tiny fish."

"My I ask the name of this professor who challenged Stanton?"

"Dr. Robert Powers. I believe he teaches mathematics there."

"But you said Stanton easily defeated him."

"Yes, he did, but post-election polls showed that Powers might have won if he'd had better financing and better messaging. You see, the Third District has always been a Democratic stronghold, but in recent years, voters have been electing more and more Republicans. This is a trend across the entire South where voters are abandoning their ties to the old Democratic Party in favor of more socially conservative views."

"What do you mean by better messaging?"

"To defeat someone such as Stanton, you need to turn his biggest asset into an even bigger liability. Stanton has seniority, longevity, and he is chairman of the House Permanent Intelligence Committee. Everyone knows that. So you find ways to turn all of those achievements against him."

"Running against Washington is hardly a new message."

"You know more about campaigns than you said," Harper replied. "It's true, running against Washington is popular. It's especially appealing to Republicans who dislike big government, and I just told you that voters in his district are putting Republicans, not Democrats, into local offices. But Powers failed to capitalize on it. He should have accused Stanton of being a 'world congressman' as opposed to being a South Carolinian congressman. He should have zeroed in on Stanton's chairmanship and how much time he spends on international affairs. You could argue that keeping the world safe benefits the good voters of the Third District, but deep down, they want their elected official to focus on their wants and their needs. That is something Stanton has left for his staff to handle. There were other issues that made Stanton vulnerable according to the polls."

"Such as?"

"Stanton's independence. He broke from other South Carolinian congressmen on several votes that mattered in his state. Again, this is because he tends to take a national view rather than a purely parochial view. As a Democrat, he also voted in favor of several social issues that conflict with traditional conservative values, such as federal funding for liberal causes that many Christian Southern voters find repulsive."

Harper rose abruptly from her desk and extended her hand for him to shake. "I'll discuss your request about your million-person march with the president and get back to you."

Standing to shake her hand, Nader said, "Ms. Harper, it is even clearer to me now why the president appreciates and depends on your political instincts."

Four hours after that White House meeting, Malik Kalb, an associate professor of mathematics at Smithville University, rapped on the office door of Dr. Robert Powers, who waved him inside. For several minutes, the two colleagues chatted about campus affairs and then Kalb said, "Dr. Powers, as you know, I am a practicing Muslim and there were some on the hiring panel here who were wary about employing someone of my faith to teach in a Southern Baptist school when I applied."

"Do you feel you are being slighted?" Powers asked, his voice suddenly filled with concern. "Has someone said something to offend you?"

"No, no. Just the opposite. I have been welcomed and have taken some joy in having first-year students being surprised that I am a Muslim." He paused and then added, "Many of my students never give up trying to convert me."

Powers chuckled. "That comes with the turf."

"I believe it is important for students to be exposed to a Muslim and for all of us to learn, respect, and appreciate our different religious traditions and values," Kalb continued.

"As do I, so what has happened that brings you to my office to discuss religion rather than Alexander Grothendieck and algebraic geometry?"

"Not long after I was hired, you took leave to run for the U.S. Congress," Kalb said.

Powers cracked his knuckles before interlocking his fingers behind his head. He leaned back in his office chair, which needed oiling and squeaked loudly. "My campaign was a disaster, but I'm glad I did it because I genuinely felt it was time for change. Our representative has been in office eighteen terms, that's thirty-six years." He unclasped his fingers and leaned forward, causing another screech. "Are you thinking about running for political office, Malik? Are you coming to me for political advice?"

"Oh no, not me," Kalb replied. "I am wondering if you still feel a change is needed and, if so, if you could be persuaded to run again."

Powers shook his head, indicating no. "Thanks, but I prefer academia, although I must confess that university politics are equally as deadly as any in Washington."

"This time around would be different for you. I have been contacted by people who are willing to donate money if you would consider challenging Representative Stanton."

"What people?"

"Muslims who are deeply concerned about Representative Stanton's recent Islamophobic comments. They believe he is reckless and is fueling anti-Muslim sentiment."

"Imagine that. Muslims wanting to help finance a Southern Baptist professor's run for political office," Powers replied good-naturedly. "Now I've heard everything."

"You looked beyond my religious beliefs when you helped me get hired here, and my Muslim friends do not see you as a Southern Baptist professor, but as a fair-minded and just man who respects religious freedom and tolerance."

"That's gratifying, but I've already been down this road, and Stanton is considered unbeatable."

"Robert, I'm not talking about a few thousand dollars. In addition to sizeable contributions, these people have access to some of the top political strategists and media experts in Washington. With their help, you would have a real chance of winning."

Powers suddenly realized that Kalb's offer was more serious than he'd assumed. "How much money are you talking about?"

"Whatever you need to win," Kalb said in a low voice. "That is what I was told to tell you."

"House races in Ohio, New Jersey, and California have cost upwards of twenty million dollars each. When I ran against Stanton, I raised $125,000 and much of that came from a second mortgage and maxing out my credit cards."

"Whatever it takes. They aren't joking."

"You didn't say who these people are or what they want in return?"

"Chairman Stanton has enraged the Muslim community. These contributions would be coming from individuals in every state. The political advisors would come from Washington and be volunteers."

"Money always comes with strings."

"Only one string—you must defeat Stanton."

CHAPTER THIRTY-SEVEN

Interstate 66
West of Washington, D.C.

Major Brooke Grant felt frustrated as she maneuvered her Jaguar XF sedan into the far left lane of the eastbound Dulles Toll Road so she could use her E-ZPass to merge onto Interstate 66 and continue her drive into Washington, D.C. It had been nine hours since the FBI's HRT unit had stormed the Perfect Hideaway cabin in southwest Virginia and rescued Cassy Adeogo. But Akbar, Aludra, and Jennifer remained at large.

Brooke tried to push from her mind thoughts about what Akbar might do to Jennifer in retaliation for Cassy's escape. Her hatred toward the radical Islamic murderer grew every day that Jennifer remained his prisoner.

It was nearly ten p.m. when she reached George Washington University Hospital to check on her uncle, and even though visiting hours were over, the security guards and nurses there allowed Brooke to come and go as she pleased.

She had known that her aunt Geraldine would be at the bedside of the still unconscious General Frank Grant in the private ICU room, but at this hour, she was surprised to see Lieutenant Colonel Gabe DeMoss with them. After giving her aunt a hug and kiss, and learning that her uncle's condition had not changed, Brooke acknowledged DeMoss.

"Colonel, don't you ever sleep?"

"I was about to ask you the same question," he replied. Glancing at the general, DeMoss added, "Your uncle is one of the finest officers I've ever known. I want to be here when he wakes up."

Brooke was not surprised by his loyalty. As far back as Brooke could remember, her uncle had been a charismatic and dynamic leader who was admired and loved by those who served under his command. Her own father had chosen to be a preacher and had been a quiet and gentle leader. Uncle Frank, aka Pooh Bear, had been the opposite. Growing up in the panhandle of Oklahoma, the general had been a rebellious teen with a hot temper. University of Oklahoma recruiters had offered him a full-tuition football scholarship, but the Vietnam War was raging and Grant knew his chance of getting drafted was high, so he opted for West Point instead of going to a state school. The military had perfected his natural leadership abilities. Grant had graduated near the top of his class and volunteered to fight in Vietnam near the final days of that conflict when everyone else was avoiding that unwinnable quagmire. Aunt Geraldine had told Brooke that her uncle had returned from Southeast Asia a much-changed man. The flash point anger and recklessness were gone. Grant had evolved into a bold and reflective leader who in the midst of chaos remained sure-footed. Shortly after Brooke's parents had been murdered during the 9/11 attacks and she had moved in with her aunt and uncle, Brooke had snuck into General Grant's study. Her eyes had been drawn to a large leather-bound Bible lying on one corner of his desk. It had belonged to her father. Inside the cover, she'd found sheets of white paper with lists of names on them. She'd never seen those papers before and knew from the penmanship that her uncle had written them and placed them there. Years later, she would ask her aunt Geraldine about the names on those pages, and she would be told they were lists of soldiers who had died fighting under his command. Every fatality. Every man. Those soldiers each had names and General Grant never wanted to forget the sacrifice that those serving under him had made to keep his family safe and free.

*   *   *

That was the caliber of man now lying before her in the ICU still unconscious.

Brooke's cell phone vibrated, shaking her from her thoughts and signaling her that she had an incoming text. She only gave her private cell phone number to a few individuals, and when she didn't recognize the digits on the phone's caller ID, she assumed it was a pesky advertisement until she read the message.

Annapolis harbor. Eastport. Slip 15. Aludra.

Gabe DeMoss was still with her and Aunt Geraldine in her uncle's hospital room and he noticed the hopeful look that swept across her face.

"Is it Jennifer?" he asked.

"I know where she is!"

"How's that possible?"

"I gave Aludra my cell number when she called me from that grocery store. She's been helping us."

"Call Agent Parker," DeMoss said. "Tell him to send the HRT."

Brooke already was dialing Parker's number at the Reston command post, but he didn't answer. The call switched over to the duty officer.

"Get me Agent Parker right now!" she demanded.

The duty officer put her on hold momentarily and then returned. "I couldn't reached him at his home and he's not answering his cell."

"He's supposed to be available at all times," she complained, clearly frustrated.

"Sometimes his cell doesn't get a good signal."

"In this area?" Brooke snapped. "Keep trying."

DeMoss, who'd overheard her part of the conversation, dialed a number on his cell phone and handed it to her. "Here's Parker. I've got him on the line."

Brooke snatched the phone from his hand and told Parker about Aludra's text.

"I'll notify HRT and meet you in Annapolis," he said.

"I know Eastport."

"That's right, you graduated from the naval academy, didn't you?"

"The marina is across the street from the Annapolis Maritime Museum on Back Creek. I'll meet you at the museum parking lot."

"Same drill as before, Ms. Grant," Parker replied. "We let the HRT guys do their thing. No cowboy antics."

Brooke handed the phone back to DeMoss.

Aunt Geraldine looked concerned. "Oh, sweetie, be careful." She quickly kissed Brooke's cheek and said, "Bring Jennifer home safe."

DeMoss chased Brooke down the ICU corridor into the hospital elevator.

"The pier where she's being held is about forty miles from here according to Mapquest," DeMoss said, glancing at his phone's screen.

"HRT will be flying out of Quantico," Brooke replied.

DeMoss hit another app on his phone and said, "That's about a twenty-three-minute trip by air according to the Internet. Probably quicker in a helicopter."

The moment the elevator door opened, Brooke broke into a run with DeMoss right behind her.

"Even in your Jaguar, we can't beat them there," he said, sliding into the passenger seat.

"Just watch me. Buckle up."

"Brooke," he said, calling her by her first name, "the last thing we need to do is arrive with a parade of cop cars with flashing lights and sirens chasing us because you've been speeding."

What he was saying made sense, but as soon as they'd crossed the D.C. limits and reached a twenty-five-mile stretch of Highway 50 that poured into Annapolis, the Jaguar's speedometer hovered at 95 miles per hour.

"Use your Bluetooth to tie into my car's dash," Brooke said. "Get Parker on the line so we can find out what's happening."

As DeMoss was linking his cell phone to the Jaguar's dashboard speakers, Brooke had another thought. "How come you were able to reach Parker on your cell when his own people couldn't find him?"

"Remember Hillary Clinton and her multiple cell phones? Parker carries two. The FBI dispatcher should have had both of Parker's numbers."

"But why did you have it?"

"I work at the White House, remember? I can get anyone's number."

Parker's voice suddenly came through the car's speakers. "Ms. Grant, where are you two?"

"A few miles outside Annapolis."

"Jeezz, how'd you get there so fast? I'm at least a good twenty-five minutes behind you."

"Where's the HRT?"

"They've been getting a positive ID on the boat that's in Slip fifteen. It's a trawler-style—another Internet vacation rental—a thirty-six-foot motorboat whose owner lets tourists use it when he's not in Annapolis. A couple named Jacob and Sally Johar from Indianapolis picked up the keys a few hours ago from a restaurant near the pier. The bartender there had them sign paperwork. He helps the owner keep track of renters."

"Let me guess," Brooke said. "You couldn't find any record of a Jacob and Sally Johar from Indianapolis. They used fake IDs."

"That's right," Parker replied. "Now remember. Stay out of the way."

Neither Brooke nor DeMoss saw anything unusual when she turned her Jaguar off Eastern Avenue onto Second Street en route to the museum visitors' lot. There were no signs of the HRT. The lot itself was empty and ghostly quiet. Brooke parked and glanced at the marina and boats that were docked directly across the street from the museum. Their cabins looked as if they had been sealed for the winter. The decks of the smaller crafts were covered with large blue tarps.

"I don't see the HRT," Brooke said.

"They might be in the water. They're trained to board ships without being noticed. They even have scuba gear that doesn't emit telltale bubbles."

Brooke glanced through the car windows again. She was trying to identify which boat was the thirty-six-foot trawler in slip fifteen. Two lights at the marina's edge cast a light over the pier.

"I think that's it," she said, nodding at an older Albin trawler. Unlike the other boats, which appeared to be empty, there was a light inside its cabin behind curtains that covered the boat's portals.

"Point it out," DeMoss said.

As Brooke was raising her hand, the trawler exploded. Yellow and red flames shot from its deck. Windows in two nearby houses were shattered by the blast and pressure from the shock wave caused the Jaguar's sensitive car alarm to sound. For several moments, smoke completely obscured the ship's skeletal remnants.

Two black vans raced down Second Street and turned into the lot, stopping directly in front of the Jaguar. FBI agents bolted from both vehicles with guns drawn

As Brooke turned off the car alarm, an agent jerked open the vehicle's driver-side door. "I'm Major Brooke Grant!" she yelled, raising her hands.

The HRT commander recognized her from the rescue at the Perfect Hideaway cabin and redirected his men toward the pier.

"What the hell happened?" DeMoss asked as he stepped from the Jaguar and hurried toward Brooke and the HRT commander.

"Was Jennifer in that boat?" Brooke asked. "Does anyone know where she is?"

"It was a trap," the commander replied. "The boat was detonated the moment two of my divers boarded it."

He turned his back to Brooke and DeMoss and ran toward slip fifteen, where his men were frantically searching for the two agents who'd last been seen climbing aboard the trawler. Brooke and DeMoss hadn't seen them because they'd boarded on the side not visible from the parking lot.

Brooke was about to follow him when her cell phone vibrated. It was another text.

USN Golf Course. 4th hole. She's still alive. Aludra

Brooke read it twice.

Brooke knew the exact location of the fourth hole because she'd golfed on the U.S. Naval Academy links as a midshipman. It was the closest green to the water's edge and the quickest way to reach it would be by boat.

Her eyes were drawn to an inflatable dinghy hanging from the davit arms of a larger sailboat docked at the pier.

"Help me get that dinghy in the water," she told DeMoss.

"What? Why? Where are you going?"

"A text. Jennifer is on the fourth green at the academy's course."

"Brooke, it's another trap."

"If Akbar wanted me dead, he would have killed me by now. He's a trained sniper, remember?"

"Let the HRT handle it. Let's wait for Parker to get here."

"Jennifer can't wait. Now help me launch this dinghy."

It took them only minutes to get it into the water. As they sped away, Brooke heard someone calling from shore. It was Agent Wyatt Parker ordering her to return. She ignored him, so he called her cell phone.

"Where the hell are you going?" he demanded when she answered.

"The green on the fourth hole on the academy's golf course. I got a text."

"I'll send the team. Return to shore. I don't want you and De-Moss killed."

"There's no time for that," Brooke said before pocketing her phone.

The water was calm and the dinghy's three-horsepower motor made good time from the creek into the Severn River and around Horn Point. They reached the entrance to Carr Creek and Brooke beached the boat on the banks of the golf club. She climbed an embankment up onto the fairway with her pistol drawn. DeMoss, who was unarmed, followed her.

The fourth hole was almost directly in front of where they had landed, and when she reached the green, she saw what appeared to be a person lying next to the flag marking its hole. She hesitated and waited for DeMoss to come up beside her.

"Someone is lying there," she said pointing with her drawn pistol. "Their legs and hands are tied."

"Do you think it's Jennifer?"

Brooke scanned the green. She didn't see anyone.

DeMoss whispered, "We should wait for the others."

"I'm not going to wait if that's Jennifer and she's hurt."

"Akbar could be hiding in the trees watching us, waiting to shoot you."

"I'm not waiting."

Brooke began moving toward the body on the green. She was more afraid about what she might find than Akbar lurking in the shadows taking aim.

Was it Jennifer? Was she alive? Why would he leave her here?

With her left hand, she fished her cell phone from her pocket and hit its flashlight app, turning herself into an even more obvious target.

Brooke was close enough now to recognize that there was a black hood over the figure's head. Duct tape had been wrapped around the wrists and legs. Tucking her pistol into the waistband of her denim pants, Brooke leaned over the cloaked figure.

"Jennifer," she said softly as she reached down to remove the hood. "Honey, it's me."

There was no response.

"It could be a booby trap!" DeMoss called to her. He had

remained several yards back. But Brooke had already gently lifted the figure's head off the brown turf and was working to remove the tape. When it was loose, she removed the hood and gasped.

It was Aludra. Her throat had been slit. Now Brooke understood.

It had been Akbar texting her. He'd gotten her private cell number from Aludra after he'd realized that she had betrayed him. He had put a bomb in the trawler rigged to explode when the cabin door was opened and then had driven here and murdered his wife. The sound of the explosion across the river at the marina had been his cue to send Brooke the second text drawing her to the golf course and Aludra's corpse.

Brooke stood and used her phone as a spotlight as she slowly turned in a 360-degree circle shining it around the perimeter of the green. She suspected that Akbar was watching them, getting a sick thrill, but there was no sign of him or Jennifer. Only blackness and silence.

CHAPTER THIRTY-EIGHT

Near the border city of El Wak
Northeastern Kenya desert

As was his custom, the goat herder rose before sunrise to pray and tend to his herd before prodding his animals toward the grazing spot outside the walls of billionaire Umoja Owiti's estate. He had been warned that today would be the last that he could graze them near the compound because a visitor was arriving there the following day. The herder wanted to take full advantage of that prime location while he could.

Walks Many Miles did not go with him. He'd stayed behind to accompany Hani to El Wak where she could place a phone call to Langley. He needed her to tell Washington that he had survived the helicopter crash and the Falcon was coming to Owiti's compound tomorrow.

After breakfast, Miles left Hani cleaning utensils near the fire while he slipped into the hut to change into the baggy clothes that served as his disguise and wrap a scarf around his head to conceal everything except his eyes.

The old man had wanted to take the AK-47 assault rifle with him when he'd left with his goats, but Miles had convinced him to leave it hidden in the hut. Owiti's private security guards might become alarmed if they spotted the herder suddenly armed the day before the Falcon and his entourage was scheduled to arrive. *How would he explain it?*

Miles had just finished tightening the headscarf and tucking one pistol in the front of his pants and the other behind his back when he heard the sounds of an approaching vehicle.

He peeked through the narrow slit between the hut's doorway and its flap covering and saw a Toyota pickup drive past the goat pen toward Hani, who was standing near the campfire. He counted two men in its cab and three riding in the truck bed. From their dress and weapons, he assumed they were Al-Shabaab fighters.

Hani picked up a baseball bat–sized stick that she had gathered for the fire and readied herself. She was standing about five yards outside the hut's doorway. If she called for help, the men would know that she was not alone. She gripped the wood with both hands and raised it back over her shoulder ready to swing.

As soon as the truck stopped, three terrorists leaped from the truck bed. They began chanting her name, taunting her. The driver and front seat passenger joined them. Hani was now surrounded by five men who had formed a circle around her and the fire. Four of them were armed with assault rifles, but only one had unslung his gun. The other three rifles were strapped over the men's shoulders. The fifth intruder had a pistol tucked in his pants.

When Hani yelled at them to go away, the man holding his rifle pointed it into the air and fired a burst of rounds to frighten her. While she was watching him, one of the others darted up from behind her and slapped her hard on her buttocks. His buddies cheered as he pranced proudly back to his position in their circle. Hani turned her head to glare at him and when she did, a fighter who was standing in front of her bolted forward and grabbed the neckline of her dress, ripping it as he passed her so that it exposed one of her breasts. This prompted more jeers as Hani was now forced to clutch her stick with only her right hand, since she needed her left to hold up her top.

It was obvious to Miles what was about to happen unless he intervened. It would be five of them against him, and he knew that he would need to kill all of them. If anyone escaped, they would return with dozens more fighters.

For a moment, he considered not reacting. Perhaps it would be better for everyone if he simply averted his eyes. What if he were wounded? Taken prisoner? He had been sent to do recon, not prevent an Al-Shabaab rape. If he was successful in killing the men, other Al-Shabaab fighters would come looking for them. How safe would Hani and the goat herder be when that happened? Still, could he not act?

He considered grabbing the AK-47, but he'd not fired that weapon since he'd taken it from the Al-Shabaab sentry at the helicopter crash site. Shooting an unfamiliar rapid-fire weapon into a circle of men surrounding Hani would be imprecise.

Another terrorist ran at Hani, only this time she had anticipated him coming and smacked his shoulder hard with her stick. He nearly toppled over, but caught himself and retaliated by lunging at her. He threw a fist at her face but she ducked, and he fell forward clumsily toward the campfire, almost diving into it. His buddies roared with laughter.

Wait, Miles told himself. He drew the pistol from the front of his pants. *Not yet.*

The humiliated fighter righted himself, turned to face Hani again, and this time when she swung at him, he dodged her club and smacked her with his fist in her chest, knocking her backward onto the ground. Rushing forward, he kicked her hand, causing her to release her stick, before he plopped onto her abdomen, straddling her. With his hands, he forced her wrists above her head. She bucked but was not strong enough to throw him off her. Two of his partners knelt down and took hold of her wrists so the terrorist sitting on top of her could rip the rest of her blouse open with his hands. Another fighter grabbed her feet and jerked them apart.

Miles was done waiting. He ducked through the hut flap into the morning air with his pistol raised.

He'd waited until this moment because he knew the terrorists would be watching Hani. The attacker sitting on her, the two men grasping Hani's wrists and the fourth, who was holding her ankles apart, would not be able to use their weapons. Miles did not run at them like some wild banshee. He stepped deliberately from the hut and began firing.

Pop. Pop. His first target was the only terrorist who was not involved in pinning down Hani. He was standing about three feet from them and was cradling his AK-47 assault rifle, which he had fired in the air earlier, in his arms. Both rounds hit his chest and he collapsed as the remaining four attackers looked up from Hani, stunned that a gunman was now firing at them.

Pop. Pop. Two more rounds. Deliberate. Well aimed. Just like target practice. His target was the terrorist sitting on Hani's chest, who had a pistol tucked in his trousers; he slumped off of her.

The attacker who was holding Hani's feet leaped up and ran toward the truck without unslinging the assault rifle on his back. He was not an immediate threat because he was running away, so Miles focused on the two men who had been holding Hani's wrists. He fired at the man closest to him, who had risen to his feet and was in the process of grabbing his AK-47. Despite the close range, both shots missed when his target twisted his body sideways. Miles fired another two-round burst and then another before the man collapsed.

By this point, the fourth jihadist had sprung to his feet, unslung his AK-47, and aimed it at Miles's chest. Miles turned his gun so it was now pointed at the jihadist, and in that moment Miles realized the terrorist had beaten him to the draw. He was about to be shot.

Still prone on the ground, Hani snatched up her stick and jabbed it upward between the jihadist's legs, smacking him as hard as she could in his groin. He fired a round from his rifle, but he had flinched when stabbed in his privates, and the bullet missed Miles. He returned fire. One shot hit, but the second missed. Ducking to his left, Miles fired a second two-round burst while the terrorist was still recovering from Hani's blow. Both slugs hit their mark and the jihadist fell forward onto the ground.

That left only the terrorist who'd run for the truck. Its tires sprayed sand from the rear tires as he fled forward.

Miles had only one round remaining in his Sig Sauer 226 handgun so he cast it down and reached for his second pistol hidden behind his back. He had to kill that driver.

He emptied the entire fifteen-shot magazine into the fleeing vehicle. Bullets shattered the Toyota's rear window and punched holes into the driver's side of the cab. As Miles watched, the truck continued moving but gradually slowed. The engine stuttered and stopped. Next came the sound of the truck's horn, a sign that the driver had slumped forward against the steering wheel.

Miles reloaded both pistols and tucked one in his pants as Hani stood, still clutching her stick in one hand, and grasping her torn top in the other in an attempt to cover her chest. Their eyes met, but neither spoke as he slipped by her and began running toward the truck. He popped open the door with one hand while using the other to aim his handgun inside. Miles found himself looking at a man with half his face missing from the pistol rounds that had cut through the cab's wall and penetrated the driver's skull. Shoving the corpse into the passenger seat, Miles climbed behind the wheel, pushed in the clutch, restarted the truck, and put it into reverse.

When he glanced over his shoulder through the shattered rear window so he could guide the vehicle back to the campfire, he saw Hani swinging her club down onto the face of one of the terrorists. In her fury, she had forgotten about her tattered dress as she swung half-naked at him to ensure that he was dead before moving to the next attacker with her club. By the time Miles reached her, Hani had finished clubbing each man. He noticed her hands were splattered with blood. He did not ask if she was okay. She hurried into the hut to change her torn clothing and when she returned, he said, "Please help me load these bodies into the truck. We need to hurry."

The corpses were heavy and Miles and Hani were both covered with sweat when they finished.

"I'll be back as soon as I can," he said. "Do your best to get rid of any tire tracks."

He drove southwest in the direction of where he'd first encountered the goat herder, and after traveling for about twenty minutes, he stopped on a barren patch of hardened desert. Miles dragged three of the dead men from the truck and positioned them around the vehicle. He staged a fourth corpse just outside the passenger door, which he left open. When he had tugged the driver back behind the wheel, he was done. Beside each of the four bodies outside the truck, he placed an AK-47. Pausing, he walked several feet away and surveyed the grisly scene. He wanted it to appear that the men had been slaughtered during an ambush. Satisfied, he fired a single round from his pistol into the vehicle's gas tank. Miles did not expect the truck to explode, as they always did in movies. He was simply puncturing its tank.

He ripped a piece of fabric from one of the men's clothing, dabbed it in gasoline spilling from the truck, and walked fifty paces away. When a trickle of the escaping fuel reached his feet on the hard ground, he lit the fabric in his hand with matches that he'd taken from the crashed helicopter's emergency kit and tossed the burning rag onto the gas.

Miles ran in the opposite direction and was safely away when the remaining fuel in the truck's tank exploded into a large fireball.

By the time he made his way on foot back to the hut, Hani had washed off the blood splatters and swept the area of any telltale tire tracks. She greeted him with a clay cup of warm milk.

"We need to go into El Wak," he said.

"They will come looking for the men you killed."

"I left their bodies at least three kilometers from here. I'm hoping Al-Shabaab will assume it was either me or an American rescue party. I don't believe they will suspect you."

"But they will come here again," she said. "They will come again and again until someone stops them." Her voice did not sound angry, only sad, resigned.

"I couldn't let them rape you," he said.

She looked at his eyes and Miles saw that she had tears in hers. "Thank you," she whispered. "But now what?"

"Now, we go to El Wak. You make the call," he replied. But he knew that she was not asking him about his immediate plans. She was asking him about her future.

CHAPTER THIRTY-NINE

A deserted road
Rural Maryland, outside Annapolis

Lying in a fetal position inside a car trunk with a hood over her head and her ankles and wrists bound by duct tape, Jennifer Conner fought the urge to cry.

Jennifer wasn't certain what had happened after Cassy left her in the cabin. Moments after she'd gone, Aludra had appeared and said the FBI was coming to rescue her. But the FBI hadn't come. Akbar had come and taken her out of the cabin to the backseat of a car where he'd covered her with a blanket. She had heard Akbar and Aludra arguing in the front seat during the drive, but they were speaking in a foreign language so she hadn't understood them.

Jennifer had needed to use the toilet after riding for what seemed to be several hours. Aludra had taken her into some woods and when they were together, Jennifer could tell that Aludra had been crying. It looked as if Akbar had struck her face.

"Where's Cassy?" Jennifer had asked her.

"Just hurry up and don't ask questions!"

"What about the FBI?"

"Don't say another word about the FBI or he will kill us both."

Jennifer had again been put into the car's rear seat under a blanket and ordered not to move or speak. After another long drive, the car had stopped and Jennifer had heard both car doors open and shut. She thought she might be alone in the backseat but she had been afraid to peek out from under the blanket. Not long after that, she heard only one car door open and close. Akbar had driven a short distance and then stopped and removed her blanket. He'd ordered her out of the car. It was dark by now and Jennifer did not see Aludra. They had stopped near another parked car. Its trunk was open and he'd made her climb into it. After covering her head with a hood, he'd applied duct tape to her wrists and ankles and closed the trunk.

She had not seen Aludra. She had no idea what had happened to Cassy. *Did Cassy escape? Or had Akbar caught her hiding in the cabin and murdered her? Where is Aludra? What happened to her?*

Jennifer couldn't stretch out in the trunk, and her wrists and ankles were swollen because of how tightly he'd bound them. The car had been traveling on a smooth road when suddenly Akbar slowed and began riding onto a bumpy one. Jennifer's head slapped against the trunk floor several times. Now Akbar was slowing down, and Jennifer didn't like that. Akbar was cruel. She didn't want him to park, open the trunk, and hurt her. *Where is Aludra?*

The car stopped and Jennifer heard Akbar switch off its engine. She heard his car door open and shut. She braced herself.

But Akbar didn't open the trunk. Instead, Jennifer smelled cigarette smoke. Her father had smoked and the whiff reminded her of him.

What was that next sound? It sounded like a car engine. Was Akbar switching cars again? Would he put her in a new trunk or in the backseat under a blanket? Was this where he planned to kill her?

She heard another car door open and close. That was followed by Akbar's voice.

"What am I supposed to do now?" he asked.

"The Falcon wants the girl alive."

Wait! That is a stranger's voice. Who is he? She listened and tried to remember the sound of the man's voice. He didn't have a foreign accent like Akbar's. He sounded American, not too much different from Brooke Grant or even her own voice.

"The American president will not free our brothers in Gitmo in return for this donkey," she overheard Akbar say.

"Shall I tell the Falcon you are questioning him?"

"No. I'm merely saying this donkey is of no real worth to us any longer."

"Don't be a fool. This was never about exchanging the girl and the congressman's daughter for prisoners at Gitmo. The Falcon never expected President Allworth to agree."

"Then why did he demand their release?"

"To send our brothers in Gitmo a message. To remind them they are heroes in this war. To give them hope. To prove that we can reach anywhere—even into Washington, D.C.—and strike. The Falcon had other reasons for having you abduct the two girls, reasons that had nothing to do with Gitmo."

"I understand. We proved we could abduct the daughter of a member of Congress," Akbar said. "We proved we could abduct the daughter of a CIA agent. No one is safe and now everyone in Washington is worried about closing their eyes at night. I will beat this girl. I will disgrace her by taking her virginity."

"No. The Falcon does not want you to violate her. You must listen to his orders. Do not risk making him angry. He already is disappointed the congressman's daughter escaped from you."

Inside the car trunk, Jennifer couldn't help but grin. *Cassy escaped! She is free!*

"Aludra betrayed us," Akbar said. "She betrayed me. She is to blame for the girl's escape, not me."

"I told the Falcon that Aludra telephoned Washington from a store in the Virginia mountains. This is why he told you to kill her. But the congressman's daughter escaped from that cabin while you and Aludra were still in that store buying groceries. Cassy Adeogo slipped her feet from her riding boots, and that was your mistake. You wrapped tape around her boots instead of her ankles. That is how she escaped from the cabin and ran into the woods, and you are to blame."

Although she was locked inside the car trunk, the two men were standing so close outside it that Jennifer felt as if they were part of their conversation. *He killed Aludra! How does this stranger know that Aludra telephoned Brooke? How had he known about Cassy's oversize riding boots? He is telling Akbar about mistakes that Akbar had made. Is he his boss?*

Jennifer continued listening. "If I had not called and warned you," the stranger continued, "the FBI would have surprised you at that cabin, killed you, and rescued both girls."

Akbar didn't respond.

"I am the Falcon's eyes and ears here," the stranger said. "If you can't do what you have been told, others will. Aludra betrayed us and now she is dead."

Jennifer felt sorry for her.

"Aludra was a woman and women have no stomach for what is necessary," Akbar said. "Even when I beat her, she did not understand. She was too kind to the donkey in the trunk but I am not kind and now the donkey must deal only with me."

"Is that where you have the Conner girl?"

"Do you wish to see her? Her head is hooded. She will not see you."

"No! I have no interest in seeing her. And you may not rape her."

"Does her age trouble you? She is an infidel. Her age means nothing to me. She is an enemy of Allah and I will gladly remove her head."

"Akbar, you failed to kill General Grant as ordered."

"It was an impossible shot."

"Do not make excuses. The congressman's daughter escaped while you were watching her. You must not fail again."

"I will not. I swear it on my life as Allah is my protector and Master."

"Study these papers and wait for my call. I will tell the Falcon what you have said, that you have sworn an oath on your life."

"And the donkey?"

"Beat her if necessary, but again, you may not take her virginity. Not yet."

"How much longer before I am rid of her?"

"Not long. Study these instructions and wait for my call. *Assalamu alaykum wa rahmatullahi wa barakaatuhu wa maghfiratuhu.*"

"And may Allah's peace, mercy, and blessing be upon you too, my brother," Akbar replied.

Jennifer heard a door open, a car engine start, and the sound of a car leaving. When it was quiet outside, she said: "I need to use the toilet."

The trunk lid opened. Akbar removed the hood covering her face.

"I heard you clearly just now. Did you hear us talking? You did, didn't you?"

"I didn't hear anything."

He slapped her. "Do not lie to me, little donkey."

"I'm not lying. I need to use the toilet."

"I am not your servant. Piss in your pants."

She could see a manila envelope tucked under his left arm. As she watched, Akbar dialed a number on a cell phone and held it down to her ear.

"Hello, who is this?" Brooke Grant asked.

"Mommy!" Jennifer screamed.

Akbar backhanded Jennifer without losing his grip on the phone, making certain the blow was loud enough for Brooke to hear.

"Jennifer! Jennifer where are you?" Brooke asked.

Putting the phone to his ear, Akbar said, "She is my prisoner and I am going to beat her."

He ended their call.

Jennifer readied herself for another slap and worse, but Akbar slammed down the trunk lid and got behind the wheel. They began riding on the bumpy road through the woods again.

As Akbar was driving, he removed the SIM card and tossed the phone out the window into the trees.

CHAPTER FORTY

Rudy Adeogo stood in the doorway of his daughter's upstairs bedroom and watched as Dheeh tucked Cassy into bed and tenderly kissed her forehead.

"Get some sleep, baby love," Dheeh said.

"I'm afraid," Cassy replied.

"We'll leave your door open. Your father and I are in the bedroom right next door."

"There's no reason to be frightened now," Adeogo added. "There are police officers stationed outside our house. No one can come inside to hurt you."

"Did you look under the bed?"

"Yes," Dheeh responded. "Twice!"

"What about Jennifer? Has she been rescued yet?"

"No," Adeogo said, "but I am certain she will be." He had intentionally kept Cassy away from watching the television news and surfing the Internet. She had no idea that Akbar had blown up a boat in Annapolis, killing two FBI agents, and that Major Brooke Grant had found Aludra's body on the Naval Academy's golf course.

"Allah is watching over Jennifer," Dheeh said in a soothing voice. "Just as He watched over you, baby love."

"But she's only a half Muslim and *he* is a full Muslim," she replied. There was no need for Cassy to explain to her mother and father why Jennifer was only half Muslim or identify who "he" was.

"No, he is not a Muslim. He is an abomination," Adeogo said. "A corrupter of the truth."

"I heard someone say that Uncle George was a terrorist too. They said he changed his name to Abdul Hafeez and he killed Americans in Somalia. He cut off a man's hands."

Dheeh shot Adeogo an anxious look. They had never told Cassy the truth about her uncle George. Her grandparents, uncles, and aunts had shielded all of the children from Hafeez's radicalization and decision to join Al-Shabaab.

"You're old enough to hear the truth now," Adeogo said. "My youngest brother—your uncle—joined Al-Shabaab in Somalia. He became a terrorist."

"Then he was no different from the man who kidnapped me and Jennifer, and beat us."

"Your uncle would not have harmed you," Dheeh answered. "These are adult matters. Go to sleep, baby love."

"If they're adult matters, that evil man should have left Jennifer and me alone."

Dheeh stepped away from her daughter's bed and joined her husband in the room's doorway, where she switched off the light.

"I don't want it dark," Cassy cried out.

"We'll leave the door open," Dheeh replied. "The hallway light is on."

"I want to sleep in your room. In your bed. Please don't leave me alone here."

Dheeh looked at her husband, who nodded approvingly.

"Okay, baby love, but just tonight," Dheeh replied.

Cassy threw back her covers and scrambled from her bed. Dheeh put her arm around Cassy's shoulders and kissed her forehead.

"Hurry down to our room. I need to speak to your father and then we can read for a while," she said. One of the ways that the two of them bonded was by reading the same young adult fiction. Cassy would read one book and then give it to her mother.

After Cassy had left them in the hallway, Dheeh said, "I'm glad you told the truth about your brother to the world and our daughter. You were brave to go on television, but it was a secret we could no longer keep."

"You never wanted to come to Washington. I'm certain you are happy now that my career has been destroyed."

"How can you say that? I have always done what a good wife does. I simply warned you when you decided to run for Congress that you could not hide the truth about your brother."

"All I ever wanted was to help our people, to do good."

"You cannot do good based on a lie. And now that our daughter is safe, you cannot do good if you retreat into self-pity and shame. You must be an example for her and the world. You must show them that not all Muslims are like your brother. Now more than before, you must speak out. Is that something a wife who wants you to fail would say?"

He touched her shoulders and pulled her close to hug her, but she did not put her arms around him. Adeogo sensed there was something more bothering her than Dheeh's uncomfortableness with physical affection.

"What is it?" he asked.

"That woman who came to the house while Cassy was still missing. Mary Margaret Delaney."

"What about her?"

"You told me after she left that night that she had threatened you. You said she had learned about George and you told me that she was trying to blackmail you. She wanted to control you for her clients. That is why you decided to tell the truth—because you were not going to be her puppet—is that correct?"

"Yes, I would not let her turn me into her pawn."

"But you have only told me about this—how she wanted to blackmail you. You have not reported her to the authorities. You did not tell the FBI agents who were here with us that night. It must be against the law to threaten and blackmail a congressman. Why are you keeping silent about this horrible woman?"

"It doesn't matter now, does it? What would be the point now?"

"To punish her," Dheeh responded.

Adeogo shrugged.

"There is only one possible explanation for your actions," Dheeh continued. "This woman knows something else about you, doesn't she? There is more that she can tell."

Adeogo released his arms from around her back and stepped back from her, but he did not answer her question.

"I remember you first telling me about this Delaney woman after you first visited Washington, D.C. You told me she was sent by Timothy Coldridge to be your handler. She was helping him—helping run his presidential campaign. She became angry with you after you refused to speak at a press conference. You told me that she was angry, bitter, and wanted revenge against you."

Dheeh looked directly into his eyes and said, "This woman's hate for you is more than politics. Did you sleep with her?"

Although Adeogo had often thought about how he would react if Dheeh had confronted him, he found himself floundering for words, and during those few seconds of hesitation, Dheeh knew the answer.

She turned away from him and walked into their bedroom, shutting the door behind her.

Adeogo retreated downstairs to his office. He tried to work but couldn't concentrate. Dheeh was right. He had not reported Delaney's blackmail attempt because he was afraid she would reveal his infidelity. He closed his eyes and rested his head on his folded arms on the desktop. His political world and now his personal world were collapsing. Dheeh would never forgive him.

A loud knock on the front door woke him. He checked the time. It was a few minutes after four a.m. He had fallen asleep at his desk.

Peering through the front door's security peephole, he saw his congressional public information officer, Fatima Olol, standing next to the policeman stationed on the porch. The D.C. police had promised to remain outside his house until Akbar either was captured or killed. He swung open the door and welcomed her inside.

"Is Cassy okay?" Olol asked.

"Yes, she's upstairs with Dheeh sleeping in our bedroom."

"There's something we need to discuss," Olol said in a nervous voice.

Adeogo led her into his study for privacy. "What's so important that you've come at this hour?"

"Ebio Kattan from Al Arabic television called me a few minutes ago. She asked me about your relationship with Mary Margaret Delaney."

"What did she ask you?"

"She said reporters had seen Delaney visit your house before Cassy was rescued. She asked me if her visit had anything to do with your decision to tell reporters about your brother."

Olol paused, but Adeogo was not inclined to answer either of her questions.

"And then Kattan said something that is really, really upsetting."

Adeogo let out a sigh. *Here it comes*, he thought, bracing himself. He assumed Delaney had told the Al Arabic reporter about their sexual affair. His indiscretion. *Was there no end to her hatred for him? No end to what she would do to destroy him?*

"Ebio Kattan told me," Olol continued, "that Mary Margaret Delaney had just been found dead."

CHAPTER FORTY-ONE

Major Brooke Grant's farmhouse
Near Berryville, Virginia

Brooke Grant's preacher father had taught her that love was unlimited. You could never run out of room in your heart, he'd proclaimed. She was learning the same could be said for hate. She had thought it was impossible for her to be filled with more hatred than she'd felt after her parents had been murdered. She'd been wrong. The heart could hate without bounds or limits, and she hated Akbar.

She could not sleep. She was sitting in the kitchen at four a.m. reviewing everything that had happened in the past several hours. The text messages from Akbar. The explosion at the dock. Finding Aludra's body. The phone call from Akbar. Hearing Jennifer scream. Checking with the phone company only to discover dead ends. What could she have done differently to protect the child she loved?

Her cell phone rang and she gasped. Was it Akbar calling again to torment her? The Caller ID showed it was FBI Agent Wyatt Parker, but that didn't ease her fear. Had Jennifer been found? Had Akbar murdered her?

She answered.

"We got a body," Parker said.

"Jennifer?" Brooke asked, her voice an instant mixture of fear and alarm.

"No! No! A Washington lobbyist named Mary Margaret Delaney."

Brooke's feelings of relief turned to anger. Hadn't Parker known she would think first of Jennifer? Was he really that stupid? Or had he wanted in some sick way to frighten her?

"I'm sorry," he said. "Still a bit groggy. They woke me up." But he didn't sound regretful.

"Who's Delaney?"

"A Washington political fixer. She ran Governor Coldridge's presidential campaign last year against President Allworth. Her body was discovered an hour ago by the Park Police. They asked us to take a look, although it appears to be a simple case of suicide."

"The Park Police?" Brooke repeated.

"Yeah, Delaney was found inside her car on the George Washington Parkway near the Three Sisters, so it falls under their jurisdiction. You need to hurry before they send her body to the morgue."

"Why are they asking us?"

"Delaney visited Rudy Adeogo's house the other day shortly before he announced to the world that his brother was an international terrorist. The FBI is assuming Adeogo was planning on hiring Delaney to help him with damage control since she was a professional spin-meister. You know, make the fact that his brother was the most hated man in America a bit more palatable for the public. Now she's dead and they want to make sure there's no possible link with terrorism. It's a stretch, but everyone's so flustered by what's going on that terrorism is the first thing they think every time a body shows up. As far as I'm concerned, you can go back to sleep."

"No, I'll leave right now."

It was a good forty-minute drive from her farmhouse, but the morning commuter traffic hadn't yet started so she reached the George Washington Parkway in record time. The "GW," as it was known, was a double-wide freeway that snaked along the Virginia side of the Potomac River and featured several dramatic overlooks. One of the most popular was near the Three Sisters, tiny rocky islands that jutted from the center of the river. Like nearly every landmark in the area, there was a legend behind them. The most popular tale was about a Native American chief who'd marooned three maidens on the rocks after they'd refused to marry braves whom he'd chosen. While most of the Potomac River near Washington, D.C., was only four feet deep, the Three Sisters were the result of a geological fall line, and the channel around them plunged to depths of eighty feet. The women could not escape because of the deep, swift currents, so they cast a deadly curse on the three rocks. Onlookers claimed a strange moaning sound could be heard whenever another victim was about to be swallowed by the river swirling around the islands. Sadly, the legend attracted an occasional despondent individual looking to end his or her life either by tumbling down the embankment into the water or by some other means.

Mary Margaret Delaney had not drowned. Brooke found her still perched behind the steering wheel of her leased BMW. There was a .22-caliber Derringer resting on her lap. Agent Parker had arrived before Brooke and already chatted with the Park Police investigators. The fatal round had been fired upward into the roof of Delaney's mouth but had not exited the back of her skull. The bullet was still lodged inside her brain.

"Some people think a twenty-two short round is fairly harmless," Parker explained as Brooke bent down to look at Delaney inside her car. He was eager to demonstrate his knowledge of gunshots. "But it can be deadly at close range." As he continued babbling about how a .22-caliber handgun had been a popular pistol used by Mafia hitmen—because its quiet discharge blended with other noises such as a car door closing—Brooke focused on the crime scene before her.

Delaney was dressed in Saint Laurent studded jeans, a button-down pleated floral blouse, and silver leather jacket. Not counting Delaney's black leather boots, Brooke guessed the ensemble had easily cost around six thousand dollars. Her bright red hair was meticulously styled and her makeup was immaculate, as were her manicured nails. There was no wedding band, but she had diamond rings on both hands, along with a gold bracelet on her left wrist. She smelled of Versace perfume.

"Was the Derringer hers?" Brooke asked.

"I have no idea and, quite frankly, don't care," Parker replied. "Delaney wasn't a terrorist and I don't see anything here that would make me believe this is linked to terrorism, do you?"

"I can't see any connection between her death, Akbar, or the Falcon," Brooke acknowledged.

"Great. I'll tell the Park Police that we're done and thank them for including us." Parker checked his watch and added, "How about breakfast? We might as well grab some before we head back to the command post."

"Let's skip breakfast, go back to the command center, and get permission to interview Mohammad Al-Kader."

"Not again! You can't just let it die, can you?" Parker moaned. "Ever since Chairman Stanton accused him at a news conference of having possible links with radical Islamists, you've been busting my balls to interview that Imam. You know we don't have any evidence that Al-Kader has ever even met Akbar. You know he has lawyered up and you know we don't have the authorization to go pounding on his mosque's door, especially with all of the media stink that Representative Stanton has raised about sending the FBI into mosques."

"But if Al-Kader does know Akbar, he might know where Jennifer is being held. We need to bring him in and find out. That's what we would do if he weren't an Imam. We need to treat him like any other suspect. Just because he's got lawyers and is a religious figure who's been thrust into the national limelight by Stanton is no reason to treat him differently."

"You're being naïve, Major Grant, and desperate, but if you insist, I'll pass your request up to the director again. But not until after I have breakfast, because I know asking for permission to interview Al-Kader is a waste of my time. Now do you want to get breakfast or not?"

"No, as long as I'm this close to D.C., I'm going to check on my uncle." Brooke was irked by Parker's timidity in pursuing Al-Kader and had no interest in watching him enjoy a leisurely stack of pancakes while Jennifer was missing.

"Suit yourself." Parker shrugged as he turned toward a group of Park Police detectives standing about twenty feet away.

Brooke started walking in the opposite direction toward her car when a young woman wearing a Park Police uniform intercepted her.

"Excuse me, Major Grant, do you have a moment?" the woman asked. "I recognized you from the television newscasts. I'm Cindy Gural, the officer who found Ms. Delaney's body this morning."

They were speaking out of hearing distance of Parker and the detectives.

"Everyone's decided this is a suicide," Gural said, "but I'm not so sure. I think this scene might have been staged."

"Why are you telling me?" Brooke asked.

"Oh, I already told them," Gural replied, nodding toward the detectives. "But I've only been working on this job for six months, so they blew me off even though I used to be a D.C. cop before joining the Park Police."

"What makes you think this scene was staged?"

"Lots of things," Gural said in a low voice, "but the biggest reason is personal. You see, my brother ended his own life and before he did it, he was a mess. He was super depressed. He wouldn't eat. Didn't want to talk to anyone. Just sat in his room with the shades drawn. He certainly didn't get all dressed up and go out bar hopping."

"I'm sorry for your loss," Brooke said, "but people react differently to depression and stress. I'm curious, who told you Ms. Delaney was out bar hopping?"

"When I discovered her body parked up here, I looked into her purse for an ID, and there was a credit card receipt in her wallet with a time stamp. It was from the After Hours, a club in D.C. Are you familiar with it?"

"No."

"It's a new place that caters to really wealthy lobbyists and other big shots. It's got a reputation for being a pickup bar. I telephoned it and spoke to its night manager."

"He was still there?"

"Yeah, the place was closed but he was still finishing up some paperwork and he said everyone knew Delaney because she was the sort everyone noticed. He said she was there with a girlfriend drinking, so I called that woman."

"You called her?"

"I know, I should have just let the detectives handle it," Gural said. "But I didn't. Like I said, I used to be a D.C. cop. Anyway, her girlfriend said Delaney had been in a great mood that night. They were having a good time when Delaney got a call from a client who demanded that she drop everything and meet him. Delaney paid her tab and left to meet this guy."

"Did Delaney mention a name?"

"Nope, just that he was a new client and she had to meet him even though it was late."

"Maybe she met him, got upset about some business deal, and drove out here to kill herself on the spur of the moment," Brooke suggested.

"You know, my brother, he shot himself and I remember the detectives telling us women used pills and always thought things through before they did it. Men, they always shot themselves and it was more impulsive. Another thing, my brother, he stuck a twelve-gauge in his mouth. I'm sure he wanted to make sure he died. He didn't want to end up paralyzed."

Brooke didn't reply.

"When I found Ms. Delaney's body, I started thinking," Gural continued, "why shoot yourself in the mouth, knowing it might not do the trick? Why use a small-caliber handgun?"

"Maybe it was the only pistol she owned."

"And maybe someone else shot her because the murderer knew

there wouldn't be much blood splatter. Blood from the wound would pool in her mouth or run down her throat and not drip all over wherever she was killed."

Brooke wasn't certain if Gural's concerns were legitimate or far-fetched, tainted by memories of her brother's death.

"Did you look at her earlobes?" Gural asked.

"No."

"The cartilage in one of them was torn. She had a dangling earring in her right ear but no earring in her left ear and the skin was torn, like someone had ripped the earring down through the skin. I think it got ripped out during a struggle. It's not in that car. She also had a missing fingernail tip—a fake fingernail had been torn off. What woman who gets all dressed up for a night at a bar leaves off one fake fingernail?"

"That does seem odd, but I really can't help you," Brooke replied. "My child is missing."

"Oh, I know, Major Grant. It's been all over the news and I know you don't have time to waste on this, but after you save your child, after you catch that terrorist, maybe you and I can take another look at this so-called suicide. I don't know the woman who is dead over in that car and she might have decided to end it all. I get that. Like I said, I had a brother who ended his own life. But if she was murdered, then the killer needs to be caught. That woman's friends need to know the truth because, trust me, after a suicide, everyone feels guilty and begins asking if they could have done something different, said something different to save that person. That's a lot to carry on your shoulders."

Brooke took Gural's number and thanked her before driving her Jaguar south on the GW parkway across the bridge into the city.

She found her aunt Geraldine asleep in the recliner next to Uncle Frank inside the ICU ward at George Washington University hospital. The general's face remained covered with bandages; he still had not awakened from his coma, but they had removed his breathing tube because he was now capable of breathing on his own, which was a hopeful sign. Rather than disturbing her aunt, Brooke spoke briefly to the charge nurse and took the elevator to the ground floor where she ducked into the hospital cafeteria. The grill hadn't yet opened, so she sat at a table and checked the *Washington Post* on her phone. A small item posted only minutes earlier on the paper's website noted the discovery of Mary Margaret Delaney's body near the Three Sisters. The police were quoted saying it appeared to be a suicide.

Lieutenant Colonel Gabe DeMoss interrupted Brooke's reading. "Waiting for one of those egg breakfast sandwiches I told you about?"

"What are doing here so early?" Brooke asked, smiling.

"Agent Parker said I'd find you here. I wanted to give you some great news." He took a seat next to her. "Walks Many Miles has surfaced in Kenya."

"Where? Has he been captured? Is he okay?" Brooke asked, clearly alarmed about his fate.

"Hey, I can only answer one question at a time. Yes, he's fine, and no, he's not been captured. We got a call from a Kenyan woman who said Miles asked her to notify us. He's been hiding in a hut with this woman and her father. They're goat herders near a town called El Wak on the border with Somalia."

"When is the agency sending a team to get him out of there?"

"Miles didn't ask to be rescued. He's going to complete his SAD mission."

Brooke's initial smile was replaced by a frown. "How can he complete a six-man assignment by himself without getting caught or killed?"

"He's proven he can take care of himself," DeMoss said admiringly.

Brooke glanced around them. Only two other couples were in the dining room waiting for the grill to open, and neither of them was within listening distance. "I'm not doubting his abilities, but he's not safe as long as someone here in Washington is betraying him by sending reports back to the Falcon and Al-Shabaab."

"The Viper," DeMoss replied. "Don't worry. As soon as her call came in, it was compartmentalized for security reasons. Only select members of the NSC at the White House were informed on a need-to-know basis, as well as Agent Parker."

Brooke sat silent for a moment thinking before she asked: "Did Agent Parker tell you why I'm up so early—that I came here after examining Mary Margaret Delaney's body at the Three Sisters?"

"Yes. He said you were angry because he won't let you drive over to Mohammad Al-Kader's mosque, throw some cuffs on him, and haul him in for questioning about Jennifer and Akbar."

"I don't see why we're not doing that."

"Have you considered the FBI and CIA might have an ulterior motive for not wanting you barging in on the Imam?"

"What possible reason would they have?"

"They could be intercepting communications between Al-Kader and the Falcon, if they're in touch with each other, or between him and the Viper. God, I hate these bird and reptile aliases," he said. "But my point is that they might have a higher priority."

"Higher than getting Jennifer back alive and safe?" she asked, clearly insulted.

"I'm just saying the agency and NSA might be keeping a close eye on him for reasons other than finding Jennifer. Have you ever heard the term 'a wilderness of mirrors'? It's from an old poem, but James Jesus Angleton, the famous mole hunter at the CIA, used it to describe the intelligence business where everyone uses everyone else and people double- and triple-cross each other."

"What do you know about Al-Kader that I don't?"

"Nothing. I really don't have some inside information on this. I'm just urging you to remember that at one point Al-Kader was recruited and worked for the agency. Now he's working for the other side. Or is he?"

DeMoss noticed the gate that separated them from the hospital grill was being opened. "Let's grab some of those egg sandwiches," he said enthusiastically, rising from the table. "I'll buy."

Brooke followed DeMoss into the grill, but she picked a yogurt and banana instead of the greasy sandwich that he was craving. As she was standing in line at the cash register to pay, she noticed a plump woman hurrying toward DeMoss, who was still waiting for his sandwich.

"Funny seeing you here, Don," the woman chirped, addressing DeMoss. "It's Rhapsody from the Bean and Bagel."

"I'm sorry," DeMoss replied. "You must have me confused with someone else. My name isn't Don."

"Honey, I may have the name wrong, but I never forget a customer's face, especially a handsome one. You're Mr. CM/CR—café misto with a cinnamon raisin bagel—remember? You used to stop at the B and B while making your sales rounds."

"I've never been to any bagel shop in northern Virginia," he answered good-naturedly. He glanced over at Brooke, who was standing close enough to hear their conversation.

"Then, honey," the woman continued, "you got a twin out there. What do they call it? A dobble-something."

"Doppelgänger," he quietly volunteered.

"I apologize. I must be losing my mind, but then what do you expect? My mother's upstairs recovering from a kidney operation and they just told me the bill is going to be nearly a hundred grand. She's got insurance but that ain't going to cover half of that. Sorry to have bothered you."

"No problem," he replied, his eyes still watching Brooke. "I get confused with other people all of the time."

PART FIVE

—◦—

TWICE BETRAYED

فالألم ليس قدراً؛ إنّه اختيار.

Al‘alam lays masir: bal hu khiar.
Pain is not a fate: It is a choice

—popular Arab saying

CHAPTER FORTY-TWO

Rayburn House Office Building
Capitol Hill
Washington, D.C.

Representative Thomas Edgar Stanton asked Robert Hazlett to meet with him privately in his congressional office in the Rayburn House Office building instead of the House Permanent Intelligence Committee's suites. Hazlett was considered the nation's most vocal critic of Islam and ranked number one on the OIN's list of Islamophobic Americans. Having Hazlett saunter through the always-bustling U.S. Capitol Visitor Center and register as a guest at the committee's underground offices would needlessly inflame critics who already were accusing Stanton of being anti-Muslim.

For more than two decades, Hazlett had worked as a Middle Eastern expert at the State Department, but he'd been fired after he published a report called *Creeping Jihadism*. In it, Hazlett warned that the steady migration of Muslims into Europe was creating a subtle but important shift in political power away from democracy toward Islamic Sharia law, which he described as being both totalitarian and repressive. The OIN had unleashed a maelstrom attack against Hazlett with Omar Nader demanding his firing. But Hazlett couldn't be let go for expressing his opinion. Under mounting pressure from the OIN, his politically sensitive bosses found a loophole. They noted that he had given an interview to a newspaper reporter without first clearing it with the State Department's public information office. While that happened frequently, it was enough of a technical violation to justify firing him. After losing his State Department post, Hazlett had used his savings to create a website also called *Creeping Jihadism*, which he now operated as his own private Islamic watchdog group.

Stanton got right to the point when Hazlett settled into an overstuffed chair. "My staff is divided about whether the Intelligence Committee should call you as a witness at the hearings that I plan to soon conduct. Some members have said they'll protest if you're included."

"That's hardly surprising," Hazlett replied nonchalantly in a nasal voice. "Predictably, your call for hearings has prompted the OIN and Omar Nader to attack you personally and call for a million-man Muslim march on Washington, although they're also inviting other religious groups to join them."

"Yes, they're angry with me, but I'm not nearly as high on the OIN's enemies list as you are."

Stanton eyeballed his guest. Hazlett was in his early seventies, thin, and mostly bald. What was left of the gray hair on the sides of his head was pulled back into a ponytail that dipped down to his open-collared shirt. He was wearing a worn navy blazer with leather patches on the elbows and a pair of denim jeans, which made him appear more like a 1960s hippie than the Rhodes Scholar he had been.

"The OIN and Omar Nader are just getting started on you," Hazlett warned. "Trust me, they are relentless and they never forget. I read that you already have an opponent campaigning for your congressional seat. Scratch the surface and I guarantee you'll find Omar Nader's fingerprints."

"My opponent is the same college professor who campaigned against me before."

"Maybe so, but if you have your people go through his financial reports as soon as they're made public, I'll wager you'll discover that he's getting contributions from a slew of newly organized PACs with patriotic sounding names. It won't be easy to trace, because the OIN is highly skilled at hiding its tracks, but if you dig deep enough and long enough, you'll find those PACs are being funded by straw men who are using OIN funds."

From the skeptical look on Stanton's face, it appeared that he seemed unconvinced, so Hazlett added, "I read on the Internet that you're having a rally this weekend in South Carolina, aren't you?"

"Some of my supporters are hosting a little get-together for me. It's backlash to the OIN's call for its million-man march on Washington."

"You should expect OIN protesters to show up."

"I've never had protesters at one of my rallies, even when I've made unpopular decisions."

"Nader and the OIN will pay them to be there waving signs accusing you of being an Islamophobe."

"Is that even a real word?" Stanton asked, smiling. "I imagine quite a few voters in my conservative district probably are Islamophobes."

"You shouldn't take this so lightly, Congressman. The OIN will be looking for your supporters who are Islamophobes. They're going to be playing to the national media, hoping for angry interactions with your people that will make for good television. You're already being cast as a new Senator Joe McCarthy. I don't mean to be rude, Congressman, but you are underestimating the OIN and Omar Nader. They cost me my federal career and they're out to destroy you too."

Continuing, Hazlett said, "The OIN will not tolerate any criticism of Islam or the Prophet Muhammad. None, and that is not the norm with other religions. The Roman Catholic Church under recent popes has been open to discussions within its ranks about such formerly taboo subjects as divorce, homosexuality, and the role of women. But no such talk is permitted inside the OIN. It's immediately called blasphemy. Can you name any other organization in the world affiliated with a religion that publishes a list of persons who it considers evil? That's what the OIN's Islamophobia list is all about—accusing anyone who dares criticize Islam of being a bigot and then going after them. The OIN refuses to admit it, but it represents Islamic supremacy. Anyone who disagrees with it becomes the enemy. Now that list includes you. Tell me, Mr. Chairman, have you ever read the Quran?"

"No, I'm Southern Baptist."

"Most Americans assume it's a book like the Holy Bible or the Torah, a collection of smaller books written by different prophets or historians that are meant to guide us through our lives. But the Quran was written by only one man, Muhammad, and it is meant to be taken literally—every word. And those words are very specific about how a person is supposed to live his life."

"I don't see how that's much different from most religions. Christians have the Ten Commandments and my Jewish friends tell me the Torah is filled with laws."

"But the Quran *is* different. It says that all other religions are an abomination and there's no divide between state and church. According to the OIN, devout Muslims are obligated to follow Sharia law and Sharia law says anyone who criticizes Allah or the Quran or Muhammad or Islam should be put to death. You've got to understand that Sharia law is not just a religious code; it's the law. It's meant to replace all governments. Jihadists don't believe in any form of societal authority or government except Sharia law, and they demand that their followers adhere to it or they will burn in hell fire."

"There's no 'Render therefore unto Caesar the things that are Caesar's and unto God the things that are God's' caveat?"

"You know your Bible."

Stanton chuckled. "I'm a forced graduate of Miss Murphy's Sunday school classes as a kid and she was a stickler for memorization."

"There is no separation of church and state," Hazlett replied. "Attempts to establish any other form of government *is* a sin."

"Mr. Hazlett, there are millions of law-abiding and peaceful Muslims living in western democracies. They aren't trying to overthrow those governments."

"Muslims move into a country and are accorded the same religious protections as everyone else. But the radicals among them demand adherence to Sharia law and that law requires a totalitarian lifestyle. As soon as their numbers start growing, jihadists begin persecuting Muslims who aren't adhering to Sharia law. Dissent is squelched, often with violence, and then jihadists begin striking out against non-Muslims. The Quran says there will never be peace until only Islam and Sharia law have been established in every nation."

"The Muslims who I know personally are not fanatics and don't fit what you are describing," Stanton replied.

"Not all Muslims are jihadists, but their leaders have done little to stop the radicals among them. Why? Because they're afraid. They're afraid of their own people because they are fanatics willing to blow themselves up. Everyone knows that these extremists will kill anyone—famous authors, cartoonists, and politicians—anyone who dares to criticize them. Drawing an unflattering picture of Muhammad is enough to get a death sentence. There's something else about the Quran that you need to understand. Other religions are based on honesty. But Islamic leaders say it's okay to lie to non-Muslims when it helps promote the spread of their religion. It's called *taqiyya* and it's why radical Islamists in Iran and other Arab states can tell us one thing to our faces without ever having any intention of actually doing it."

After their meeting ended, Stanton wasn't certain what to think about Hazlett. His initial reaction was that his guest was both obsessed with Islam and paranoid about the OIN, but what he'd said was definitely chilling. While he was mulling over Hazlett's warning, an aide entered Stanton's office and said that Representative Rudy Adeogo was calling.

Stanton picked up the line. "Mr. Adeogo," he said, "I'm happy your daughter has been returned safely to you. I know her kidnapping and your public revelation about your brother have made this an extremely difficult time for you. It's certainly not how most freshman congressmen envision spending their first months in office."

"Thank you, Mr. Chairman, for your concern; the matters you have just mentioned are why I am calling. I've heard you're having a rally in South Carolina this weekend, and I am wondering if you would be willing to invite me to appear on stage with you?"

"For what purpose?" Stanton asked.

"The last time we spoke—when my daughter was still being held hostage—I promised to support your call for committee hearings. I can speak freely now that she's been rescued, and I have a lot to say about the insidious spread of radical Islam."

"Having you attend would certainly stir things up in the media. You haven't appeared in public since your statement about your brother, am I correct?"

"I have remained sequestered inside my house, that is correct, but it is time for me to speak, which is why I am asking to appear with you in Smithville at your rally. As you just noted, it would be my first public appearance since my statement about my brother and my daughter's rescue."

"Tell me, what do you hope to accomplish coming to my rally? What sort of statement would you be making in Smithville?"

"I would condemn radical Islamists and explain how extremists, such as Mohammad Al-Kader, are corrupting the minds of our youth. I know this personally because my own brother was seduced by radicalism. I would repeat that I never supported what my younger brother did, and I certainly never betrayed our country."

"I gather you think appearing on stage with me—the so-called new Joe McCarthy—would send the public a clear message. If I think you cut muster as a Muslim, then you must be okay, is that what you're after?"

"I would not put it that way, but yes, I believe appearing with you would reinforce to the public that I am not a radical like my younger brother."

"In essence, I'd be giving you my seal of approval, so to speak."

"And my appearance would give you my so-called seal of approval as a Muslim," Adeogo replied. "The OIN and Omar Nader are accusing you of being Islamophobic. Having a Muslim standing shoulder-to-shoulder with you, saying you are not an Islamophobe and your hearings are not anti-Muslim but merely an examination into whether political correctness is hampering our country's efforts to ferret out radicals—yes, that could help your cause, as well, at the rally."

"What happens if reporters accuse you of hypocrisy?"

"Because I didn't tell authorities about my brother?"

"That has been a hot topic in the media. Commentators are condemning you for not speaking out earlier about him, for not identifying him during the Somalia embassy crisis."

"And what would that have accomplished? I now regret my silence, but I had no real information to provide, other than to tell authorities that Abdul Hafeez had changed his family name. Let's not forget that radical Islamists abducted my daughter and are still holding Jennifer Conner captive. I am not only the one member of Congress who is a Muslim, I am also the one member whose daughter has been threatened and terrorized by these animals. Fighting them is personal to me *because* they corrupted my younger brother, stealing him from our family with their radical teachings, and *because* they later kidnapped and beat my only child. I believe that takes precedence over the fact that I didn't mention that Abdul Hafeez and I once shared the same last name."

"I've been warned that Omar Nader and the OIN will be sending protesters to my rally. Are you prepared for what they will throw at you?"

"I have never cared for Omar Nader's bullying tactics and I will tell the media that the OIN squelches dissent. I will read a personal e-mail that Omar Nader sent me. In it, he tells me specific words that are acceptable for me to use as a Muslim when discussing terrorism and words that the OIN actually forbids Muslims from saying about Islam. Of course, I will also condemn the OIN for its attacks on you. This is America. No group should ever be able to censor anyone simply because it doesn't agree with what you are saying."

"If you are willing to say all of that about the hearings and the OIN and Omar Nader, then, Representative Adeogo, consider yourself invited to Smithville."

CHAPTER FORTY-THREE

En route to El Wak
Near the Somalia-Kenya border

The four Land Rovers speeding in the direction of El Wak fit the intel description that Israeli intelligence had sent to the CIA. The Falcon and his entourage were returning to the mansion of billionaire businessman Umoja Owiti.

At 12:32 a.m., when the vehicles were within a mile of the border, a Hellfire missile streaked through the black sky. It smacked into the lead SUV with such force that the vehicle seemed to vaporize in a burst of flames. The Land Rover traveling directly behind flew from the road. It performed a backward flip that ended with it lying upside down and on fire. A second missile smacked into the third SUV in the caravan, destroying it and causing the fourth Land Rover to swerve out of control off the road before it came to an abrupt stop. Within seconds, two Apache attack helicopters swooped over the carnage, firing their 30-millimeter chain guns at the three men who'd survived the missile attack and were scrambling for cover. On the Apaches' black-and-white night cameras the fleeing terrorists glowed white and shook uncontrollably when the burst of rounds ripped into them.

Next to appear was a Bell UH-1 helicopter, the military's workhorse, which landed near the first destroyed vehicle while the two Apaches circled above with their guns ready, all under the watchful eye of a Predator drone flying high above them on alert for possible insurgents. A six-man SAD team disembarked and immediately confirmed that all occupants of the four Land Rovers had been killed. Because the Falcon had never appeared in public without covering his face, the CIA knew it would be difficult to positively identify him. The team photographed every corpse, including those in the burning wreckage, took body measurements from the victims not incinerated by the Hellfires, and retrieved DNA samples before returning to the Huey. CIA forensic specialists would compare that data to what was known about the Falcon based on digital imaging and computerized reconstruction techniques.

Miles had been told to position himself near Owiti's estate. His assignment from Langley had been relayed to him through Hani during her brief telephone call to Washington. He was to monitor the billionaire's compound to learn if any vehicles arrived in advance of the now destroyed Land Rovers. Although unlikely, it was possible the Falcon might have traveled in a separate convoy. He was also instructed to watch for Owiti on the chance the billionaire might leave the compound to meet the Falcon in some other location. He had been hiding on a slight bluff some two hundred yards outside the compound since daybreak with instructions not to leave for any reason.

Having destroyed the convoy, the three helicopters and Predator swung west across the Somali border into Kenya to collect Miles. He heard the sound of the aircrafts' blades before he could see them. Thanks to night vision and thermal imaging equipment, the pilots had no trouble spotting him. While the two Apaches and the Predator drone kept watch on the compound for Owiti's private guard force, the Huey swept down.

Miles removed the material covering his face and lifted both of his hands above his head to show that he was not carrying a weapon as he ran to the now hovering helicopter. He didn't want to be mistaken for a terrorist. As soon as he boarded, the helicopter lifted upward.

Strapped into a seat and handed a headset, Miles found himself speaking to the commander of SAD operations as well as CIA

Director Payton Grainger, who was monitoring the mission from Langley.

"Good to have you back with us, Miles," Grainger said. "Or should I call you 'Chief'?"

"Nice to be back, sir." Having dispensed with that greeting, Miles said, "No vehicles have arrived at the Owiti estate since first light yesterday morning, sir. There's no evidence that the Falcon is inside the compound." His eyes-on-the-ground report confirmed what satellite images and drones had noted during the past thirty hours watching the estate.

"Sirs," Miles said, "I did observe two Land Rovers carrying what appeared to be members of Owiti's private security force exit the compound about an hour ago heading in the direction of El Wak. But that was the only movement."

"If the Falcon was in that convoy as reported by the Israelis, then there's no reason for us to engage Owiti's private army or spark an international incident by attacking his residence," Grainger replied. "You're free to head to Nairobi."

Miles was disappointed. If Owiti was bankrolling the Falcon, both men deserved the same Hellfire missile fate.

It was the SAD team leader aboard the Huey who spoke next. "Sir, there were only six insurgents in the four Land Rovers."

"Are you certain of that count?" Grainger asked.

"Yes, sir, six tangos, and that includes the ones who were crispy."

In the past, the Falcon had never traveled without at least twice that number in his entourage.

No one responded, but everyone participating in the call understood the implication. It was possible they had missed the Falcon.

"Sir," Miles said, "the woman, Hani, and her father who have hidden me here in Kenya, I'd like permission to take them with us to Nairobi."

"For what reason, soldier?" Grainger asked.

"El Wak is a tiny town, and it's only a matter of time before someone realizes Hani made a telephone call to the United

States—something she'd never done before. They could link her to tonight's attack on the convoy."

Grainger considered the request but only for a moment. "We can't just swoop in and pick up two locals."

"Couldn't we arrange safe passage for them through the State Department as political refugees?"

"It could take months to get through all the necessary hoops. And we have rules about who this agency resettles. We can't accept someone simply because they provided you with temporary shelter."

"With all due respect, sir, I feel a moral obligation. I believe the woman already has been beaten by Al-Shabaab. It's just a matter of time before she and her father are murdered."

Grainger considered the urgency of Miles's request. "The best we can offer is a lift to the American embassy in Nairobi. I'll talk to the State Department, but no promises of resettlement. Is that clear?"

"Thank you, sir."

It took less than ten minutes for the Huey to reach the hut that Hani and her father shared. As they circled it, the SAD team's leader asked through his headphones: "Do goats sleep on their sides or are those goats down there dead?"

Miles felt a sense of alarm.

"Our heat sensors are not detecting anything from the goats," one of the Apache pilots said. "They're definitely dead."

There was no sign of Hani or her father when the Huey landed. The SAD team moved methodically across the hard-packed earth toward the flap that served as the hut's door. There was no outside morning fire, which Miles took as another worrisome signal. Hani usually kept the embers burning throughout the night.

"We got no thermals from inside that hut," an Apache pilot said through his mouthpiece as the two attack helicopters circled above.

"Hani?" Miles called from the entrance. There was no answer. Two SAD squad members ducked under the flap. Miles followed them. The first body that Miles spotted was the goat herder sprawled on the floor surrounded by spent AK-47 cartridges. His rifle had been taken by the men who had killed him. Hani's corpse was lying close by. She had been stripped naked and her breasts had been cut off, which was another trademark of terrorists in Africa who raped and mutilated women. Her face was frozen in a silent scream.

"Don't touch anything," the SAD leader warned. "Good chance they're booby trapped."

There was nothing any of them could do but to return to the Huey. As the aircraft rose, Miles tried to quiet the guilt rising within him. The fate of the old man and Hani had been set before he'd chanced upon them, he told himself. Jihadists had been harassing the goat herder before Miles first spotted him. He assumed that Hani had been assaulted by insurgents on the day when the old man had first taken him to see Owiti's mansion. She'd had bruises on her face and puffy eyes. Their cruel deaths were not his fault. And then another thought came to him.

He had watched Owiti's private security guards leaving the compound earlier that night. Was this their handiwork or Al-Shabaab's?

And still another thought. Was the killing of Hani and her father coincidental or had Owiti's goons been told that they were hiding Miles and come searching for him? Had they tortured Hani to learn where he was hiding?

He pictured Hani's face. Imagined her torture.

The violence that he had watched against the old man, who simply wished to tend his goats, and Hani, who had suffered so much even before she'd died, made him furious and physically ill. He thought of Brooke Grant. He thought about Jennifer.

It was time for him to return to Washington.

CHAPTER FORTY-FOUR

Sacred Seas, *a yacht*
Off the Somali coast

S ome eight hundred miles away from Walks Many Miles, a
Eurocopter EC175 approached the top deck of the ninety-foot
luxury yacht *Sacred Seas* in the Gulf of Aden. No other private boat would have dared anchor so close to the Somali shoreline. But billionaire Umoja Owiti wasn't concerned. Al-Shabaab
had warned pirates not to approach his yacht, and piracy was much
better organized and controlled in Somalia than was often believed
in the West. No Somali pirates acted without permission of their
financiers—warlords or corrupt business owners and government
officials. The pirates relied on Al-Shabaab to guard ports in Somalia's most southern tip where captured vessels were docked while
awaiting ransom payments. If some renegade Somalia pirate had
taken it upon himself to attack the Owiti's boat, he would have
been greeted by a battery of sophisticated weaponry and a security
force eager to draw first blood.

The helicopter landed on an upper deck where Umoja Owiti's
chief butler was waiting with warm hand towels to greet the Falcon
and his bodyguards.

"Welcome to Mr. Owiti's pleasure craft," the butler said in his
formal English accent. "May I say it's good to see you again, sir?"

"No diamond-encrusted floors to walk upon barefoot?" the Falcon asked, glancing at the polished teak decking that edged the
helipad.

"No, sir, but the parlor where Mr. Owiti is waiting does have a fourteen-carat gold-covered ceiling and walls decorated with hand-painted porcelain tiles. I'm certain you will feel quite comfortable there."

Owiti was speaking on a satellite phone when the Falcon joined him. Owiti nodded and held up a finger, indicating that he was almost finished talking, as his butler offered the Falcon tea and cookies, which he declined, preferring to keep his face covered except for his dark eyes. He sat on a white leather sofa monogrammed with Owiti's initials, which also had been painted on the porcelain tiles on the cabin's walls as well as inlaid into its marble floor.

Ending his call, Owiti greeted his guest. "Welcome, my friend. I have just learned that your four-vehicle caravan was attacked and destroyed by American helicopters near the border less than an hour ago. You sent six of your men to their deaths."

"I sent them to paradise. They answered the call of Allah."

"His call or yours?"

"I am His humble servant, as are you."

"Everything happened just as your American spy warned us it would," Owiti replied. "Your decoy fooled them. As you assured me, this source of yours in Washington is highly placed."

"You asked me to demonstrate what I am capable of and I have shown you, beginning with the attack at the Mandera college. Are you satisfied now—enough that we can move forward?"

"How close is this serpent of yours to the American president?" Owiti asked, dodging the Falcon's question.

"If I gave the order, she would be dead tomorrow. His breath is warm on her neck."

"Then why not strike? Why bother killing students in Africa or abducting girls from privileged schools. Kill President Allworth."

"Killing a president only gets us a new one. What I need from you will enable me to cripple their entire nation."

"That is a very ambitious goal, my friend." Owiti chuckled, taking a cup of tea and raising a cookie to his lips. He was now sitting across from the Falcon on a matching white sofa. "With my money, you hope to buy something exotic. Perhaps the recipe for a deadly virus with no known cure. A poison to dump into an American city's water supply."

"That is a plot of a bad American movie."

"A bomb, then. A nuclear bomb, perhaps?"

"It is also a movie plot, but one that can actually be put into action," the Falcon replied. "It can be done."

"Oh, my friend, you do have big ambitions. Others have tried to buy nuclear devices from Russia or even Pakistan or India, but the Americans have always caught them. What makes you believe you can do what others can't?"

"The Americans keep track of known nuclear weapons and the raw materials needed to make a bomb. They follow the money everywhere in the world. But Allah, bless His holy name, has shown me a way to make them blind and avoid detection."

"I'm listening," Owiti said, finishing another cookie.

"I will go to where the Americans cannot see, to the only country where the Americans have no eyes, and I will buy my bomb with currency the Americans cannot track."

Owiti wiped his lips with a linen napkin and leaned forward. "And where is this place where the Great Satan is blind?"

"It is not Russia, which is always suspect. It is North Korea. For the right price, anything is possible when dealing with the eternal president and supreme ruler of the Democratic People's Republic of Korea."

"And what is the right price?"

"A billion dollars."

Owiti chuckled. "You are ambitious, my friend, but that is a large sum of money even for me."

"You are a businessman with companies and investments in

many nations. We've already discussed the advantage of knowing a cataclysmic event is about to strike the United States economy."

Owiti thought for a moment and said, "Yes, there would be ways for me to earn a profit knowing an American city is about to be destroyed."

"Not one city. Many American cities, all simultaneously, and not some insignificant ones. Boston, New York, Philadelphia, and Washington, D.C., gone forever."

"I'm sorry, my friend, but I do not believe that even with the help of the North Koreans, you will be able to obtain multiple nuclear devices and transport them into the United States. It is improbable and, quite frankly, impossible."

"Not many. Only one."

"With only one nuclear device," Owiti said in a clearly skeptical voice, "you are going to destroy major U.S. cities, including New York and Washington? How is that possible?"

"I will explain after you agree to give me one billion, but I can promise you, it is not only possible—with Allah's help, it will happen."

"Let's assume, for the moment, this scheme is achievable—that you have found a way to destroy cities with one bomb. Let's say I give you a billion dollars. You just said that the Americans follow the money. How am I supposed to deliver one billion dollars to you without being arrested or worse?"

"You own the largest oil producing companies in Africa," the Falcon said. "One of your ultra-large crude tankers can transport three-point-seven million barrels of oil in one delivery. As you are keenly aware, the price of oil is currently hovering around a hundred dollars per barrel, after recovering from years of being much cheaper. A tanker at that price is carrying the equivalent of roughly three hundred and seventy million U.S. dollars."

"You would use my tankers of oil to pay the North Koreans?" Owiti asked.

"Three of your tankers leave from African ports," the Falcon said. "Why would the Americans care about that crude oil? In their entire country there is only one port in Louisiana that can accommodate one of your ultra-large tankers so they pay little attention to those vessels. It is a big ocean. Big enough for a supertanker to deliver oil without being noticed."

"As you say, it is unlikely they will track my tankers. However, there is a fatal flaw in your plan. North Korea doesn't have a port large enough for an ultra-tanker to dock and unload its cargo," Owiti said.

"This is what the world has been told," the Falcon replied. "But you and I know the world is wrong. Don't we?"

Owiti sat silent for a moment and then said, "How did you find out this information? Was it your precious Viper in Washington who told you?"

"Allah sees everything."

"Let's not play games, my friend. Tell me what you know."

"I know that one of your construction companies is finishing work on enlarging the port in Rason, which is perhaps the most important seaport in North Korea because it remains ice-free in the winter. I know that North Korea is thirsty for oil. And I know something more."

"More?"

"I know that you have access to North Korean officials, and if you speak to them about my plan, they will agree to it. You can arrange this for us and, in return, your wealth will be greatly increased."

"I am impressed, my friend. You have done your research," Owiti said. "You have tied all of the pieces together. You have found a way to avoid the prying eyes of western money trackers by using my oil tankers rather than U.S. currency to pay for a nuclear device. You have learned that one of my subsidiaries is finishing work expanding the port capabilities in the city of Rason. Very clever of you, my friend, very clever indeed."

The Falcon nodded.

"But even if you obtain a single nuclear device, you must still get it into the United States undetected, and no one has been able to accomplish that. How will you perform this miracle?"

"I have said enough tonight. There is a way to avoid detection, a weakness the Great Satan has not seen. Be patient. Tomorrow I will share this final secret with you."

Owiti threw up his hands in mock resignation. "Ah, you will keep me waiting, then. Perhaps that is best. Anticipation is exciting, is it not? I have a woman waiting for me right now. I have kept her naked in my bed anticipating my arrival long enough. Would you like a woman tonight, my friend, or does your infamous piety keep you from the pleasures found between a woman's legs?"

"While I am grateful for your offer, I would rather have three tankers of your oil."

Owiti laughed loudly. "Always jihad with you, my friend. Tomorrow, you will tell me the remainder of your plan, and if you convince me that it can inflict as much damage on the United States, as you claim, then we will discuss my three tankers of my oil."

CHAPTER FORTY-FIVE

Gated neighborhood
McLean, Virginia

The Honorable Thomas Edgar Stanton had never been awakened by a CIA director arriving at his house at four a.m. on a Saturday morning. Nor had Director Payton Grainger ever made such a house call. The reason for his urgency became clear moments after Stanton opened his front door.

"You woke me up to tell me someone is going to try to assassinate me," Stanton said, "and you learned this based on a single telephone call, is that correct?"

"This is the first time we successfully intercepted one of the Falcon's calls. An NSA computer was able to match his voice with one of his Internet rants."

"You make it sound as if I should feel honored."

"I simply meant to convey the gravity of the threat," Grainger replied.

"You're sure this isn't jihadist jibber-jabbering?"

"We don't believe the Falcon engages in bluster when it comes to ordering people murdered. To be clear, he didn't mention you by name. He said he wanted a congressman killed at your rally later today in Smithville, but that pretty much narrows it down to you."

"Representative Rudy Adeogo will also be appearing on stage with me. We were keeping it a surprise until we walked out together. Makes it a bit more dramatic."

Grainger felt his face starting to flush. "I should have been aware of that information. Obviously, he needs to be warned."

"Do you know who the Falcon was telling to arrange my demise?"

"A man here in Washington is responsible, but we haven't been able to identify him."

"Who else knows about this?"

"I came directly to you," Grainger replied. "I'd like to ask you to cancel your rally."

"Like hell I will," Stanton snapped. "This is our country and I'll be damned if I'll be afraid to walk the sidewalks in my own district because of some religious fanatic making a phone call from Africa."

"With all due respect, your rally has become much larger than a walk down a sidewalk. Protesters are planning on demonstrating against your call for investigative committee hearings."

"So you've heard the OIN and Omar Nader are busing protesters into Smithville to picket."

"Your rally has turned into a tinderbox and this new threat only exacerbates the danger. If you go forward, you will be putting your community and constituents at risk."

"Director Grainger, don't try to lay that at my door. I'm confident the U.S. government and South Carolina authorities can keep Representative Adeogo, my constituents, and me safe. We can't run and hide inside a hole every time one of these Islamist jackasses says he wants to kill one of us, nor can we cancel a political rally simply because protesters will be there."

Minutes after leaving Stanton's house, Grainger alerted FBI Agent Wyatt Parker, who in turn, asked Brooke Grant to report to the Reston command post.

"The Falcon has put a hit on either Representative Stanton or Adeogo or both of them," he explained. "It's supposed to happen today at Stanton's rally in South Carolina."

Brooke checked her watch. It was a few minutes past five a.m. The rally was scheduled to happen in less than twelve hours.

"There's more," Parker continued. "We suspect the Falcon is sending Akbar as his assassin."

"If Akbar's in South Carolina, then Jennifer can't be far away."

"Unless Akbar has—" Parker caught himself before stating the obvious.

"She's not dead," Brooke replied. "She's still valuable to them as a bargaining chip. Besides, I can feel it. She's waiting for us to come get her. If Akbar is going to be at that rally, so am I."

"I've already got a helicopter standing by."

By seven a.m., Agent Parker and Brooke had arrived in Smithville, and Parker had briefed the counterterrorism branch of South Carolina's Law Enforcement Division and had alerted a myriad of other Palmetto state and local law enforcement agencies.

By eight a.m., a command post had been established inside the Smithville Police Department to parcel out assignments to all of the different law enforcement agencies being called into town. Special Agent Parker had put himself in command.

By nine a.m., a local television reporter had learned from a talkative Smithville police officer what was happening. The reporter had tipped off the major television networks. Word spread quickly through the national press corps that a terrorist threat had been lodged against Stanton and that Adeogo would be speaking at the rally and also could be a target.

At 9:15 a.m., one of the networks broadcast a story about the threat.

Shortly after ten a.m., the president of Smithville University announced his school would not allow Stanton's supporters to hold their rally on its campus because of threats of violence. Six busloads of Muslim protesters also were spotted arriving in town.

An hour later, at eleven a.m., Smithville's mayor revealed his city would not allow Representative Stanton's supporters to host their rally inside its municipal auditorium or at any city-owned facility, including public parks.

Shortly before noon, a spokesman for Stanton's supporters proclaimed that the four thirty p.m. rally would be held on an undeveloped plot of land located not far from the university campus near the Smithville Medical Center. The property was owned by a staunch Stanton supporter. Carpenters already were busy erecting a stage.

At one p.m., after initially saying the city would not issue the necessary permits for the rally, the mayor reversed himself. He'd received a private phone call from Chairman Stanton and the rally was back on.

A half hour later, a local news station reported that FBI Special Agent Parker had distributed photographs of an Al-Shabaab terrorist identified as Ahmadullah Aba-Jihaad, aka Akbar, to all local lawmen. The station broadcast Akbar's mug shot and informed viewers that the FBI had offered a $1 million reward for information about Akbar when he'd first become a suspect in the shooting of General Frank Grant. That reward was still waiting to be claimed. Almost immediately, armed residents were spotted patrolling Smithville's streets.

"If I see that Muslim bastard, I'll shoot him dead for free," one man gushed to a network television reporter. Resting his palm on a .45-caliber handgun in a holster strapped to his waist, the longtime Smithville resident added, "I'm a damn good shot and I got plenty of ammo."

At 2:22 p.m., Omar Nader held a hastily called news conference to announce that Muslim protesters would not be attending the rally but would be demonstrating at a different location in town. With his supporters clustered around him waving brightly colored posters that read: MUSLIMS ARE PROUD AMERICANS TOO! and STOP DISCRIMINATION! END PREJUDICE, Nader explained that the Smithville police had cautioned him against confronting rally-goers. "We were told it wouldn't be safe for Muslims to show our faces there," he claimed. "We might be beaten or shot."

Twenty minutes later, Nader again appeared on television, this time standing in front of several buses that OIN protesters were boarding. "A city official has informed me that it is illegal for us to demonstrate without obtaining the proper city permits. But the office that issues that paperwork is closed on weekends. We have been threatened with arrest if we demonstrate, but nothing is being done to stop Representative Stanton from holding his rally. This double standard is a clear violation of our rights to free assembly as Muslims."

Pointing to the buses being boarded, he said, "Given that armed citizens are walking the streets and there is open hostility toward Muslims here, we have decided to leave Smithville peacefully. We do not want to incite violence or be falsely blamed if there is an assassination attempt or a terrorist event later today, as the media has speculated might happen."

At three thirty p.m., Smithville police slid two wooden barriers aside for FBI Special Agent Parker and Brooke Grant so they could enter the main street leading to Stanton's rally. Parker had ordered local law enforcement to establish a one-mile perimeter around the rally location and detour all local traffic around it. As he drove his unmarked car, with its blue lights in the grill flashing, through a steady stream of spectators walking in the middle of the street toward the rally grounds, Parker noted the festive air in the crowd. "These people look like they're going to a rock concert. They aren't scared one bit."

Brooke quietly wondered how many rock concerts Parker had attended. He struck her as more of a *Lake Wobegon* fan than a rocker.

Parker stopped their car about twenty feet from where three walk-through metal detectors were being used to screen rally-goers. The edges of the grounds had been roped off with brightly colored plastic police DO NOT CROSS tape that was being augmented by uniformed officers standing about ten feet apart to ensure no one slipped under the flimsy barrier without being cleared. At one end of the football field–size property was a stage that rose about four feet above the grass. The hastily constructed platform was twenty feet long and eight feet wide. A red, white, and blue banner that read FREEDOM DEMANDS VIGILANCE! was draped on ten-foot-tall posts behind a podium in the center of the stage. The afternoon temperature had risen to a high of sixty-five degrees outside and many rally-goers were bringing bags of fast food and carrying blankets to spread out on the grass. Based on the number of people in line to pass through the metal detectors, there would only be standing room. It looked as if much of Smithville's population of 29,000 had turned out. Many were carrying American flags. Brooke also spotted a large DON'T TREAD ON ME banner being paraded around the field by two stocky men.

"Let's walk," Parker said, pushing open the driver's door. As he stepped outside, a bomb-sniffing dog hurried up to him, and a South Carolina state police helicopter flew over their heads.

"If Akbar is stupid enough to show," Parker said, "he'll head for high ground." He pointed a finger on his right hand south toward the only tall building in the neighborhood. It was the Smithville Medical Center, a six-story brick building about a half mile from where they were standing. "I've sent teams to the hospital to stand watch. Got three agents with field glasses on its roof monitoring these grounds. If Akbar goes anywhere near that hospital, he'll be shot on sight. And we aren't going to let him infiltrate this crowd either."

Brooke did a 360-degree visual scan. The lot being used by rally-goers was in a neighborhood of mostly 1960-era, rambler-style houses. Three sides of the field were edged by homes and tall elm trees. The only opening was a swath in the northeast corner that butted up to a parking lot that served a half dozen mom-and-pop shops in a tiny strip mall.

"I've had people look up every tree and under every rock," Parker bragged. "And I'm not going to let Akbar pull any Hollywood antics."

"What sort of antics?"

"Posing as a cop and slipping through security. We've issued every law enforcement officer a red interactive chip that we brought down in bushels from Washington. It's the latest technology." He pointed to a red button attached to the shirt collar of a nearby Smithville police officer stationed outside a metal detector. "Each chip is being tracked by a computer at the command post. Each of those buttons contains a sensor that uses cutting-edge DNA technology to positively identify and monitor the officer wearing it. We can identify each officer by name; know where he or she is stationed, when they are moving, even when they duck into a Porta-John to relieve themselves. If Akbar shows up disguised in a police uniform without one of our red buttons, we'll spot him, and if one of our people disappears and Akbar or any other terrorist puts on his uniform or takes that chip, we'll know instantly."

"What about a suicide bomber?" Brooke asked.

"No way a vehicle can get through our roadblocks. We have sentries standing by with fifty-caliber rifles capable of stopping any motorized vehicle short of an Abrams tank, so a suicide driver will not make it inside. As you can see, we have bomb-sniffing dogs going through the crowds, and we have security checkpoints at every possible entrance into this rally."

Brooke watched as a thirty-something couple walked through a nearby metal detector. The woman was holding hands with a boy who looked as if he was about four years old.

"Don't touch that doggie!" the mother exclaimed while simultaneously jerking her son's arms away from a police dog who was busy sniffing rally-goers for explosives. "Them is attack dogs and they'll bite your head clean off."

What kind of parent brings a four-year-old to a rally after being warned a terrorist might be targeting the event? Brooke wondered.

A skirmish suddenly broke out about twenty yards from where Brooke and Parker were standing. Two uniformed police officers were wrestling with a bearded, heavyset man in overalls and a wool plaid shirt. They knocked him to the ground, and when he continued to resist after they had pinned him down, an officer repeatedly jabbed him with a 50,000-volt Taser.

"I'll hit you again!" the officer hollered after two jolts. "Stop resisting."

Parker and Brooke reached them as the two officers were helping the now handcuffed and compliant suspect to his feet.

"What'd he do?" Parker asked.

"He's carrying a gun," an officer explained.

"Yeah, that's right, and I got a permit to carry it too," the man complained. "I'm going to sue your asses!"

"Didn't you read the posters?" Parker asked him.

"What posters? And who the hell are you?"

"FBI, and there are posters clearly visible everywhere around here that prohibit anyone except law enforcement officers from carrying firearms within a hundred yards of this designated area, even if they have conceal gun permits."

As he was being led away, Parker turned to Brooke and said, "Akbar would be a complete idiot to try anything. Not even a cockroach could crawl into this rally without us noticing."

The radical Islamic terrorist Ahmadullah Aba-Jihaad, aka Akbar, had enjoyed watching two policemen stun a redneck South Carolina rally-goer with a Taser before handcuffing him. He'd watched the dust-up through field glasses from his vantage point roughly a half mile away. He'd also spotted Brooke Grant hurrying over to confer with the policemen. He only wished that he'd been given permission by the Falcon to shoot her as well as his congressional target.

Akbar had been watching Brooke and FBI Special Agent Parker since they had stepped free of their unmarked car near the front gate of the rally. He'd seen Parker point toward the Smithville Medical Center, the highest vantage point in the area. It is where Akbar had expected the FBI to post agents.

Did they think him stupid enough to go there?

He had not scaled a tree nor hidden himself under a rock. He had found a safe haven inside one of the Smithville infidels' most sacred refuges. The Smithville Church of Believers was a colonial, rectangular brick building, northeast of the rally grounds. It was across the street from the strip mall parking lot, and its towering white steeple was clearly visible from the rally grounds. It was home to one of the town's most prominent and largest congregations. The two-story, redbrick sanctuary had a decorative portico with four gleaming white columns outside its oversize double front doors. On the roof a few steps behind that portico was the church's steeple, which looked every bit like the spires found on thousands of other churches in American cities. It was what had caught Akbar's eye when he'd first surveyed Smithville for a shooting spot. It rose high above the sanctuary's pitched roof and had been built in diminishing sections that could have easily collapsed into each other.

The base of the steeple was a redbrick square with a single octagonal porthole on each of its four sides. It stood about eight feet above the black shingled roof. Rising atop it was a section called the "lantern" because in colonial days this was where lights had been hung to guide churchgoers toward God's house at nighttime. Each of its sides was an open archway and birds often could be seen resting on the edge of the two-foot-high wall that ringed its base.

Atop the lantern was the belfry, an enclosed wooden square that housed electronic bells that could be heard through large vents cut inside its facade. Rising from the belfry was the final level, the spire, which resembled an upside down ice cream cone. At its peak was a narrow four-foot-tall cross painted bright gold.

Construction workers had added the steeple to the church's roof in four sections with a large crane. The only piece of it that a man could hide inside was the lantern, and that was where Akbar had crawled, having scaled the building on Friday night under the cover of darkness. From the street, an onlooker could see through the lantern's four open sides. But from the street no one could see behind the lantern's two-foot-high knee wall that formed its base, and that was high enough for Akbar to duck behind.

From his perch Akbar had an unobstructed 360-degree view when he peeked over the lantern's knee wall. When he'd heard through the earbuds he was wearing to monitor police calls that the university president had cancelled the rally at Smithville University, he'd given up hope of having a shot at either congressman. The campus where the rally was originally scheduled to take place was about a half mile east of Akbar's steeple hiding place. By then it was daylight, so he had no choice but to remain hidden.

It was at that point when Allah had smiled on him. The rally had been moved to an even better location directly west of the steeple. In fact, the stage being built was an even closer target than the university's outdoor arena to Akbar's east. The only adjustment Akbar had needed to make in his hiding spot was to turn his body from facing east around to the west.

He checked his watch. It was 3:45 p.m.

It was almost time.

CHAPTER FORTY-SIX

Stanton political rally, vacant lot
Smithville, South Carolina

Representatives Stanton and Adeogo sat across from each other on matching tan leather chairs inside a forty-five-foot-long luxury motor coach provided by one of Stanton's supporters. The bus was parked about fifty feet from the rally grounds, where the crowd was becoming more and more boisterous in anticipation of their arrival on stage.

Stanton's private cell phone rang. It was President Sally Allworth.

"Mr. Chairman, I've just been informed by my chief of staff that our intelligence services have intercepted another telephone conversation between the Falcon and his Washington contact," Allworth said in a concerned voice. "This traitor with the code name Viper told the Falcon that Akbar is in Smithville and ready to shoot his target."

"Did he mention whether the lucky fellow is me or Representative Adeogo?" Stanton asked in a cheerful voice.

"Thomas," she replied, calling him by his first name, "this is not a game. This is not a joke. The assassin shot General Grant and murdered Jennifer Conner's nanny. Director Grainger is telling me that his agency has one hundred percent certainty that Akbar is going to attempt to murder you and Representative Adeogo when you go out on that stage. You must call off your rally."

The seriousness of her tone disturbed him, but it did not shake his resolve.

"I appreciate your concern Madam President, and your call is touching, but I am going to repeat to you what I said earlier this morning to Director Grainger. I am not going to be intimidated by a terrorist talking on the phone to another terrorist. This is America, and we cannot allow a radical jihadist to frighten us or disrupt our democratic process. I am confident in the FBI's ability to protect me."

"I appreciate your bravery, but I will urge you once again to cancel this rally until we have a chance to catch this killer."

"And when will that be, if ever?"

"If you aren't going to cancel it, then delay it until next week. I have just gotten off the phone with the head of the Secret Service and I've instructed him to get his people involved in protecting you."

"Thank you, but we've already got a nice crowd here, and I'm not going to disappoint them. Representative Adeogo is sitting here with me. I will pass along your concerns to him."

"I have a better idea: If you don't mind, let me speak to him directly."

Stanton passed Adeogo the phone.

"Congressman," Allworth said, "I have been trying to talk some sense into Chairman Stanton. We have just intercepted a second phone call from the Falcon instructing his followers here to assassinate Stanton and you. I have urged him to postpone the rally until I can get both of you Secret Service protection. Hopefully, you can talk some sense into him. But I'm asking you to not go forward with this rally. These terrorists have caused enough suffering and havoc."

"I have listened to Chairman Stanton's side of your conversation, Madam President," Adeogo said, "and I must agree with him. We should not have to hide our faces on our own soil. Much of a terrorist's power comes from scaring people, making them afraid. If the Chairman cancels this rally, it will show that we are afraid, and that will send a horrible message to Americans that we are incapable of protecting our own people. That the terrorists have won."

"And what sort of message will you be sending if either of you is shot?"

"A message that says boldly, we will not be afraid."

Adeogo handed the phone back to Stanton, who said, "You have your answer. It's not the one that you wanted to hear from either of us, but I expect that is not a surprise to you or Ms. Harper. Recently, I have been giving her several answers that she doesn't like."

"That's politics. This is about life and death."

"No, Madam President. It's about freedom."

Rumors began sweeping through the crowd at 4:45 p.m. that something was wrong. Why hadn't the four thirty p.m. rally started? Inside the luxury motor home, Chairman Stanton finished the last of a bottle of water and said, "These vests are darn uncomfortable." He was referring to the bullet-resistant vests that the FBI's Parker had insisted both of them wear under their white shirts, ties, and suit jackets.

For a man who had been warned by the president that an assassin might be lurking outside to end his life, Stanton seemed oddly at ease, even jovial. He had been all morning.

When he'd arrived in Smithville by private helicopter near nine a.m., Stanton had ignored Parker's request that he remain in seclusion and instead had strolled down Main Street. He'd entered Smithville's most frequented coffee shop, where he'd taken a seat at a corner table and had proceeded to hold court for several hours, listening intently while his constituents told him their concerns.

Stanton was an old-school politician. A gifted extemporaneous orator, he could speak passionately about any current event, but especially about intelligence issues. In Washington, he was known as a tough, sharp-tongued inquisitor who could make even the most veteran federal bureaucrat squirm. But a different side of him emerged when he was listening and talking to voters in his South Carolina district. He was one of them, and despite the status and acclaim that he had achieved in Washington, D.C., which allowed him to rub shoulders with the president, foreign heads of state, and the nation's most elite intellectuals and power brokers, Stanton felt most at home with blue-collar workers and South Carolina farmers in a greasy spoon café that smelled of bacon.

When he'd finally been forced to leave the café and wait inside the donated RV for the rally, there was no doubt in his mind that he had made the right choice in coming to Smithville despite the threats being made to him and Adeogo.

Adeogo also seemed happy that he'd been included. He had been greeted by Stanton's aides when he arrived in town shortly after two o'clock. He had left Washington Friday night in an unmarked police car with two D.C. patrol officers. They had driven halfway to Smithville before stopping for the night in a hotel. Dheeh had not said much when he had left their house. She was still furious that he had slept with Mary Margaret Delaney. But Cassy had begged him not to go and had cried and refused to stop hugging him when it was time for him to depart.

If President Allworth had wanted to change his mind, Adeogo thought, she should have put Cassy on the phone.

Adeogo had come to Smithville to redeem himself, but he'd also come because he despised Omar Nader and the OIN. He suspected that Nader had somehow been involved in providing Mary Margaret Delaney with the sealed court transcript about his brother Abdul Hafeez. The OIN's insistence that every Muslim fall in line with its decrees was no different, in his mind, from the demands made by radical Islamist extremists who insisted everyone obey their self-righteous dogma. They were twin sides of the same coin. When he learned that Delaney had been found dead on an overlook along the George Washington Parkway, he had wondered if Nader and the OIN were involved. But when the Park Police announced that Delaney had taken her own life, he decided that his initial suspicions had been based on unfounded paranoia.

Just the same, he was eager to verbally attack both Nader and the OIN at today's rally as well as lend his support to Stanton and his call for closer scrutiny of radical Imams and mosques.

"Let's wait until five o'clock to start this show," Stanton said.

"That's a half hour later than we planned," Adeogo responded. "Are you having second thoughts about going outside? Did the president's call change your mind?"

Stanton laughed. "Naw, it has nothing to do with President Allworth's call. That crowd isn't going anywhere, and making them wait will only get everyone more excited and hyped up for when we finally do go out on stage. I'm certain reporters are already on the air speculating about whether we've changed our mind. Might as well not let all that conjecture go to waste. Getting out there by five will still give us time to appear live on the local news and make the national newscasts at six."

Adeogo was impressed by Stanton's savvy. "I can see why you have been so successful, but I'm afraid your tutelage is being wasted on me. My chances of being reelected are nonexistent despite the opportunity that you are affording me today at your rally."

"You call possibly being shot an opportunity?" Stanton chuckled.

"Given my popularity right now in America, it might be best. Some political commentators are suggesting that I staged my own daughter's abduction to cover my complicity with my brother and Al-Shabaab."

"You can't control either the news or what people say about you. The media is calling me the new Senator Joe McCarthy, and I've been warned the OIN is going to pump millions, if necessary, into defeating me. I've also heard the White House is conspiring behind my back on the Hill with my colleagues to strip me of my chairmanship. I suspect Mallory Harper is behind Omar Nader's decision to come down here and protest, and I wouldn't be surprised if she isn't secretly advising him about how to defeat me. So, my friend, we're in the same boat, and you might have a better chance of getting reelected than I do."

Adeogo shook his head, indicating no, and said, "I didn't realize the ugly side of politics. Given all that has happened, I regret ever running for Congress."

Stanton knew about regrets. The lengthy time that he had spent in Washington had taken a huge toll on his personal life. His had been a long-distance marriage and he had been a long-distance father to their children. His beloved spouse had stuck with him, and his kids greatly admired him. But there was no way that he could reclaim the thousands of hours that had taken him away from them. He could not and would not give in to those regrets. The trade-off had been a life that mattered in his eyes, a life of true public service.

"Let me give you some advice," Stanton said. "Never underestimate the American people's willingness to forgive. This great nation of ours was settled by people seeking second chances and redemption. Forgiveness is in our blood, and we appreciate someone who gets up after they get knocked down. You can come back from all of the negative press and attacks, but only if you talk directly to the people and speak to them from your heart."

"If that is true, then why are you concerned about losing to a college professor?"

"Because the second thing that Americans love after redemption is a fresh face spouting new ideas. With longevity comes blame for everything that has gone wrong during my tenure. Voters believe the next politician who comes along must be better than the one in office, especially if they haven't held public office before, only they rarely are." Stanton laughed and added, "Your election is a prime example. Didn't you come to Washington with a broom in your hand ready to sweep all of us veterans out the door?"

Stanton's chief of staff appeared. "It's five now. Are you ready?"

"Okay, Representative Rudy Adeogo," Stanton said, standing, "it's time for us to see if these bulletproof vests work."

Adeogo didn't smile at his humor. As they stepped from the RV, which was parked in the strip mall lot adjacent to the field, Stanton and Adeogo were enveloped by five South Carolina state troopers and two FBI agents. A path had been cordoned off for them, and as they crossed the asphalt, both noticed two ambulances with their engines running. Those were the only other vehicles in the parking lot and, along with Agent Parker's unmarked car, the only ones permitted within a mile of the rally. Homeowners had been told to keep their cars locked in their garages and not attempt to drive them before or during the rally. All vehicles parked on the streets or in driveways were driven or towed outside the area. The FBI was taking no chances with car bombs.

"Let's hope neither of us leaves in one of those," Stanton said as they stepped by the two emergency rescue vehicles. When they reached the field, they moved quickly through the gauntlet of police officers separating them from the crowd. Stanton was the first to climb the four steps to the platform, appearing before the crowd at the same moment his local campaign manager was finishing his recitation about the wonderful job "the Chairman" was doing for South Carolinians in Washington.

Applause, cheers, whistles, and a few air horns that his staff had discreetly distributed greeted Stanton as he stepped behind the wooden podium, borrowed from a local high school, with his hands raised as if he were a prizefighter who had just scored a knockout. For the moment, Stanton took pleasure in soaking in all of the sights and sounds around him as he searched the crowd for familiar faces, whom he then waved to while mouthing their names. He loved this and it showed on his weathered face. Directly before him were his people, the reason why he served in Washington. To his right on another hastily built platform were television cameras from all of the networks, and in a separate area roped off from the crowd were the media. Stanton recognized several of them too. Until this controversy, he had considered many of them his friends, but they had turned against him, reminding him that no politician could ever truly be a friend with those who earned their living praising or skewering them.

After basking in the revelry, Stanton quieted the crowd.

"It is my great honor to represent you in Washington. What you believe and what you want is what I believe and what I *deliver*."

Cheering and clapping interrupted him.

"Thanks to you, I have been your public servant—and I do believe that I am your servant—for eighteen terms, but I'm here this afternoon to tell you that I am not done yet. Our nation is not safe, and I am determined to continue working in Washington to make it safe."

Someone began chanting his name and others joined in, repeating it over and over, until he waved them quiet.

"Today, I have brought a colleague with me. He's also become my friend, and he's the only practicing Muslim in Congress." Afraid that someone might boo, Stanton added, "He's an American first, and he's here because both of us believe Muslims and Christians can and must work together to create a better and safer America. He's supporting my efforts to identify radical extremists in our country. This is not about persecuting anyone because of his or her individual religious beliefs and values. It is about identifying radical Imams and other terrorists who are poisoning our young people's minds on our American soil in mosques where hatred toward our beloved country is preached. What's being taught is not religious instruction and training; it's radical political dogma and indoctrination. It is hate mongering, and as such, it should have no place in any legitimate religious group, and it shouldn't be protected simply because its proponents want to hide behind the Quran."

Once again the crowd began to cheer.

"I do not fear my American brothers and sisters who are followers of Islam. But I do fear extremists who twist that religion into an excuse to steal, maim, attack, torture, rape, and destroy anyone who doesn't blindly accept their beliefs."

Stanton rarely used notes, but as the crowd applauded, he glanced down at the podium, where his aide had left biographic information about Mohammad Al-Kader. Stanton intended to name Al-Kader specifically as an example of a dangerous Imam. As he raised his eyes to re-engage with the crowd, a round from Akbar's sniper's rifle struck the Chairman in his head.

CHAPTER FORTY-SEVEN

Stanton political rally, vacant lot
Smithville, South Carolina

Representative Stanton collapsed.

Standing near him, Rudy Adeogo dropped to his knees to help Stanton. That kind move saved the Minnesota congressman's life. Akbar's second shot whizzed inches above his skull. The two FBI agents who'd helped escort the congressmen from the motor home to the stage leaped forward and crouched over Stanton and Adeogo, shielding them with their bodies.

The sniper's two rounds ignited a stampede. Panicked rally-goers bolted in every direction. Several were knocked to the ground and risked being trampled. Smithville police officers standing watch along the field's perimeter were shoved out of the way by a frantic mob that ripped through the yellow DO NOT CROSS tape.

Akbar did not risk firing a third shot. Instead, he placed his rifle next to him in the base of the steeple's lantern section and grabbed a black remote control. A quad-copter drone hidden outside the Smithville Medical Center nearly a half mile away soared upward from where he had placed it earlier near a large green dumpster. Its arrival above the hospital roof shocked the three FBI agents stationed there. They had been watching the pandemonium at the rally grounds through field glasses and had not noticed the drone approaching until one of them heard its four propellers and glanced upward just as Akbar touched a button on his controller. The hobby aircraft had been built to hold a camera for aerial shots, but Akbar had reconfigured it to carry an explosive device the size of a hockey puck. He detonated it.

The mini bomb was designed more to create noise and smoke than to maim or kill, and it exploded with a thunderclap that could be heard at the rally grounds. A black cloud instantly rose from the hospital roof.

The explosion set off a new round of screams as rally-goers continued to scatter from the field. Several police officers pointed toward the black cloud. Television crews documenting the panic turned their cameras toward the rising smoke. A few onlookers raised their cell phones to document the chaos. Thinking the hospital was being bombed, the FBI agents inside began evacuating the building, causing even more panic.

The drone attack had created the diversion that Akbar had expected. It would be too risky for him to continue hiding in the steeple after firing two shots from it. At some point, the FBI would calculate the trajectory of his gunshots. He needed to escape while everyone was focused on the rally grounds and hospital. For a moment, he considered leaving his Dragunov sniper's rifle behind in the lantern. But like many soldiers, he felt a kinship with the weapon and foolishly slung it over his shoulder as he stepped over the lantern's knee wall and leaped down onto the church's roof.

Mason Jeffrey Lee happened to be in the church's parking lot when Akbar appeared on the sanctuary roof with his rifle. The forty-year-old Smithville plumber noticed the terrorist scampering across the shingles toward a corner drain spout. Lee had intended that afternoon to be part of the crowd inside the roped-off area where Stanton was speaking. But when he'd reached the one-mile perimeter where police officers were turning vehicles away and everyone had been required to proceed on foot, he'd read a poster warning him that rally-goers would have to be cleared by metal detectors before they could enter the assembly. Anyone who was armed would be arrested. Initially, he'd ignored those warnings, much like the rednecked Smithville resident who'd been wrestled down and stunned with a Taser near the field's heavily guarded entrance. But as Lee walked closer to the field, he'd lost his nerve and had stopped at the church parking lot a half mile away from the metal detectors. He'd been afraid to go nearer because of the 9mm Glock hidden under his wool shirt. Instead, Lee had elected to watch a simulcast of the rally on his Apple iPhone. Within seconds after seeing Akbar, Lee connected the dots and realized that he was watching the assassin attempting to escape. Drawing his Glock, Lee ran toward the corner of the church where Akbar was now shimmying down a drainpipe.

Akbar saw Lee coming for him, but could not unsling his rifle because his hands were grasping the drainpipe. He let loose and fell the last ten feet from the brick wall to the parking lot pavement. Akbar was quick with his rifle, but Lee already had his pistol raised and he began firing. The first two shots missed, and for a second Akbar thought he might be able to kill the man rushing at him.

But Lee stopped and emptied the clip in his handgun. Three of the shots grazed the terrorist and one hit his abdomen. A veteran of Desert Storm, Lee charged in an adrenaline-fueled panic and threw himself at the now bleeding terrorist, knocking him down onto the asphalt. Lee slammed his empty Glock against Akbar's skull, striking him again and again until he was satisfied that Akbar was either unconscious or dead.

Tucking his pistol between his pants and boxer shorts, Lee snatched Akbar's Dragunov rifle from him and hoisted it into the air with his left hand. With his right, he took hold of Akbar's shirt and pulled the ragdoll-like terrorist into a sitting position. Waving the rifle above his head while gripping Akbar's collar, Lee hollered: "I got the bastard! I shot him!"

A young couple who were fleeing from the rally grounds saw them and reached for their cell phones. One dialed 911 while the other began taking video of a triumphant Lee holding Akbar as if he were a prized hunting trophy.

FBI Special Agent Parker and Brooke were moving through the

last throng of panicked rally-goers toward the stage when Parker learned through his earpiece about Akbar.

"We got the sniper!" he exclaimed, stopping midfield.

Along with Brooke, Parker had been watching Stanton speak on stage from the rear of the rally near the metal detectors and Parker's unmarked car. After Stanton was shot, they had been unable to reach the stage because of the fleeing mob. They were now about twenty yards from the stage.

"The sniper—is it Akbar?" Brooke yelled.

"It could be," Parker called back.

Just then the two ambulances from the strip mall parking lot cut between them and the stage. As they watched, a lifeless Stanton was carried into one of the emergency rescue vehicles and Adeogo was escorted into the second. With lights flashing and sirens wailing, both vehicles raced from the field en route to a nearby town's hospital that, unlike Smithville's, was not being evacuated.

"I got agents heading to that church," Parker told Brooke, raising his right hand and pointing it toward the white steeple to their immediate east. "That's where the sniper is. We think he's the only one."

"Is he dead?" Brooke demanded.

"Apparently a local good Samaritan saw him climbing off the roof and did us all a favor by killing him."

A look of horror appeared on Brooke's face. "Where's Jennifer?" she asked. "Was she with him?"

"Come with me," Parker replied, turning and now running away from the stage toward his parked unmarked sedan.

She rushed after him and reached the passenger's side after he'd already slipped behind the wheel.

"Where are we going?" she asked, entering the sedan. "Is it Jennifer?"

He started the car, turned on its sirens and flashing lights, and then turned to face her.

"She's been spotted. My people can mop up here. Let's go get her!"

CHAPTER FORTY-EIGHT

Outskirts of town
Smithville, South Carolina

Where's Jennifer?" Brooke demanded, her voice a mixture of excitement and trepidation. "Is she okay?"

"She was spotted five minutes ago by a woman riding through some woods on a trail bike. She saw two men pulling a girl from a car at a farm on Bell's Road not far from here."

"Backup?"

"Haven't called any yet. Let's check the scene. We don't want to rush in and spook the two men holding her."

Brooke had a horrible thought. "Do you think they're watching the news?"

"I would be."

"If they hear Akbar is dead, they might decide to hurt Jennifer and run."

Parker turned their car onto Bell's Road and accelerated. He switched off the vehicle's flashing lights and siren, and when they had gone about three miles, he pulled to the side of the road. "The woman said the house is about a hundred yards through these woods. Let's walk."

They moved rapidly through the foliage.

"There it is," Parker whispered when they reached a clearing.

The old farmhouse was about fifty feet from the woods where they were hiding. It was in rough shape. Shingles were missing from its gray roof. The upstairs windows in the two-story house were covered with plywood sheets. Trash littered its unkempt yard. The only evidence that someone was inside was a silver Chevy Silverado truck parked near the back door.

Touching his earbud receiver, Parker whispered, "The media just reported Akbar has been killed."

Brooke fiddled with her earpiece. "Why are you getting this and I'm not? I haven't heard the last three or four messages you've told me."

Parker gave her a blank stare. "I'm going to call in the HRT," he said. "I don't trust anyone else. It will probably be two hours before they can get here."

They heard Jennifer scream inside the house.

"We can't wait," Brooke said, drawing her pistol.

"No. Stop!" Parker called out, but he caught himself. "Go ahead, I'll come after I call for backup."

Brooke was already dashing across the clearing toward the farmhouse. She threw herself against the building's back wall and hesitated in order to catch her breath and focus. She slowly edged her way to the house's back door, where she peeked through a sagging wire screen door and dirty window in the upper half of the door. She didn't see anyone inside the kitchen. Brooke gently opened the screen and tried the knob. The door was unlocked and creaked when she opened it. As she entered the house, she heard the sound of footsteps. A man was running down a hallway toward the kitchen with a raised pistol. He fired and Brooke could feel the shock wave caused by the bullet as it sailed by her left ear. Ducking, she shifted her weight and fired her handgun. Her aim was better than his, and he hit the floor and didn't move again.

Jennifer screamed.

Her voice was coming from upstairs. Brooke hurried from the kitchen, down a hallway into the front foyer of the house where a staircase would take her up to the second level. But she paused at its first step. Parker had mentioned two men, and she assumed the second terrorist would be waiting upstairs with Jennifer. He would have heard the gunfire.

"Ayub, did you kill her?" Brooke heard a male voice call down.

He would know when there was no answer that his partner was dead. He would also know that she would have to climb the stairs to reach him and Jennifer. Brooke didn't have a choice. She raced up them as fast as she could.

She reached the top step at the same moment the second terrorist appeared on the landing. Before he could fire, she threw her shoulder into him, hitting him in his groin with such force that she lifted him off his feet. He tumbled backward and instinctively lowered his hands to break his fall.

Now towering over him, Brooke fired twice. The terrorist gasped and began gurgling from the wounds in his chest. He glared at her. She fired a third shot into his forehead.

Only one of the upstairs bedroom doors was open, and Brooke darted through it. She spotted Jennifer sitting on the floor. Gray duct tape was wrapped around her wrists and her right leg was chained to an old-fashioned steam radiator in the room. The terrorist had taped Jennifer's mouth after her last scream.

Dropping to her knees, Brooke laid her pistol on the floor and drew a pocketknife from the pocket of her denim jeans. She removed the tape from Jennifer's mouth and freed the girl's wrist.

Jennifer grabbed Brooke with both arms and burst into tears.

"I've got you now!" Brooke exclaimed, squeezing the teen as they hugged. "You're safe. Those men aren't going to hurt you anymore." Jennifer held on tighter.

"I knew you'd come," Jennifer whispered.

As they held each other, Parker entered the room, causing Jennifer to flinch. "A man!" Jennifer said in a frightened voice, unsure who Parker was.

"What?" Brooke asked, turning her head to look behind her. "Oh, don't be afraid, Jen. That's FBI Special Agent Parker. He's one of the good guys."

"Yes, I am," Parker declared, as he walked closer.

Jennifer's traumatic brain injury had robbed her of many cognitive abilities, but it also had forced her to develop new ones. She remembered voices, even ones that she'd only heard once. It was as if voices became recordings in her brain, much like old LP records that could be pulled from a mental shelf in her head, dusted off, and played.

Jennifer knew instantly that she had heard his voice before, and she knew where she had heard it. She had been locked in a car trunk, still a hostage. It was when Akbar had parked his car and stood outside the trunk talking to another man. It was the same night when Aludra had disappeared. The voice of the other man belonged to Agent Parker.

"He's one of them," Jennifer cried. "A bad man."

"What? What are you saying?" Brooke asked, clearly confused. She was still on her knees facing Jennifer with Parker standing behind her. When she turned to look up at him, she noticed that he was holding two guns, and one of them was aimed at her.

"Lower that gun," she said. "You're frightening her."

Parker didn't respond, and she saw that he had put plastic surgical gloves on his hands. She also realized that the pistol he was pointing at her was not his service weapon. It was the handgun from the dead terrorist at the top of the staircase.

"What's this about?" she asked, slowly turning on her knees to face him.

"The Falcon asked me personally to kill you. Both of you."

"The Falcon?" Brooke stammered.

"You didn't have a clue, did you?"

"You're a traitor?"

"Let's just say I recently decided to switch teams. You should feel honored. The Falcon called me directly. Always before, I've gotten my orders through an intermediary. But he called me personally because he really wants you and this girl dead."

She glanced at Jennifer, who seemed paralyzed, and then returned her gaze to him.

"You bastard!" she said. "You're the Viper. All this time, you have been right in front of my eyes."

She shifted her eyes to look at her handgun lying about a foot from her reach on the floor. He noticed and said, "Go for it. I can shoot you here, but I'd rather do it at the top of the staircase."

"Why?"

"Because then I won't have to drag your body there. I'll admit, it's not the most original plan, but it's a plausible one. I'll tell them that I was on my cell phone in the woods calling for backup when you ran ahead. You have a reputation for being impulsive. I discovered your body at the top of the stairs where you'd been shot with this handgun." He raised the pistol slightly to make certain that she realized that he had taken it from the terrorist whom she'd killed. "Regrettably, I found Jennifer fatally wounded as well."

"You're the reason my headset doesn't work, aren't you?" she said. "You are why I've not been getting messages and you have."

"There's nothing wrong with your headset." He snickered. "I was making up those messages. I knew Jennifer was being brought here. I lied to get you to come with me. Now we're on a bit of a schedule. I can't have our backup storming in while you both are alive."

"You actually called them?"

"Of course. But don't get your hopes up, Major Grant. I can tell what you are thinking. If you can stall long enough, they'll arrive in time to stop me from killing you. Not a chance. Now, it would be easier for me if you would stand and walk to the staircase. I'd rather not risk having someone noticing drag marks on your skin during your autopsy."

"You're asking me to help you cover up my own murder? Go to hell!"

"Perhaps you need an incentive." He pointed the pistol at

Jennifer. "Do you want to see her die first? Getting shot in the stomach, I've heard, is especially painful."

Brooke glanced at Jennifer, who was clearly terrified.

"Why?" Brooke asked him.

"Now, now, do you really want your last thoughts to be about such trivial matters as my motivation? In a few moments, none of this will matter to you—not even Jennifer. Ticktock, ticktock. We're on a schedule, remember?"

"You owe me an explanation."

Parker burst out laughing. "Owe you? Okay, how's this. Cold, hard cash. Short and simple answer. Lots of it, and I have you to thank for it."

"Me?"

"Remember when you returned from Somalia? You'd stopped the Falcon from exploding a bomb in Mogadishu that would have killed hundreds, and I got to thinking, what would this new Islamic mastermind terrorist have been willing to pay for inside information? If I had been providing him intel about you in Somalia, he would have been able to set off that bomb."

"You contacted him and offered to spy?"

"No, I offered him a business deal, my information services for cash. Why do you seem so surprised? John Walker Jr., Aldrich Ames, and Robert Hanssen were all Americans who sold secrets to the KGB during the Cold War. Wake up, Major Grant. Terrorists are the new marketplace for information—the new enemy—and for the right price, I have been willing to sell that information to them. Do you know why jihadists have been able to avoid detection in Europe and the U.S.? Edward Snowden. That young, naïve American posted information on the Internet that exposed our secret communication system and showed them how to evade detection. Many Americans call him a whistleblower, a hero."

"You're not a hero. You're a Judas."

"Oh, Major Grant, sticks and stones, really? Trust me, the Falcon paid me much more than thirty pieces of silver. And before you get too melodramatic, don't forget that Osama bin Laden was once on our side fighting the Russians in Afghanistan. Once upon a time, we hated Iran but we ended up fighting with them in Syria against ISIS. One day our enemy, the next day our friend. That's how international politics work."

"Stop trying to minimize what you are doing. What's the going rate for betraying your country?"

"Why, you interested in joining the team? Ha. Two million dollars as a retainer, plus another million for eliminating you and the girl. A million-dollar bounty—you should feel honored."

She glared at him. "With you, it's more than the cash, isn't it? I've been around you long enough to know that it's ego too. You get a kick out of going to work each day fooling everyone around you, don't you? It makes you feel important, doesn't it? It makes you think you're special, smarter."

"Enough psych 101. Enough stalling. Raise your hands and walk to the top of the stairs, or I'll shoot the girl first so you can watch her die."

Brooke turned and positioned herself between Parker and Jennifer as a shield as she slowly rose to her feet.

"No heroics," he warned.

Brooke lunged at him. He fired at the same moment her body struck his. She had never felt anything as painful as the slug that ripped into her abdomen. It was as if she had been hit by a speeding car. Despite the intense pain, she grabbed Parker around his neck with both hands as they tumbled onto the floor.

He landed hard on his back, with Brooke now lying prone on his chest. She felt the air escape from his lungs when they hit the floor, and she tried to tighten her grasp to choke him. But her fingers failed her. The initial shock of being wounded caused her entire body to shake as she fought to remain conscious.

Parker momentarily gulped for air but quickly regained his composure. He released his grip on both handguns—his FBI service weapon, which he was holding in his left hand, and the terrorists' pistol in his right—so he could pry her locked fingers from around his neck. He shoved her from his chest and rose up on his knees so he could face her, turning his back on Jennifer. He stared down at Brooke, who was now immobilized by her wound.

"Had to play the hero up to the end," he snarled, mocking her.

Brooke's white cotton blouse under her navy blazer was turning dark red from her blood. Her breathing was labored and irregular. She looked up at him half conscious and wanted to speak, but couldn't.

"Stupid bitch," he snapped. "Now I'm going to have to drag you and clean up your blood."

He bent forward and retrieved the terrorist's pistol from the floor. He pressed its barrel against her breast not far from where the first slug had pierced her. "I think I'll just leave you dead here. I'll tell them you were protecting the girl when you and the terrorist exchanged gunfire. It will take some staging, but everyone will want to believe you died being a hero. They'll want to believe my story."

As he started to pull the trigger, a piece of chain flew over his head and caught itself around his throat.

Parker had been kneeling with his back to Jennifer so he had not seen the teen gather up the excess chain that ran from her leg to the radiator and fashion it into a garrote.

Parker instinctively dropped the pistol and grabbed the chain collar now choking him. He tried to pry it free with both hands but Jennifer pulled the chain with all of her strength. Now panicking, Parker stood and began twisting and turning, shaking violently in a failed attempt to toss Jennifer from his shoulders. She tugged the links tighter against his throat as if it were a bridle on a horse that she had mounted. The traitor's face turned bloodred as he threw his hands behind him and grabbed Jennifer's hair, causing her to scream, but she did not loosen her grip.

Parker suddenly remembered the pistols at his feet near where Brooke was now lying. He bent down and reached for one.

Brooke saw him. She'd recovered slightly from the initial trauma of the gunshot, and although she didn't have the strength needed to rise from the floor to challenge him, she called up every bit of energy that she could muster and forced her hand to respond. Sliding her fingers across the floor, she searched for the pistol grip. She felt it just as Parker was about to seize it. She pointed it upward and fired.

The last sight Brooke saw was Special Agent Wyatt Parker's chin exploding.

She blacked out.

CHAPTER FORTY-NINE

"For a while, we thought we'd lost you," Walks Many Miles said when Brooke opened her eyes.

Seeing him momentarily confused her before she realized he was standing next to a hospital bed that she was lying on. Her arms were attached to IVs and monitors. *Being shot. Parker. The Viper.* Now she remembered. She tried to sit and a sharp pain shot across her abdomen like 50,000 volts of electricity.

"Easy now," Miles said when he saw her grimace.

"How long have you been here?"

"Landed an hour ago. Came right over."

"You get shot in Africa?" she asked.

He slapped both hands against his chest as if he were searching for holes and said, "No bullets. I'm still in one piece."

"Not me. I got shot."

Miles couldn't tell if Brooke was cracking a joke or was simply being serious. She seemed groggy from the morphine being pumped into her arm.

"How long since that bastard shot me?" she asked.

"Three days," Aunt Geraldine announced, stepping toward the bed next to Miles. "Everyone thought you were going to die—even the paramedics who flew you here—but not me. I told them—she's a fighter. It isn't her time to die. They operated on you for nine hours straight, sewing up everything and rearranging your insides. You've been knocked out for two more days because of all the pain."

"Where's Jennifer? Is she okay?"

Miles nodded to his right, and Brooke glanced past him and her aunt and spotted Jennifer standing at the foot of the hospital bed. The teenager was clutching a bright pink stuffed animal—a unicorn.

"This is for you," Jennifer announced, lifting the mythical animal in front of her as she edged forward. Geraldine and Miles moved aside so the teen could be closer to Brooke. "Unicorns can do magic," Jennifer announced.

"Have you named her?" Brooke asked, reaching for the toy.

"I call her Brooke the Unicorn."

With her free hand, Brooke took Jennifer's and squeezed it. "I'm pretty fond of that name. How you doing, peanut?"

"Aunt Geraldine is letting me stay in your old room."

"That's wonderful. There's still a lot of my stuff there. Board games I used to play."

"That's really old stuff. But it's okay."

Geraldine said, "It's like we're having a family get-together in the hospital, isn't it? Your uncle is directly down the hallway."

"Is he awake?" Brooke asked in a concerned voice.

"No, child, not yet," Geraldine replied. "But his eyes have been twitching and the nurses tell me that's a good sign that he'll be coming out of his coma real soon. But don't you worry yourself about him."

A nurse joined them, saying, "Sorry, but I need to check our patient's vital signs and apply fresh bandages."

Brooke released her hold on Jennifer's hand. She didn't want the teen to see her wounds. "Are you hungry, peanut?" she asked.

"I bet Mr. Miles here is as hungry as a dog in a bone factory," Geraldine volunteered. She'd recognized Brooke's reluctance at having Jennifer in the room when the bandages were changed.

"A bone factory?" Jennifer said, giggling. "Is there such a thing?"

Geraldine snickered. "You can't get much past this child. But c'mon, we need to let this young nurse do her job while we go downstairs and get some breakfast."

"I definitely could eat," Miles volunteered, placing one of his hands on Jennifer's shoulder and rubbing his stomach with his other one.

"Do you think it would be okay if I took Brooke the Unicorn with me?" Jennifer asked.

"Yes, peanut," Brooke replied, handing the stuffed animal back to her. "What do you think unicorns like to eat?" she added with a wink.

"I'll ask her when we get downstairs. Probably ice cream."

Everyone laughed.

Miles said, "Jennifer, why don't you and Mrs. Grant go downstairs right now? I need to tell Brooke something really quick. Then I'll join you."

Geraldine led Jennifer out of the room.

By this time, the nurse had finished checking Brooke's vitals and was ready to slip back the covers and apply fresh bandages.

"Would you mind giving us a moment before you change the dressing?" Miles asked.

The nurse frowned. "The doctors will be making their rounds soon and I'll get in trouble if the bandages aren't fresh."

"I promise, only a few minutes."

Letting out a sigh, she said, "Be quick, please."

As soon as they were alone, Miles said, "Jennifer has regressed. Physically, she's okay but she won't talk to anyone about what happened in that bedroom with Agent Parker."

"Is he dead?"

"The backup agents who Parker called found him dead and you unconscious. Half of Parker's face was blown away and Jennifer was on his back choking him with a chain. She was covered with blood splatter when they pried her loose from him."

"No wonder she doesn't want to talk. She's blocking it out."

"What happened in that bedroom?"

"Parker was the Viper. He fooled us. He planned on murdering me and Jennifer and blaming it on the terrorists."

"But why?"

"Money. He sold us out for money. Plus, I think he was a narcissistic psychopath who only cared about himself, his own wants, his own needs. Just because he was wearing a suit and tie and had a badge didn't change that."

From the troubled look on Miles's face, Brooke could tell he seemed unconvinced.

"It doesn't fit," he said. "I mean, he tried to kill you, so there's no doubt he betrayed us, and because of that I'm glad he's dead. But are you sure he was the Viper?"

"Why are you questioning it?"

"Because Parker knew what the FBI was doing here in the U.S., but he couldn't have known what I was doing in Kenya. He certainly wouldn't have had access to our flight plan when we were sent to watch that billionaire."

"Maybe he got access to it through the FBI computer system."

"I doubt the agency and Pentagon shared that information. And he certainly wasn't told about the goat herder and woman who were protecting me in Kenya."

"Woman?" Brooke asked through her now partially closed eyes. She was fading. Miles leaned down and kissed her forehead.

"We'll get it straightened out after you're feeling better."

Miles found the nurse waiting impatiently outside the door.

"Thanks for giving us a moment," he said. "Can I bring you back something from the cafeteria? Some coffee, fruit, toast, a bagel—anything?"

"Actually, a bagel would be great. I've not eaten this morning. But have them put the cream cheese in a container on the side. I'm watching my calories and they smear it on really thick in the cafeteria. I'll pay you when you bring it upstairs."

"No way are you paying. I'm happy to do it. Thanks for taking such good care of our patient."

"You the husband?"

"Hope to be someday."

When the nurse began the painful task of changing the bandages, Brooke opened her eyes. After the dressing had been changed, Lieutenant Colonel Gabe DeMoss arrived.

"Major Grant," he said cheerfully, "I wanted to check on you and General Grant before heading to the White House this morning. Representative Stanton's murder and all the rumors about Agent Parker have everyone alarmed, especially the president."

Before Brooke could reply, the nurse interrupted them. "I need a new bag of saline for you. I'll go get one. I'll be back in a minute."

The nurse scooted by DeMoss and out the door. "Actually, I'm surprised you're alone here," he noted. "Every time I've stopped by, one of your cousins or your aunt Geraldine and Jennifer have been here. Your aunt drew up a round-the-clock family schedule so you wouldn't be alone."

"She's a sweetheart," Brooke said. "You just missed her, Jennifer, and Walks Many Miles. They went downstairs to get breakfast."

"Your aunt Geraldine is not with the general?" he asked in a startled voice.

"She's downstairs."

"That's unusual. She eats, sleeps, and showers in his room. I've never known her to leave that room unless there's someone watching him."

"She doesn't want him to wake up and be alone, I suspect. Isn't there a Pentagon security officer stationed outside his door?"

"Not any longer. Only a hospital security guard who's got a desk near the elevator."

DeMoss seemed fidgety, and the morphine was making it difficult for her to keep focused.

"Did you miss me?" the nurse asked, returning with a fresh saline bag for the IV.

"I'll go check on your uncle now," DeMoss volunteered. "I don't like him being alone. You need to rest."

As soon as DeMoss left, the nurse said, "Now don't be getting all jealous, but I've got to tell you that your boyfriend—he's a keeper. He's not only handsome, he's thoughtful. He asked if there was anything from the cafeteria he could bring me, and when I told him a bagel with cream cheese, he refused to take any money from me. Now that's a gentleman."

Brooke was only half listening. She closed her eyes. *A bagel with cream cheese. A bagel. Mr. bagel. No. Wait!*

Brooke popped open her eyes. *Something isn't right. Bagel. What is it?* Brooke tried to focus. The last time she had gone to breakfast in the hospital, Gabe DeMoss had been with her and a woman had spoken to him. *What had she called him: café misto with a cinnamon raisin bagel. Mr. CM/CR. No, she'd called him Don and he said they'd never met but she'd said she never forgets a face. Why had he lied? What was he hiding?*

Another memory popped into her head. It was of her fatal encounter with Agent Wyatt Parker. He was pointing a pistol at her. What had he said?

"The Falcon asked me personally to kill you. Both of you."

"The Falcon?"

"You didn't have a clue, did you?"

"You're a traitor?"

"Let's just say I recently decided to switch teams. You should feel honored. The Falcon called me directly. Always before, I've gotten my orders through an intermediary. But he called me personally because he really wants you and this girl dead."

What had Parker said? *Always before, I've gotten my orders through an intermediary.*

She thought about what Miles had said minutes ago.

"Because Parker knew what the FBI was doing here in the U.S., but he couldn't have known what I was doing in Kenya. He certainly wouldn't have had access to our flight plan when we were sent to watch that billionaire."

Parker couldn't have known all of the information that the Viper had known. He wasn't the Viper!

The nurse had left her alone. Brooke pushed the call button, but no one responded. She pushed it again and again. Finally, she forced herself into a sitting position. The throbbing in her abdomen was excruciating, and for a moment she felt as if she was going to pass out. *Stay awake. Stay focused.*

She carefully began disconnecting the IV tubes and various wires attached to her and swung her legs over the side of the bed. Another debilitating jolt.

Brooke slid off the mattress to her feet and staggered toward a tiny closet. It wasn't clothing that she was after. She didn't care that a gaping hole in the back of her hospital smock exposed her bare buttocks. She was searching for her pistol. It wasn't there.

General Grant can't be left alone.

She forced herself to walk across the room and into the hallway. *Where is everyone?* There was no one at the nurses' station. *Where is the hospital security guard?* Touching the hallway wall to support herself, she moved as quickly as she dared toward her uncle's room. When she reached it, his door was closed, so she pushed inward.

Gabe DeMoss was next to her uncle's hospital bed holding a syringe.

"It wasn't Agent Parker," she said. "You're the Viper."

She expected DeMoss to deny it, to tell her that she was mistaken and delusional. Instead he asked, "What proof do you have?"

"The woman from the bagel shop. She recognized you."

"A simple case of misidentification. You're cold, Major Grant."

"Parker said his orders always came through an intermediary. That means he wasn't calling the shots here in the U.S."

"Warmer, but still chilly."

"Parker couldn't have been the Viper and I can prove it. Akbar and Aludra were holding Cassy and Jennifer captive in a Virginia cabin. Cassy managed to escape and was hiding in the woods. Akbar had just started to search for her when he got a telephone call on a satellite phone warning him that the FBI was on its way to the cabin to rescue the girls. Parker couldn't have placed that call because he was with me. We were in a helicopter flying to that cabin. Someone else warned Akbar. The NSC was monitoring our every move. That means you knew we were heading to that cabin. You warned him."

"Ah, you are turning up the heat."

"Parker didn't have access to what was happening in Kenya, but you did. As a member of the NSC, you knew about the SAD team's flight to El Wak and you also were briefed about the goat herder and woman who helped Miles."

DeMoss smirked but did not challenge her reasoning.

"And I saw you sitting next to my uncle at Decker Lake's funeral. It was you who sent that text to Fawzia Samatar telling her to light herself on fire and attack the president."

"Congratulations, Major Grant," he said sarcastically. "You've pulled together all of the pieces. It was that text to Fawzia that caused your uncle to become suspicious of me. During the funeral, he saw me reach into my pocket and fidget with a cell phone. I'd already written the message. All I did was hit send, but in the short time it took for me to do that, he noticed. He thought it was disrespectful for me to be sending a text."

Brooke interrupted him. "Let me guess, he began zeroing in on you when he learned the text to Fawzia had been sent from a burner phone—a phone bought by the president's reelection committee and stored in a box at the White House—a box that you had access to."

"Bravo. They were careless. There were no records kept of who took one of the burner phones to use when they were conducting campaign business versus doing their government jobs."

"Were you responsible for my uncle being shot?"

"I had to do something, and killing him made the most sense. So yes, I arranged for him to be attending a meeting at the CIA that morning and then I told Akbar and the others where they could trap him by having that rented truck dump debris on the highway. I hadn't planned to go with him that morning, but then he invited me."

"And you opened the passenger door to the car so Akbar could get a better shot at him, didn't you?" she demanded.

"Yes, it was a game time call. I opened the passenger door and then Akbar failed to kill him."

"Why? Why would you do it? Parker was in it for the money. Is the Falcon paying you too?"

"No, I don't give a damn about the money. Don't you get it, Major? I am your worst nightmare. I am an American jihadist."

"That's impossible."

"Why? Because I am not an Arab or a Somali?"

"You weren't raised as a Muslim."

"But I am one now. I thought I was going to die when I was captured by the Taliban in Afghanistan. Have you ever been tortured, Major Grant? Denigrated? Abused? There are things worse than death. They twisted my arms and legs and tied them together, leaving me hanging inches above the ground for hours. No one can stand that much pain. They beat the soles of my feet. You can't imagine how many different ways a man can inflict pain on another human being. One morning, I asked for a copy of the Holy Quran. I hoped maybe they would stop beating me if I acted interested in their religion. But then I began reading it."

"And you became a Muslim?"

"Not at first, but I began feeling at peace. I actually started praying for them. They didn't believe me at first, but they kept me alive, and when they became convinced that I was not deceiving them, they began teaching me, explaining why they—why we—must fight against infidels, against the Great Satan. I began to understand. I

TREASON   357

became one with them. It was a biblical-like transformation. My torturers became my saviors."

"I was told you escaped after being held as a prisoner for nine months," Brooke said.

"I didn't escape. They forced me out. I wanted to stay with them and fight with them, but the Falcon convinced me that I could help them more by staying in the Army and working in the Pentagon."

"Stockholm syndrome."

"No, not at all. I am not a victim, Major Grant. During those nine months, my entire perspective changed. I became a true believer."

"In what? Murdering innocent children and families?"

"I don't expect you to understand. You and your uncle are blind to the truth, to our higher purpose. You are like a robot programmed to believe democracy and capitalism are superior when neither is." DeMoss glanced down at General Grant. "I've been waiting to be alone with your uncle. I can't afford having him wake up from his coma. But until this morning, every time I came to visit him, your aunt was standing guard. And then finally, she leaves him alone and now you've interrupted us."

Brooke felt weak, as if her legs were about to go out from under her. She grabbed onto the bed's foot railing to steady herself.

DeMoss was still holding the syringe in his hand. "There should be enough in this shot for you too," he said. "I've been told it's quick, painless, and untraceable. You'll be found at your uncle's bedside. What a touching end to the Brooke Grant story. Here with her beloved uncle. I will be gone before anyone finds either of you."

She tried to stop her legs from quivering. She failed. One of them buckled and she was forced to tighten her grip on the rails to continue standing.

DeMoss snickered as she swayed, helpless.

Brooke did not have enough strength in her legs to attack him. She didn't have enough to flee into the hallway for help.

She screamed.

What came from her mouth was a guttural noise from deep inside, a blending of rage, fury, and frustration.

The hospital security guard, who'd been taking a bathroom break earlier when Brooke had come down the hallway, heard her. He nearly knocked Brooke over when he flung open the door to General Grant's room.

DeMoss had just inserted the needle into General Grant's skin but he hadn't yet pushed in the syringe's plunger.

The guard reached for his pistol, which was in its holster.

"Don't be a fool!" DeMoss threatened. "You know who this patient is. If I inject him, you'll be responsible for killing him."

The officer lifted his left hand away from his sidearm.

"It's over," Brooke said. "Give up."

"It's not over until I say it's over," DeMoss replied.

Brooke was only half listening now. She was focusing on what she needed to do to save her uncle. In one quick motion, she removed her right hand from the bed railing and swept her fingers up the security guard's left leg, plucking his sidearm from its holster. She had not been watching DeMoss when he'd been talking. She had been staring at her uncle's twitching eyelids, and she had seen the general open them.

As she raised the guard's handgun, General Frank Grant jerked his hand upward from the bed, shoving DeMoss's hand away from his chest, taking the syringe with it.

Brooke fired the pistol as a startled DeMoss looked blankly at the now fully awake general before slipping backward into a heavy machine monitoring the general's vitals. He slid down its front to the floor with the syringe still in his fingers.

Brooke's body began to tremble and she collapsed.

The gunshot drew other security guards and nurses. Within minutes, Brooke was back in her hospital bed. Miles burst into her room. Her first impulse was to think that she'd been dreaming. None of that could have happened.

"Brooke," he said, "how did you know about DeMoss?"

During the next several moments, she explained the clues that had convinced her that DeMoss was the Viper. "All this time," she said, "I thought he was coming to visit my uncle because he cared about him, about both of us. All he was really looking for was an opportunity to murder him. When I told DeMoss that the three of you were downstairs having breakfast, he saw his chance."

"Agent Parker, and now Colonel DeMoss," Miles said. "How could we have been so easily fooled?"

"Because we are Americans. We believe people are good and decent until they show us otherwise. It is one of our greatest virtues and our greatest vulnerabilities."

CHAPTER FIFTY

U.S. Capitol Rotunda
Washington, D.C.

An American flag was draped over Representative Thomas Edgar Stanton's casket, which was on the catafalque that had been built to hold President Abraham Lincoln's remains when his body had lain in state.

Thick red velvet ropes encircled his coffin. Inside that oval, soldiers from each branch of the armed services stood at attention facing inward.

President Allworth and Congress had agreed that "the Chairman" should be granted the honor of lying in state, a privilege only automatically granted to presidents. This was the final night for viewing, and a select few had been invited to pay their respects after the rotunda had been closed to the public.

As Walks Many Miles pushed Brooke Grant forward in a wheelchair across the highly polished marble floor directly under the Capitol dome, they saw Representative Rudy Adeogo, his wife, Dheeh, and daughter, Cassy, standing outside the velvet ropes paying their last respects to Stanton.

"How's Jennifer?" Adeogo asked when he saw Brooke approaching.

"She's doing better," Brooke replied. "But there are days when she retreats into her fantasy world."

"A happy world of unicorns and rainbows," Miles said. "I'm sometimes envious."

"How are you, Cassy?" Brooke asked, reaching over to affectionately touch the girl's shoulder.

"I miss Jennifer," Cassy answered. "I hope she's not angry that I left her in the awful cabin. I had to!"

"She understands. Don't you worry one little bit."

"Do you think you could enroll her in my new school? It's in Virginia, and my father said it's not far from where you and Jennifer live—and it has horses. She won't find a unicorn there, but we got plenty of real horses and I could introduce her to the new friends I've made. Everyone is nice."

"What a thoughtful idea," Brooke replied. "I'll talk to her about it."

Cassy grinned.

Glancing at Stanton's closed casket, Adeogo said, "I respected the Chairman. He was a good and decent man."

"He made a lot of enemies as soon as he began questioning whether radical jihadists were infiltrating our government," Miles said.

"Yes, he did, but I was not one of them," Adeogo replied. "And I would say the events of the past several days prove he was right."

"What happens now?" Brooke asked.

"The fight between good and evil continues," Adeogo replied, turning philosophical. "The Falcon will kill anyone who doesn't submit to his radical perversion of Islam. In my eyes, the OIN is equally tyrannical when it smears anyone who dares question its viewpoint and tactics. I'm only a freshman member, and who knows if I will be reelected if I decide to run again. But while I am in Congress, I will push for the investigative hearings that the Chairman wanted held. We should not be afraid to ask tough questions during dangerous times. It is the only time that tough questions really matter. And we should never be bullied by thugs who wrap themselves in religious garb but are the opposite of everything that is holy."

"We are trapped in a violent circle," Brooke said. "First there was the violent embassy attack in Mogadishu and then the Falcon sent that Somali American couple—Cumar and Fawzia Samatar—to kill President Allworth at Decker Lake's funeral. My uncle is shot. Jennifer's nanny and my friend, Miriam, is murdered. Cassy's school is attacked. Our girls are abducted and finally Representative Stanton is murdered. Will there ever be peace?"

Glancing around them, Adeogo said, "How many great American patriots have lain in state in this magnificent Capitol building? Three immediately come to mind. Abraham Lincoln, John F. Kennedy, and Ronald Reagan. Different generations, different political parties, different personalities and ways of governing. But each faced very real threats to our government. It was men such as them, and men such as the Chairman, who held up a lamp during dark times. They were human. They made mistakes, but they believed in our great nation and our right to direct our own futures. I am proud to serve among such men." He looked at Brooke and added, "I am proud to be among such men—and women."

"I don't know why we simply can't live and let live in peace," Dheeh Adeogo said. "It could be so simple. Love one another and treat your neighbors as you want to be treated. It's a tenet of all great religions."

"There will never be peace as long as there are men in this world like the Falcon," Brooke answered. "He cares nothing about love or peace. He only lives for his empowerment and personal gratification. To me, he personifies evil. Not because he hates America but because he hates everyone who doesn't bend down to him."

For several more moments, they spoke in hushed voices about Chairman Stanton. When they parted, all of them had tears in their eyes. The emotion inside them had welled up because of his death. But those tears were not signs of resignation or of defeat. His assassination and the discovery of treason inside the FBI and NSC had caused them to become more resolved in their fight against terrorism and oppression.

Brooke was not ready to return to her hospital bed after they left the Capitol grounds. She had spent nearly eight days there, was tired of the confinement and eager to be discharged.

"I want a hot dog," she declared to Miles as they were leaving the Capitol. "Let's go to Ben's Chili Bowl."

"No way am I buying you a spicy hot dog smothered in chili," Miles replied. "Your doctors have you eating bland food for a reason. You'll be out in a couple days and then we can go there."

"Let's compromise. We go to Ben's and you eat a chili dog and I'll get a milk shake."

Because of its notoriety, Ben's Chili Bowl stayed open long after other well-known eateries had closed. It was after midnight by the time Miles wheeled Brooke inside the eatery with its 1950s diner decor. He helped her into one of the booths that lined the wall across from the bar where a half dozen customers were perched on chrome stools eating.

"Ah, that smell," Miles said

"Aroma, not smell," Brooke said. "Comfort food."

"I've never thought of hot dogs as comfort food," he replied.

"They are to me."

From her seat inside the booth, Brooke could watch a television mounted on the restaurant's rear wall near a bright red-and-white backlit plastic menu. Brooke glanced at the screen at the same moment Al Arabic reporter Ebio Kattan appeared.

It was too noisy for them to hear what Kattan was saying, so Miles slipped from the booth and walked over to the television to listen.

"Kattan's done it again," Miles said, when he returned to his seat. "She's gotten a scoop and every network is rebroadcasting her report."

"What now? Is it the Falcon?"

"I'm not sure. She's discovered three supertankers carrying crude oil have vanished somewhere in the Pacific after leaving an African port."

"An African port? Did she say who owned them?"

"Some African oil company. I didn't recognize it."

"Where were they last seen?"

"Heading north toward the Sea of Japan."

"How about the tankers?" she asked as she fished her cell phone out of her pocket. "Did you catch the names of any of them?"

"Ah, one was called *Sea* something."

"That's not real helpful."

"Why does it matter, Brooke?"

"Because three supertankers carrying millions of dollars worth of oil don't just disappear, especially in waters frequented by Russia, China, and North Korea. Something is going on."

"One of them was named *Sea Master*, I think. I'm sure that's what one of them was named."

Brooke typed `Sea Master` into an Internet search engine on her phone.

"Oh no," she said seconds later.

"What?"

She slid the phone across the booth's red Formica tabletop separating them so he could read the name.

"Umoja Owiti," Miles said aloud. "He owns those ships."

Suddenly, neither of them was hungry. Their minds were on more important matters than chili dogs and milk shakes.

EPILOGUE

Rason Seaport
Democratic People's Republic of Korea

Hakim Farouk, the Falcon's most trusted envoy, stepped from the deck of the patrol boat that had brought him ashore from the *Sea Master* supertanker anchored a mile off the North Korean coast. His traveling companion, an Iranian nuclear physicist in his sixties, followed him onto the recently completed dock.

A diminutive official dressed in a black topcoat, black suit, white shirt, and narrow black tie was waiting to greet them. Atop his head was a black fur hat that either had been imported from Russia or sewn in a North Korean knock-off factory. Armed soldiers flanked him on either side.

"*Annyeong-hasimnikka*," Farouk said, having memorized the formal version of saying "hello" in North Korean while making the long voyage from the African port of Durban. (The supertanker actually had been too large to enter the Durban port and had been moored at a single buoy at Isipingo, some nineteen kilometers south, but still had listed Durban as its port of origin.) Farouk had read in online travel guides that he would be expected to bow, and he'd practiced in a mirror in his berth aboard the tanker. Keeping his legs straight and pressed together with both arms at his side, he now bent down from the waist with his eyes cast downward so as to not look at the older man.

"*Kam-sa ham-nida*," his host replied, which Farouk knew when translated meant "Thank you."

"You do not speak Korean," the man said, "and I do not speak Egyptian Arabic, so we will converse in English, which I understand is a tongue familiar to both parties."

"Yes," Farouk said.

"My name is Pak," the man replied. "Please allow me to welcome both of you to the Democratic People's Republic of Korea, a genuine workers' state in which all the people are completely liberated from exploitation and oppression. Only here will you discover that workers, peasants, soldiers, and intellectuals are the true masters of their destiny."

Farouk nodded. Privately, he had little use for the man speaking to him. Pak was an infidel no different in Farouk's eyes from the infidel Christian Believers of the Book and the much-hated Jews. But the Falcon had sent him to trade with the North Koreans, and he took some comfort in knowing they would eventually be subjugated.

"My name is Runihura," Farouk said, and my traveling companion is Hassan Yazdi." Farouk assumed that Pak was not the actual name of his host just as Runihura and Yazdi were not their true names—an acceptable subterfuge, given the serious nature of their business.

"Please follow me inside to an accommodation where we can be more comfortable," Pak said.

Farouk and his companion were eager to oblige. The afternoon sky was overcast and it was only seven degrees Fahrenheit on the dock, with a strong wind blowing off the Sea of Japan making the wind chill factor several degrees colder. The patrol boat ride from the *Sea Master* had taken them by tall stacks of white, red, blue, and yellow shipping containers that had been unloaded for transport. Although North Korea controlled the port, Farouk knew that it allowed both the Chinese and Russians to transport goods through it inland, making it one of the country's bustling seaports.

Yet Farouk had not seen a single worker, not even on the tugs tied to piers or manning the two giant floating cranes used to lift containers from ships. He assumed Pak had sealed off the entire area to dockworkers and allowed only DPRK soldiers to be present.

Pak led them into a nearby four-story concrete building at whose entrance two soldiers stood guard despite the bone-chilling weather. Farouk noticed that they, like the two soldiers with Pak, were armed with North Korea's copy of the Russian AKM assault rifle called the Type 68. Once inside, Pak guided them along a vacant corridor into an office that contained only a table and three chairs. Nothing else. Pak waited for his guests to sit first before joining them at the table with his two guards taking positions directly behind him. The soldiers stared straight ahead and did not look at either guest.

"The occasion of our meeting today is filled with the dignity and self-respect of being victors in our glorious Workers' Party of Korea struggle against those enemies who would destroy our socialist Korea and the sun of Juche. We welcome you today at the request of our trusted and mutual friend, Umoja Owiti, the builder of the magnificent and most glorious socialist port where you are now sitting and the arranger of this exceptional meeting."

Although Farouk suspected Pak was sufficiently conversant in English to speak unscripted, it was clear the North Korean was following dialogue that had been carefully crafted for him.

Farouk reached inside the heavy wool coat that had been lent to him by the captain of the *Sea Master*. He had little use for such a heavy garment in his native Egypt. From a pocket inside, he withdrew a folded document: a bill of sale for the oil. He remembered to present it to Pak with both hands, as etiquette required.

"The cargo aboard the *Sea Master* can be released when you produce the object of our desire," Farouk said. Because both of them were speaking a language that was not their native tongue, their conversation contained words that would seem stilted by Western standards.

Pak returned the bill of sale with both hands without reading or signing it. "Our glorious people's republic has no need for documentation of our mutual objectives."

In a symbolic gesture, Farouk ripped the document and dropped its torn pages onto the concrete floor.

Pak said something in Korean to one of the armed guards, who left the room. No one spoke while they waited. It was overly hot thanks to a vent blowing warm air into the room, yet none of them removed his coat, and Farouk noticed sweat on Pak's forehead directly under the brim of his heavy fur cap. The guard returned with three soldiers who were pushing a bright red cylinder loaded on a waist-high steel cart. Farouk estimated the missile-like device was about six feet long and two feet in circumference.

"I believe this is the object of your desire," Pak said, referring to the thermonuclear device that bore Korean markings.

Farouk spoke in Persian to the Iranian nuclear physicist with him, and the scientist rose from his chair to inspect it. As he did, Pak issued another command in Korean to the guards, and one of them produced a packet of schematics and papers written in Arabic. For the next forty minutes, Farouk and Pak watched the Iranian study the tube. He used instruments that he had brought with him to verify it contained fissile material. When he was satisfied, he addressed Farouk.

"This is legitimate," he said.

"Are you one hundred percent certain?" Farouk asked.

The Iranian grinned. "The Koreans built it based on plans that our nuclear scientists gave them. It is like one of my own children."

"Where must this item be transported?" Pak asked.

"Our benefactor is arranging delivery from the airplane hangar he constructed near this port for use when he flew in and out of Rason to supervise construction."

"I am intimate with the hangar," Pak said. He spoke to the soldiers and they began to wheel the device from the room.

"No!" Farouk exclaimed, rising abruptly from his chair. His

sudden movement alarmed the guards standing behind Pak and they began to lower their weapons.

Speaking in a calm voice, Farouk said, "With much respect, I am required to be married to this container now that you have completed delivery. It must not leave my eyesight."

"Just as I am required to be with you," Pak replied. He ordered his guards to stand down and explained to the soldiers that they were to wait with the device until his guests were ready to accompany it to Umoja Owiti's private hangar.

"With your kind permission," Farouk said, "before departing, I will use my satellite phone now to inform the *Sea Master* captain that our exchange has been achieved. He is authorized to make his way into port. Two other ships are in international waters nearby. They will be notified by him. I will inform Mr. Owiti's employees and tell them to be ready for our arrival at his airplane hangar so our flight will be ready for exiting."

Pak nodded his approval and waited while Farouk made those two calls. When he was finished, Farouk said, "There is one more message I must deliver."

Pak again nodded and sat patiently, his face now glistening with perspiration from the heat blowing into the tiny room.

Farouk dialed a third number that was answered by a computer in Belgium. He typed one word into his phone's touchpad: Runihura, the pseudonym that he had used when introducing himself to Pak. The computer immediately sent that word to another machine in France, which relayed it to yet another in London, which relayed it to a fourth in Taiwan. Farouk had no idea how many more times his message would be bounced around the world. All that he knew was that his message would eventually reach the Falcon and that master terrorist would be well pleased.

Pak stood and asked, "Are you ready to go with the object of your desire?"

Farouk rose from his seat. Within the hour, the nuclear device had been loaded on one of Umoja Owiti's private jets and the two envoys were ready to depart.

"*Kamsa ham-nida*," Farouk said to Pak, bowing.

"Our glorious Workers' Party of Korea and our supreme leader hope your visit to the Democratic People's Republic of Korea was most enjoyable and fruitful," Pak said, returning the bow. Then he added, "Have a pleasurable flight, Mr. Runihura."

As he boarded the aircraft for takeoff, Farouk wondered if the North Korean had learned enough about Egypt to realize the significance of the name *Runihura*.

In his native tongue it meant "The Destroyer."

ACKNOWLEDGMENTS

The authors wish to thank Joe DeSantis for his contributions to the development, writing, and editing of this book. His political experience and insights were invaluable.

We also are grateful to our agents, Kathy Lubbers and David Vigliano, as well as Kate Hartson, our editor at Center Street, an imprint of Hachette Book Group, and our copy editor.

In addition, Newt Gingrich wishes to acknowledge: Steve Hanser, who for forty years taught him to think historically; General Chuck Boyd, who tutored him about national security; Joan Dempsey, whose long career in intelligence has been dedicated to protecting America; Congressman Bob Livingston, who was in many ways the model for "the Chairman"; Barry Casselman and Annette Meeks, who introduced us to the vibrant and exciting Somali community in Minneapolis; daughters, Kathy Lubbers and Jackie Cushman, and their husbands, Paul Lubbers and Jimmy Cushman, who have encouraged all of his adventures; grandchildren, Maggie and Robert Cushman, whose future safety keeps him focused on national security and politics; and his wife, Callista Gingrich, whose companionship and love make it all worthwhile.

Pete Earley wishes to thank: Dan and Karen Amato, William Donnell, Amanda Driscoll, Walter and Keran Harrington, Marie Heffelfinger, Michelle Holland, Don and Susan Infeld, Kelly McGraw, Dan Morton, Richard and Joan Miles, Jay and Barbara

Myerson, Bassey Nyambi, Nyambi and Atai Nyambi, Mike Sager, Lynn and LouAnn Smith, and Kendall and Carolyn Starkweather. He also is grateful for the love and support of his wife, Patti Michele Luzi, and his children, Stephen, Kevin, Tony, Kathy, Kyle, Evan, and Traci, and granddaughter, Maribella.